ONE SMART INDIAN

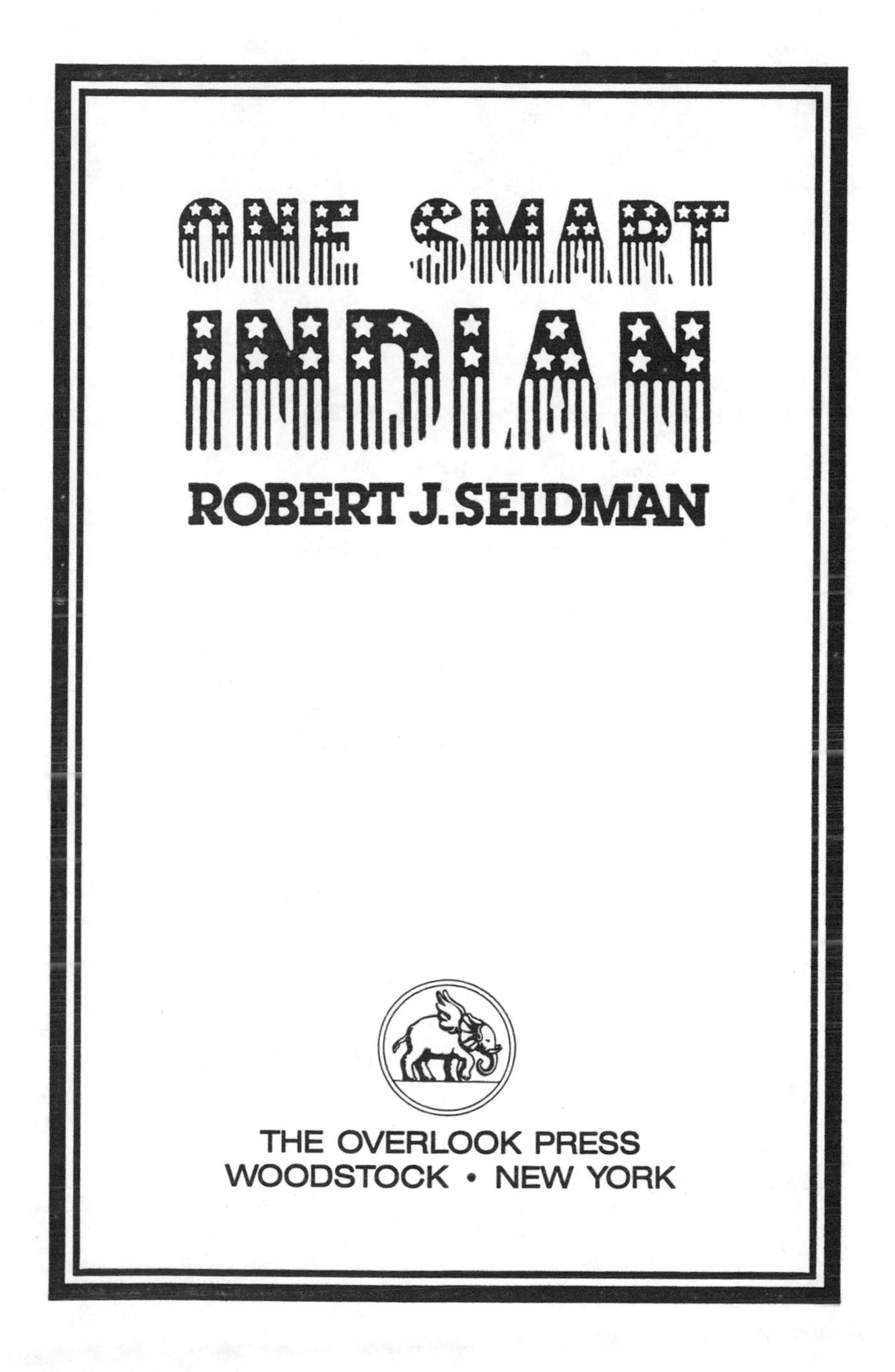

ONE SMART INDIAN

ROBERT J. SEIDMAN

THE OVERLOOK PRESS
WOODSTOCK • NEW YORK

First published in paperback in the USA in 1979 by
The Overlook Press
Lewis Hollow Road
Woodstock, New York 12498

Published by arrangement with G.P. Putnam's Sons

LIBRARY OF CONGRESS CATALOGING IN PUBLICATION DATA

Seidman, Robert J
One smart Indian.

I. Title.
[PZ4.S45850n 1979] [PS3569.E532] 813'.5'4 79-14987
ISBN 0-87951-099-4

Printed in the USA

Second Printing

To Harry and Giff

This story was told to Tumbling Hawk by his grandfather, Mohe, on the occasion of their flight from a cavalry detachment out of Fort Sheridan, Nebraska Territory, in 1847.

COYOTE AND WHITE MAN

COYOTE AND WHITE MAN walked across a broad plain, each lost in his own thoughts. As they passed under a large tree, Coyote said, "I have reached a new agreement with our world. Would you care to know what it is?" Before White man could reply, Coyote cried out, "Let my eyes sit on that juniper branch." Suddenly Coyote's eyes left his head and flew to a high limb above them. Of course White man was astounded. He begged Coyote to let him know his secret, already imagining what he himself would do with this power. Coyote was tempted to keep the power for himself, but he knew he'd have no peace if he did, so he said, "I'll teach you how to send your eyes flying, but you must promise not to use the power more than three times a day. For if you do, something strange might happen." Of course White man had no trouble promising, and after Coyote called his sight back into his head—"Eyes, shoot back!"—he taught White man about his agreement with the Earth.

As soon as he could, White man left Coyote and wandered off on the prairie, eager to test his new gift. First he startled a jay by sending his eyes into her nest, then he burrowed along with some frightened prairie dogs through their underground villages. But when he realized he had only one more use of this marvelous new power, White man grew restless. Suddenly the day ahead seemed very long. "I have only one more," he told himself. He walked along until he came to the shore of a lake, where he was distracted by trout jumping. Enviously, he watched them flick their tails in the air and plunge into the cool water until, unable to resist, he sent his eyes flying out of his head to swim with the fishes below the surface; his sight dove down into the deepest water and stirred up a dour old catfish. This time White man examined their world very carefully and saw many things he hadn't known about before. He was very pleased to be able to see like a fish.

When his eyes were back in his head, he couldn't help thinking that he'd squandered his opportunities; how vast the day seemed as it stretched out before him. White man wondered how he would be able to wait until the next day before he sent his eyes flying again. Sadly he walked through the woods, annoyed at the briefness of his time as a bird and a prairie dog, and even as a fish. Very soon he was furious at himself for having squandered his great new power.

He reached home in an ugly mood and immediately picked a fight with his woman. He stormed out and walked toward the village. By this time he was telling himself: "Perhaps Coyote lied when he made me promise not to use the trick more than three times. Maybe he was afraid I would have more power than he has. Besides, he said something strange *might* happen, not that it *would* happen."

He found a number of his acquaintances gathered around the fire. Bear was there, and Porcupine, Squirrel, White man's brothers, and a few others. For a while they chatted about commonplace things—the weather, their health. The longer they spoke, the more impatient White man grew. Meanwhile, his conversation with himself changed. "That first trip to the jay's nest didn't count, since Coyote did practically the same thing on that juniper branch. My guess is I've only used up two flights, not three." Still he didn't do anything, trying his best to listen to what bored him, increasingly annoyed with the empty chatter. Ahead of him the day seemed a vast desert, behind lay three wasted opportunities. Finally he could wait no longer. "I have made new and powerful magic today," he said, interrupting Porcupine. "Now watch me; wonder at my strength!"

He did as Coyote had instructed, saying, "Let my eyes sit on that hickory branch!" And his eyes went flying over the clearing and landed in a small tree on the far side of the village. White man was pleased that his eyes had done as he commanded and felt greatly relieved when nothing strange happened. He was glad that Coyote was such a cautious fool. But he had little time to think about that before everyone crowded round to praise him and to beg for the secret of his incredible power. He teased the villagers, boasting about his own greatness but telling them nothing. He reveled in their praise until he decided it was time to have his eyes return. Then he called out as Coyote had taught him—"Eyes, shoot back!" Nothing happened. He called and called again. His eyes remained high in the tree at the opposite side of the clearing. Some of those who, a moment earlier, were fawning about him, now laughed at the poor blind man. A few, including his brothers, tried to comfort White man, but even they left him about the time his stranded eyes began to bulge and sweat. Then, all alone, White man lay down on the ground and cried.

He cried for a long time, until a mouse who was happening by heard him sobbing and started the journey over his body to see what was the matter. He climbed on White man's face, walked up his cheeks, and began to lick away his tears. To steady himself, the mouse put his tail in White man's mouth. This was a mistake, for White man clamped his teeth around the mouse's tail till he could grab him with his hand. Then White man demanded that the mouse take him to the tree where his eyes were.

White man held on tightly while the mouse led him to the foot of the hickory. They stopped there while the mouse, whose own eyes were not very strong, squinted up to see if he could make out the state of White man's eyes. Unfortunately, they'd swollen to an enormous size and flies were already gathering on them. When the mouse offered to climb up to retrieve them, White man refused. He knew if he released the creature he might lose his guide.

Still holding onto the mouse, who by then was bruised and sore, White man considered what to do. Finally he said, "You will have to give me one of your eyes!" The mouse struggled and tried to escape, but White man gripped him so tightly that the mouse eventually gave up and let his captor pluck one of his eyes out of its socket and place it in his own. The mouse's eye was much too small; it set back too far in the socket. Through it, White man could see only very mistily, as through a cloud.

Discarding the miserable mouse, White man wandered off crying. He trudged across the prairie until he bumped into something large and shaggy. It was a buffalo. The buffalo, a compassionate animal, asked White man why he was crying, and White man told the buffalo the story of how he'd lost his eyes. The buffalo thought for a long moment (he always deliberated very slowly and very surely), and then said, "White man, you are always wandering around alone, and you live mostly by yourself. But I am always in the company of so many friends that I believe I can afford the loss of one of my eyes." With that the buffalo allowed White man to help himself to an eye, which White man did. But the buffalo's eye was too big, cf course, and when White man placed it in his head it bulged out of its socket.

That is why White man sees the way he does, with one eye that's too small, that looks at things too closely, and one eye that's too big, an eye that sees too far away.

BOOK ONE

THE WHITE SOLDIER

The jackrabbit crouched so close to a tuft of bunchgrass that the grass twitched with his breathing. His nose sampled the air for a clue; the ears rotated ever so slightly forward, then slowly back. Still he didn't move as the four boys crept up on him, even when two of them broke from the group and began to circle apart. When they drew even with the rabbit, they stopped to wait for the wind.

The rabbit quivered violently–his ears swung forward, then seemed to extend as they swept back; his hind legs knotted as they dug into the sand. Then the wind died. The lead pair moved out ahead of him. The other two held their places, then fanned out quickly. Their noose set, they drew it tighter until, several steps away, they all rose to a crouch, nocked the arrows and drew their bows.

For an instant the animal quieted, then he sprang forward. He took three unhurried bounds at one boy, then his ears went flat, he veered sharply and darted between them. They released–all four missed their shots, the arrows momentarily gathering in a disordered sheaf as they crossed the spot where the rabbit had been, then skidding off in separate directions. Takes-the-Pipe and Small Deer streaked up the slight rise after the rabbit and Lightfoot trotted after them. Tumbling Hawk hustled off to gather up the precious arrows.

When Tumbling Hawk reached the top of the sand hill, which sheered off steeply on its far side, Lightfoot was laughing too hard to speak. He could only point weakly down the steep side of the hill at the bottom of which lay the poor stunned rabbit, his legs hopelessly splayed behind him. Struggling down after the animal was Takes-the-Pipe, ankle-deep in the sand. Behind him came Small Deer. Suddenly Small Deer stopped, drew his bow and fired. His arrow took one hop and skidded into the dazed creature.

At the top of the sand hill Lightfoot danced up and down, slapping Tumbling Hawk on the back and yelling to the others: "At least you hit him on a bounce! It's a good thing the jack's legs are shorter in front." He put his hands up to his chest, a pair of limp paws. "Otherwise he couldn't have killed himself for you. First his head, then his legs, then the head—hop, hop, hop—like tumbleweed, over and over all the way down."

He ran down the hill, then hopped over to Takes-the-Pipe, threw his arms around him, and collapsed on the ground. "I've captured the tribe's great hunter." They wrestled until Takes-the-Pipe flipped the big boy over, and Lightfoot promised to stop.

Lightfoot took the occasion to lie back in the loose sand. He was a big formless boy who needed more rest than the others. Small Deer, frailest of the four, dropped to the ground next to Lightfoot. Tumbling Hawk followed. Since early morning they'd stopped only twice, once for a crow they couldn't scare from its high nest and again for a turkey they'd flushed, then missed. They had seen an antelope lure a lone coyote away from her young, but hadn't been close enough to head her off.

"A rabbit isn't a deer," thought Tumbling Hawk. But every kill went into the family pot, and Tumbling Hawk was particularly glad Small Deer would have something—even that mutilated rabbit—to add to his father's.

Takes-the-Pipe sat there too, moody that he'd missed his shot and impatient to be off as soon as possible. He was slightly older than the other three, and he took leading them for granted. His father was a headman of the Elk Horn Society.

"He knew where we were," Tumbling Hawk said, pointing to the tawny broken body, "but he thought about it for too long."

When they had rested, they rose to move off, but Lightfoot couldn't resist twirling the rabbit over his head and presenting it ceremoniously to Small Deer, who stuck its head through his belt.

Then they were off again, laboring over the last of the sand hills. They were glad to get onto the firmer footing of the Nebraska plain, and glided along smoothly, like slow-moving antelopes. As they ran they hunted. They checked the openings in the rimrocks for bobcat, eyed every hole for fresh signs of badger or weasel. They knew where the mule deer might be lying in the long grass and broke off into pairs to scour the bedding spot of a dwarf deer in a stand of chokecherries. They gauged the age of all droppings, knew the size and weight of a gray wolf from the depth of its tracks on the windward side of a ravine. Their skin, their noses relayed slight changes in the air's texture—a dryness where a rattlesnake had lain under a rock, an acrid bite still lingering near the bleached bones of a ground squirrel.

They slowed to scramble down a dry streambed, displacing only a few pebbles as they climbed up the opposite bank. On the other side of the stream the mood gradually changed—the air was clammier, thicker here. Cautiously they moved ahead until a slight nod from Takes-the-Pipe led their eyes north to the tracks of a horse. As they drew closer, they could see the animal was shod with the heavy shoes of the white man's soldiers. The tracks were fresh, the horse had been galloping in the heavy sand. Silently they moved around islands of tall bunchgrass over a slight rise until they crawled by a gopher hole that had broken the horse's leg and sent the rider hurtling to the ground.

The dead horse lay on its side, its right foreleg bent impossibly back through the joint. Its throat was cut in a straight line. ("A good knife," Tumbling Hawk thought.) Just below it, a pool of blood soaked into the ground. Only a few ants were on the body and there were no buzzards, for the horse was still warm.

The rider's tracks led away from death. ("It's wise to get clear before it starts to smell," thought Takes-the-Pipe. "He must be a good warrior.") But the trail was written so clearly in the sand it seemed he beckoned them after him. It made them cautious. "A whole tribe could move without such marks," Tumbling Hawk continued to himself, remembering a story about Wolf Tongue who, when wounded in Cree territory, brushed away his tracks as he crawled back to camp, three days' ride away.

They were trained for this moment. Their options were perfectly clear—they could send back to camp for help, or they could face the danger themselves. But camp was far away, and soon other Waschita might come looking for the soldier. Besides, this was too good a chance to miss. The white man might be dead already, or almost dead. And there had to be a pistol, maybe even a rifle. Counting coup on a white soldier and capturing a gun were strong incentives, more to boast of at the fire than deer or a stringy rabbit.

They followed the tracks of the soldier-crawling-on-one-side until his trail snaked into an island of bunchgrass. Tumbling Hawk and Lightfoot split apart and crawled on ahead. Just as they hoped, there were no tracks leading out.

The four boys tightened the noose until they were close enough to hear the soldier's labored breathing. So he was alive. But could he shoot? Or had he seen them crawling toward him and set up this deep-breathing trap? They waited; after what seemed a long time the man's groans quickened; he began to reach for air with shallow rattling gasps. As Takes-the-Pipe came into a crouch, Tumbling Hawk was up and running toward that island of grassy plumes. Braves waited all their lives for a soldier, a gun; men went to noble deaths this way. But Tumbling Hawk felt no fear: though the air they moved through was laced with blood and death, they could have been racing each other anywhere.

Even when Tumbling Hawk saw the soldier propped up against the log, the army pistol in his hand, he didn't swerve but ran straight at him. The soldier didn't fire. As he dove, the boy didn't know if the body was alive.

He hit the man with his shoulder, lifting him off the log. They crashed to the ground, the soldier emitting a flat sound as the air went out of him. They rolled over once and the white man landed on top. The limp heavy body, the thick smell suffocated Tumbling Hawk, and he fought back wildly, kicking and clawing at the man's face. Takes-the-Pipe dragged the soldier off, then Lightfoot took over, stomping the big, soft body till he was all but dead, lying limply on his back.

Now Lightfoot began to dance around the white, grimacing and making thrusts at the man's throat. Takes-the-Pipe had the army pistol pointed professionally at the soldier, who lay without moving, looking up at them with pained, terrified eyes, babbling. Sometimes his lower body would twitch and a tiny stream of blood would spurt out of the corner of his mouth. Standing over his broken enemy, looking at the flat colorless skin, Tumbling Hawk wondered why he felt so little excitement.

Lightfoot brandished his knife blade in the soldier's face. "Let us take Waschita's scalp," he yelled ferociously.

But the word "scalp" sounded strangely foreign to Tumbling Hawk. Scalp had always been an adult term, far beyond their world of rabbit and squirrel.

He watched Lightfoot bend down over the body, run his fingers over the cropped hair, and prod the back of the head with the point of his blade. The man shifted violently, kicking up sand. With his teeth clenched into a macabre smile, Lightfoot pushed his face up next to the soldier's and let loose a war cry. He made a feint at the man's face, moving his knife blade in an ugly circle as if he intended to dig the eye out of its socket. Through it all, Small Deer kept his distance.

Takes-the-Pipe indicated officiously where the cut should be made—a little less than halfway up the base of the skull. He had his knife out and was ready to break the skin when Lightfoot interrupted. "Tumbling Hawk took the first coup; he must take the scalp." Takes-the-Pipe drew himself up in dignified assent and let his tensed right hand fall to his side. Only then did Tumbling Hawk stoop down next to the soldier. The others looked on respectfully as he pressed the blade to the head, a little above the spot Takes-the-Pipe indicated. "It's hard to gather such short hair," he thought with muted technical interest. He understood why white scalps weren't very highly regarded. He made the two curved cuts—the paired half moons—and the knife skimmed a circle of flesh from the skull. The man writhed like a broken snake. A dying noise escaped him—hardly any sound, only a deep lingering sibilance.

The flap of skin and hair still clung to the head. Blood tipped the edges of the scalp when Tumbling Hawk completed the work with a shallow slice of his knife. It came away into his hand with a plop, ripping off a little more hair and flesh. Thrusting it above his head, he reached inside himself for an expression of triumph. "HOKA HEY! HOKA HEY!" His war cry startled him even more than the others. It broke his trance.

Takes-the-Pipe followed with another war cry, and together the three who'd touched the man, and thus counted coup, began to dance around the soldier. At first they moved slowly, restraining themselves so as not to burst into a jagged childish dance. They planted their feet cautiously, their arms pumped slowly as they felt their way into the rhythm. They'd never done the Scalp Dance before, only seen it, for a man could not move through those sacred steps until he had severed hair from head.

Then Small Deer joined them, and the four moved around the dead white together. Like a strange rhythmic insect, four feet touched the ground together, then the other four. Their feet began to stamp and raise dust; they let out cries. Heads dropping forward, then falling back, feet thudding, they circled their dead enemy in gradually quickening rounds. Their bodies tensed and sprang like bows, their feet brushed over, then crashed into the dust. They danced until the sun started toward its place of going over in the west, until one by one they sank exhausted to the ground.

Afterward they felt refreshed. Takes-the-Pipe and Tumbling Hawk picked through the soldier's belongings. They had difficulty opening the buttoned pocket of his tunic, which revealed a small rectangular notebook. Tumbling Hawk was about to open it when Lightfoot, arms outspread like an eagle, swooped by and snatched it out of his hand, then awkwardly groped through clumps of pages. In the pockets of the coat they found a key (totally inexplicable to them) and a dirty kerchief of faded red calico. They agreed to give the hunting knife to Small Deer, who could use it for his carving. Takes-the-Pipe got the strange blade that carried its own sheath (a razor), and they all took turns at opening and closing the smooth steel. They could make nothing of the paper money, rolled tightly into a cylinder and held together by a small gold clip. But the coins fascinated Tumbling Hawk, who had never seen things so perfect. He rolled them round and round, searching for the tiniest irregularity. Nothing he knew was that faultless. Or symmetrical. A raised part on one looked like a face; on the other he saw something which might have been a bird, perhaps an eagle. He stood without moving until Lightfoot said, "Tumbling Hawk grows giddy following the round of their skimming stones." In response Tumbling Hawk stuffed his hand down into his quiver, letting them drop from his fingers one by one. Long afterward, his fingertips remembered the feel of the metal, and often that day his hands itched to touch them again.

Three nights later the men of the Cheyenne camp assembled in the lodge of Takes-the-Pipe's father, Man-Who-Runs-the-Farthest, then a leader of the Elk Horn Warrior Society but already considered likely to become a tribal chief. His lodge was quite large, made of nineteen mature buffalo skins, which befitted a man of importance. His antelope shield hung from the central lodge pole, and under it dangled a pair of dry, shrunken-looking moccasins, which had once belonged to a Crow chief. At the back of the lodge near the host's bedding was a high stack of beaver and muskrat skins which he meant to give away to poor villagers. The fire was hot and the guests, lounging on their mattresses and backrests, were sweating freely.

Man-Who-Runs-the-Farthest wore only breechclout and moccasins; his hair was drawn back into a tight scalp lock. He was a large man who looked as if he had been cut from a great slab of slate. The sharp economy of the father's features had been passed to the son. Neither wasted gestures. But on the night of his son's first public honor, the host was expansive. For him there was no better celebration than one that jointly honored his tribe and himself. For three days he'd worked hard, and already he felt rewarded by the expectant hum that filled his lodge. He knew his guests were pleased with what he set before them.

The boys were seated in places of highest honor, to the left of the host and the chief shaman—first, Takes-the-Pipe, then Tumbling Hawk, Lightfoot, and Small Deer. In corresponding positions to the right sat their fathers, with one place left empty for Wolf's Tooth, Lightfoot's father, who'd been killed in the previous summer's raid on the Pawnee. An extra place had been added for Hankering Horse, who'd taken his brother's son into his lodge. In front of the boys, on a white antelope skin, lay the soldier's revolver, his knives and scalp, while next to them—right next to them—was Rumbling Wings, the most powerful medicine man in the Cheyenne nation.

As soon as the medicine man rose, the hum stilled—a wind might have sucked their voices out of the smoke hole. When the old man began, his voice was parched, dusty as if from long disuse. As he continued his sounds began to irrigate themselves.

"Our sacred ceremonies can dry into dust and be blown away by one strong wind if celebrated by a hollow voice and attended by a step without spring. Better to thank the buffalo in the moment of kill, the hunter sprayed with the victim's blood, than to mark his agony in songs without music. Better to stumble on the growing ear and greedily tear through its flesh than to walk with empty tread through the steps of the Corn Dance, kernel without seed, following footsteps but not where they lead. We cannot excite the cracking land with promise of rain that does not come. That is why I do not often attend these feasts; it is not my place to drain the ceremonies of their blood. I am here because I look for power in this deed. Perhaps these boys will spread new power across the Plains, and a time will come when Waschita fall to the youngest of the Cheyenne."

Bowing his head, Rumbling Wings let his hair fall until it almost touched the ground. The black hair framed a shower of bone necklets; in the middle of the string was a deep smoky stone. Only Small Deer and Takes-the-Pipe had seen the Healing Stone before, when they were very sick. Both had tried to see through it while Rumbling Wings searched for the evil inside them. Now, as the medicine man swayed, the stone came alive with quick darting lights. The shaman sang, his eyes closed:

"We call upon our Helper
In strength, in need.
We should not call more strongly
In triumph than in pain,
In pain than in triumph,
Or through the sound of our voice
He will hear the gap in our hearts."

When the old man took his seat, the eating began.

The feast was impressive—there were baskets of rainbow trout and bass and carp and catfish; there were turkey, elk, bobcat, and dog, and the fine-grained meat of the dwarf deer. Three buffalo had been butchered—the ribs roasted, the hump boiled, the lungs cut open, dried and roasted on coals. Sparrows and blackbirds were roasted on skewers and served in their charred skins. There were bear root and turnips, grapes, plums and chokecherries, as well as unfamiliar delicacies like the tongue and nose of the young bull buffalo, liver sprinkled with gall, and the roasted intestine of a yearling. For the boys the meal improved each time their names were mentioned, whenever their courage or cunning was commended by the warriors. Which was often, since they were the main conversational topic. There were two sour tastes: Strong Left Hand was strangely quiet, as if to suggest one dead white wasn't worth all the fuss, and Small Deer's father, Hard Ground, looked uncomfortable among the other fathers. He was a poor man, a cripple, and thus something of an outcast.

The guests ate and joked until they couldn't eat anything else, then forced themselves to suck on lingering marrow in a particularly sweet bone or cracked open another nut. Not until then did the host stand up.

"If I didn't hope to make you at least as comfortable, I wouldn't take you away from what is before you." He spoke with good feeling and characteristic awkwardness. Everyone knew what he meant, and no one needed more. "My son's deeds made me as happy as when I shot my first buffalo calf. I feel as if I was with them on their rabbit hunt, as if I walked in my son's tracks when rabbit turned soldier. I feel this, yet I take no glory away from my son except for the borrowed light a father basks in as his son grows." His pleasure halted him there, so he ended: "My son took second coup, so I gave the best horse I had to Walking Crow. He captured a gun, so I gave a fine pony to Cross Beak. I welcome to my lodge the men of the Cheyenne. I am honored to have you here."

Many of the older men had the same thought: "A chief grows happy making his people happy." Others, including Tumbling Hawk's grandfather, Mohe, had different views: Big Road had given up his right to hold the banquet, though his son had taken first coup. Man-Who-Runs-the-Farthest had come to him and asked for the privilege. Big Road deferred because, as he told Tumbling Hawk, a man who wanted to be a chief could make better use of the occasion. He'd asked his son not to be too disappointed, and Tumbling Hawk tried not to be. But it did not seem altogether just to the boy.

In the order of things it was Big Road's turn to speak, though it would have been hard to tell by looking at him—he was so relaxed it seemed he wouldn't move for days. He had on a worn buffalo robe, his "feasting dress" he called it, which gave him ample eating room. He was a big man who grew larger, more solid, as he aged, as if he accommodated more life as he came to live it more fully. Then suddenly—Big Road had a way of sitting with his left leg under him and springing up off it—he was on his feet. Since he never thought of a gesture until he made it, everything came as a little surprise to him. And so, of course, to others.

To his host he said, "The fruits of your lodge are blessed gifts to your brothers." He touched the words lightly and continued, yet they lingered like a benediction. Big Road made clear that he was perfectly satisfied with these arrangements. "I too have a son who has filled my heart with the youth Man-Who-Runs-the-Farthest know so well. Yesterday I thought of Tumbling Hawk as a boy, the day before I called Tumbling Hawk child."

The father's face was full, almost chunky, his features open and amiable. His son resembled him, only Tumbling Hawk had a thinner, more delicate face—the jaw less assertive, his cheekbones not so full. Father and son shared generous mouths, though Big Road's was less clipped at the corners and even fuller in the lips. Tumbling Hawk studied his father, but if he'd looked at Mohe he would have seen an even closer likeness—the longer, tighter face, the same prominent expressive nose with finely arched nostrils. The boy's broad forehead and rich copper skin came from his mother, Shell, as did his eyes, which slanted ever so slightly down, as did his droopy lids, which never seemed altogether open.

"One white soldier is not an army. But even a father who fights being overproud knows that nothing passes without tracks. And to follow those tracks is always a step toward virtue. A sign, as clear as the iron hooves of the horse, led our boys to the fallen Waschita. The wind held the soldier's hand as they raced each other to the body. May many more white hands be stilled by the grip of the wind. May our sons always race one another toward glory."

A lot of chatter followed Big Road's speech. No one noticed that Hankering Horse had risen to speak and he, in turn, probably would have stood on his feet all night if someone hadn't whispered, "The Horse!" Still he stood silently, looking out at them. He said nothing, just smiling to indicate how pleased he was to be there. Eventually they were smiling too. Then he began to chuckle, quietly to himself until a few men joined him. Then, with them, he began to laugh louder, and then louder until his laughter was swallowed by theirs.

Later, when the lodge grew quiet, he said, "My son Lightfoot has tended my herd and lived at my fire since he came to me. I did not have to treat him like a son, for he is my son, nothing else. Today he rewards me with a great honor. I thank him for that as I thank him for sharing my lodge. As I thank you for being here—as you can see—"

Grinning and embarrassed, the Horse sat down to their cheers and laughter. The next speaker was to be Hard Ground, a short grisly man with scaly flesh and a torso wizened like a bad ear of corn. Sensing Hard Ground's mood, the warriors kept up their clapping, hoping to humor him, hoping to cajole and persuade him to share their mood. But he stood up torturously, exaggerating his deformity—shoulder tilted too high, the hump thrust out. He knew how much the sight disgusted them.

All night Small Deer's father had brooded that his presence was a temporary concession, that the warriors allowed him to sit in the lodge only because his son had trailed after theirs.

He spoke with vicious self-effacement: "I am pleased my son went with the party. I am glad he took his rabbit and returned safely."

Small Deer cringed and looked down. But even if he'd searched for help, the others would have avoided his eyes. A father's words could not be countered.

Hard Ground grunted brusquely as he sat down, "It is my pleasure to be here."

The community recoiled. An affront to ritual was an affront to all. Good observance pleased the ancestors, for through it they lived again. The bitterness of Hard Ground's words was an attack on the host and blasphemed Rumbling Wings, their spiritual guardian, who was never to be exposed to such a tone.

The shaman's irritation was only momentary. With casual dignity he inclined his head toward his host and whispered something. Man-Who-

Runs-the-Farthest turned to his left and said, "Will our sons and younger brothers follow their fathers with words of their own?"

Tumbling Hawk was up before he finished. "Three days ago we tracked a soldier to his place of dying; we closed the circle around him as we were taught by our fathers. Four of us crawled within a few paces of a living Waschita, and each held one of the cardinal points. It took four of us to cut off his escape." He started firmly, but his voice trembled slightly as he insisted on the number. "Then two of us, eager for glory, raced to the body while our brothers, a few steps away from the Waschita and his gun, held their points to keep him from breaking out. Together we share all honor, whatever honor there is."

The older men approved. One whispered that Tumbling Hawk was surely his father's son.

Takes-the-Pipe took his turn, as always, in dignified possession of himself. "Fathers, we are honored to be here among you. All of us are honored. After the hunt I had only one doubt." His tone was uncompromising. "That was in myself. A better tracker would've known by the soldier's trail that his back was broken."

Lightfoot thanked them for the excellent feast, his chin still glossy with grease. Then he mimed the vicious feints with which, he said, "I scared a dying man to death."

They laughed again, but guardedly this time. Every eye was on Small Deer as he rose. His tawny skin was a little flushed as he said, in a quiet but audible voice, "On that day my part seemed small: one rabbit and holding the south as I have often done. Thank you, fathers and brothers, for telling me just how large each part really is."

That was enough for Rumbling Wings, who stood up beaming, delighted they'd answered the challenge in its own terms. It was the first time many of the company had seen the medicine man smile. "Our young men did what they should always do, show us what we fail to see. We are in their debt." He paid tribute by bowing to his left, though the smile would have been enough for the boys. "To settle some small part of the debt, I offer a story. It tells the youngest what has passed with the oldest in the earliest days we know how to speak about. If some of you have heard the tale before, listen as your fathers do, for the time of telling can change the story as much as the age of hearing.

"In the days when breezes brought children to surprised women and the tongue of all animals, two-legged and four-legged, was still the same, in those early days of this earth and our people, red man was very weak. All the animals, especially the buffalo, ate us just as we eat them today, for we had just emerged from underground and had only recently become accustomed to light. In those days we were without bow or arrow or horse. The buffalo so terrorized the Indian that the Great Power began to fear he might lose one of his offspring. So he called the world to him and told them to arrange for a race to be run around the edge of the Black Hills. If the four-leggeds won, things would continue as they'd been; red man would have to take his chances. But if the two-leggeds won, they were to be given power over the buffalo and the other four-leggeds. And so it might be to this day—so we might be delicacies at the buffalo's banquet.

"All animals and all people gathered at the edge of the Black Hills, in a place you know as the Race Track at Buffalo Gap. Preparations were elaborate, for the winner was to be given great power. The bald eagle took white clay and rubbed it over his head and neck, even adding a spot back on his side, then painting the rest of his body dark brown. The antelope colored herself yellow with patches of white. The coyote swore if he didn't win he would give up his way of life and climb to a hilltop where he would sing a plaintive song. The gray eagle whistled like a falling arrow, promising to nest between earth and sky if he lost. All preened and primped and painted themselves for, though they didn't know it then, the markings they wore that day were to become theirs forever.

"Before the start of the race the animals lined up. Using their strength, size, and numbers the buffalo moved themselves in closest to the hills, in the best positions. Whenever another creature came near the inside positions, the buffalo chased them away. Soon everyone was pushing and squirming and jostling to get the best places. Only red man stood apart, quite far away, for he was still too weak to compete. Then magpie asked the buffalo to play fairly and be less greedy. They mocked her openly, called her names—black beak, white flasher, long tail. Annoyed with the buffalo, magpie quit her place among the animals and joined the humans, saying she too had two legs and would race with man. The others only jeered. But her human friends greeted her warmly. Finally, when all were ready, Thunder gave the signal to start.

"Slim Walking Woman, a fine buffalo cow, took an early lead, with the swift birds and fast animals close behind her. But the fastest animals and birds tired quickly, and soon Slim Walking Woman opened up a big lead. Meanwhile, the magpie flew steadily higher as she went forward; her pace never changed. By the time they reached the west point, halfway round, many had already fallen exhausted. In the west, magpie reached her greatest height. There she also passed the first runners, though they were far below her. At the third corner, the south, even Slim Walking Woman's pace was faltering; she was beginning to tire. Meanwhile, magpie gathered speed as on and on she flew, gliding, then darting on with a smart flap of her wings. Faster and faster she flew until she passed the whole of creation, even Slim Walking Woman herself. She reached the place in the east where they'd started—far ahead of the others.

"So magpie and her friend man triumphed, and they made the buffalo teach them the Sun Dance in order to thank the Great Power for their victory. Since winning that race we have had the right to eat the flesh of all four-leggeds and most birds, though not the magpie, with whom we have a bond of friendship. And so every summer we hold the sacred Sun Dance with all the creatures who ran against us at the circle at the foot of the Black Hills."

He paused a moment, then slyly added, "Of course the buffalo's character has changed greatly since those days. He has learned humility, and humility has made him a friendly creature. We too must be careful not to be cruel, for it's impossible to know when we may have to run for our lives again."

Afterward the talk turned, as it should, to battles. The men spoke of great deeds they'd done and, for the first time, the boys heard the formal recitation of their father's stories. The tales of coup and scalp and captured horses continued long into the night.

Eventually the host and the shaman moved to the flap of the lodge, and waited there for the guests to file out. They gathered again outside, then everyone looked up at the sky. It was a beautiful night—brilliant, clear. They gazed up in silence awhile, then Man-Who-Runs-the-Farthest sang:

"My boy has found game
My son has come upon the enemy.
Protect him always,
He has faced death and returned."

His guests, the fathers and the sons, carried his song back with them to their lodges.

BUCK'S HEART, THE EXERCISE MASTER

FOR THE REST OF the tribe, the winter's hibernation was just like any other—the slow familiar round of daily activities, the women working the buffalo hides in the half outdoors of the roofless enclosure of buffalo skins, the warriors sitting around the lodge fire retelling their deeds and every second or third day venturing a short distance into the deep snow for whatever game they could kill. The four boys, coming into their twelfth year, waited expectantly through the Moon of the Frost in the tepee and into the Moon of the Dark Red Calves. Then Takes-the-Pipe, three months older than Tumbling Hawk, received a sign from his ally: the elk promised him a stately future, power, and protection as a warrior. Soon afterward, a crow spoke mysteriously to Lightfoot.

Through these long winter months, Tumbling Hawk waited for his vision. But no ally spoke to him, and none offered him its powers. He slept poorly during the Snowblind Moon.

Early in the Moon of the Grass Appearing, as the foothills soaked up the snow, a beaver instructed Small Deer to go to a certain stream and to stay there and watch for his brothers. Small Deer was gone five days. When he returned, he told Tumbling Hawk that he had watched the beavers slide down the banks on their tails like they had as children on their buffalo-rib sleds. He'd seen the beavers wrestle and swim, diving and steering each other around in the water. He'd observed them navigate their system of canals and watched his allies' patient craft as they cut down trees, chopped them into manageable lengths, dragged the logs to the water, and ferried them onto their new home. They fitted the lengths as carefully as lodge poles, pushing in the smaller twigs and dredging up patching mud. He left them only after every chink had been sealed and the roof completed. Tumbling Hawk listened carefully to his friend, ransacking his own dreams to be certain he hadn't missed any signs. He turned up nothing.

Tumbling Hawk didn't think he slept at all that night in mid-April. He saw the eagle raise wings to break flight, the hawk swoop to clutch at a flash below, the deer leap so gracefully the air seemed to hold her up. His mind was so full of whirr and motion he didn't know he slept until his pictures were interrupted by Buck's Heart's sharp taps.

With a snap of his wrist and a threading motion of his finger Buck's Heart told the boy to rise and go to the water as fast as he could. The silent one was gone from the tepee before Tumbling Hawk had slipped out of his buffalo robe.

As he ran toward the stream, Tumbling Hawk was vaguely conscious of the sun being lower than usual, which was why, he thought sleepily, none of the warriors were down at the water. But after a few strides he was no longer alone. With him, converging on the stream, were his friends–Lightfoot, Small Deer, and Takes-the-Pipe. All sensed each other at the same moment and looked around to find themselves nearing the water from four equidistant points–as if started by Buck's Heart at exactly the same instant.

Identical strides brought them to the bank and the same leap sent them into the air. Together four boys hung over the water until together they all took the shock of the flowing ice water. The cold smashed them, chilling their hot flesh.

Takes-the-Pipe was the first to notice Buck's Heart standing on the bank. His hands told them they needn't be in a hurry, but when they finished bathing they were to join him on the warriors' field. They lingered in the stream until the older men began to drift down for their morning baths.

The tall, gaunt brave with the deeply pitted face stood before them on the prairie about a half mile east of camp. The same white man's disease that chiseled into his face had silenced his tongue. But in spite of his ugliness, Buck's Heart was a favorite with the boys. When they were very young, he had taught them how to stalk the deer, how to move together in the surround. Though he wasn't the strongest Cheyenne (Strong Left Hand, for one, was far stronger) the Buck knew so much about the movements of all creatures that it was said he could turn the power of an enemy against itself. Because he understood how things moved, he was the tribe's best tracker. He was also one of their finest riders. Which was why the four of them stood before him. Before they could pledge themselves to a warrior society and join their elders in battle, they would have to learn to ride like warriors.

Two years before, a boy called Yellow Wolf had fallen from his pony and broken his neck. He'd been trying to "make the switch," the Cheyenne's most important battle maneuver: the rider drops his body on one side of his horse, hooking his heel over the pony's back. With just that hooked heel for support, he could either rise and shoot his arrows over the pony's back or under its neck. And with that heel alone he could heave himself up again and switch to the opposite side. Naturally, with the pony's body between him and his enemy, he made a difficult target. The maneuver was difficult enough for a grown man with full strength. On their own, all four of the boys had practiced "making the switch" for almost a year now, though only Takes-the-Pipe and Tumbling Hawk could get off any accurate shots and neither had done it at a gallop.

They were surprised they hadn't been told to bring their ponies. But that didn't lessen their excitement—being called by Buck's Heart was the beginning of the practices and ceremonies that led to manhood.

Buck's Heart stood with his feet apart, his arms raised at right angles to his body. He pivoted his upper torso, rolling from left to right and cocking his hips slightly. His right arm swept downward, the hand followed after until it appeared that the ground itself came up at it and patted it gently in the palm. Raising himself easily, he returned to his starting position, then repeated the movement to the other side. The exercise was simple to begin with. The boys followed with a less precise version, arms flailing, hips jerking.

Buck's Heart continued for a while, absorbed in his own movements. Then he arched his back and brought his neck forward in front of the plane of his body. That way he could keep up the rhythm as he watched them.

He observed each boy carefully. Lightfoot had too much curve in his back. So Buck's Heart exaggerated the sway of his own back, forcing his behind to stick out and up. That cramped his arms by pushing them too far back in their sockets. He did the exercise a few times from that swayback position. Then he began to straighten his spine. Slowly he coaxed Lightfoot's back into its proper line. He looked like he was being pulled up by a rope above his head. As his back came into place, his rear settled into the base of his spine; suddenly his arms were free again. He worked with Lightfoot awhile, then acted out in turn the others' faults. He was patient, so willing to drop back to lead them forward that in time they all did it fairly well. He led them through many simple movements, exercises they'd done before (or thought they'd done), and a few difficult ones, contortions they could hardly believe possible. He somehow demonstrated to them what stretched and what contracted and took care to indicate how parts of the body were paired to work together.

Sometimes the boys could feel the map of their own sets of muscle inside them. Sometimes they got only an interrupted outline of what he suggested was there. Occasionally the muscles didn't seem to exist at all. There was one exercise where he pulled his right arm up and down behind his back with his left, moving it almost the length of his back. Small Deer was the only one who could move his arm at all. Takes-the-Pipe could hardly touch one hand to the other.

Of the four, Small Deer generally had the least trouble. The others were stronger and could keep it up longer, but Small Deer fell into the rhythms easily and usually let the others set the pace. Buck's Heart was very pleased with him. Takes-the-Pipe mastered a lot of the exercises quickly, but those he didn't he tended to massacre, exhausting himself trying to overpower them. Lightfoot began enthusiastically but got distracted quickly. Tumbling Hawk was the most reflective: he studied the movements as if to think them into his body. He hated the awkwardness of beginning. Once he mastered them, he did them well but had difficulty keeping time.

The morning was long and hard. They did a scrambling exercise on all fours until their thighs felt waterlogged. Their knees could hardly open and shut. Finally, when only Tumbling Hawk and Takes-the-Pipe were still going, both missing every other beat, Buck's Heart sprang up and stood perfectly still. One by one the boys shifted into standing positions.

It felt good at first. For quite a while it was pleasant. Then they began to tire. They all fought off the first waves of fatigue, impressed by their master's comfortable stance. Then their points of contact with the earth seemed to shrink; the arches of their feet rounded underneath them, toes curved up; they tottered and shook. Finally, the earth itself gently tipped them off. Small Deer was the last to move. Buck's Heart jumped and landed, jumped and landed, his knees flexed. He instructed them to find the place where their feet sank into the earth, where their legs were cushioned by the ground. There they could make peace with the earth they walked on. They stood searching for their stance until the sun was halfway up the morning sky, until Buck's

Heart swung out of the circle into a run. The boys broke from their places even before he waved for them to follow.

Tumbling Hawk felt the tightness ease from his lower back; his mind cleared. He felt good on the flat ground, moving without having to think where what hand went on which count or where to put which foot on what beat. He'd never realized how fine running was, or any of those things that came without training, or whose training was so long past it came to the same thing. Then he understood that for Buck's Heart each exercise was as natural as running. Unable to think of how he ran, his breath coming in its proper place, his legs and arms moving as they had to, suddenly Tumbling Hawk's body filled his mind with happiness.

SMALL DEER AND HORN, THE BOWMAKER

SMALL DEER WAS WELL named—quiet and shy, with unobtrusive but profound pockets of strength and a fiercely understated sense of determination. He was easily underestimated by those who didn't know him, but rarely by those who did. People were always surprised how close he and Tumbling Hawk were. There were many reasons for that, though ultimately it wasn't a question of reasons. For one thing, Small Deer lived with more difficulties than the others, although no one knew whether that made him more mature or whether he would've been so anyway. In any case, Tumbling Hawk relied on his friend's quiet good judgment and sense of fairness.

Small Deer's problem was his father. Hard Ground's cruelty to his son was rare among the Cheyenne, who sternly assumed a proper relation between parent and child. What made the situation worse was that the tribe strictly forbade interference in family matters—except by other members of the family. But Small Deer's father was a poor man, without relations, and his mother was a Crow. So he had neither uncles nor mother's family to escape to. Yet Small Deer never complained. He never said a word against his father, not even to his best friend. At the same time he made plans. At the age of twelve he decided to become a bowmaker.

He then went to Horn, the tribe's bowmaker, and explained why he thought he would be a good apprentice. After presenting Horn three bows he'd made, Small Deer asked permission to visit Horn's lodge on a regular basis. He was still too young to be formally apprenticed and took care not to put Horn in too awkward a position.

The bowmaker was tempted to think the boy presumptuous, but he was more impressed by Small Deer's self-assurance. Like everyone else in the village, he knew the boy's family situation and wasn't anxious to take on what might be a very complicated responsibility. There was also a question of the boy's frailness. Horn was amazed, then, that Small Deer went on to say he had to conserve energy in a way his friends didn't, but believed he could develop his endurance slowly, over a long period of time. Therefore, bowmaking seemed the most sensible thing he could do. Besides, Small Deer concluded, he liked it. Hesitantly Horn agreed to let the boy observe him. They made no other arrangement at that time. A month later the bowmaker admitted to being impressed by the way his instruction found form in the boy's work. One day Horn realized he appreciated having the boy's quiet around him. Still he hesitated—the burden of accepting Small Deer, he feared, would be almost as great as having a son. (Horn had three daughters.) He had plenty of time for a decision, and his uncertainty about the boy's stamina persisted. A few days later, Horn realized he didn't like his reasons for turning the boy away. He announced this by pointing to the sheepskin bow case that hung on the center pole of the lodge. "I think it's time I told you the story of my bow."

It was one of the glorious moments in Small Deer's life. He lifted the bow from its place and carried it over to where Horn sat by the fire.

A little roughly Horn pulled the bow out of its sheepskin case; it sprang into his hand. The bow, made entirely of the horns of a giant mountain sheep, was a startling white.

Horn braced it against his thigh then bent it sharply. The string sinew slipped into the notch. He let the bow tense. "He likes to flex his muscles sometimes. Seems only fair not to leave him defenseless when I talk about him." The point of the bow rested on the ground, the curve across Horn's thigh.

"When I was a few summers older than you, the Pawnee raided our camp on the Cow and made off with my father's elk-horn bow. It was his ceremonial bow, used to Renew the Arrows as well as to call Thunder. Walking War, my father's father, had given it to him.

"Bent Straight was beside himself with grief and rage. Each night for a month he danced in the Medicine Lodge to purge the tribe of its loss. For another month he fasted and took the sweat bath. During that time hard rumors ran through the camp, declaring my father's power ended. He was sad—I never saw him so sad—yet whenever I asked if I might go and recapture the bow from the Pawnee, he told me to be patient and wait; a sign would appear. He was that certain his power hadn't left him.

"One night in the third month of his trial a strange vision came to me while I slept." Horn tapped the bow lightly. "I was on a high mountain far north of this place, somewhere in the Wasatch range. I don't know how I knew it was the Wasatch, but somehow I recognized it. So I found myself working up a steep rock face. I climbed until suddenly, above me, a great mountain sheep appeared, snow white, with the largest horns I'd ever imagined."

His left hand curved into place on the gleaming bow. "I was surprised that when the sheep saw me he didn't run, but I didn't think much about it—I was very excited—and kept climbing up the face, trying to get into position for a shot. I remember my great hurry to get close to him. He moved up slowly, staying just out of range and using the rocks as cover, though I really didn't think of that at all then. Yet, as I climbed, I suddenly got the notion he was teasing me. I told myself that was crazy. Finally I reached the place where the rock split. I was at the narrow end of a funnel, and at the top stood the sheep. Just as I was about to start up, a shower of rocks fell down at me. I heard it coming, looked up—and there he was, staring down. If I'd had the time I would have been frightened, but I didn't, so I dove for cover behind a large boulder just outside the funnel.

"I waited until all the rocks skittered by, then started up into the funnel. The sheep was really angry now. Every step I took was such an insult to him I knew either he'd kill me or me him. That was very clear. It was like fighting a man.

"All the way up the sheep patiently watched me climb, screening himself so well I didn't have a shot. He just let me come on. I should've known the creature was letting me trap myself. I was less than one hundred paces from him when he backed up against an enormous boulder, planted his front legs and began to push against it with his hind legs. He pushed regularly, but he didn't seem in a hurry. As if he knew it would move.

"I was terrified. Alone, with no angle for a shot, on sheer mountain face, caught in a rock funnel, a bewitched sheep aiming boulders at me. On the way up I'd watched carefully though, and noticed a cut in the opposite rock face, at a point not far below where I stood. The slit was large enough that I might be able to hang on there—if I had to. If I could jump across the gap. So I slid down fast, looking up all the time since I couldn't turn around, and watched that sheep deliberately step back from the boulder and kick. Each kick sent loose pebbles down, and I had to duck them. Finally I got to the spot where I'd have to jump. The sheep moved around on the rock to get a better position and his cover broke. I had to thread two overhanging rocks to hit him, but at least I had a shot! By then bigger stones were coming down, then a huge rock bounced by just missing me. I heard the boulder shift, realized he had it loose. I tensed the bow, looked up through the slot, thought about all the shots I'd made in my life, and thanked the spirits for the chance. Then I heard the boulder come loose. And I released.

"I never saw the arrow after it left my bow. I never saw the boulder bouncing down. I just dove. Somehow I made it. I hung by my fingertips over the drop knowing nothing. Behind me I heard the whole mountain give way. And over it, I heard a scream, not like the cry of a sheep but like a man being strangled.

"The slide took away the funnel and sent the mountain down halfway into the valley. I worked my way down the rock face I was on. Way below, on top of the slide, I found the sheep, even bigger and whiter than I expected. My arrow had gone right through his throat. That might explain the strange scream." Clearly he didn't believe that was true. "Or maybe he was surprised by my shot.

"His horns—"

Horn touched the bow as he'd touched it that first time. "There's not much more to tell. My father urged me to go to the mountain and be found by the sheep on the rock face. We prayed and fasted and made sacrifices together until we believed the time had come. Then I set off, dressed and armed as I'd been in my vision. Everything happened exactly as I'd seen it, every detail absolutely in place. Afterwards I cut off his horns. I had to remove all my arrows to fit them into the quiver. When I finally got back to camp Bent Straight greeted me with great joy. There was feasting and dancing, and I was asked to fashion this bow."

He patted it again. "When I was finished I was given a new name and made a bowmaker, like my father. The day I was made bowmaker my father told me it was good for his father's bow to remain with the Pawnee, for its horn had become too brittle and its time was past."

The approach of Small Deer's formal apprenticeship only fed his father's fury. Hard Ground objected to giving Horn three horses, wanting the gift reduced to two. He declared the ceremony "demeaning to the natural father." Hard Ground was disgusted that the quiet independence which had patiently outflanked his authority was about to escape and render his strongest weapon—parental disapproval—

useless. Their battle was as brutal as all extended mismatches are. The last two months Small Deer spent as much time as possible in Horn's lodge to keep out of his father's way. Even so the village heard Hard Ground yelling at his son every night. Sometimes he even struck Small Deer, an unheard-of thing for a Cheyenne. Yet Small Deer never said a word about these things to his friends. And the only noticeable effect was that he grew still more committed to his principle: once he escaped the ugly tone of his father's lodge, he wanted never to hear it again; and Small Deer was certain he would never sound it himself.

Tumbling Hawk and Small Deer were often together during Small Deer's last days in his father's lodge. Often they walked in the woods while Small Deer searched for the best juniper saplings or the straightest cherry shoots for arrow shafts. Small Deer gave his friend new eyes. Soon Tumbling Hawk could tell when they were approaching a likely juniper, or guess which split branches would make the soundest bows, or which shoots could be peeled and straightened with the least trouble. He learned how to make the overlapping cuts to check the run of a tree's grain, how to close those flaps to keep the insects out. He began to notice minute differences in each tree's texture, could tell their densities from their grains. He bit bark, chewed on shoots from trees. He learned to avoid the marsh and soggy bottom, to prefer the high well-watered ground, to never use heartwood—"... made to carry food and life, not to kill." Together they cut trees as Horn had shown Small Deer, taking great care as they made the first notch.

"It lets the tree know how it will be taken. Never slash around, for the sap runs in the wood long after it's separated from its root."

As often as he accompanied his friend to Horn's lodge, Tumbling Hawk ,never lost his fascination for the place. Bows were everywhere, in all stages of completion—some barely off the tree, others beginning to bend into their curving forms, waiting for a binding sinew or a warrior's patron animal. In the village Horn appeared squint-eyed and abstracted to Tumbling Hawk; he always seemed to be looking off somewhere. To the boy he'd always lacked a little dignity. But inside his tepee, sitting cross-legged, his tools in an orderly row before him, his concentration found its focus; the bowmaker drew on the space around him like a robe. As he worked, his face grew more intent, which emphasized the way it pulled back away from the point of his thin nose, as though he'd been walking into a strong head wind all his life. But the more intent the face became, the more relaxed the hands. The face did the worrying, the hands, the work.

Tumbling Hawk first saw Horn lift a bow out of a tree on the day the bowmaker was working with hickory. He remembered only that they were already at work when he entered and that Small Deer first directed his eyes to the strange piece of hickory in Horn's lap, then looked at Horn quizzically, prompting his master to take the cue. Horn smiled, shook his head slightly, and said, "Usually I wouldn't use a wood like this—" The hickory's grain was crosshatched with dark lines that looked like termite holes. "But I'm curious to know how strong it is. I remember an old southern Cheyenne bowmaker telling me these markings sometimes make for a good long-range bow."

Horn picked up one of his worn knives from the buffalo robe in front of him. The master began to scrape the hickory along the grain in a long sweeping arc. Even his first cut made the curve of a bow. Small Deer picked up a blade then too and made similar arcs on his own wood, surprisingly long and well curved, though not as deep or steady as Horn's. Most of the time Tumbling Hawk watched the master, he was so caught by the contrast between the emotions of his face and those moodless, steadily working hands. He didn't know how long he sat there before he realized the shape of the bow had already emerged; he couldn't understand how he'd missed its forming. A little later Small Deer stopped and then he too watched Horn. But his attention was better informed; he saw more and knew how to impress each of his teacher's movements into himself. All the while Horn was pulling from the tree the form he found imbedded there. The tree seemed to contain nothing else—all the rest was to be stripped away to free the bow.

Horn spoke once: "I don't like this very much. Too mushy for hickory. I don't think it'll be very good." After that he worked more quickly. They watched the wood bend under his hands as the blade took off one continuous curling piece. The wood ribbon didn't stop until Horn's thumb and index finger lifted a bow into the air.

Horn passed his fingers over the shavings and sang:

"The tree that held you
Relinquished you to me.
The scar I cut—forgive.
Fly like a falcon
to your new home."

Within the bowmaker's lodge time was much the same. That was one reason Tumbling Hawk liked it so much. Sitting in that still bright light, quietly intoxicated by the smells, Tumbling Hawk lost all interest in time. His only measure for it was Small Deer's increased skill, or his friend's stronger grip (he religiously squeezed wads of buffalo hide when he wasn't working with Horn), or those small hands growing callused. Even those markers grew less distinct as time passed and the movements of the hands became more and more like one.

Technique, Horn said, is like a muscle; it grows stronger with use. As Tumbling Hawk saw Small Deer's skill grow, he understood. What impressed him about his friend's apprenticeship was the way their work accommodated those days when Small Deer's fingers stumbled over each other and Small Deer seemed to be back at the beginning again, or the days without energy, and even those without interest. Somehow their craft assumed and incorporated all days.

As the blade settled into the apprentice's hand and bowmaker's tools became longer, stronger fingers, Small Deer changed—he knew where to look and how to place what he saw. Subsequently, he forgot less, wasted less. The boys' roles reversed, the hardest time for friendships. But Tumbling Hawk and Small Deer enjoyed each other's company more than ever before. Their conversation became what seemed to them more grown-up. They came to appreciate why the repetitions in Small Deer's work were infinitely more interesting than Tumbling Hawk's endless playing at games he'd outgrown. Tumbling Hawk was bored with stealing pieces of buffalo meat from the drying rack or capturing berry baskets from the girls when they came home from their picking—this did not satisfy any longer as his imaginary coup. All that was for children. Tumbling Hawk was too pleased with Small Deer's escape and his winning a new father to begrudge him anything, but Small Deer's presence in that other world made Tumbling Hawk more aware of how arbitrary the boundary was and fueled his urge to spill out into manhood.

Yet, no matter how impatient Tumbling Hawk became, he always felt soothed when Small Deer imparted his master's wisdom: "Horn said that craft is a path through a trackless world; by following in the steps of those who went before, you brush up against all the mysteries they never understood and which you probably won't either. Sometimes you can even use things you don't understand. With me, that happens most of the time. Horn says you can make a pleasure out of what you don't know by working with it. I like that. Does that makes sense?" Tumbling Hawk sensed it did, but he was even more taken by the way Small Deer's eyes narrowed as he spoke, by the way he kept rolling his thumb over his fingers as he would to determine if the arrow shafts were smooth enough. Small Deer had never seemed more himself, yet these mannerisms were his master's. "He said you have to reserve the right to be ignorant. If you don't reserve that completely and absolutely, if it embarrasses you as often as it does me—and I know from long experience it does that to you at least as much—then it makes it harder to learn. You put something between yourself and what you want to know. Sometimes that's so powerful you spend your time worrying about it and don't even start on the thing you're interested in."

The curious thing for Tumbling Hawk was the difficulty he had in isolating Small Deer and Horn in the present; past and future kept breaking in too. One of Tumbling Hawk's recurrent images of master and apprentice was of the day when they first made glue together: Small Deer kept bumping into things and getting in Horn's way. But that was overlaid in Tumbling Hawk's mind by their growing grace with one another; the last few times he'd seen them do it—gluing the sinew to the bow required delicacy and perfect timing—they'd slipped by each other like disembodied figures. In the future Tumbling Hawk could imagine them as clouds. He could also imagine a time when Small Deer would no longer cut, but would coax the wood to strip itself from the tree, when the hands that reached out to reposition the apprentice's would be Small Deer's. He recognized that beauty with a slight ache, pleased by its clarity for his friend but knowing it wasn't for him. His future would be less settled. His uncertainty was growing. Tumbling Hawk had a reserve of past successes to draw on, but he knew he was borrowing from a place that meant less and less to him. And still there was no sign of an ally, though nightly his dreams were filled with the same stately parade.

THE BATTLE

On a clear June morning, in the Moon of Making Fat, Tumbling Hawk wrestled with Lightfoot in the stream. "Too long!" spluttered Lightfoot as he struggled to heave his bulk on top of his friend's slippery back. He had almost shoved Tumbling Hawk's head under when he was interrupted by terrified cries. He froze, his friend's head still clutched in his hands.

"Waschita! Waschita!" "Waschita! Waschita!" Instantly the village came alive: a stream of naked, dripping men and boys rushed from the water. Babies cried, dogs barked, horses whinnied and shuffled, everyone yelled directions at the same time. The camp was big, which meant there were many lodges to move. They'd been gathering families for the summer buffalo hunt and the tribe was just under full strength. Horn and Small Deer had made nothing but arrows for the last month.

The path was so crowded the boys could not move faster than anybody else, so they padded along with due restraint until they reached the silent warriors around the dead campfire. Tumbling Hawk stood very close to Strong Left Hand. Beside him, Tumbling Hawk felt Island move up on to his toes to see better. There would be no debate about tactics, not even among the highest chiefs. If there had been time, the young braves would have certainly clamored for a fight; just as certainly the older ones would have insisted that their first responsibility was to the women, children, and old people. Now only one man spoke, Able-to-Reach-the-Cloud, the chief in charge of the buffalo hunt.

"They ride quickly from the south. Dog soldiers will stand at the southern edge of camp to give the Elk Horns time to lead everyone across the water and over the eastern ridge. Kit Foxes will ride behind the people in case the Waschita break through the Dogs."

The younger braves were angry—Running Bear beat his thigh with a tense palm; Torrent scowled. Since battle was their only chance to distinguish themselves, they hated to pass up any opportunity to make their warrior societies. Tumbling Hawk and his friend would soon be in the same position, so he felt the others' impatience as he would feel his own. Finally he understood what had happened on the last hunt. They had taken half the morning to station riders, for the buffalo were spread out all along the Loup River. Just before the surround was closed, Running Bear broke cover and stampeded the herd. Important occasions in the life of Cheyenne warriors—the hunt, the battle—were meticulously organized. But the chiefs only formulated strategies: they gave no binding orders. And the only real enforcement of these orders was the others' disapproval, which was bound to come after the fact. At the time of the stampede, Tumbling Hawk had been furious with Running Bear. But now, watching the balked, disgruntled faces of the younger braves, Tumbling Hawk understood the tension between their desire to distinguish themselves and the demands of discipline. Voluntary agreement was for cool mature heads; discipline was easily accepted once you had taken a scalp.

The present problem was more complex than the impatient young men realized. If they fought and won, white man would pursue them. That was the trouble with him: He changed the meaning of battle. Against him there was no victory—he didn't know when to stop. The younger braves did not understand this yet, but some of the older warriors were beginning to fear a victory too. Because of this and the vulnerability of the camp, Able-to-Reach-the-Cloud determined to delay the whites with a rearguard action, to try to minimize losses while covering the people's escape.

As the chief worked out strategic details with leaders of the warrior societies, the boys threaded their way through the glistening tangle of bodies over to their fathers. Tumbling Hawk touched Big Road's arm and whispered, "I'll bring the ponies down." Lightfoot said the same to Hankering Horse. The fathers approved.

The boys pulled themselves out of the crowd. Already a few tepees had been stripped of skins, so now their path was more jammed with small children, dogs, goods, and horses.

"I'll meet you at your grandfather's," Lightfoot said.

Tumbling Hawk shook his head no. "You'd better get up to the graze right away. I don't know how long it will take me."

Alone, Tumbling Hawk moved more quickly. He knew the arrangements of the circle well enough so that he hardly saw the things he dodged. He jogged, his mind so busy ordering the sequence of his chores he was surprised how soon he reached home. He didn't bother to look inside, but deftly unhobbled the three horses in front, tying their reins to a beech tree. Then five quick paces east and he entered Mohe's lodge. The floor was almost bare, the backrests and mattresses were rolled up and tied in bundles for the travois. Mohe sat cross-legged and impassive; a dry old doll in the dust in front of the fire.

Shell was busy laying out Big Road's weapons. Tumbling Hawk took this in quickly and was gone before either spoke, carrying out Big Road and Shell's saddles, one in each arm. A moment later he was back, for he had to saddle Mohe's mare too, and prepare her for the travois. As soon as he finished with her, he started around the lodge, shaking loose the ground pegs and plucking them up as he went. He circled the lodge once, then loosened the skins while they were still on the frame. His first fold revealed Shell and his grandfather.

She said, "We'll go as soon as the poles are down. You'll come with us."

She spoke so shamelessly that for a moment Tumbling Hawk actually believed it. That was how she wiped out all the years he'd spent preparing to be of use, how she eradicated even his father's orders. She made him start all over again, from back beyond a point she'd accepted without question months before. If he'd been a little older, he would've laughed at the irony. Instead, all he could muster was, "I have to bring the ponies down." His words sounded petulant, which made him feel like hurling down the wooden pegs in his hand.

"They are few and not our best." As Shell spoke, her hands were laying out Big Road's arrows in perfectly straight rows of ten. Before her, on the buffalo robe, were her husband's moccasins, a wrapping for his hair, strings of sinew, as well as his bow, pistol, and shield. In the middle of the shield stood the great round ball of the sun; leading to it was a painted path of stars. The circular piece of bullhide was crested with an eagle feather, for swiftness and courage, and a bear claw hung from it threateningly. Big Road killed the bear to take its toughness for himself. The thought filled Tumbling Hawk with pride and a vicarious elation. At the same time he was infuriated by her meticulous attention to Big Road's war preparations while she denied his own.

Uncertain what to say next, the boy strode inside and stood before Mohe, silently demanding his help. But the old man was occupied with his own thoughts about white man—which were really quite mad. Mohe's expression suggested he'd seen the mother-son struggle too many times to have much interest now. He thought it timeless, irresolvable. But at this moment Tumbling Hawk didn't want wisdom. He knew he was right and insisted on support. He soothed himself by thinking, "Old people are useless in the end."

Shell felt her old depression settle over her. It always came when she gave in to the feeling she existed as a force against the men. Mohe understood. He said to her gently, in a voice almost sexless, too old to be partisan, "Let the boy go."

But Tumbling Hawk was too young not to be greedy. He hated to see Shell's mouth grow taut; it made her look old. "Don't worry, Mother," he said in the most patronizing manner. "The horses are pastured north of here, and the soldiers come from the south."

"Don't speak to me about north or south!" She wouldn't let him have it both ways. "The best place for you is with us!"

Big Road entered and took in both sides of the argument. Of course they said nothing further. Big Road briefly outlined the battle plan. At the same time he tested his bow, loaded his pistol, checked and smoothed the turkey feathers on each of his arrows. Big Road was still an able warrior, though he was one of those said to have "no interest in dying." Having distinguished himself years before, he was a model of what irritated the ambitious younger braves.

Tumbling Hawk asked: "Is there anything else I can do for you?"

Shell was very businesslike: "Put the travois on the mare, then strip our lodge. I'll finish here."

Tumbling Hawk was relieved to get out of Mohe's lodge. Still he did not escape his anger at her meddling even as he unloosed the first peg. It broke the rim of the circle and the skins sagged with a dull thunk. He disliked being drawn to his mother at such times, since that was the measure of how much a child he remained.

Around him, in undignified haste, the camp was being stripped down. The dogs were nervous; many whimpered; Lightfoot's puppy tirelessly chased its tail. A handsome bull buffalo, a yellow moon, and an elk were speedily folded in on themselves as Able-to-Reach-the-Cloud's lodge came down.

For a while Tumbling Hawk patiently unbound each buffalo thong. But he began to cut them the moment he noticed a few families moving east. He felt humiliated having to move out of the way of those unsavory white creatures with their heavy horses and their faces covered with hair. His grandfather said they were once few and weak, but now, everywhere, they seemed countless. When the skins hung limply from the poles, he shook his head at the miserable sight. Then he took down his home without much more emotion. He untied the poles, laid them down side by side, except for two, which he dragged to the mare and set up as the travois. A moment later he stepped back into what remained of Mohe's lodge.

His father was dressed and painted for battle, his hair wrapped and pulled to the shield's side—the left. A single eagle feather was poking up from his headband; his pistol was stuck in the waist of his leggings, his quiver strapped to his back. The crier was just starting to call the warrior societies together, so Big Road had to go.

Tumbling Hawk wished Mohe a good journey and was moving toward his mother when she got up. "Come back quickly." Shell gripped his forearm forcefully.

He followed his father outside. Big Road carefully checked the saddles and glanced at the travois fittings. Then he gestured for his son to come closer. With his back to Mohe's lodge Big Road reached into his shirt and pulled out a thick picket pin attached to a short cord. "I have the Dog Rope," he said simply. No obligation was more coveted or dangerous—once the pin was planted in battle, a warrior could not retreat beyond the radius of the cord until a fellow Dog soldier pulled the Dog Rope out of the ground and whipped the warrior with his quirt to drive him from the field. Big Road was a trifle embarrassed. "I'll tell you the story quickly. Remember those two horses I gave Bold Eagle for a gambling debt?" Tumbling Hawk did, though he remembered thinking it strange at the time. His father rarely gambled, and he'd never known him to lose anything larger than an arrowhead. "In fact, Fishing for Fire wanted the Dog Rope, and couldn't make his bid attractive enough to get Bold Eagle to give it up. He came to me and asked that I give the two horses. I did. Then Fishing for Fire insisted I take it first. So here I am, hiding it in my shirt."

To his son Big Road's tone was altogether as amazing as the story. There was no concern in his voice, not even much interest and certainly no bravado. The boy thought about how the younger warriors—like Fishing for Fire—would have responded to the privilege, and felt foolish for underestimating the merits of age.

Even those in the position to do so, which Tumbling Hawk definitely was not, were not allowed to wish a warrior good luck. So they mounted their horses and said good-bye as they would have done on any other morning. Big Road added, "Ride well." It was intended for both of them. The father turned south; the son headed Cloud in the opposite direction.

Tumbling Hawk looped west to keep out of the way of the families moving eastward. He tried to hurry, but since he was running against a stream of ponies, his progress was slow. Other boys greeted him with shouts of "Turtle foot" and "Snail slow," which he ignored.

Tumbling Hawk dropped below the rim of the plateau, picked his way down the hill, and crossed the rocky gully. As he started up the opposite hill he was passed by the last strings of ponies being hurried down. Someone shouted, "Lightfoot's up there waiting for you." Another boy laughed.

The meadow was empty except for Lightfoot, who trailed after Big Road's youngest filly on foot, a rope in his hand. He was chucking to her gently in a strange tongue. Tumbling Hawk couldn't suppress a smile at his friend's tactics, but more to the point, he kicked Cloud forward and raced by him. The idea was to drive the nervous filly into a heavily wooded corner of the pasture, but it took a number of passes before she retreated in that direction. Together they moved in on her—Tumbling Hawk shifting Cloud to cut the filly off each time she tried to break out while Lightfoot drew nearer, talking all the time. They'd backed her almost to the trees before Lightfoot got a rope over her head. She bolted and dragged him a few steps, but finally he quieted the filly by stroking her and gurgling in imitation of Hankering Horse's pony language.

Sweating and exhausted, Lightfoot looked up at his friend. "All of them spooked. Must be something in the air." That seemed to revive him, for he laughed enthusiastically at his own joke. "They had me running all over the mountain. I could've used you."

"You could have used a horse."

They added the filly to the middle of the second string, sticking her nose into the rear of a well-broken mare. There were four bands of six ponies each, Hankering Horse's and Big Road's ponies mixed together. On the way down they said little. Near the bottom of the hill, just above the thin skirt of walnut trees that cut off their view across the gully to the plateau, they looked south to where the camp had been—it was gone. In its place stood a broken ring of lodge poles—some slashed diagonally as if they wanted to break free of each other; some were crossed, as if jousting, while others thrust helplessly at the sky. Methodically spaced around the rim of the former camp circle were smaller circles composed of three concentric rings—the outside earthworks rim that kept out the rain, the lowered circle that had been the lodge's floor, and the charred center ring, hardly larger than a dot, where the fire had burned.

"Someday we won't move." Lightfoot spoke intensely, the pudgy comic face surprisingly reverent. Which made Tumbling Hawk feel cynical: he didn't believe it. White man brought a new threat. Lately Mohe insisted that something was shrinking around him, like a buffalo robe that got wet and then dried out too quickly.

Farther south the Dog soldiers, Big Road among them, waited on their ponies, like a fringe hung at the edge of the bare camp. To the east the last stragglers were crossing the stream. The fleeing tribe stretched up the ridge like a long snake. Tumbling Hawk watched the last families across the river, saw the snake's head touch the top of the ridge, looked south a final time. Still he saw no white man, only a slow dust cloud rolling toward the Dog soldiers.

An island of rocks and thicket forced them due south across the gully, though the more direct way would've been to push east and avoid the climb back up the plateau. Their ponies slowed them down, and they couldn't see anything below the level of the plateau. As they neared the top of the rise, the boys were stunned by the sound of a pistol shot. Then another. Then too many to count.

Just below the lip of the plateau they heard the Dog soldiers shout their retreat: "Hae! Hae! Hae!" Tumbling Hawk knew it was the usual lure—he could almost see them gallop away, pretending to be routed. He knew his father wouldn't plant the Rope until the Dogs charged back. But the boys didn't actually see the retreat racing toward them until they were up on level ground. By then it was too late. Before they knew it the boys were colliding with their own warriors.

Then Tumbling Hawk saw his father, the Dog Rope wound around his left forearm, its pin hanging down in front of his shield. At the same instant Big Road realized his child was in the midst of those milling ponies. Desperate tension fractured Big Road's face. Tumbling Hawk saw this expression and it mortified him. For despite his posturing, he knew he was too young to fight. For one bitter instant the boy was tempted to die in battle just to show his father. But he dropped the thought immediately. Besides, he couldn't move, he was so mixed up in lead ropes and horses. As was Lightfoot.

The whites picked that moment to charge. The warriors wheeled around to meet them. Tumbling Hawk watched the pain on his father's face intensify as Big Road charged forward with the Dog soldiers. His face seemed to float above the backs of the ponies as he galloped away, looking back at his son, concentrating all his energy to will the boy away from there. For an instant all motion stopped for the boys, then the terrified ponies stampeded, sweeping Tumbling Hawk and Lightfoot into the battle, as helpless as two twigs being swept downriver.

Terrified by the cloud of sound, the Indian ponies swept forward. Or rather came sidewise, an enormous crab mounted on an assemblage of kicking legs. The two forces met, and the Cheyenne line gave way, sliding west with the pressure. The soldiers' momentum carried them east, into the stalled bank of ponies. As the Indians looped around, suddenly they found themselves behind the soldiers. They quickly herded the whites into the natural corral. The pack grew solid. Most of the soldiers couldn't turn their horses around; they all faced in one direction. And facing them, just out of sword's reach, in the middle of the four hopelessly tangled strings of ponies, sat Tumbling Hawk and Lightfoot.

High above, the midday sun was brilliant. But in the diffracted light of that dust bowl, forms moved like slow ghosts. Or broke up into fragments. Tumbling Hawk saw the vertical yellow stripe on a blue background of a uniform pitch up horizontally, then dive down toward the ground. He saw a yellow kerchief slashed with a running line of red. A knife reached out to a flat-brimmed silhouette; a pistol dissolved into a halo of light, a lance skewered empty air. Though Tumbling Hawk wasn't certain who was winning, he knew from sounds he'd never associated with death before that many whites had fallen. Then the trumpet went still. A few moments later the ponies danced on the cavalry flag.

The ground grew red; dust turned everybody, red and white man, a dull red gold. There was too much blood for the air to hold, so it deposited a warm sticky glue on each of them.

Finally the red-gold cloud thinned. The well-trained ponies shifted their ground a little less. The boys could occasionally spot each other bobbing up and down in the midst of the ponies. Their legs were bruised from being crushed against the animals' sides, their arms were about to pull out of their sockets, their hands raw, but they held on because they had to.

When the dust cleared, the few surviving soldiers tallied the mutilated white bodies strewing the ground. Out of ammunition, as they reached out with useless swords at an enemy who loved to fight hand-to-hand and who had the further advantage of striking them from behind, the soldiers knew they were dead. Suddenly three braves leaped off their horses and raced for the handful of white men. The soldiers experienced a horrified confusion when, instead of being tomahawked or clubbed to death, painted warriors shouted war cries and reached out to touch pant legs with coup sticks and slapped officers' thighs with bare hands. No soldier could reconcile a warrior's wild, wild joy with his own death. White man died with a quizzical expression on his face.

One soldier backed his horse out, spun around. The warriors, who had the remaining whites completely ringed, gave him a measured head start. Then Strong Left Hand went after him, twirling his hatchet.

Strong Left Hand hit the soldier with the back of the hatchet at the top of his spine; the neck broke with a sharp crack and the head dropped to the man's chest. Before the soldier hit the ground Strong Left Hand struck him two more times, rising up off his saddle for each stroke. He cleaved the skull into an open X that hung apart like a quartered apple.

The white survivors witnessed it all. Then the Cheyenne backed two more soldiers out. The braves cheered as the warriors ran them down, smoothly, faultlessly.

That left only two whites, and the cheering turned into a chant—the Dog soldiers began to wail for their dead. At a moment too late for understanding, the whites were included in the intimacy of the ritual. Not that it mattered. The end came quickly.

Tumbling Hawk didn't spot his father until Big Road was making his way toward him, shoving ponies out of his way, slashing taut ropes as he came. He was blind to everything but his son. The danger was past, but Big Road felt it wouldn't be over until he intervened and ended it. He reached Tumbling Hawk, lifted him off Cloud, and pulled the boy's body fiercely to his chest. He held Tumbling Hawk off the ground a long time, hugging and rocking him back and forth, then he remembered himself and gently lowered the boy to the ground. He carefully patted and felt his body all over to assure himself each part was in its right place and there were no hidden wounds. Big Road felt he ought to be mad at the boy, though he was too relieved to pursue the point, and his pride in what his son had accomplished compromised him.

Tumbling Hawk seized on that pride. "It would've been best to ride east with the ponies, Father, but we had to run south along the edge of the walnut trees. We came up onto the lip of the plateau just as the Dogs shouted their retreat. Suddenly we were in the middle of the fight. If we'd come a little earlier or later, the whole thing would've been a story warriors told at the fireside, something for boys to listen to. But the way it worked out, we couldn't escape—like the white soldier."

Tumbling Hawk had dug up that corpse so often that year Big Road knew it was coming before the boy said it. "Will you ever lay that soldier to rest?" he asked with a smile. For the first time he felt at ease.

"As it happened," his son replied, "we helped out a little."

"As it happened..." Big Road mused. He couldn't help being impressed—twice now his son had been in the center of white man's defeat. The father philosophized. "As it happened... But then much of war is good fortune—being in the place you do not know is crucial until the enemy tells you it is."

Behind them, as the others made the body count, the battlefield grew peaceful again. Two warriors were dead—Burnt All Over, who'd been shot through the heart, and Snake. So with eight lodgepoles they raised two death platforms, laid the bodies out full length, hands at their sides. Each man's medicine bundles were placed beside him, then both war-horses, standing dazed nearby, were led under the platform and shot. Snake's brother, Short Body, chanted to himself until Plenty Crows spoke:

"Two of our brothers have started on the trail where all footprints point the same way. We have lost two of our best friends and finest warriors, and we mourn for them under the open sky, on the ground where they fell. Yet even with their loss, what could have been great trouble was not. Eighteen soldiers lie dead, none have escaped. We shall disguise our glory by taking scalp like the Pawnee, and will rub out the rest of our marks like a heavy snow. It has been a good day, a good day to win, a good day to die. The dust blinded our enemy, our two boys set the trap with their ponies. As the spirits of this place have been good to us, so we have watered it with our tears and blood, leaving the bodies of two brave Dogs—and many dead enemy. Our brothers are now high above the earth; soon the platform will crumble and they will join all flesh in returning to the ground."

There was no signal, but the men began to chant:

"Earth that carries us
Earth that makes us
Earth to which we return
Thank you for your gifts,
We sing of the day you give to your sons."

They wailed the song over and over until they began to sway in place. Slowly, hardly moving at first, they shuffled their feet. Only they knew when they began to move around in a circle, for their movement was hardly more than a swaying, yet slowly all were shuffling forward, almost on the heels of the next man. Through the dance the tempo never changed; they only strengthened it. Feet began to pound; they danced on the blood of dead enemy and brother, coating themselves in its thick red gold, stomping to place their footprints down with the dead.

The boys had seen the warriors dance many times before, but never had they felt so called to the prohibited ceremony—now it was theirs too; they had helped in the fight. Each beat became an urging, each stomping foot such an invitation that as tired as they were they were never certain they'd be able to resist violating the sanctity of the ceremony until the dance was over.

After the dance, the warriors put the finishing touches on the disguise, removed all identifying marks from Burnt All Over and Snake, even shifted the position of the few remaining lodgepoles to imitate the Pawnee, and after the two travois had been made up for the wounded, the company set out after their fleeing tribespeople. They followed the trail quickly, pausing only to pick up discarded Cheyenne belongings.

They hadn't been riding long when Big Road dropped back to his son. Tumbling Hawk had been thinking he hadn't seen his father fight even though Big Road was only a few paces away from him. "You didn't get a chance to plant the Dog Rope, did you?"

Big Road said, "There never was a position to hold, so we didn't charge." Though Tumbling Hawk knew this, he was nonetheless disappointed.

"I've planted it before," his father went on with unassertive confidence, "quite a few times. Perhaps I'll do it again. I would've been pleased to today, but I'm just as glad I didn't. Either way now it's very much the same to me." Tumbling Hawk never doubted his father's bravery, but such thorough professionalism was hard for him to appreciate at a time when he wanted a little more romance.

"It has something to do with your mother," Big Road offered reflectively. They talked about Tumbling Hawk's part in the battle. Big Road insisted that this second event was a sign too powerful to ignore. The boy loved his father's expansive moods. At the same time he knew Big Road was temporizing, for he did not want to talk about Shell or what she would say. They rode in silence awhile, then Big Road said, "Mohe will be there. He may think of some way to appease your mother." The boy looked skeptical. "These days he only speaks when necessary. He's got to pick targets carefully now, he doesn't have the strength he used to."

Somewhat comforted about the coming meeting with Shell, they rode together until they met the returning scouts, who told the company to make preparations for their entrance, for camp was just ahead. As the men gathered on the slope, Tumbling Hawk caught up with Lightfoot, who was already down at the stream with his ponies. They let the animals cool off before they drank, then Lightfoot led one out past the shallows into deeper water. Together they began to scrub the animals, removing the blood and dust. The chore required effort; the coat was thickly layered.

They worked without talking. Tumbling Hawk, in particular, felt relieved to be working hard at something uncomplicated. They scrubbed until they heard a great splash, then another. A ghostly file of warriors streamed down the banks and plunged into the water. The men ducked and jumped and splashed, rubbed themselves free of their clinging coats; they poured water over their heads, massaged it into aching muscles, rolled it deliciously through their dust-caked mouths.

Downstream the boys watched the water redden. Then the acrid smell of battle floated to them. Suddenly they both felt unclean. They worked faster after that, pulling the ponies out into deeper water, scrubbing them feverishly. Finally they too were free to dive in and wash away that lingering battle cloak in the clear, cooling water.

They lay in the stream a long time. On the bottom of a shallow pool, his back resting lightly against a rock, Tumbling Hawk rose and fell with the water's motion. Farther out, Lightfoot was stirred around in his seat at the foot of a small funnel, where a miniature falls cascaded down the length of his body. The boys didn't leave until the warriors called them. By then the Dogs had blackened their faces for the return. Since they had lost two men, it wasn't a day for painting the robes, so they finished the simple preparations and rode off.

The people pretended to be surprised when the warriors drew up on the ridge overlooking the camp. Of course, those who watched the trails had already reported the approach of the Dogs, and one Dog soldier had already slipped into camp to inform the families of the deaths and prepare them for the ceremonies. But that had no effect on the appearance—women waved, children pointed, old people nodded their heads.

They waved the black death blanket twice, then the families of the dead warriors were led out to the mounted troop and there, in sight of the tribe, they joined the Dog soldiers' lament:

> "We cry for a brother who has left us,
> Bold warrior close to our heart."

Short Body shouted the war cry, and all answered together:

"Whenever his friends were afraid,
He made it easy.
Only stones stay on earth forever."

Hair-with-Many-Tangles, Snake's wife, gashed herself on both calves; White Moon, wife of Burnt All Over, was handed his lance by Plenty Crows. She took it as if she didn't understand, then raised it into the air. Still clutching the lance she fell, screaming for her husband:

"Come back to me,
Return to me,
You who will soon be earth."

Relatives fell to the ground alongside her and began chewing the dust. So the families mourned and cried and rolled about on the ground. They would continue to wail for a day, after which the intensity of their mourning might begin to lessen, the first day of death being the hardest, when the wanderer searches for the trail where all the footprints point the same way. The women might not wash the blood from them for weeks, and all would go barelegged for months, publicly showing the scars of their suffering. The old men–fathers, grandfathers–would wear their hair unbound, flowing like tears. At the end of a year all mourning would cease abruptly: the warrior had reached his new home in the stars.

The mourning continued until the families were led back to camp and into their tepees, to take up their private grief. Then the wave that ran together with the mourning swept over them. Their joy at victory hadn't been suppressed by the death ceremony, and their present feeling did not contradict their mourning. Instead, their joy expressed the way in which the two feelings stood side by side, for they knew this day so full of grief was also rich in glory, and the death of two loved brothers came enmeshed in victory.

Then the entire tribe cheered and sang and shouted to the phalanx of warriors spread across the ridge. The greatest fighters–Big Road's name was prominent–were celebrated loudest and longest. And when, in the second file, the crowd recognized two small but exultant boys, they sang:

"They came among men,
The little warriors who fought well."

For the first time the boys heard their names run up the hill to greet them:

"Tumbling Hawk, Lightfoot
We honor you."

At the height of their intoxication, Plenty Crows' war cry rang above the people's voices, and the entire party, the boys among them, charged down the hill at the crowd, shooting captured guns in the air, shouting wildly. Warriors who'd taken scalp waved them from the end of poles, men who'd counted coup thrust lances in small circles by the right ear of their ponies. So they announced their valor even as they streaked down at the camp, then into it, dodging the fire, through the village and back outside the circle again, recklessly racing around the ring of the lodges.

They rode until they were dizzy, then beyond, before Plenty Crows reined up smartly and vaulted to the ground. When all the Dogs were by his side, the battle began again. This time each warrior acted out his part as the tribe looked on. Plenty Crows wrestled hand-to-hand with a soldier, turned the man's own pistol on him and shot him through the heart. Cries-for-Perch struggled with a very brave white who, knocked from his horse, pulled two Cheyenne to the ground. He killed Snake, and was about to kill Two Feathers when Perch speared him with his lance. But even with it in him, the white fought until Cries-for-Perch struck his knife into his throat. Big Road demonstrated his attempts to plant the Dog Rope, but brave men were always fighting in front of him, not behind, and there hadn't been a second charge. So he couldn't find an honorable position to hold. Tumbling Hawk felt mortified as the entire tribe laughed—he hated Big Road's buffoonery until the boy watched him laconically touch an imaginary white soldier with the palm of his hand, then take a scalp as easily as he himself scooped a fish out of water.

They didn't reenact the battle simply for those who weren't there. Piece by piece the warriors were able to fill in the parts of the battle they hadn't seen. So Big Road understood that Cries-for-Perch had saved him from the Man with Much Yellow Braid; that Plenty Crows had killed the officer with his hatchet.

The boys drew laughter, too, since they did such an elaborate job with their imaginary ropes and got all tangled up again. But the joke did not diminish the importance of their trap, and everyone knew that. They had defeated white man—many Waschita—a second time, which confirmed their powers. The boys could almost hear the emissaries telling Rumbling Wings the news. Later, after much celebrity and many earnest congratulations, Tumbling Hawk and Lightfoot parted with a sense of their own and their shared importance.

Alone, Tumbling Hawk walked slowly. He was in no hurry to get back to his lodge, where he was anything but a hero. He paused to nod more aloofly than usual at Bear Child, Cries-for-Perch's daughter. But he was too anxious to stop to chat.

The tepee was already in its position in the circle. He entered and found Mohe sitting next to his mother, obviously arguing with her. They stopped abruptly. The floor was clear of brush, but the beds and the backrests were not set up yet. For some reason that annoyed Tumbling Hawk. He started toward his usual place next to his mother, but his grandfather motioned him to the place of honor to the left of Big Road's seat. Shell's expression made clear that was what they were fighting about. He sat down and waited. The silence was terrible. Mohe was in a difficult spot. He didn't want to anticipate what Big Road would say. Tumbling Hawk didn't consider that. He was mad at the old man for not making it easier for him. Shell's feelings were more complex. She was furious about what had happened with the ponies—exactly what she'd been afraid of. And she was tired of her son holding on to childhood intimacies while claiming he was a man. She hated that duplicity—only men allowed themselves that.

Big Road entered much later. He took his place, glanced reassuringly at his son, then used his right to speak first to ask Shell, "Do you want to know what happened?" The question was as reasonable and conciliatory as it could be.

She bridled at his tone. "You both were in the fight." It was both question and statement.

"Yes," said Big Road, not wanting to offend her. "The two of us."

"Did the boy fight well?" she snapped.

Big Road felt slapped. "He sat well. He didn't fight." He was exercising enormous control and delicacy, for he recognized whatever lived inside her was more erratic than anything he'd ever faced.

"If they have not reached the age of initiation, are they still given the death rites of warriors?" Her question was so unreasonable, it reflected how gratuitous her position was. Big Road knew there was no answer and both the lack of an answer and her recklessness frightened him.

Tumbling Hawk didn't understand. Only very rarely had he been forced to withdraw from adult things, because Big Road and Shell had never made distinctions between them and the things of his life. But this time he really didn't understand. He felt as though he'd lost his parents.

Mohe was the only one who could respond. "That's no question. It asks nothing, tells nothing."

Ordinarily Shell would've withdrawn at this point, for ordinarily she took pride in not offending their sense of fair play. But now she thought everything they did was unfair. A song she'd sung for Big Road, often before moments of great pleasure, snaked vilely into her mind.

You fought bravely,
Now I will sing for you.

Once, Big Road had come in sheathed in dust, his leg caked with blood. It had taken two men to get him off his pony and into the lodge. He was in terrible pain, but he'd forced a joke about how lucky they'd been—the wound was high on his thigh. She'd cut away his chaps and delicately washed the wound, then had taken him, half risen, into her mouth. Slowly she slid along that hard length with the child's soft skin, driving away all pain, taking him away from battle. The mockery gagged her now—all her being aroused by it, giving in to it. The child of that impulse sucked milk to become a great warrior; her child sent off to die, mothers throwing away their fruits of love singing vile, killing songs:

I fear only old man's teeth—
Ride hard and die!

"I will say yes to his becoming a man because I have no choice," she said bitterly. "And Mohe and I will hold hands in age. But I will never sing the songs you love, of a woman burning to see her brave warrior home."

Big Road had no reply. He got up and went outside. His son joined him, leaving Mohe with her. They stood by the lodge saying nothing. They couldn't even look at each other. Inside, they heard her weeping.

Big Road thought: it had been sixteen years since he had taken Shell away from the southern Cheyenne. Over the years he'd lost the blood lust his son now felt. Big Road wondered if he would have softened so much if she hadn't been lonely for her home, if there'd been other children. Having lived through those years of his riding off to war and having seen him dragged back with his skull split open, his chest pierced by two Pawnee arrows, and his right leg smashed by his pony's fall—having helped him survive that—Shell did not want to go through it again. Not with her son, their only child, whom she felt was reckless. Big Road understood that. If he felt she was just attacking the boy's part in the battle, or even the ways of warriors, the situation would've been different for him. But he knew she was talking about them, that had been the question all along, though they hadn't realized it, not even Shell herself until that moment. Though it had gone unrecognized, he knew the problem had existed the whole time they'd been together.

That was what he thought as he stood just outside his tepee, hearing her weep, his son beside him. Big Road felt duty bound to do something, but he didn't know how to change a tribe's history or how to change a life. He hated the resentment his failure would bring to them, hated that almost as much as he hated that sense of incompletion they had just discovered had always been there. He feared that resentment in both of them as much as he feared her power to see. In the moment she had blurted out her words, their life had changed. Ironically—he cracked a bitter smile—he knew the confrontation had been formulated long ago, and because he knew the moment she spoke that there had been a lack they both had sensed long before they knew it existed.

What made things worse was that he was glad his son couldn't see because he knew a boy couldn't understand; only his softening toward her allowed him to understand. He wondered if he were the only man in the tribe who understood and suffered it. He wondered if everyone suffered it, had suffered it all along.

RUMBLING WINGS

The boys on Takes-the-Pipe's side stood in a row watching the last two hoops roll toward them. Closest to the enemy, on point, Lightfoot tracked the second wheel. If he really concentrated on the spot in the center, he would hit it this time. Three times he'd thrown his sticks and missed, not much of a record for the man honored with the point. Another miss and his side might lose, for they were only one ahead of Tumbling Hawk's.

"Point throw wide again!" Tumbling Hawk waved his arms and jumped up and down, trying to distract his friend. He wasn't sure that was fair, but he hated to lose to Takes-the-Pipe. As long as Tumbling Hawk could remember they'd been rivals—ever since the play wars of their childhood, they always led opposing sides. In the past few months Takes-the-Pipe had grown taller and filled out, and lately to show off his strength he had taken to lifting Tumbling Hawk off the ground every occasion he got.

Lightfoot let the weight of his best stick nestle into his palm. As the hoop spun toward him, he drew back and whipped his arm forward. He released, and the slender stick spiraled straight to the heart of the wheel—its "blood." The wheel ran by him, spinning his arrow in tight little circles. "The blood," he thought with satisfaction, "I drew blood."

"It's about time," Tumbling Hawk shouted, annoyed that his team lost. Takes-the-Pipe looked over at Lightfoot, Lightfoot looked back; they scooped up two hoops and started after Tumbling Hawk.

They chased him across the prairie and on into camp. Tumbling Hawk dodged around Old Man Afraid of his Horses, then set up Yellow Fox as a screen before scooting around behind a tepee, so they didn't corner him until they were near the middle of camp. Lightfoot had the best shot and whipped his hoop sidearm, hard and fairly low. Tumbling Hawk sidestepped as he ducked, and the hoop sailed by him, landed on its rim and began to roll. The three of them watched it roll, then, terrified, they froze. The hoop kept carrying on and on, and ahead of it, in its path, was Rumbling Wings' lodge—the sacred skins of the chief shaman.

The instant the wheel struck the lodge, a strange double note sounded—a bass bellow from deep inside while the thin skins rang, as if plucked. The note still sounded in their ears as Rumbling Wings emerged.

His face was drained, his skin the color of weathered wood. His hair stood up in squat, carefully spaced tufts; his deerskin shirt had thin lines marking diagonals across the front and the back, and tiny painted signs, all different colors, ran up the sleeves to the yoke. The shaman looked deeply disturbed. The boys would never know what they called him away from—he could have been talking to the Power of Thunder, communing with those in the House of the Dead, or sitting on one of the cardinal points hearing of the wanderings of its wind. They knew nothing, only that the most powerful medicine man of the Cheyenne had been distracted by their game.

Rumbling Wings immediately picked out the offender, then looked deep into Lightfoot's heart. Yet all he said was, "We have very little time. Listen to me carefully and do precisely what I say."

His eyes still lingering on Lightfoot, he pointed Takes-the-Pipe south, Tumbling Hawk north, and told them to go until they came to a flint in their path, which they were to pick up and return with "just as they had come." They stepped off in opposite directions.

Now the shaman's gaze rummaged inside Lightfoot's blubbery body, prodding his inner being as the old man searched for pockets of disrespect or ignorance. Lightfoot didn't know how long the examination went on, he simply gave in to it.

"Only if you act correctly now, will we be able to turn this to our use." The voice held no anger, it was beyond exasperation.

The boy was ordered to walk east out of camp until he came to the buffalo chip that would fall under his right foot. He could not stretch or shorten his stride at all, he just had to walk naturally.

Lightfoot went a short distance from camp; his foot came directly down upon the chip. He picked it up and turned back, madly elated. Approaching the spot where Rumbling Wings stood, Lightfoot found his friends converging with him. North, South, East closed on Rumbling Wings until they all stopped an arm's length away from each other.

The old man first took the chip from Lightfoot, examined it and said: "It is dead enough, it is live enough." He placed it on the ground in the middle of them, then ordered Takes-the-Pipe and Tumbling Hawk away again, telling South to bring him the dry white sage "that lies scattered in your path" and North to return with "two arms brimming with sweet grass." Tumbling Hawk had a brief confusing moment when he wondered if the shaman was mocking them, but he had no way to pursue that thought and headed off to get the sweet grass.

Lightfoot then watched Rumbling Wings kneel and strike the fire flint on stone. The old man didn't breathe on the spark, he didn't fan it, but suddenly the smoldering buffalo chip leaped into flames. An instant later it was blown back to smoke by a puff of north wind. Rumbling Wings sang:

"Fire, do not die
Stay with us
Mother, wife, child
Warm our life
As you take
Your own away."

The shaman's song soon became the fire's fuel, for as his voice rose and fell so did the small flame. Fire and song worked so powerfully on Lightfoot he didn't hear North and South returning until they stood beside him.

Without hurry Rumbling Wings interleaved the sage and the sweet grass, then laid it on top of the chip. By the time he finished, the chip looked dead; no smoke rose from it. But the shaman sang to it secretly, and it revived. He reached over the fire and purified both sides of Lightfoot's hands, palms first, then did the same to himself.

Rumbling Wings explained what he wanted—they had to run through their chase exactly as it happened. "That will be easy," he said, studying them with cold, commanding eyes. "Then, at a certain place, I'll ask you to do something difficult and unusual. Don't be afraid. Don't even think. Just do what I ask as best you can, then a little better, and all will be well. The important thing," he concluded as if offering them a deep secret, "is to remember." Then he whispered, "Remember! Remember!"

Rumbling Wings knew the spirit hadn't caught them until they entered the circle itself, so they moved out just beyond the edge of camp and started from there. Lightfoot and Takes-the-Pipe carried their wheels under their arms, and Tumbling Hawk led them into the circle just as he had before. He took only a few strides before he knew he was running in his own tracks. As he took a step the next one became clear, but only the next one, so he ran on the verge of overtaking what he remembered. As he dodged the sweat lodge, he was caught by a desire to make a misstep. That frightened him and made him giddy. Tumbling Hawk couldn't help thinking about all the steps he hadn't taken, because now he could see them, feel them, and as he stretched out his legs each unexplored step seemed a tantalizing opportunity. He ran in this heady mood, not knowing what he was going to do, until he remembered his obligation to the tribe's medicine, to the great shaman, to Lightfoot. He sprinted toward Rumbling Wing's lodge, his friends trailing him.

They moved into their places, but at the very last moment the shaman cried, "Don't throw it. Do it all but don't let go of that hoop."

Lightfoot wound up as he had before, twisted his back and hip to get the proper whip and pretended to throw the wheel. He saw the disk spin slowly toward Tumbling Hawk, who apparently saw the same thing, for he ducked and sidestepped just as it was about to hit him. All three boys watched it land and roll slowly past Plenty Crows' lodge, that thin line of dust for a tail, on and on until, just before it reached the magic hides, Rumbling Wings shouted: "Stop it! Stop it before it touches my skin! Make the wheel spin all the way back till it rests in Lightfoot's arms."

At the very last instant Lightfoot remembered how he'd tensed his body to try to force the wheel down. This time his body's follow through worked, and just as the wheel's shadow touched the skins it developed backspin, then moved back the way it came, back, back until it lifted off the ground as it reached Tumbling Hawk, who rose up quickly and stepped closer to the hoop as it almost grazed him, the wheel rising a little higher before settling into Lightfoot's arms. He found his back still twisted from his throw and straightened up gently.

"You've done well," Rumbling Wings congratulated them. "Things are now replaced. Good may even come of it."

On their way to their homes, Lightfoot was too distracted to speak.

That annoyed Tumbling Hawk, who was anxious to tell his friend what he felt while he was running. He had no desire to speak to Takes-the-Pipe. Tumbling Hawk never did get a chance to unburden himself, for Lightfoot was never the same again.

Every third night from then on, Lightfoot had dreams. The next morning Hankering Horse would emerge from their lodge to report, "He had another one last night." That was all. No one knew what the dreams were about; naturally, that added to their mystery. Before long the rumor started: Lightfoot had the calling of a medicine man. The villagers were not surprised: since the defeat of the white soldiers, Lightfoot and Tumbling Hawk had been watched with special interest.

The time was difficult for Tumbling Hawk, who had to contend with his own and everyone else's expectations. Usually he kept silent when his friends talked grandly of their futures—he felt he'd fallen woefully behind, and that humiliated Tumbling Hawk. The merest trifles jarred him—his father's reasonable counsel to be patient, Lightfoot's pretensions about the days when he'd become shaman, even the way Takes-the-Pipe stiffly strutted around camp, showing off his muscles in his new jerkin. Tumbling Hawk despised his own lack of generosity for it deprived him of dignity. For weeks he did not rest well. He had no trouble falling asleep for a short while, but then, for no reason, he'd wake. The rest of the night was spent trying to coax himself back to sleep. Just before dawn, in the coldest time, he'd finally doze off. That second sleep was a heavy blank, and he got up each morning feeling waterlogged.

One morning in the second month of Lightfoot's dreams, they found him crouched outside Rumbling Wings' lodge, looking like he'd just thrown the hoop.

Two dreams and five days later the great event was announced—Lightfoot was called to the shaman's lodge. Of course he was jubilant as he strode through the village, yet outwardly Lightfoot remained calm until he reached the sacred tepee. He hesitated outside the open entrance hole, suddenly terrified. Then he took a deep breath and stepped inside.

A moment passed before he could see; the firelight was dim. The lodge, the largest in camp, was entirely painted so that, all across the roof, bright bands alternated with black strips. The wide bright bands were days, or some measure of time, while the black strips were pierced by brilliant points of light from their planets, stars, and moon. The night sky felt immensely deep, and as he stood looking up, Lightfoot felt as though the strips had been peeled off and he was being projected into the mysterious night.

The days started in the east, just above the entrance, where the earth was entirely covered by water. From there the adventures of the world marched across the sky. He saw Cheyenne being eaten by Buffalo, Coyote stealing fire from the gods, Sweet Medicine riding the North Wind back home to his people. There were many other stories he did not know.

Lightfoot was so impressed, he didn't even look at the great shaman. Rumbling Wings sat like a stone by the fire. Finally his eyes moved. They seemed like a snake's, slow and cold, and as they reached the boy, Lightfoot half expected to find a cold wet trail in the air. The shaman drew on his pipe; as the bowl glowed, so did his eyes. The bowl was stone, yet was as fluently worked as soft wood, with colored tracings curling down the stem and minute designs circling the bowl. As the bowl cooled, the shaman's eyes died through a series of shades down to a weird half tone. The shaman let the boy stand transfixed before he broke the mood and beckoned Lightfoot to sit down to his left. He began without further explanation:

"Long ago there were two brothers camped on the Snake. Both wanted to learn about the river, so the first day they came down to its banks together. The older brother plunged in and swam out into the water, though not too far this first time, since he wanted to test its force against his strength, search for eddies to rest in, and ride with the current. That day the younger brother didn't swim, but sat on the shore and looked at the colors of the stream or walked along its banks and talked to the flowers and trees and grass, especially those that grew along the river's edge. From then on, each day the older brother would swim out a little farther, and each day he became a little stronger. Each day the younger man would listen and look; he would smell, touch, and talk to everything that grew near the water, or watch the shifting shadow and light or wander along its banks. And each night they would share what they learned, agreeing before they slept to continue their work much as they'd done that day."

Rumbling Wings stopped; Lightfoot waited and waited; the shaman puffed on his pipe in reply. At some point Lightfoot realized that the shaman thought the story finished. More time passed. Finally, when he couldn't stand it any longer, the boy asked, "Did they ever cross the stream?"

The old man's eyes churned his soul. "How would you end the story?"

The question confused Lightfoot. He didn't understand what was wanted.

The old man considered the boy another moment, then his patience snapped. He cackled sharply: "Let me ask you another way then, little man." His face caved in around the mouth; wrinkles slashed up his forehead. Then the face relaxed again, the voice softened: "For me the story ends well, I wouldn't have it another way. Your question surprised me." He hesitated, expectant, then continued, "But I was pleased by your boldness and your desire to relieve what you regarded as something uncomfortable. I thought, 'You will rid yourself of the useless old. A privilege of youth.' I was pleased with that until I realized how you'd change the story." His voice tensed till Lightfoot feared it would choke the sound. "To you it is a story without end, as jarring as a drumbeat broken in midstep. So jarring you would put another tail on it, and thus unbalance it and make it laughable."

Lightfoot was terrified. He also knew there was no way to hide from the old man and vowed never to try.

"Let me put it another way." Rumbling Wings started again. "We see only a small part of a thing and in our foolishness often mistake that small part for the whole. When we live with people or things we see a little more clearly—we can't help moving around them so we see what we think we know from many different places, at enough different times, and in enough moods to begin to do justice to what we see. But with the unfamiliar a single view is often convincing just because the view is most striking, because you haven't seen or imagined it. Always remember that the single view is too simple. Remember that as you listen to me and I will be a little more at ease as your teacher.

"For I dislike my voice when it reaches you ripe with the wisdom of the single striking picture which may stand in the way of your own discoveries. That deprives you and it of life, like a bad ending to a good story."

The shaman's lips lifted a little, as if considering a smile. Suddenly above Lightfoot the alternating bands of day and night shifted as a wave rippled down the covering. The sun beamed, the moon shone, the morning star appeared, and a brown bull buffalo near the entrance flap led his cows across a morning sky. Then it all stopped. It might have been a wind lifting the skins.

The voice continued: "You must learn to sift what I say. For I know how to sing the song and dance the dance. Take my words seriously or I will come against you—against those who know nothing, a powerful enemy. Take them too seriously, young man—" Lightfoot felt he was being mocked, though the lined face remained absolutely blank "—and I may begin to despise the blood of my own life. For I carry within me our people's memory, all those things we hold as treasure, which hold us more strongly each day."

He folded himself into silence, apparently exhausted. For a long time he leaned limply on his backrest while Lightfoot sat perfectly still, afraid to breathe. At one point the boy was afraid the old man might be dead. Much later, with great effort, Rumbling Wings gestured to him to go.

A few days later Hankering Horse asked the shaman to accept his son as a follower and gave Rumbling Wings five horses. From then on, every third day, Lightfoot went to the medicine lodge. Shortly after the beginning of his formal apprenticeship, Lightfoot's friends began to gather in his tepee to listen to his stories about the shaman: how Rumbling Wings caused the Pawnee arrows to turn aside; about the time he was buried beneath a giant rock by a southern Cheyenne magician, but was found sitting by the sweat bath the next morning, the boulder still in place. The stories prompted Tumbling Hawk to ask Mohe to tell him about Rumbling Wings. The boy sat through an afternoon listening to familiar stories. That night, when they assembled, Tumbling Hawk volunteered his own tale: about the time Rumbling Wings blinded the Crow scouts so that they rode right up to a Cheyenne war party caught out in the open. Tumbling Hawk thought his story at least as well told as Lightfoot's, and so it surprised him that his friends' response was cool, even embarrassed.

During the weeks that followed, Lightfoot would often stare blankly at Tumbling Hawk as if looking out from a trance or would pretend not to hear when Tumbling Hawk spoke. By the time the fledgling shaman's audience was hearing stories about the ups and downs of Coyote, with his talking excrements and his bodily members as advisers, a few warriors had joined them. As the tales of Coyote's cunning continued, Lightfoot's manner grew secretive, mysterious, as changeable as his teacher's. Suddenly he'd jump up and shake and twitch convulsively. Or, while he was talking, his jaw would lock in midsentence, and he'd start to rock back and forth, absolutely silent. One day they found him shivering in his lodge and piled on one buffalo robe after another; he cold-sweated through that night and the next day, Hankering Horse and Takes-the-Pipe attending him.

While Lightfoot struggled with the entering spirits, Tumbling Hawk was battling against his old picture of Lightfoot. His fat friend had always been a little foolish and vulnerable, so Tumbling Hawk felt genuinely fearful watching Lightfoot's immersion in that deep world of magic.

One afternoon Tumbling Hawk returned home from a solitary ride. For some reason he picked up his old quiver and reached down into it. The white soldier's coins were gone. The boy groped in the dust at the foot of the center lodge pole where the quiver hung—he turned over the willow mattresses, moved backrests, lifted up the edge of the hide liner that kept out the rain. He thrust his hands into every crevice and storage place, he poked frantically around in the fireplace rocks. Yet even as Tumbling Hawk searched, he knew it was futile. The day before he'd argued with Lightfoot about the white man's goods. Lightfoot swore, when he was shaman, to banish coffee, the metal ax, and the rifle, to dry up every drop of "the filthy trickle fouling our lives." So Tumbling Hawk knew Lightfoot had stolen his faultless disks.

In the end Tumbling Hawk gave up the search and sat down by the fire, despondent. After two years of fingering their perfection—gone! He felt his first real fear: His stomach jumped and began to flutter down through bottomless space.

As he sat there, Tumbling Hawk grew angry with himself—why did those rounds mean so much to him? Would he continue to play the infant and brood over the loss of a toy? Or was he ready to be a man? a warrior? If so, the loss of the disks might be his signal to start. Finally he had a way out of this paralyzing self-contempt. It was time to search for his vision. Tomorrow he would ask Rumbling Wings to help prepare him for that search.

The next day, standing alone inside the shaman's tepee, Tumbling Hawk mentally congratulated Lightfoot on the accuracy of his descriptions. Lightfoot had become such a potent storyteller that Tumbling Hawk felt like he'd been in the lodge before—the earth covered with water, the Dark Cave.

Rumbling Wings was dressed in deerskin leggings and shirt. Only his moccasins were worked at all, with delicate chips of abalone which sent curved beads of light across the floor whenever he moved his foot.

The boy came to ask about the future, and Rumbling Wings sat considering the past. The shaman knew that Shell had wanted more children, but had not been able to have them, that she was sometimes lonely among the northern Cheyenne. He knew that Big Road no longer loved war, understood that Shell had brought about that softening, and knew that Mohe regarded it as the one slight defect in his son. The boy was both reckless and discerning; he was not well trained in waiting, for he'd done well in early life. This was the boy who captured the white soldier, then sprang up at the banquet to answer Hard Ground. The recent battle with Waschita promised much.

Tumbling Hawk asked the shaman what he had to do to search out his vision. Rumbling Wings suggested Mohe as his sponsor, saying that his grandfather was the best man to supervise him. Then, step by step, the shaman detailed the preparations.

"Go on," Rumbling Wings said when he finished. "You may look. Since we are at the beginning, today should be a question of beginnings. You can look up and see the beginning with the earth covered with water, and that might be a place to go forward from.

"Or you might begin with the tribe whose origins, like your own, are lost in mystery. The Tsistsistas, the real name of our people, lived in a great, always dark cave. Far above, higher than the highest mountain, was a distant brightness not yet called light."

Tumbling Hawk saw that the first strip of day, in the east, was painted on the skins in the blue greens of deep water. Water covered everything. Only Heammawihio and a few animals, the largest a white duck, floated on it. There were no trees, no land. A great black hole spiraled upward, narrowing like an inverted funnel, as darkly threatening as a twister. The light that cut into the cave thinned and seemed to unravel as it fought down into the gray black until only a feeble strand touched the bottom.

"For many generations the council debated the wisdom of sending a party of warriors up toward the darkness. In the end, a single brave, Laughing Child, dared to start the long climb upwards."

The boy saw a group of men huddled together at the bottom of the hole. They were arguing, their feet planted, torsos lurching forward, their blunt faces frozen in looks of discord. One man, painted an impossible blue, broke away and began to move up the sheer walls. Up and up he climbed, a tiny blue fly on the glistening gray black, the light first silhouetting and flattening out his form, then enlarging him until he cast an enormous shadow on those who looked up, tinted, just slightly, with that color from the world beyond the cave. Below, on the crowd's faces, looks of fear, begrudging belief, icy smiles of envy.

"But the light from above was too bright for him."

Tumbling Hawk's eyes were fixed on the pictures even while the shaman spoke. Above, Laughing Child burst into the light, light that struck him in the eyes like a club. Brilliant, clear, too lucid, the searing fire yellow of the sun (not at all what it seemed from below). His arm thrown up to shield his eyes, Laughing Child retreated in pain to the edge of darkness.

"When he recovered the use of his eyes, he returned to the others and immediately urged the tribe to move up out of the darkness."

He climbed back to his people who waited for him, quarrelsome, will-less. He led the whole tribe—a long winding line of old men and women, the younger children paired. All were helped up by the footsteps of the one who had gone before. Each one in the line now touched with a shade of his blue.

"At first the light burned, and many urged a retreat. But Laughing Child told his people to shade their eyes. While they debated the pain subsided and their eyes grew accustomed to the light. When they could see clearly—that may have taken a long time—they found themselves in a dry, bare country, surrounded by rocks and stones."

Near the top Laughing Child left them bunched together in partial darkness, then led them out of the neck of the cave one by one, each with his back to the sun and with forearm raised to shield the eyes. The pictures were beautiful here—the gray fog of dry land slowly coming into focus until the painted rocks grew solid and the gray blur of the barren land etched itself into a fixed line.

"There was nothing to eat except rabbits, so they took to stoning them."

Then the Slaughter of the Rabbits—thousands of the long-eared furry creatures falling to their stones. Rabbits covered in shades of drying blood, rabbits heaped up on each other covering each patch of open ground. Yet always more. No matter how many they killed a shower of life rose to answer their plague of death.

"They stayed in that country for many generations, until the warriors tired of life in that bare dry land and led the tribe west.

"Moving was difficult in those days, for they had no dogs or horses then. Finally they came to a large river where timber grew all the way down to the water. They'd never seen that before.

"The river was so far across they couldn't see from one bank to the other. They stayed on its bank. How much time passed before they fashioned a canoe is a question like how much time passed before the Tsistsistas climbed out of the cave or how soon their eyes became accustomed to the light. Many generations may have flourished and died before they learned how to float a tree in water, to hollow out a tub from a tree trunk, to narrow and lengthen and draw out the beautiful body of the canoe. All good things come slowly."

Tumbling Hawk stared. The abrupt ending jarred the boy, who felt deprived of something and wanted to ask for more.

Rumbling Wings was not used to having children sense when he lost interest, sense when they were being fobbed off with a tag line. Tumbling Hawk was subtle and quick, as Mohe said, with the healthy impatience of those who know their own minds, who anticipate where the story leads and object when it does not get there. Just the sort of virtue that curdles if thwarted too long. Tumbling Hawk would make a fine alert follower—as long as he agreed, as long as nothing was left out. How different from Lightfoot, who had the true disciple's nature:

malleable, reverential, so awestruck or intent he had no inclination to let his own thought come between himself and his master. Suddenly curious, the shaman tried to recall which type he'd been as a young man, but he could not remember.

Without looking up, the shaman saw the painted sky above his head, each image locked in its rightful place. Not long ago there had been an agreement between the pictures and his stories. Now he felt a force outside that the pictures did not incorporate, something new—old, new, he'd never had to think of it like that before. Now he sensed two realities—the old one fixed, immutable, which he'd contemplated for years inside his lodge until the images were locked behind his eyes; the other outside, in a world terribly changed.

"Telling a story is a curious thing—so much depends on where you have to go and how quickly you must get there. There is always so much to choose from, so many paths that might be taken, and so many stories. If you stay with our fathers and describe some part of their lives on the east bank of the Great Water, there are tales of Laughing Child's life—" Above him Tumbling Hawk could see many more spots of that distinctive blue. "There Branching Tree made the bow, and Sweet Medicine tricked the bird whose wings made the wind into becoming a steady breeze by taming the bird after breaking its wing. But if you lead the tribe quickly over the path of the sun, toward our present home, those lives on that far shore will mean very little to you.

"Only words hold those times—words that have begun to mock us by changing in our throats as we speak them, words that will no longer hold their shape in the thoughts of others." Was this too difficult for the boy? There was more, much more to say—that each man understands only according to what he can see; that a man's thoughts tend to circle around his greatest concerns, round and round till they wear a track so deep his thought rarely climbs out of it; that the world around the Cheyenne had undergone startling changes in the few short years since that first wagon of the white man rutted their hunting range. The shaman's people no longer listened as they once had; the origins of the stories, the truths they had always held, seemed a long way off. "Stories are arrows which rarely find their mark, a heavy sadness for a man of stories. Yet something remains. Look above—" Tumbling Hawk followed the old man's eyes "—see the stories lighting up the sky like one of the night stars. See the trail of heroes whose names have faded to a shadow of their former brightness. A story loses one kind of truth to gain another; outlines get clearer as details fade.

"That arrow above—" Rumbling Wings pointed to the first strip of day in the east and his finger described the arcing flight of an arrow across the sky. Through alternating bands of day and night a track of displaced air grew visible to Tumbling Hawk, like the path of a comet whose blazing tail curved finally into the last night of the west.

Why hadn't he noticed it before?

"That arrow does not pretend to be the wood we balance in our hand before we let it fly from the bow; it is only a way of sending an arrow which will not kill through the air of the mind."

THE VISION

A FEW DAYS AFTER Tumbling Hawk's visit to the shaman's lodge, the Moon of the Falling Leaves displaced the Moon of the Changing Seasons. Each day before the sun was up Tumbling Hawk went to the hills to care for the horses; as before, he went shooting and hunting and riding with his friends. He visited Small Deer at work, watched Takes-the-Pipe's untroubled readiness with a bit of envy and some surprise, and spent every third evening listening to Lightfoot. Though he occupied himself as before, time was different for him. He became sensitive to his family's desires that he take his true path. They were too good and too subtle to tyrannize him with their hopes, yet somehow the awareness of how much they wanted for him projected Tumbling Hawk still further into his loneliness. Life no longer seemed simple.

He felt closest to his grandfather. He began going to Mohe's lodge each day at dusk to learn how to prepare for his vision. The grandfather listened patiently to the grandson's impatient demands that his ally appear; he sympathized with Tumbling Hawk's struggle to appreciate what Lightfoot was undergoing. Yet the old man feared the boy's restlessness would cause him suffering. Mohe recognized Tumbling Hawk's habit of mind, the impulse to fasten on the imperfection of a thing, to worry it. Mohe thought assuming perfection was even accessible was foolish. For himself, he preferred to enjoy the virtues of the thing rather than wrestle with that endless turnover of flaws. He never really liked that insistence on perfection, but eventually came to believe it was bound up with his grandson's willingness to take risks.

Of course Mohe was right. Tumbling Hawk did nurture a secret pride. He was almost glad he didn't know what would be his. But that pride haunted him. Was it too fickle, too greedy? For that grain of pride was he doomed to miss the heart of the mystery? A part of him remained fearful, afraid of his own undefined ambition. Yet another part hated the others' gray smugness as they sat around the fire, speaking furtively of a mystery they could not or would not name, agreeing with each other about the singleness of a face which seemed to the boy myriad-minded, unlimited.

Two weeks passed in the peculiar intimacy bred of crisis and an old man's desire to help a young one. As much as possible, Mohe screened Tumbling Hawk from the pressures surrounding him, trying to let the boy be as free as he could, knowing that was the best way for the vision to come to him. Tumbling Hawk had no idea how hard his grandfather worked.

Camp was almost ready to break up and Rumbling Wings preparing to go into his winter quarters when, in the middle of the Moon of the Falling Leaves, Tumbling Hawk's day arrived. He prepared as he'd been instructed—taking his morning bath alone, in the holy pool upstream from where he usually swam. Afterward, standing naked on the drying rock, he fanned his body with sprays of white sage. Tumbling Hawk should have gloried in his body that morning, but he felt dull and heavy. His scrotum contracted with the cold, and the right testicle threatened to float back up to his childhood. It bothered him so much he kept pushing it down on the long walk to Mohe's lodge. He spoke to no one.

Mohe's hair was braided, one braid wrapped in red-and-black striped hide, the other in red. He sat facing the rising sun with his yellow breechclout spread in front and behind him in a gesture to past and future. A leather chain of herringbone weave circled his head. Dangling from it, over his ears, were two short weasel tails.

To the boy his grandfather's lodge had always seemed beautiful and mysterious, with that hint of pressure which attaches to the exemplary. It was a little archaic; thus slightly too formal. All Mohe's cutting tools were bone or stone or quartz, many so long used they were as thin as sinew; his dishes were clay. Only what nature placed in his hand, the old man said, was allowed inside his home—buckets of buffalo paunch, a bladder waterskin, bowls made from tortoiseshell, cups hewn from box elder, wonderful to hold.

As Tumbling Hawk's eyes wandered attentively over these familiar things, he couldn't help remembering the old man's furious fight against the white man's trade beads: "You give away your power for a little sparkling stone. Better to chip the rock with the fingernails than with their iron blade, better to pull each porcupine quill with your teeth than to accept these gifts with two edges." Tumbling Hawk believed his path required his grandfather's sheer determination. The boy found speaking difficult; his brow furrowed like Mohe's but with wrinkles that wouldn't hold their crease.

Mohe relieved him: "Put everything but your own desire from you now." His coal eyes lit up the dark bed into which they settled a little deeper each season. "Think your own secret thoughts, be fearless in the face of your own desires. This is to be your vision, the sign from your allies–no one else will stand beside you on the hill. No one can find fault with what comes from within and is answered from without."

Much of this advice failed to penetrate, but suddenly the boy wanted to thank Mohe for everything he'd ever done. He walked over to the old man, stooped down and gripped his forearm. "Grandfather, you have always given me the rich gift of proper instruction." That was all he said; Mohe smiled. Then Tumbling Hawk left the lodge, feeling surprisingly hopeful.

He walked out of camp according to his instructions–on foot and naked except for the string around his waist, carrying his spray of white sage in his left hand. The day was perfectly clear, without a cloud, and as he moved across the prairie Tumbling Hawk watched the familiar blue haze at the edges of the sky climb until it merged with the darker blues above. To Tumbling Hawk the sky was a giant lodge, that light border a pale lining of airy skin. Once Mohe suggested he become like that blue–consistent, complete, unbroken. Now he wished for a cloud. Not rain, just something to interrupt that limitless sameness, some tension in that vast indifferent blue.

He walked west, trailing his own long shadow through early morning. The light, with autumn's clarity, washed up the sides of the distant mountains and touched their peaks. He pushed on through hard-baked dirt, sun-strangled grass. His shadow began to shrink back into him. About midmorning the landscape hardened; the light became a grindstone, which sharpened all the world's edges. The hills were suddenly spiked. The gully straight ahead opened like bloodless old man's jaws, with broken rows of rock teeth. Trees grew blades; bushes stuck out barbs. Tumbling Hawk felt real fear and with it a sharp pain in the pit of his perpetually falling stomach. Yet he followed his instructions, forced himself to go where he was told his future lay. There was satisfaction in that.

When the sun caught up to him, the edges dulled. Those mountains on the horizon lightened and seemed ready to float up off their bases. His landmark slowly rose up before him—a patchy bald line of hills running southeast, stubbled with the black hairs of dwarf pines; he turned north. Ahead loomed a long gray escarpment, its vertical columns of bisalt a standing file of skeletons locked forever in place. The buffalo grass no longer smelled sweet to Tumbling Hawk.

He picked his way through the bunchgrass and stepped carefully to avoid the lizards and crickets whose paths crossed his. Then the stillness of the wash-blue horizon was broken by flecks of white. Antelopes on the run—scores of them. Flare after flare swam through the pale blue as they ran from something he couldn't see. The boy's nostrils filled with the imagined musk they gave off in flight. He watched until the last white flash disappeared and the sky returned unbroken to the horizon. Feeling very tired, he trudged on.

A few miles farther, the tawny prairie was broken by mounds of dirt. A colony of prairie dogs met him with chattered warning. A single voice passed through them, then a wave of buff bodies crested just ahead of Tumbling Hawk as he stepped delicately through their village, avoiding the openings to the burrows from which a hand could reach out and drag a man or even a horse to the underworld. He walked on, feeling he was slowly making his way across a giant's palm.

He was relieved to get off the floor onto the first slopes, where the mesquite gave way to short grass. But the footing loosened, and making headway was difficult. He fought his way up one sandy hill, he slipped and slid down the other side, up and down, up, down. On top of each hill he had a view of hills ahead, in the troughs he lost sight of his landmark.

Finally he reached the base of the escarpment; up he climbed toward the barren platform where he'd stand alone and naked for four days. When he searched for his place, Tumbling Hawk had come upon an overlook and found it was just what it was supposed to be—desolate and grim and dry, with a commanding view back over the foothills to the plain below. Back at camp the boy had described the place to Mohe, who approved it and located the spot where Tumbling Hawk was to stand, looking east, in the direction from which he'd come.

His ledge, actually a niche, was poised under an overhanging rock, halfway up the escarpment. Standing there, the boy etched the rise and fall of the hills into his mind, traced the clumps of trees in their places on those hills, added the giant switchback wash that opened a red wound in the side of a distant southern ridge, the two great gullies studded with boulders that joined in a V to form a giant necklace. Once the outline was set, he filled in the largest boulders and table rocks, the stand of osage orange trees roughly three hundred paces away and seventy-five to eighty-five paces straight down; the hummocks of yucca holding on where there was no grass; the bushes and lone trees and the scattered islands of grass or weeds. He shortened his focus until he saw only the world that grew up around his feet.

In his terrible haste, he demanded that the land come to him at once, and since he asked too much he felt rebuffed by his chosen site. The boy did not know what he sought, which made him feel small and naked and useless. Still he forced himself to start the ceremony of welcome, following Mohe's instructions dutifully. He was not inspired, and that troubled him too.

To prepare the ground, he brushed it with sage, singing the song Mohe had taught him:

> "Ground be my breast
> Sky my blanket,
> Cardinal points, point me
> In your ways."

He greeted the ground, the sky, and the cardinal points with outstretched arms, palms up, then, palms down, he turned and bowed to the east, west, north and south.

Facing east again, he chanted: "Spirit of this place, welcome and support me." Then, to offer himself to the Spirit, Tumbling Hawk opened his mouth as wide as he could, spread his fingers and toes, rolled his neck back while stretching open his eyes. He arched his back and threw his arms all the way back. He held this stance until his eyes began to burn, then Tumbling Hawk started a game of catch with the place. He caught the air gently, sometimes with one, sometimes with two hands, plucking air out of the air, scooping the air near the ground and reaching above his head and turning all the while from cardinal point to cardinal point. He tried to make sure nothing escaped him. With a snap of his neck he doubled over, tensing his muscles in an effort to catch whatever the place offered. But when he took up his squatting position, left leg bent under the right, he felt unnaturally fatigued and knew he hadn't gotten hold of the spirit.

His blood hadn't yet contracted to fit the space, which was five or six times as wide as his body and four times his length. He began pacing his ledge, gazing out to the far ridge and mesa, scanning the vacant sky for the slightest change. He measured those osage orange trees and explored the contours of the wash, but those gritty undulations held no miracles.

He'd been roaming restlessly, trying to appreciate what this particular expanse of tawny indifference held for him, when an overhanging rock jutted into the known contours of a hill. He backed up half a pace. The landscape resumed its old form. With an eye to these changes, the boy began to move about, disrupting the old panorama when possible, encouraged by this new variety. He surveyed the rocks at his feet, the skunkbush fingering into a cranny, the lichens bearding the gray rock face. As he circled a rock, Tumbling Hawk stepped closer to it, then backed off, stood on his toes, then gradually lowered himself into the dust, moved his head up and down and around. A single small stone became a wolf, a buffalo hump, infant, cliff, all these as well as each seen and unseen possibility. He loved the changes in the thing that remained the same.

The day passed. Just before the sun was to drop out of the sky, Tumbling Hawk stared intently west. He knew that if he looked closely enough he might be able to see the end of light and the beginning of dark, for day and night brought on the ancient monumental battle. Sometimes there was extended sparring, sometimes a siege was laid until one streaked terrified from the heavens. But always, with the next challenge, the other returned. Occasionally a man was blessed enough to see them stand up to fight. Then the outlines clarified—and the edges of day and night became visible. At that instant a man could see them and beyond them as he looked into the crack that cut through to chaos and the beginning of all things.

The wind blew up; the shadings slipped imperceptibly from yellow to bright orange to light rose to a dark blood red—the color of the death of day—then from red to a rich, layered violet. Between the violet and the gray, and the gray and the black, Tumbling Hawk strained to scrutinize each unstable hue. At one point his head snapped back—for an instant he thought maybe he saw something. But it passed like a running shadow.

The day's concentration wore him down—his eyelids tingled with dry fire, his legs ached; all he wanted was sleep. The first cool stars pleased him, but soon they turned to shimmering points of fire. He felt the warmth steal out of the earth; even before total darkness, cold night began to fall upon him. The sky was pitch black before he moved from where he stood naked and shivering.

First, Tumbling Hawk raked together a pile of rocks and small pebbles, then spread the rocks into three rows the width and length of his body. He lay down. Even on that bed it felt good to take the weight off his legs and stretch. But as the boy relaxed, he cramped. To fight the spasm Tumbling Hawk straightened his legs through the joints. The movement was incredibly painful, but slowly his feet and ankles and calves and, finally, his thighs relaxed. He then slipped off his moccasins, forced pebbles between his toes, and lay back, cold sweating, to rest.

The night passed in quaking misery. Where his back touched the earth, in spite of the stones, his body felt almost warm. But his front lay open to the night's falling damp. All night the stones wedged their way into his flesh. After an unaccountable length of cold pain, he picked out the pebbles and began to think about standing again. This was hours before the sun would rise.

Somehow he got the half-frozen muscles thawed enough to function and push the joints past their cracking agony. When he finally stood, the pain was excruciating. "Old age must be like this," he said to himself. Exhausted, Tumbling Hawk realized that was the first thought he'd had all night, which seemed a considerable triumph. Then he realized it was only the second day, his first morning. He wanted to smile, but found he couldn't.

A moment later his knees went liquid, he felt delirious. So when the pictures came they brought Tumbling Hawk some relief, wiping out the unyielding line of those foothills, that boulder necklace. Not that the terrible pain went away, but the images distracted him, and pain was secondary.

He saw a tree hung with infants' cradles, a child strapped to each board, the board suspended from a limb. An old oak that bore children for fruit. He saw it all, yet he was small again too, rocked in one of the gently swaying cradleboards watching the leaves in a green-yellow sea bob up and down in time to the song whispered by the leaf to his ear. Then the leaves vanished, and cold white pieces of gray sky fell down at him, delicate chips from an ice block above.

Suddenly he was running, his father's face tilted up like his at an orange-and-black butterfly that danced against the sky. They chased it in and out of bushes, shooed it from a low branch and across a stream. The butterfly must have known they wouldn't harm it, for it stayed near the boy all the time, dodging, diving at the ground, or fluttering just out of reach above his head. How cunning the lovely thing was and how fast. It led them out into a high-grassed meadow where it swooped between Tumbling Hawk's legs, then spiraled up into the blue sky. The boy finally caught up with it at the edge of the high grass and cupped its fluttering colors in his hands. Big Road said, "Don't hurt it, but now rub its wings over your heart, Tumbling Hawk, and ask the butterfly to lend you its grace and speed."

He was pulling on his first moccasins, with a star of red and white porcupine quills on the instep; he saw his mother stooped over a buffalo hide, resting her weight on an elbow-shaped elk-horn scraper as she slowly plowed the skin into hairless rows. He felt his ears being pierced. He was bawling out loud, feeling power as the salt tears stung his eyes, when he heard his name being called once, twice, then felt the freezing air slap his face as Shell whisked him out of the warm glowing lodge into the white woods where he cried himself out. He saw himself inside the circle of the buffalo hides where women sat tanning hides; Tumbling Hawk remembered how proud he'd felt to stay within the sight of his grandmother, whose eyes had grown cloudy with the years.

Mohe led him to the sweat lodge, and when they emerged from the steamy dark, his grandfather rubbed him from head to foot with the fat of a wolf killed the day before. On their way to the eagle pit Mohe explained that he'd dug Tumbling Hawk a little cavity at the end of the pit, which meant there had been more dirt to hide from the keen-sighted bird. But he'd planted it under bushes and spread it about until everything looked as it had.

So he sat patiently while his grandfather positioned the wolf carcass, then filled in the branch lattice overhead with mats of fresh long grass. They waited under the thick thatch until just after midday, when the heavy bird hit the ground close above them with a wild chirrup. The sunlight grew vague as the bird mantled, shading the thatch with its huge wings. After a long, cautious pause, the child heard the bird tear into the wolf, dragging its innards apart and ripping away at its flesh.

Soon the wolf's blood was trickling through the thatch onto Mohe's back and onto the boy. The eagle danced around the carcass, scratching up tufts of their grass roof until Mohe's arm shot up through the thatch and grabbed the bird by both legs, pinning them together to protect himself from the talons. Once again the sky darkened as the bird unfurled its wings, squawking madly and straining desperately to fly. The struggle pulled Mohe almost to his feet. Then, with a crash of branches, he dragged the huge bird, squawking and flapping, down into the pit. Tumbling Hawk held his grandfather's shield only inches from that slashing beak, that icy riveting eye as Mohe deftly slipped a noose of buffalo hair around the eagle's neck. The old man yanked with all his strength.

The bird's wings filled the pit, its head pivoted to wound the old man, but Mohe pulled until the eagle's clear eye clouded, then the wings moved heavily.

In his dream Tumbling Hawk saw his grandfather and his grandmother, his mother and father. Then the four faces began to float before him, whirling into a blur of the single face that was his family.

They were gone, and Tumbling Hawk found himself climbing through the picture stories in the sky of Rumbling Wings' lodge. He was in the east, at the first streak of day, being pulled out of the right side of Heammawihio. As Laughing Child he made his way up toward what was not yet called light; as the Duck, he dove down to the lowest depths of the water-covered earth to return with the little piece of mud that made land. Then he was in many places at the same time—he stayed on the east bank of the Great Water to fashion the canoe while he moved west across the flooded Misi Sipi, planting poles to mark his way back. He saw the first rifle reach up and pick a bird out of the air even as he ran from the hostile Pawnee who fired a strange stick that barked thunder.

Then the Contrary appeared to him, his bow drawn backward as if to shoot himself, his headdress completely hiding his face, and his shading palm extended upside down to cover the eyes he believed he'd found on the back of his head. As Tumbling Hawk hung in the sky, the Contrary faced him, looked at the boy, then scuttled backward with surprising speed. He seemed startled by what he saw, for he raised his lance as he retreated from the boy, pulling it back over his head till he disappeared into that first band of night.

Tumbling Hawk felt unsettled. Did the backward man come to mock or to warn him? Or was it to teach him something? Contraries acted out what no one wanted to happen—through the Magic of Reversal they lamed powerful adversaries, dragged enemy chiefs from their ponies. And they could seal a past action and anticipate evil, for the Contrary's magic made an enemy unable to substitute what he wanted for what had actually passed.

The sky was bright when Tumbling Hawk's thoughts began to clear. He guessed it was the afternoon of the third day. He wasn't certain but thought he'd shivered through another damp night, and he believed the sun had dried him when it rose. Time passed before Tumbling Hawk considered further—the slightest effort exhausted him. When he decided to examine himself, the boy found he was lying face down on the rocks. His chin had dug into the ground, coating his lips and teeth with dirt. He thought he remembered spitting. His feet bled, his stomach was shredded; inside he felt like an enormous cave. For three days—if that was right—he'd had no food at all, no water. Worse—most horrifying of all—there'd been no announcement of his future. His dreams had been rich, but they told him nothing he had not already known.

The day passed and, except for that brief moment of lucidity, he had no knowledge of its shadings, its changes in temperature. He stood without thought, totally emptied. Day gave way to night, but the change was of as little interest to Tumbling Hawk as it was to any other stone around which the crickets poked, on which the flies and chiggers landed. He felt nothing, saw nothing. He simply was.

The fourth day broke on him like thunder. He heard the day come on—he heard the night give itself over with a crackling yell that coursed through him. He did not see the chasm between the two worlds, but he clearly heard the scream of defeat as night fled the sky. For that he was grateful, he was glad to be given that much. As the understanding passed into him, Tumbling Hawk realized he was standing. Then the earth made a sound beneath him. At first he thought it was the dying scream of night. But light was already up; besides, this noise was different. It came too regularly, in precise intervals, a sound he'd never heard before in a rhythm steadier than that of a trotting horse. The noise was like a good knife blade being drawn backward over stone, or a kind of scraping.

Near him stood a figure. Or rather half a figure—its near side was perfect and whole, but the being's far side was darkened by a thick night fog. The left half of his face had a prominent jaw and solid high cheekbones, a full mouth.

On the warrior's left cheek there was a Cheyenne battle mark—two yellow lightning flashes. A red coup count tipped the warrior's nose. In his left arm the figure cradled a shiny new rifle. Where his right hand should have been he held an arrow painted with the circle of all beginnings and ends and the double eagle feather of the sacred arrows. Meanwhile the noise continued, penetrating, unnerving.

When the figure finally spoke it uttered sounds unlike any the boy had ever heard. But the sound didn't come from his half mouth; his lips didn't move. Instead it issued from the air around him. A moment later the voice merged with the strange rhythmic noise and the two became indistinguishable. As it grew louder the sound became a chilling squeak, like a mouse crying when clutched by a hawk, but much more horrible because it was louder and more insistent.

Terrified, Tumbling Hawk forced himself to fix the warrior's single good eye. The left eye flared like a fire-fed kindling. As it did Tumbling Hawk saw the right eye glow. For an instant he thought that if he concentrated intently, his concentration might burn off the cloud shrouding the figure. Then it vanished—sound, figure, all.

His head ringing with the silence, Tumbling Hawk groped to understand. He realized that this figure was his vision. He had received no signs, no directions. There had been no promise of valor or victory, only a mystery he couldn't begin to understand. Bewildered, flooded by disappointment, he forced himself to say his final prayers, trying, as graciously as he could, to make his peace with the place. Then he started the long slow trek back to camp, walking back along his faded footprints. He went directly to the shaman's lodge.

As Rumbling Wings listened to the elusive story, the shaman found himself slightly annoyed that he couldn't easily comprehend the vision. He was surprised to stumble over a particle of vanity he thought he discarded years before.

"I cannot tell you all of this story." The shaman began circumspectly, aware of the effect of his words on the tense child. He didn't tell Tumbling Hawk there might have been ways to pursue the vision at the time because that time had passed. "The clouded half must remain in shadow until burned away by the fire of time within. I myself do not see all that the shadowed part holds. But I have seen a stone for grinding corn which makes a noise like the one you describe, and I have heard of desert tribes who use a stone wheel for turning clay into bowls. That wheel might make a similar sound.

"Probably, the sound will soon become clear to you." He hesitated before he added, "but that would be far from here. To the east." Rumbling Wings turned his worn stone of a face toward Tumbling Hawk, trying to comfort him. "You were born with the rising sun, with the hawk and his kind, in the clear cool light of morning. But you will have to travel toward the sun, back to yourself, in order to come west again, to the dark cardinal point where the heart knows itself from the inside out.

"Your journey will be arduous, with much confusion, but the difficulty of the journey is the test of the man."

Then Rumbling Wings softened. "But if you go away, you will return to us. The arrow speaks of your coming back. We will talk together then—many words. Then you will teach me and I will have little to say." The shaman was pleased to be able to promise that.

The idea of leaving was so incomprehensible that Tumbling Hawk didn't immediately grasp it. Dumbfounded, he asked his most obvious question: "But what about glory and honor? Won't I be a warrior among my brothers?"

The old man replied gently, in a voice that disguised his own sense of anticlimax, "I have always been certain—as you have—that there would be honor enough in your life. You have overlooked your ally's arrow and gun, and also he bore a coup mark."

The boy chafed under the shaman's prophecy. How could the medicine man be so sure? This vision was so extraordinary, so unimaginable. And if he was to leave, where would he go?

Rumbling Wings knew he wouldn't be able to convince the boy. The shaman did not bother to explain that the sound wouldn't enter the Cheyenne world—that was virtually impossible since Rumbling Wings knew their world as a wild turkey knows the call of every bobcat in his range.

"Will I be away a long time?" Tumbling Hawk asked with false assurance.

"If you go away," Rumbling Wings answered, "you will go to a different people. You will live on a different soil, so you will be able to tell how great the changes are among us. With your help I might be wise enough to guess what time has done. Remember, Tumbling Hawk, whatever happens, remember how you have begun."

Rumbling Wings then questioned the boy about his vigil. Did his right arm tingle and have short spasms? Were his arches sore? Did wavy lines run west to east at sunset? Had he noticed any sparrows? Larks? He was asked to reconstruct his suffering instant by instant. Tumbling Hawk realized he'd forgotten a lot already. At that point Rumbling Wings' injunction began to sink in.

"Remember," the shaman insisted again. "And do not plague yourself with what is to come. It needs no excuses. You have much to do. Someday there will be more to say. We can wait till then."

That was clearly the dismissal, so Tumbling Hawk rose to go. Rumbling Wings raised a scaly index finger: "As for the vision, it is better kept between ourselves. Do not take it away from here in words, only in your heart. Think of it and see it many more times, hear it over and over. And, remember, you will always see only a part of what is before you."

Later when asked to tell about his vision, Tumbling Hawk said he'd been sworn to secrecy. Impressed, they agreed he had to honor his vow and asked no further. He spoke to no one about what had happened, not to his father or grandfather, mother or friends.

THE RAID

At the beginning of the Moon of the Popping Trees the Cheyenne split into their winter hunting bands. Tumbling Hawk's party of eight families traveled south and west to the Slim Buttes country. There the fire burned brightly, and the camp gained the clear quiet air of a home. The circle was beaten flat and cleared of snow, and in the upper pastures the ponies nosed down to the green beneath. The younger boys spent their days sliding down hills on their buffalo-rib sleds. The men wore out the time with stories set in warmer seasons, and the women worked in the half outdoors of the unroofed circle of the buffalo robes. Game was sparse, so, providently, they nibbled away at their dwindling supplies.

Tumbling Hawk waited moodily for the season to give way to spring, for with it would come the first set of trials for the entrance into the Dog Soldier Society. Throughout this winter, the strange shadow man appeared frequently in his dreams. Twice the shadow teased him into believing it was about to reveal more of itself, but the promise was never fulfilled, and the secret Tumbling Hawk nursed continued to disturb his winter's sleep.

Spring was herding the snows north when Tumbling Hawk's band moved west to rejoin the party of Takes-the-Pipe's family. Near the Chalk Cliffs they camped long enough to see the green spread over the low places and to gather more of their people to them. For the first time the boys were included in the spring buffalo hunt. Tumbling

Hawk returned with a fine buffalo calf, Takes-the-Pipe took two. That made their fathers very happy.

Early in the Moon of the Blowing Snow, Man-Who-Runs-the-Farthest proposed a raid on the Shoshoni. Winter lingered so late in the Wind River mountains, Man-Who was certain the Shoshoni would consider themselves safe from attack until well into the spring; he also knew their ponies would be thin from lack of grass and weak from lack of exercise, and thus unable to pursue his party. But what made this raid so special was that Man-Who instructed the crier to announce that Tumbling Hawk and Takes-the-Pipe would go along with the warriors to Shoshoni country.

Since they weren't members of a warrior society, they could not take part in the ceremonial preparations, though Man-Who-Runs-the-Farthest would recount these events in careful detail. The boys knew when he held conferences with his warriors, knew when he entered the sweat lodge with the shaman to consecrate his battle shield, and afterward they heard the prayers that had been offered to protect their leader from arrows and bullets, and the shaman's promise of many horses awaiting them in the Shoshoni mountains.

Tumbling Hawk held conferences with Big Road and Mohe about his weapons. Together father, grandfather, and son decided how much food Tumbling Hawk could carry, which pouch he should take, how much weight he could run with, the best place to store his second pair of moccasins.

Often Tumbling Hawk sat with Shell as she stitched these new moccasins and talked of village gossip and other small things. Neither felt they had time to waste on what had passed. They were closer than they had been in a long time. Tumbling Hawk was tied to her by the sinew she pushed through the holes she'd awled in the hide. As the parfleche sole grew together with the deerhide, the boy knew these moccasins like his own skin. When the porcupine quills formed the five-pointed star on the instep, the time had come for him to go.

By then they'd said their good-byes. Shell was quiet as Tumbling Hawk stood beside her on that last morning, his bow slung over his shoulder, newly feathered arrows dressing up his quiver. She was able to view the dark intense figure almost as she would another boy. Of course the parting saddened Shell, but it also brought relief. Her struggle to keep him a child was over; Tumbling Hawk would return a man. Their relationship would be different then; they would see little of each other.

Mohe stood erect next to the pony, checking the bridle and reins with auspicious attention. He was proud to be wearing the fringed robes of a sponsor. Big Road blew on the arrows' feathering for good luck. (Tumbling Hawk had taken a sheaf of ten from Mohe, another ten arrows from Small Deer.) Big Road felt blessed that Tumbling Hawk was to become a warrior while Big Road was still young and vigorous.

They said good-bye, then Tumbling Hawk hoisted himself up with one hand. Feeling the solid pull across his chest and down the muscles of his arm, Tumbling Hawk realized how much stronger he'd grown in the past year. "The body of a man," he thought, gripping his horse with his knees and tensing his thighs to keep his hands free. Beneath him, Cloud shifted her weight.

Sitting above the painted and robed warriors, the older men and mothers saying good-bye, the young boys staring up envyingly, having listened to the Wolf songs all through the night, Tumbling Hawk felt like the boy who'd raced so well for the white soldier's body. His future was out there, ahead of him; all he had to do was ride into it. When he came back he'd be mounted in the first row; the villagers would call his name again and again; it would roll up the hill to him; and the wave, begun that day, would never crest, for he'd return many, many times to the top of that hill.

From Cloud's back Shell looked small. Strands of hair—the wind was gusty—kept whipping across her face, hiding her eyes. Tumbling Hawk was glad Takes-the-Pipe, his old friend and rival, was riding with him, for he had a score to settle about their buffalo hunt. Tumbling Hawk still smarted from missing a second shot at close range and needing four arrows to bring the calf down. Well, he would change that. Older braves nodded at him, men who'd won their fame and taken their places at the council fire. Your turn has arrived, they seemed to say.

The party numbered nine, led by Man-Who-Runs-the-Farthest, his pipe cradled in his right arm, his battle shield swinging loosely from its strap over his left shoulder. Behind him came the scouts, Island and Two Children, and after them Hard Rain, a strong quiet brave. In front of the boy sat Short Body and Running Bear, hardly older than themselves, then Tumbling Hawk and Takes-the-Pipe and, finally, Hankering Horse with his two "catcher" mares as rearguard. Except for the leader, each rider carried his own arms, food, clothing, and two ropes. The youngest were also responsible for carrying the leader's gear; he carried nothing but the shield and pipe, not even bow and arrow.

When everyone was mounted, Man-Who-Runs-the-Farthest threw a handful of dust into the air and, without another word, they rode out of camp.

The company headed south and west, dropping toward the Wind

River country where they'd ride west up the valley, avoiding the high mountains and coming upon the Shoshoni from the south. They loped along through the familiar flat country, pushing through swirls of snow that still gripped the brown ground, sidestepping the deeper drifts. Tumbling Hawk tried to keep Cloud's fetlocks dry. Meanwhile Hankering Horse entertained the boys with his chatter about his mares, whom he'd trained to lure away enemy horses. He talked to his ponies as he did to the boys.

Shortly after midday, by a creek that had eaten through limestone until it produced a pebbly reddish beach, they stopped for water. Running Bear, a big nervous youth who still had not been admitted to the Elk Horn Society, sauntered back to the boys. Stepping up to Takes-the-Pipe's pony, he shook the load on the pony's back to test the cinch, then slapped the animal a little too hard on the rump. It made a loud sound—the older men turned to watch.

"Is this how our children go to war—carrying households on their backs like their mothers?"

Takes-the-Pipe stiffened, but he held back remembering that boys on their first raid were often subjected to such hazing.

"You hit the pony too hard!" Tumbling Hawk growled, stalking over to the older boy. He was furious and almost as annoyed that Takes-the-Pipe accepted the insult.

Running Bear involuntarily stepped back and, as he did, his foot skidded on the smooth pebbles; he fell backward, catching himself by sticking out a hand. He rose slowly, trying to reclaim his dignity. A fight was in the air.

Hankering Horse stepped closer to his mare, directing his loud aside into her ear: "If the two young braves loose that on the Shoshoni, we will return with many new lovers for you."

The warriors' laughter gave Running Bear the opportunity to withdraw, but by then Tumbling Hawk had made an enemy.

When they stopped at dusk, the youngest pair took over the women's work of making camp—fetching water, chopping kindling, preparing and serving Man-Who's food, for he wasn't allowed to ask for food or water. After they'd eaten, Man-Who-Runs-the-Farthest scratched himself all over with a small pointed stick (he wasn't permitted to use his fingernails, for they were reserved for the enemy). Then he filled his pipe, lighting it with an ember from the fire. He pointed the stem to the sky and chanted: "Spirit above, smoke," pointed the stem down: "Earth, smoke." He puffed again and pointed west, north, east, south—"Four cardinal points, smoke!" The circle completed, he handed the pipe to Hankering Horse, who sat on his left. The Horse passed it on to Island, then it shuttled to Two Children, Hard Rain, Short Body, and Running Bear. The Bear left only enough room at the top of the stem for Tumbling Hawk to take it with difficulty. But the boy pinched the stem with his thumb and index finger and, holding the bowl upright, drew deeply and solemnly before passing it on to his friend. After Takes-the-Pipe took his puff, the bowl came back to his father, who tapped the ashes into a pile by his side.

The stories began with Man-Who-Runs-the-Farthest's tale of his raid against the Crow, but by then their smoke on the battle pipe was working on the boys—Takes-the-Pipe's eyelids felt weighted; Tumbling Hawk's moment of anxiety had passed, and now he felt he was floating a couple of feet off the ground. The pipe circled around. In turn each warrior asked, "Shall I tie another story to it?" Then he told of his act of war, or of capturing ponies, or counting coup. The stories followed the path of the sun until Running Bear's turn came, but he was silent; which made it that much worse when Tumbling Hawk told about the white soldier and Takes-the-Pipe enlarged on it. After a second round of stories, Man-Who-Runs-the-Farthest told his men the time had come to rest.

When the moon shouldered its way into the middle of the Hunter's belt, Tumbling Hawk still lay awake. He felt he had two heads, one of which goaded him to plan wild revenges on Running Bear, while the other lectured that such foolishness was not important enough to keep him awake.

The debate raged until he heard Man-Who-Runs-the-Farthest shift a little, then saw him sit up. Only Takes-the-Pipe's sleeping body separated Tumbling Hawk from the leader, so the boy could watch the older man by turning his head ever so slightly to the right. Man-Who looked around the circle to see if anyone was awake, and when he'd passed over Tumbling Hawk, who feigned sleep, and his son, he began to sing quietly to himself:

> "You have entrusted me with the lives
> Of brothers and sons, Great Spirit.
> Give me strength with good will, patience, and courage,
> Graft to my strong body a mother's tenderness.
> Great power, my brothers, sons, help me."

He continued in a low voice: "For my son I ask little. I know he will be courageous and strong, a fine warrior. Soften him, Mystery, bring him a joy less grim, a fulfillment that may sometimes smile." The granite profile, which had been rigid in the moonlight, slackened with sadness. "The other boy sees sharply, clear, a good and dangerous boy. Keep him beside us." Tumbling Hawk caught his breath when he heard the whispered words—there they were again. "Running Bear is strong, for him I hope the best. Short Body is ready, the Horse a brother, with Island and Two Children great gifts for a man. Protect the steady one. He always does well."

Tumbling Hawk heard no more, for Man-Who-Runs-the-Farthest's voice dropped as he began to speak rapidly. His drone became an incantation, and soon the boy drifted off, his mind uneasy with words that echoed Rumbling Wing's prophecy.

After that, the days fell into an exciting routine. Each morning the scouts were sent ahead to clear the way for the company's advance. The pair would move through the wooded valleys keeping to the low places and ravines to escape being seen until they scaled the south or western wall up to the top of the hills to check the next valley beyond. The lightest breath of smoke, some timber wolves looking back as they slinked off, a keen-sighted antelope poised to examine what the men could not see would stop Island and Two Children until the invisible resolved and they could move on again. Behind them they left messages, a tiny cut across the grain of an oak running southwest, a slight rearrangement of a deadfall to point the way over the next ridge; an oddly broken branch parallel to the trail. Thus the feelers spoke to the body as they tentatively felt their way forward.

The raiding party twisted through a canyon of brilliant red cliffs and moved up the steep-sided Wind River valley hugging the wooded northern slope to avoid the southerly camps of the friendly Wind River tribe. They reached the head of the valley and were almost to the foothills of the Absarokas when the scouts came hurrying back, and all knew as they approached that Island and Two Children had seen the Shoshoni camp. By sunset, Island reported they were within attacking distance; a half day's journey until they reached the spot where they'd leave their horses, then move on foot to the place where they'd wait for night to fall.

They rode in absolute silence, with Island and Two Children going ahead only a few hundred paces and waving them forward. Like the others, Tumbling Hawk made his own pictures of the ground over which they passed, knowing he'd need to be thoroughly familiar with the land to make the retreat. For the first time he felt what it meant to be in enemy territory, in the honey-thick air of danger. He modulated his mood, aware that too great a change in his heartbeat or temperature or body smell might raise a signal into the air as intelligible to the Shoshoni as the messages Island and Two Children sent back to his party. For the space through which he moved was inhabited by a people who knew the moods of its winds. Beneath his pony's hooves lay a ground so well acquainted with those who walked on it, it could always detect the footsteps of intruders.

A thoroughly alerted company of Cheyenne halted when the scouts flung up their arms and noiselessly flopped onto their bellies. Man-Who-Runs-the-Farthest crawled forward to join his scouts at the edge of the jagged ridge. The rest held their positions—frozen in stride, each with a hand cupped over his pony's mouth—until Man-Who crawled back to them. A detachment of cavalry had set up camp on the valley floor—thirteen soldiers, two officers, seventeen horses, two with full packs.

Then they understood why their movements through the Shoshoni country had been strangely unhindered. The Shoshoni had pulled back to the higher ground at the northwest rim of their hunting range, hoping the Waschita troops would pass by them. So there'd been no sign of their hunters or scouts at the eastern end of the valley. Tumbling Hawk was enraged that white man had interrupted his first raid, yet it was odd to resent Waschita's presence in Shoshoni territory.

The ponies were led down the ridge out of earshot; the men took their habitual positions in the circle to wait for Man-Who-Runs-the-Farthest and the scouts who busied themselves with the final inspection of their weapons. All wondered if they would attack the soldiers.

Man-Who-Runs-the-Farthest came back with Two Children, leaving Island on the ridge to watch the soldiers. He looked his men over carefully before he whispered, "At night a Cheyenne looks much like a Shoshoni to a soldier—tall and straight with feathers in his hair." Man-Who-Runs-the-Farthest flipped the two eagle feathers in his headband. It was the funniest thing Tumbling Hawk had ever seen him do. "We must be certain they think we're the mountain Indians. We take all their horses but one; while the soldiers are stranded we slip by them up the valley and take the Shoshoni's ponies from the white hills. We will be home at the campfire before more soldiers return with new mounts. After that, the Shoshoni will have a hard time coming after us."

They waited joyfully for the night, the boys working their ropes around the trunks of pines to loosen them up. The leader spent much of his time with the younger braves, making them repeat their instructions until they could never forget them. Finally, when night came on, they chanted a few short words of prayer and moved up the ridge, then slowly crept down toward the soldiers, forming a loose loop around the camp, then gradually tightening it until they could see the saddle marks embossed on the horses' sides, the wide cinch marks disappearing under their bellies, the white breath steaming in the dark air.

Their positions on the surround were the same as their places at campfire. Hankering Horse and Man-Who came up from the east, upon the soldier who guarded the horses; he was sitting on a log, his back to them. Next to his father was Takes-the-Pipe, then Tumbling Hawk. Man-Who-Runs-the-Farthest crawled forward until he was two body lengths away from the sentry; all the while Tumbling Hawk lay amazed that the soldier didn't turn and fire into the grass. So white man was deaf as well as blind!

Man-Who rose off the ground a little, so it looked like he was making his way up a slope that wasn't there. As he rose and moved the last short distance he drew out his knife. His left hand whipped around the front of the soldier and gripped his chin, wrenching it all the way back. The knife point pierced the large vein on the soldier's neck, then the blade pushed the head forward until Man-Who's right arm was fully extended. The knife took the sentry's last breath with it; there was no sound. The body slumped back into its sitting position.

As Man-Who snatched the guard's rifle out of his hands, four shadowy forms were on their way to the horses; they began cutting pickets and collecting bridle ropes. Tumbling Hawk and Takes-the-Pipe still lay in the brush next to Running Bear, waiting to take the second group of horses. They caught the flash of Man-Who's hatchet as he took the sentry's scalp like a Shoshoni. Then the first four slid silently past the boys, leading off eight horses.

A moment later the three boys were in among the skittish army horses, cutting the pickets and holding the smooth bridles in their own hands. The boys had one bridle rope in each hand, and Man-Who-Runs-the-Farthest and Hankering Horse both had two horses when suddenly Tumbling Hawk slipped one of his leads to Takes-the-Pipe, the other to Running Bear and, before they could react, he headed toward the dead sentry.

Tumbling Hawk dropped down behind the sentry to survey the camp's layout. The rest of the soldiers slept on the far side, away from the horses, and above the fire was a squat ugly thing that the boy guessed was their tepee. His eyes searched the ground around the sleeping men till he spotted what he was after—a long rifle barrel glinting in the firelight.

Tumbling Hawk knew he was taking a risk, knew what he asked of the others. Tumbling Hawk thought of Running Bear. Yet the white soldiers were not as alert as the buffalo; all the sleeping Waschita seemed as deaf as the sentry. And the prize was worth it—to capture a rifle on his first raid. That was repayment for women's work and Running Bear's abuse, that would make up for Takes-the-Pipe's second buffalo.

As he lay calculating each step to the gun, Tumbling Hawk became aware of a strange life lingering about the sentry. The man was dead, his scalp already dangling from Man-Who's belt, yet some part of him was still alive. Tumbling Hawk's thoughts wavered. He knew very little about white man, only that his power was considerable. Perhaps this was a sign of his strength. Behind him the boy could feel the passing eyes plead with his back. But he did not turn. Instead he forced himself into a low crouch and started toward the line of sleeping white bodies.

He passed the first soldier and was almost up to the second. Just ahead, beyond the next sleeping form, it lay. A step and a half and he was over the gun, above those pallid sharp faces. As he stooped down one of the whites rolled toward him. The soldier's eyes were closed, the lids barely touching in relaxed sleep. Tumbling Hawk could not tell if they'd flickered open enough to mean his death. His breath left him, his pulse died, he stiffened, lifeless as a stone.

At least a minute passed before he leaned down again. Then he gently lifted the rifle, balancing it in both hands. It felt cool and smooth, its stock so highly polished it seemed a new kind of wood. Tumbling Hawk reversed himself and, carrying the weapon in front of him, crept back along his own footprints. Not until he crouched behind the dead sentry did he allow himself to breathe.

Then it was there again—that strange little sound, very small, like a tiny madly racing heart. The noise coming from the dead man distracted Tumbling Hawk from the glory of his prize. He could feel the others slipping away up the ridge, but still he could not pull himself away. Terror fused him to that sound which came from the front of the body, someplace near the stomach. He cautiously reached around the soldier; both hands awkwardly explored the folds of rough cloth. They encountered a short metal rope. His fingers guardedly slid down it. They were stopped by a round metal disk—the round thing that was alive, the thing that made the sound.

Tumbling Hawk tried to jerk the chain loose but it held when he pulled. For a moment he wondered if the circle was part of the man's body. But he had seen whites without such a thing, so he pulled again, harder. The cloth ripped slightly—still the chain did not come free.

Sweating, Tumbling Hawk gathered his strength and pulled the chain upward. There was a sickeningly loud sound as the man's clothing tore; then the body swayed and toppled and, as it fell, the chain pulled free.

He knew he had to run, but instead he could only stare at the small ticking circle in his hand, trying to comprehend its regularity, its life. Mesmerized, Tumbling Hawk stared at it until he almost became aware of another sound—almost, for he only really heard it afterward, when it was too late. A sound of warning not heard as warning because not truly listened to, like any one of the thousand noises passed over and never heard again.

The shot startled the boy more than the searing in his thigh. He was up with the sound and away, dropping the gun but still clutching the gold disk. He ran only a few steps before he crumpled in pain. He dragged himself forward and tried to scramble back up to his feet but the thigh kept caving in under him. Then the butt of a rifle smashed into the back of his wounded thigh, and a soldier stood over him.

Tumbling Hawk waited without fear to be shot. Mortified at being caught, he anxiously awaited the crack of the rifle that would grant him a warrior's death and deliver him from this pain. Instead of firing, the soldier pinned him roughly to the ground with the rifle butt. A second soldier appeared. They spoke together and the first man stripped him of his hatchet and knife, yanked him up by one arm and angrily dragged him toward the low fire in the middle of the clearing. The throbbing in his leg drilled through his body like an awl drilling into his bone marrow.

The camp was alive with soldiers running in the many directions they guessed their horses had been taken, scrambling up into the total darkness to search for those who had long disappeared into the night. In the fire's shifting light their shadows seemed blind angry giants stumbling about.

At the campfire stood a spare weasel of a man with a sharp nose and a tiny chin, gesturing with authority while shouting orders. Tumbling Hawk knew he was the leader. By the time the wiry little man turned away from the soldiers, the boy had slumped pitifully onto a log. And when the officer looked at Tumbling Hawk, it was clear he didn't like what he saw. But he examined the boy professionally, quickly yet thoroughly, then took the weapons from the soldier who'd taken them. The officer inspected the hatchet and knife.

Tumbling Hawk was furious he hadn't followed his impulse and plunged his knife into the dead man's body. Their believing he'd killed the soldier would have meant instant death. Which would have been satisfactory. Either that or turning him loose. He had the absurd thought they might go away and leave him.

Colonel Benjamin Hyde looked down at an Indian child of twelve or thirteen, who was in great pain and rapidly losing blood. He wished Symonds, his surgeon, had not remained at base camp. Now Sergeant Medwar would have to do. He studied his prisoner: The boy's straight long black hair framed a longish face. The eyes slanted slightly downward, the lips were full, almost unnaturally full. Looking at the boy, you definitely focused on the mouth first. His nose had the characteristic flatness, to be sure, but the nostrils were well arched. The eyes glowed that fierce black, more angry than afraid. Had the others sent him to murder the guard and get the watch, some horrible initiation rite? The colonel doubted it. They wouldn't take the watch for gold. Hyde wondered what to do with him, and his thoughts drifted indecisively until he focused on the gold watch chain dangling from the boy's fist. He reached out and forced the fist open.

A big man appeared, carrying a flat black case. He looked at the colonel for instruction and, receiving only a curt nod in the boy's direction, opened the case with a snap. The sound was foreign to Tumbling Hawk, who'd never heard a metal clasp. The inside of the case held sets of knives arranged in neat rows, curiously small and flat and thin blades. The sergeant prodded the boy's thigh with a long piece of metal, then picked a narrow knife from the case and made a deep cut in Tumbling Hawk's thigh. A thin sharp pain started from the center of the wound and spurted through him.

The slug out, the boy's thigh throbbed hotly, his head reeled as he watched his leg rhythmically wrapped in a cool, perfectly white skin, lighter than any hide he'd ever felt. It must have been skinned from a giant animal, he thought, seeing it unwind from a long roll. The sergeant's hands went round and round his thigh, shuttling the hide back and forth around the leg. Watching this, Tumbling Hawk grew still more light-headed. He thought he saw an enormous snow beast, a giant white bear, attended by a strange little man with quick unceremonious hands. He heard voices speaking a strange tongue, and shouts and heavy noises. Then he heard and saw nothing for a long time.

BOOK TWO

BENJAMIN HYDE

In 1848, at the age of thirty-four, Colonel Benjamin K. Hyde assumed command of Fort Laramie in what later became the Nebraska Territory. The post was small, but Colonel Hyde rightly regarded Laramie as an indispensable link in the defenses of the western frontier. Hyde was a passionate protector of his realm and in five years had extended Laramie's sovereignty west from the foothills of the Rockies to the forks of the Platte. His troops had chased killers and scoundrels more miles than they deserved on the principle of what he called "preventive expense." The cost to the United States Government might be more than it was worth, but it deterred others from stealing the next saddle or raising the next gun. Hyde knew that his protection encouraged migration and that the more movement, the safer things became. To Colonel Hyde, that formula was an indisputable law of progress.

In September 1850, Hyde brought together ten thousand Sioux, Cheyenne, Arapaho, Pawnee, Snake and Crow, the largest gathering of Indians America had ever seen. It was an extraordinary event—there were so many ponies that they overgrazed the fields around the fort and the colonel had to move the council lodge to the meadows at Horse Creek, thirty miles east of Laramie. In two weeks Colonel Hyde had won from the tribes the right for settlers to travel unmolested over the wagon trails and the freedom to hold the established forts, all in exchange for an annuity of fifty thousand dollars in goods.

The nation's press believed that the unprecedented treaty would bring lasting peace. Hyde was less certain. In 1851, encouraged by the treaty, forty thousand people drove west over the Oregon Trail. In 1852, Hyde's count topped forty thousand. He watched the trail widen, saw settlers swallow the land forbidden them by the treaty, saw ranches and farms spring up all down the line; he saw game become scarce and disease begin to devastate the tribes. The Indians watched too; they grew surly and suspicious; begging and thievery increased; fights broke out between settlers and Indians; there were occasional skirmishes with the soldiers.

Hyde considered the humors of those wild Indians the most predictable of his problems. In the past year pressure had developed to speed the settlement of the Plains, and the Senate Committee on Territories had asked Hyde, as the man in the field, to draw up a plan to organize a new Territory. The colonel proposed a Territory of the Platte which would provide permanent Indian lands north of the Niobrara River and encourage settlement to the south. A reasonable plan, one so persuasive that Stephen Douglas, chairman of the Senate Committee on Territories, had blessed it. Blessed until the Platte bill's provisions for Indian lands ran into time-consuming debate. Douglas—and others—could not wait.

At stake was the richest plum Americans had yet invented for their fiscal delectation, the transcontinental railroad. The phrase itself made men sweat greed. Every thinking citizen could calculate the advantages that would accrue to those whose doors fronted on the first coast-to-coast rail link. Each mile of the slender right of way was freighted with fantasies of princely fortunes—towns and cities would mushroom, hotels and saloons and shops spawn, real estate values multiply. But the railroad right-of-way could not be laid out until the territory was organized.

In this matter of the transcontinental railroad, Colonel Benjamin Hyde and Stephen Douglas were natural allies. Douglas' residence was Chicago, his political support drawn largely from the old Northwest. Douglas' growing empire in Chicago and on the Great Lakes dictated that he favor the midwest route which ran almost in a straight line from his city to Des Moines to Omaha, up the Platte River, through Laramie and over South Pass. Moreover, Douglas' committee coordinated the railroad surveys, the legal means by which the great sectional interests entered their bids in the transcontinental railroad sweepstakes. Douglas wrote Hyde: "The proposed Southern route lacks only that strip of desert south of the Gila River. If Jefferson Davis could purchase the tract as *military land,* which appears to be his legal prerogative as

Secretary of War, the Southern transcontinental *package* will be complete. In that case, all the Friends of the Laramie route will have to look for another way to organize the Territory—fast." Hyde replied: as the man who administered the annuity and fought and negotiated with the Plains Indians, as the man whose word of honor was violated when settlers wandered into lands interdicted by the treaty, he felt a responsibility for the tribes' future. He wanted the railroad to pass through Laramie, indeed he sincerely believed that the Overland Trail made the best route. But Indian lands had to be secured. No other treatment was equitable or politic. Stephen Douglas had never replied to Hyde's letter.

Just then the watch stopped. The jagged edge of silence tore into the boy's thin delirium. That ticking regularity had worked its way so deeply into his own rhythms that suddenly he felt deserted. The watch started again and ticked precisely for a few seconds before, again, it quit. It ran too fast, too slow, then stopped altogether. Tears burned his eyes as he picked it up. It sputtered erratically for a second or two, then died absolutely still.

Tumbling Hawk found himself resting on a soft platform. "I'm dead," he half wished. Beneath him was something snow white, yet dry and warm. On top of him was more of that same white stuff. His right thigh throbbed hotly. It felt raw and tender, although (only after a few minutes did he comprehend this) there was something hard all around it. Still clutching the watch, he forced his free hand to creep down into the whiteness and cautiously touch his thigh. A strip of fine white skin wound down from the top of his thigh almost to his ankles. The material was totally foreign, but it too was white. He vaguely recalled something about a great snow beast, "a bear." But nothing helped explain the two staves of wood that stiffened and weighted the length of his leg.

Trying not to panic, he slowly started to sit up. But the sheets bound him, reaching down into the place between his legs, clinging to his back. He moved and the nightshirt gathered, pinching tighter under his armpits till, terrified, he wrenched away. Pain blasted from his wound—raking claws struck all over his body. He forced himself to relax until the pain grudgingly retreated back to the thigh.

He couldn't understand the shape of the place. White man had cut down a forest—barked the wood, hewn it to sharp angles, and put it up all wrong. Wood covered the ground, the sides, the top where the sky should have been. Nearby some strange white thing stood shakily on four skinny posts. This table had a number of objects on it, one of which the boy guessed was for holding water. But the rest, for all he knew, were part of the table.

The hot tongue of white man's smell licked at his nostrils. The room began to swim before him. Suddenly Tumbling Hawk understood why white man ripped up trees, stripped them naked, laid them side by side in rows; why they made the round tree straight and raised a roof between him and the sun. Two reasons: Red man, at the world's creation, had promised to protect weaker white man from the sun; the other—it bothered him he couldn't remember whether Mohe or Rumbling Wings had said it—the other went, "No man should ever live outside the circle. For the circle contains all things. From that first great circle, the sun, comes all beginnings and ends, all journeys and all lives forever." Yet here he was, lying between their straight walls while white powers lurked in the four dark places outside the circle. White man had taken him out of the sun deliberately. Tumbling Hawk had to escape the white man's trap, had to reach the sun whose light burned high above him. He tried to move but his arms and legs turned boneless and fluid; he moved in thick slow motion, turtle-like. He inched forward and felt his strength gaining when a tiny, barely visible sun of his own grew larger and larger until it exploded in his head.

"Eight months! That bloodless doctor tosses off eight months like it's a prescription for heartburn!" The boy had almost fallen out of bed, yet Hyde's post surgeon offered only cold medical testimony: "The thigh is badly shattered. If the boy keeps calm and does not move excessively, it will take a good eight months before he can put any weight on that leg."

"How in the world can I hold a man-child Shoshoni already in too much of a hurry to be a warrior for eight months?" To make matters worse, the boy would not eat and grew weaker every day. They could not even speak to the child until Bushnell got back, the scout being the only one on the post who spoke Shoshoni. Except for the Pawnee, whom Hyde did not trust. Everything depended on Bushnell, already three days late.

Given any other possibility, Bushnell would not have been Hyde's choice for such a delicate job. Bushnell wasn't exactly steady—or grammatical. He drank too much, spoke bastardized English, was uncouth. He created in the colonel that sense of moral superiority that polished people feel toward the rough. Curiously fitting, though, it all resting on Bushnell, a mountain man filled with the lore and half filled with the beliefs of the Indians, perhaps more savage than the savage since he had been given his chance to be a civilized human being and half rejected it.

Eight months. Hyde's eyes questioned the familiar room. Two walls displayed solid files of books. The other two bore large maps—one with flags representing permanent Indian camps and a color-keyed latticework of hunting grounds and seasonal migration routes; the other featuring forts and ranches on the prominently marked trail along the Platte. This second map had three names: Overland Trail, Platte Trail, Oregon Trail. Hyde did not care what the settlers called it as long as it remained the primary migration route.

"Never can tell how things will work out." Near the colonel's desk stood a tall upright slanting desk, more like a lectern than a desk, which served as his adjutant's working space. Matthew Sherrin, Hyde's aide, stood 6 feet 2 inches, a gangly youth trying to grow into features too large for him. His knees were knobbed with boles which balanced uncertainly on twig calves; his broad shoulders lay like a yoke over a birdcage chest. Hyde believed he looked structurally unsound. His most striking feature was his face: wide and flat like a plate with a wavy bow mouth which neatly sagged in the middle.

In Hyde's nineteen years in the cavalry (not including his four years at West Point), he had developed an exact idea of proper military deportment. Sherrin's deportment was not exactly military. Not at first anyway. The boy's oversized feet constantly abused the rugs. He dropped things; when he bent to pick them up, tables overturned, files splayed like fans. During his first few weeks with his adjutant, Hyde felt he had been sealed in an envelope with an ungainly leaping frog. And just when the order the colonel had labored so diligently to establish seemed ready to collapse, the boy scaled himself down to fit the office. His body memorized routes around obstacles, his feet struck the right paths. Once his body agreed, his mind followed. That had been seven months ago.

As Hyde considered how pleasant and profitable those months had been the anteroom door burst open and Matthew Sherrin strode in, flushed and winded. "Sir," he exclaimed, catching his breath, "excuse me, sir, I'm afraid Bushnell's been in Laramie since last night."

At that moment Hyde would have given anything for an insolent aide, someone to upbraid. But Sherrin stood at attention, his face burning with contrition. Hyde knew from his expression Sherrin had followed military procedure correctly. "He's on his way?"

"Yes, sir. The runner just went after him."

"Where did you send the runner?" Hyde wondered if he was commanding an army post or a grammar school. He wondered if he would always have to catechise his aides.

"First to the barracks, then to the Prairie Belle."

"Check," thought Hyde. In the same mood he added, "Did you check the sign-in list this morning?"

"I did, sir," the boy replied, falling into the colonel's absolving catechism. "His name wasn't on it."

Since Sherrin could not be blamed, Hyde dismissed him with an unanswerable riddle: "How long do you think it will take him to get here?"

Matthew Sherrin shrugged. "I don't know, sir." Hyde murmured, "Unreliable sot," and turned back to the details of a wagon-train escort. First came the orders, troop assignment, alternate routes for heavy snow, then the sticky question about the price of wheat flour. The wagonmaster had been haggling for a lower price with a local merchant named Isaac Straw and finally had pleaded with Hyde to intervene and set the figure. Hyde hesitated; he disliked using military authority in civilian matters.

Forty-five minutes later Bushnell sauntered into the colonel's office. He was a sampler of furs and skins from his beaver cap to his doeskin moccasins. His hair, which cascaded in greasy yellow ringlets over his shoulders, looked like wet fur; his beard, an extravagant red, might have been a prize fox pelt. His mouth lay tucked away between the overhang of lip and underbrush of hair. Powder horn, flint, and two knives hung from his furs; though a big man, Bushnell had a wizened quality, which made him seem weighted down by the gear he carried. His eyes had that alert but slightly vacant expression of people who spend their time alone and seem surprised to find others nearby. But his most overwhelming characteristic at that moment was his smell—a brew of cheap whiskey, bear grease, filth, and sweat that threatened to combust in the colonel's cramped quarters.

"You're three days late."

"Colonel, sir," Bushnell began, "run into trouble down on the Middle Fork. Party o' Oglala bucks backed me into a draw for near three days. Snuck ou' at night, ou' the back door. Lucky to be back so early." His eyes proclaimed perfect innocence.

"Why didn't you report when you got back?" Hyde knew the ritual was pointless.

"Got in mighty late las' night, and I 'uz comin' over just when . . ."

"When the corporal found you in the saloon."

Bushnell looked sheepish. "Some men take breakf'st afore they parlay."

He always managed to get around his most direct questions. "Have you heard about the Shoshoni child?"

"As a matt' o' fact, that did set a tongue or two waggin'." As he nodded, his greasy yellow ringlets bobbed thoughtfully.

"I'm relieving you of scouting duty."

The way his stomach tumbled, John Bushnell didn't feel the slightest bit relieved. He felt as nervous as a coyote at feed since he learned the colonel had dragged a Shoshoni buck back to the post.

"On this new assignment you'll be ordered to do two things: the first and the simplest is to feed the boy. I want buffalo meat and game fed to him just as they would in his village. You can do that, can't you?"

The scout nodded yes.

"Second, you will be my interpreter."

This time Bush's nod lodged somewhere between yes and no.

"I've had the head and the hump of a buffalo deposited in the storeroom. The surgeon advised a liquid diet. There is a broth, if I remember correctly."

Bushnell assured the colonel, "You remembered right, sir."

"Can you make it quickly?"

"No more than a couple of hours."

"There are questions of delicacy here," the colonel began stiffly; he proposed to continue: "that are beyond your experience," but that sounded condescending. He changed it to: "that you've never had a chance to consider before." He paused, not certain he had made his point. "I'm trusting you to always behave like a gentleman."

Bushnell felt stung. The scout had known Hyde a long time and had respected him from the very beginning. Of course the colonel always considered Bushnell beneath him and the scout had accepted the colonel's appraisal. But this seemed unnecessary. He had been raised by a mother too. Even if he wasn't the brightest man in the Territory, he wasn't fool enough to forget what a fine lady Mrs. Harter was or who her best friend was. So the colonel's injunction only made Bushnell more nervous. He was ordered to be at Mrs. Harter's by three, then sent off to his soup pot. During the next hour, as he flaked rawhide from the bull's neck, he tried to forget all the swear words he ever knew.

The next time the boy awoke, he hardly had time to notice the watch on the table beside his bed—it was ticking again—when the door opened and a white woman entered carrying a platter. Her eyes caught Tumbling Hawk—he had never seen that color before: gray like smoke and also green.

The woman smiled, pleased to see him awake, and placed the tureen on the night table. The aroma reached him before she took off the top.

Until that moment, Tumbling Hawk had been tempted to starve himself. Before, refusing to take their power into him had been easy; he'd been afraid and what they brought hadn't seemed like food. But now he smelled the unmistakable tang of buffalo broth and, as she ladeled it into the bowl, he saw the color, the gummy texture.

Hot as it was, he drank the broth, slurping greedily. She filled his bowl again, then another time, but when he pointed to the bowl to ask for more she put it back on the tray and left the room. She returned with the weasel man and a white man dressed entirely in skins, his face hidden under a great mat of red hair.

The weasel looked strange to Tumbling Hawk. His nose was delicate and very long, his chin receded sharply, so that nose and chin seemed set in opposition. His face was deeply tanned, almost matching the color of his light brown hair and hazel eyes. Though he was small (he stood only 5 feet 6 inches), his spare erect body managed to convey authority. But as peculiar as the colonel looked to the boy, Bushnell looked even more peculiar.

Tumbling Hawk could not help staring at him. He had seen only one hairy face before, a trapper with whom his father had traded one winter. Mohe told him men grew bushes on their skins because they were ashamed of their faces, but the boys said white man let the hair grow so they could hide shit in it, then pick it out later.

The colonel's voice carried portent sufficient to the occasion: "Do you think we can get his name?"

Bushnell responded like a diplomat. "Mos' likely ain't good to ask yet." Half to himself he said, "Knew a Sioux once didn't tell me his name for better 'n a year."

For Elizabeth's sake—this woman with the gray eyes was Elizabeth Harter, and the three whites stood by the boy's bed in a second-floor bedroom of her house—the colonel explained, "They believe that anyone who knows their name has power over them. They never tell enemies their names. But we will get it eventually." To Bushnell he said, "Tell him we intend to keep him dry and warm and to feed him with his own food until his leg heals."

Tumbling Hawk couldn't understand what was going on. Why did the woman watch him so intently? What did the weasel want from him? Then the other one, with the shitbush on his face and his slicked-down yellow hair, uttered sounds more like those which the tongue was formed to make. The boy strained to understand, yet he could not catch a word. That Bushnell's words meant nothing to the boy soon became clear to the whites. Bushnell repeated it; again, absolutely no response.

Hyde wondered if the boy had lost his hearing. Bushnell had another suggestion. "It don' make no sense to me them Shoshoni attackin' you at night. 'Specially after yo' goin' to all that trouble makin' yo' camp signs so clear. Warn't that long since the treaty, and them bucks don't forgit all that quick." He paused like a lawyer picking the right spot for his clinching argument. "If they was Shoshoni," he reasoned, "why they take them big hosses o' yours? They ain' no good" (he checked himself from saying "no damned good") "up on that high ground. Let me try one o' my Injun lingoes out on him."

Hyde nodded. He felt extremely foolish.

In Sioux, Bushnell asked the boy what tribe he belonged to.

Tumbling Hawk could not believe it—a white man stood before him, a white man in hides with a full red shitbush on his face who spoke the Cheyenne sister tongue. Proudly the boy answered, savoring the taste of his moving tongue again.

"Says he's Cheyenne, Colonel."

"Tell the boy we would like to be his friend. He shouldn't be afraid of us, make that clear, and say we will do anything we can for him if he communicates his needs to us. Our medicine man will examine his leg. He will not want to hurt the boy, only see that the leg heals perfectly—insist on that. If he does what we tell him, he will run as fast as he ever did. If not, he will never again walk like a man. Make that clear; insist that this is not a trick."

The hairy white man opened his mouth and out came the long fluid phrases of his language. The sound of word succeeding word transported him to his parents' lodge; he felt overjoyed at being able to speak again. Yet what they told him was bad, very bad. He had to remain a prisoner, though that was for his own good, they said. White man's medicine made the lame walk, they said; without it he would hobble forever. "Like Hard Ground!" he thought.

Rampaging fear seized the child, who sensed many things beyond his understanding here. How could he know if they lied? What power did he have against those who fed him his favorite broth?

"Tell him we want to speak with him, and to do that he must learn a little of our language. I know he will be upset, Bushnell, so please make a point of just how *little.*"

Tumbling Hawk felt upset to the point of panic. But silence seemed pointless once he had spoken. Besides, he might be with them for many days. Did white man's words poison the palate? Was he too weak to reply? This man could speak both, jump back and forth between them without harm. So he thought he might try.

"Tell him our word for Waschita is white man. Say it as one word—whiteman—and say it over and . . ."

"I got it, I got it, Colonel. That ign'runt I ain't. I know at least eight Injun lingoes and I reckon I got consid'able mo' trouble with the one white one than the whole pack o' others."

When Tumbling Hawk tried to imitate their word, his tongue turned unmanageable, his lips could not make the same contours as the weasel's. In his mouth their sounds felt cool and slippery, smooth pebbles at the bottom of a streambed. His tongue bumped along them, a hook not catching what it sought. The colonel recited the word and once again the boy tried, testing those new places in his mouth. More words followed—whiteman split into "white" and "man," which proved easy enough. Pointing to Elizabeth, they added "woman." When they went on to names—Hyde insisted on giving him their names—the strain that had been developing in Tumbling Hawk's jaw shifted to his head; he felt a pain he had never known before, a little knot just off center in his right temple. He kept on because he now believed their words gave him power over them. The thought never occurred to Tumbling Hawk that they could give their words away so easily because words had little power in their tribe.

At six o'clock the next evening, Hyde rode out of the stockade's main gate. A great many arms saluted in his wake. He turned north and cantered a mile before the church spire rose before him. Ordinarily, its crisp white lines seemed droll to him, but tonight the cool westerly light honed it to sharp edges which cut into the bare snow-flecked hills beyond. He rode toward the steeple till it grew life-size. Next to the church, a little less grand, stood the whitewashed one-room schoolhouse, and beside the school a white frame house. The colonel paused to review the row of shops and houses that moved in double column out toward the hills. Main Street halted abruptly before a scrubby open space, the Green, as it was optimistically titled. Beyond rose the first courses of the new Town Hall, the first brick building in the Platte Territory. "If there ever is to be a Platte Territory."

A couple passed arm in arm and greeted Hyde. He returned their "Good evening" extravagantly, feeling personally congratulated by their assumption of ease and safety. A few years ago this was Indian land; soon the vast bowl that held Laramie would be filled to overflowing by this town. The single brick building would spawn more brick, more permanence. Of course, if the Platte bill ever got out of committee, if the railroad came this way . . .

His horse shook itself, telling Hyde he had been frozen in his saddle for an unaccountable time. "Must look like an equestrian statue," Hyde thought and chuckled all the way to the frame house where the Indian boy lay.

Hyde had known Elizabeth Harter since 1838, when he and Elizabeth's husband were stationed together in Louisville. That he disliked Jerome Harter even before he met Elizabeth had always been a consolation. To Hyde, Harter was a man of promise intent on consuming it. He never got over the novelty of his decline, and his self-pitying disbelief only accelerated Harter's attempt to forget what he might have become. Harter's behavior pained Hyde; he suffered deeply for Elizabeth.

During the three years they shared the Louisville assignment, he called on them frequently until Harter went off to fight with the Texans. Hyde opposed the annexation on principle and violently opposed the use of regular officers in a pro-slave land grab. For this and a less political reason, he requested an immediate transfer. Later, in 1842, they were assigned together at Fort Smith, Arkansas, where, again, he took up calling on the Harters. In the fall of that year Harter was killed on patrol—he rode out with his troops and three days later they carried him home, a Cherokee arrow through his chest. Hyde thought it a merciful death.

A year passed and in 1843, on November 11, Elizabeth's birthday, Hyde asked her to marry him. She replied: "If I ever married again, Benjamin, I should like to marry you. But I will never be a wife again—I do not want that."

Hyde remained at Fort Smith for the next three years, and he proposed to her each year on bended knee on the eleventh day of the eleventh month. She refused his offer, accepted his birthday gift of sheet music or a picture album or dried flowers, and their conversation continued as before. In the summer of 1846, Hyde's orders dispatched him to the Mexican campaign, and when he returned in early March of 1848 he was a colonel, with the command of Fort Laramie. He asked her to come west with him and share the same arrangement there. She had said, "Yes, of course," and arranged for the shipment of her piano.

Outside her door, Hyde pulled down the edges of his jacket and straightened his cravat. The slight flush that always accompanied his visits warmed its usual spots on his ears. When he was away from Elizabeth he often saw her in that mental album of characteristic expressions and gestures he kept of her. But he could never keep the impression whole until he actually saw her; only then would the pieces fuse with a palpable charge. He knocked and her door opened to him.

"Good evening, Benjamin."

She led him inside, never quite presenting her back to him. Her scent lured him on, the tantalizing musk of opopanox. He knew the paths through the rooms as well as she so he followed without watching where he stepped, seeing only her neck's slight turn. They slipped through the hall and passed together into the sitting room. He moved around a chaise a bare step behind. As he caught up to her they halted, she in front of a high-backed rocker, he to her right by a stumpy chair with pudgy arms. He waited for her to sit; then sank into the chair. He felt limp.

Hyde had stopped by that seat for five years, as often as three or four times a week. As long as they moved, as long as he stood, the impulse to cross the forbidden zone between them never entirely disappeared. Once they took their places, time immobilized them. A screen rose between them, one he had helped construct as much as she.

Their barrier was a curious one, for it let in most of the intimacies that two people share while excluding only one thing. In the fifteen years they had known each other, they had never touched except for a social purpose—when she offered her arm while walking or shook his hand to greet or say good-bye. So he clung to her movement; it was his indulgence, his vice. How that slight turn of her body stirred him. Yet he could always put it aside.

"Well, how is he?"

"Resting."

"Wish I could say the same for the town."

Elizabeth shot him a glance which said, "I know what you're getting at but don't like it."

The colonel leaned toward her, intent. "They're probably already jabbering about our little red killer."

"Killer!" she protested. "Mr. Bushnell said he had no feathers, no marks."

"Coup marks," Hyde corrected.

"Ben, must we go over it again?"

"I know how you feel. You don't want to think about it. But don't forget how it hurts to see people you once liked behaving like swine." Because of him, Hyde thought, she would never forget that feeling. Always he placed her in untenable positions.

"Ostracism looks simple compared to the horrors you prepared me for—torture, boiling in my best stock pot, my scalp dangling from the hatstand." Her fatigue made her harsher than usual. Yet she knew he feared saying one thing, meaning another. He had not wanted to force the child on her.

"I'm tired of these play battles, Colonel. And I do not enjoy being treated like an incompetent. Together we made a decision, and together we'll stick to it." She smiled, knowing they could both consider the issue settled, knowing that they now had the moral equivalent of insurance against mutual accusation and self-recrimination once the town started jabbering and squawking.

As the chair rocked she came toward him and fell away against a backdrop of navy drapery bordered by a soft green wall. The room's constant colors held still as her vivid composure flowed across them. She was not a beautiful woman, though Hyde thought so, but everything about her face had purpose. There was humor in her mouth, direction in that long emphatic nose, determination in her chin, and in the gray-green eyes an understanding of her possibilities.

He watched her closely, proud of her courage while alert to the ugly rumors already swirling around the white frame house. Again Hyde felt wrenched between the impulse to protect her and the positions which they invariably struck. Like the welcome he had prepared for her in Laramie.

Elizabeth faced ugly rumors when she arrived. She responded by buying the house and letting Laramie know she would be giving lessons in piano, lute, and voice. Elizabeth allowed Hyde to visit every other day. Each day she shopped on Main Street, each Sunday she took her place in church. She did only what the town expected of a reasonably well-heeled woman from a good family in Boston who taught music because she loved it and believed one ought to be useful.

Six months passed before Elizabeth received her first invitation to tea and another three months before she had her first student. After a year of rapt scrutiny and flawless conduct, Elizabeth was widely, if grudgingly, accepted as all that she appeared to be—a woman of high moral character.

Hyde wondered what enabled her to endure the rumors and fevered fabrications. In this he underestimated her feeling for him. He alone redeemed the ill-founded, presumptuous calumny. If she had been obliged to explain her devotion to the colonel, she might have said, "I give him something and he gives me something back." But she didn't put it to herself that way; after knowing each other so long and living as closely as any couple she could imagine, giving and taking intermingled. That they avoided the one great impossibility never struck her as a sacrifice for him. Partly because of that unspoken and seemingly immutable agreement, she felt more deeply married to Benjamin than she ever had to her husband.

"White, man," "white woman"—the words kept wedging into his febrile brain. He fought valiantly but there was no eluding, no outflanking them. Did speaking their words bore a tiny hole into his being through which those sharp ghostly faces could gain access to his thoughts? Did this speech make him unfaithful to his people? If so, would the Cheyenne powers rise up against him as they had done to torture Sun Child when he had prayed for the Dog soldiers' defeat? Tumbling Hawk doubted the Cheyenne magic could reach him so far from home, surrounded by dark wood squeezed and teased into curves, by all those unnamed horrors—drapes and rugs and chairs and a looming mahogany armoire.

Those things in the walls? At first all three looked like holes. But a few slight movements of his head convinced Tumbling Hawk only two cut through to the outside. He felt no draft, no wind, but could look outside at the indecipherable buildings and track the sun's shadow as it edged along the high pitch of a roof, yet he could not fill his lungs with one breath of fresh air.

One of the windows framed a school, sliced off a corner of the church, and revealed a teasing beginning on the steeple. Whenever he moved his head, various parts of church and school elongated. (Good glass had been difficult to come by when Elizabeth first came to Laramie.) At first the boy feared that they had bewitched his eyes. Now he guessed that this unnameable thing was a distorting skin white man set over his world.

Other mysteries unnerved him. On the white building which narrowed like a tepee there was a black circle much like the one on his ticking disk, with giant gold lines that kept matching the positions of his little gold lines. Tumbling Hawk did not know what this meant. Nor did he understand about that third larger cut in the wall, the one that wasn't a hole but a mass of color that stopped abruptly at four straight edges.

The painting troubling Tumbling Hawk was a monumental representation of a naval battle which had been presented to the Harters on their wedding day by Jerome's father. Commodore Harter objected to his son's choice of West Point instead of Annapolis, and he said so. A violent quarrel followed in which son defended the past, present, and future superiority of land to sea warfare and father just as vehemently claimed the reverse. They had not spoken again until the day of the wedding when the commodore arrived at Elizabeth's father's church carrying the painting as a peace offering. It depicted the commodore's thirty-eight-gun frigate, *The Tempest,* engaged with His Majesty's ship of the line, *The Wellington,* off Hampton Roads on August 12, 1812. Artistically, the painting had no value. Elizabeth never liked it and Jerome scorned it more and more madly as time passed, sometimes addressing it with profanity, sometimes with detailed accounts of historic infantry battles.

Tumbling Hawk guessed the foreground might be water. But he had no idea what those two ungainly brown hulks were, certain that nothing that cumbersome could actually float. On both ships he saw men, but the riggings and masts looked so battered, the sheets so torn, the jumble of ropes and ladders and cannon and bodies so confusing, he had no idea what the men were doing. In the midst of the tattered but jauntily flying ensigns and to the side of four broadside cannons, stood the brave man on the deck, the commodore, unconvincingly heroic. Apparently the painter cleared a last-minute spot for him amid the sea of gore and limbs and blood, and transferred him unrumpled and unsmudged from a safer place, thus avoiding all mortal threats to the gallant leader.

Every day of her adult life Elizabeth Harter sat down at five-thirty to practice her piano. That day she was working on the piano part of Beethoven's Fifth Concerto. As Tumbling Hawk contemplated the mysteries of sea battle, suddenly his room was struck by a wave of rippling sound. The concussion staggered him, the riptide tempo buoyed him away. He wondered if the watch had run wild, for those tiny ticks seemed to be roaring now, howling through a range of sound without interval or rhythm. The pincers of pain that struck continually at his thigh found voice in piercing clusters of notes. The whites promised not to hurt him, but now a terrifying equivalent of his pain swelled up through the floorboards, a ceaseless force that scraped on his bones as it threatened to pulverize his body. His head grew hotter, began to ache, the ache turned into a tripping corrosive wail.

Cheyenne music moved with a steady insistent tempo, one that his body could absorb. The sound of the piano was too fecund and prolix, a force without form. Not until the adagio did he begin to pick out sweet notes and dumbly cling to them. But this pathetic flotsam kept being swamped by rough discords, which altered the memory of the sound even while he fought to hold on to it. Never before had he heard so much of anything; it had to die down, he thought. But the sound flowed on and on without regard for him.

Tumbling Hawk buried his head in the pillow, and for the first time in his life he wept. He wept for his weakness, wept for his fear, terrified that while he stayed in this place he would always be too weak to resist them.

Meanwhile, another piano banged out another tune in another part of town. Bushnell leaned up against the mahogany bar of the Prairie Belle Saloon, not even hearing the piano in the background. He had planted himself at the least-visited end of the bar, turned his back on as many of the people there as he could, and set to work to drown his headache.

Behind him, though it had just turned six, the Prairie was mobbed. Tables full, card games underway; even a scattering of evening drunks present. The women were decked out in their satins, eyes shaded in those colors that made it nighttime even in broad daylight. But none of that occupied Bushnell, not even the women. Lavish pouring would be required to insulate his poor head, to drown his picture of that Cheyenne boy sitting up in bed, casting about for answers he'd never find with those dark startled eyes. Bushnell had begun to quench his demanding thirst when he found two men crowding his elbow.

The scout was annoyed to be surrounded when his smoke signals read so clear. He kept at his drink, drained it, poured another quickly, then shook his head with disgust, and turned back to his glass.

A throat cleared. "Buy you a drink," the voice came uncertainly. That had to be Isaac Straw, a "rancher" who made buckboards of money supplying the wagons with whatever they couldn't get through more sanctified channels. He always turned up with hay or beef or horses or timber, and sometimes ammunition, always at the right moment. He was the one holding up the first spring wagon train over the price of hay. In acquiring his fortune, Straw hadn't neglected himself and had grown grotesquely fat. Lately he had gotten so gross he walked with mincing steps with his torso angled backward as though afraid he'd pitch forward onto his stomach and never be righted again. Which would have pleased a number of people in Laramie. Now, while standing, he wedged his belly up against the bar and used his arms as brackets—he thrust them straight out to the sides, elbows bent at right angles, and grappled his bulk to the bar with fat, pink, jeweled fingers.

"Buy you a drink," his voice sounded again.

Bushnell didn't bother to turn. "Straw," he said, eyeing the gilt mirror directly ahead of him, "I'm a standin' here with a bottle locked b'tween my elbows; reckon that'll hold me for a spell."

"Nobody means harm here, but a number of citizens like to know what Hyde wants with that Injun."

"Look, hoss," Bushnell said to him, still not turning, "I don' see why my bizness is any mo' interestin' to yo' than yo's is to me."

The speech made his head pound, so he poured another round. It hadn't even reached his lips when Straw interrupted again.

"Bushnell, come on. What the hell's going on with that tomahawk?"

The tone annoyed Bushnell and he was weighing his reply when Ord Cobb joined their party. Cobb in his way was as devious as Straw. But his way was significantly less prosperous. He spent all of his time sponging, talking, and drinking. He never had a job, except for a very odd one or two, never had any money, but was clever enough to scrape by. To an instigator's cunning and an investigator's curiosity, he added a restless compulsion to keep things lively. Cleaned and polished, he might have been a decent-looking man, except for his teeth–sawed-off stumps sunk in a pestilential swamp of a mouth.

"Leave the stuffy old bag of flatulence alone," Cobb intervened. "He's tired o' knockin' roun' Injun country with a flea-bitten pelt on his back and some surveyin' tool in his hand. He come in t' retire and die. After all his service to his country, yo' ought'n grudge him nothin' in the soft and cushy line."

Their laughter prompted a dignified response: "I neveh touch no surveyin' tool."

Cobb kept up: "Ain' such a bad ride yo' got, Bush, sittin' round all that day in that plush lady's bood-wah swillin' coffee."

Bushnell retreated into silence.

"Yo' jus' keep an eye on him, he'll be fatter than a sow in three week."

"Won' never get fat," the scout growled, bouncing Cobb a lethal look off the mirror. "I'm all gristle."

They laughed with him this time. Just down the bar, Hinman, the German, spoke up. "Vy he brung dat Injun here in da first place? Vat gib him dat right?"

Hinman was a bullwhacker, of squat body and wide girth. Coming upon him on the road he took up as much room as the other members of his team, was just as broad-browed, dull-eyed, and slow. But he had a suspicious malice Bushnell wouldn't have tolerated in an ox.

"Bush," wheedled Cobb, "Hyde ain' crazy 'nuf to want t' keep that kid 'round here, is he?"

"S'pose I tol' yo' the colonel want t' learn that Injun English?" Not the politic thing to say, but the guessing game tired the scout and the talking wasn't aiding his head. Besides, Bushnell could never resist the impulse to brag.

"English!" Hinman spat. "Mit Injun he's not possible."

Straw thrust a fat beringed pinkie at Bushnell. "How he know for sure he don't got no white blood on his hands?"

"Cause I looked." The scout spoke in his official capacity. A legitimate question, he felt, one that came from all of them, from all the respectable citizens too. "It was this bucko's fust war party—he got no coup marks, no feather, no lodge sign."

Half-crocked Bushnell wasn't fully persuaded by his own arguments. To defuse his own uncertainty more than anything else, he volunteered, "If any yo' be interested in a small wager concernin' this here Injun's chances o' learnin' the King's English . . ."

Even with the scouting pay he just pocketed, Bushnell had more takers than he could cover at 6 to 1 against. A round of bad jokes commenced about the disadvantages of having Bushnell for a tutor, then the assembled got down to serious drinking. The piano tinkled on unnoticed until three in the morning, which was when Bushnell pursued his wavering route back to the fort.

When the shirt from the General Store turned out to be too long in the sleeves and too tight across the chest, Elizabeth had asked Bushnell to take the boy's measurements. Now she deliberately cut out the gusset. A person can never tell how things will turn out, she thought. Obviously she had to give up her music lessons. Already the schoolchildren next door paid an inordinate amount of attention to her upstairs window, and yesterday she found a boy encamped on her front porch. There would be confusion enough without children trooping through the house. She would miss her students and the modest victories of their progress, but her seclusion would provide a well-timed escape from Laramie gossip.

In two hectic weeks she had begun to appreciate why Benjamin was such a highly regarded officer. Joining him in action enlarged Elizabeth's understanding of the colonel, which brought her closer to him. Even when they had their disagreements, even when Hyde acted the pedant schoolmaster, or behaved like an overexcited child with too much of the bully in him.

Ben, for all his intelligence, sometimes missed the most obvious things. Like the time he and Mr. Bushnell lifted the commodore's ship off the wall and moored it alongside the boy's bed. While Hyde labored to explain perspective, the boy reached out to touch the sharp flakes of pigment. Watching his head move back and forth, Elizabeth could almost see the commodore's face break up into splotches of pink and black, white and blue. Meanwhile, the men droned on about ships and battles on water, telling the mesmerized child that the ships held one hundred men, could float like a canoe yet go faster and never tire. While all he wanted to know was how one thing got behind the other when all of it looked and felt flat. And she had blurted out that she would teach him to draw. The answer, sometimes, seemed so clear.

Other times, however, she had no answer. As when the boy told Bushnell that he longed "to see the buffalo skins sag and lift as the lodge breathes with the wind," or when he said he missed the "soft light" inside the tepee. Elizabeth thought of it as soft scattered light, "diffused light," and assumed it must be very beautiful. What could she say to that?

Upstairs she heard his bed creak, heard him reach for his water pitcher and pour. "How quickly, mercifully, things are absorbed. He doesn't use that glass any differently than I do." Yet Hyde's introduction of the drinking glass seemed, now, a sideshow magic trick—clever, productive of desired ends, yet somehow unfair. The second day of the boy's stay they entered his room and found the nightshirt on the floor. The child would not speak, would not answer their questions, would not repeat "white man," "white woman." At that point Hyde ordered Elizabeth to the kitchen to get the glass pitcher and a drinking glass. She would never forget the child's expression as he watched the clear fluid climb up the sides of the transparent glass. He waited underneath, desperate to feel a single drop. It never fell.

Until he touched the glass, he told Bushnell later, he prayed it was frozen water—even though he knew better, though he watched the colonel handling it like pottery. Finding the glass warm, he accepted their magic with doomed, unquestioning resignation. He fondled the glass dumbly, slipped his fingers in to wet them with the feeling he had been ordered to do it. The glass felt impossibly smooth, dry, round in his hand. As the boy finger-pondered "this clear thing that held its shape," the colonel stepped to the window where he tapped the pane and laid his hands flat against it to establish the plane. The colonel said: "The world on the other side of it is just as you see it, just as it would look through the opened flap of a tepee. But in our world no one has to lift the flap."

"Clever," she thought as she ripped out the back seam of his shirt. The grandfather's clock chimed the quarter. When the boy asked about the ringing, Hyde took the occasion to explain about the chimes, the watch, the church clock. Next day the boy wound the watch himself. Hyde claimed this as proof of the boy's genius.

She visualized the long bronze face, the salient shelf of cheekbones. Yesterday, for the second and last time, Hyde asked if she was afraid of the child. No, she answered honestly. She had expected him to be more savage and shy; but this child was the most dignified she had ever met, more like an adult than a child, self-contained yet sensitive and obliging. Even when he suffered terrible pain.

Not afraid of the child, yet afraid. She had never considered education overbearing. But it was, terribly so. At the moment the boy was caught up in his new world and his studies. But later, when the child understood more, she wondered if he would feel tricked, manipulated. If she had her way, every step of his education would be fair and responsive to his questions. But that ideal seemed hopelessly unwieldy. And Hyde, she admitted, knew how to work wonders.

Mr. Bushnell. At first, when he still felt out of place in her home, she had done her best to put him at ease. Appreciative, he had responded with awkward, touching gallantry—delicately patting his outlandish beard with the serviette, springing up with alacrity whenever she entered a room. He caused her to smile the least condescending of bemused smiles. He became more candid with them, or rather, with her. That proved helpful, for it reduced their chances of misinterpreting the boy. Witness the question of the piano. Bushnell kept fidgeting while she played her scales and finally she stopped and asked him if something was wrong. In his most charming no-offense-intended manner he said that the boy was probably terrified of "that pie-ano of your'n ma'am." The sound made him feel like being "shot through with fire arrows." Momentarily, Elizabeth's face caught fire. Recovering, she replied, "Will you please explain the piano to him, Mr. Bushnell? I can't insist he like it, though if he does not I will always believe he disapproves of my playing. But there is no earthly reason why it should torture him." Bushnell now told them everything the child wanted, when he was fatigued, what they should and should not ask him. The boy trusted Bushnell. Bushnell, for his part, remained most antagonistic to their ambitious educational plans. She laid out the boy's shirtsleeves on the table, contemplating images of the three men of her household with a thoughtful smile.

Hyde sat at his desk before his open diary, a satisfied victim of fatigue. He had just completed this entry:

21 April: Introduced maps; at first he couldn't understand why we wanted these "line pictures." Once he got it, he seemed to believe he could get back to his tribe by stepping into the map. The Niobrara country in half-inch scale made him homesick.

Once again impressed by Bushnell's phenomenal visual memory. He knows every pass, gulch, draw, mesa, "crick" between the Rockies and Kearney. Wish all his talents like this.

Elizabeth affecting the boy like a good penetrating oil, sinking deeper into his workings. He's far more comfortable with her than with me. (Down self-regard, comfort is not what this instruction demands!) She will continue to spend as much time as possible with him.

In spite of Bushnell's objections, I must have his name! B. fears a relapse, cites his old friend the Sioux. I bridle each time I have to call him *boy* or *child.*

In the next week, the diary swelled:

23 April: He's blessed with a fine memory. He can name all bedroom furnishings, objects in paintings, many objects in the books.

24 April: How do you tell a savage that the earth revolves around the sun, horizon line curves with unobservable subtlety, heavy bodies do not fall to earth simply because of heft? Why do we not topple off a spinning globe?

Don't feel discouraged. Our most concrete scientific theorems are also most abstract. Copernicus and Galileo had one hell of a time persuading their contemporaries & they spoke the native dialect.

25 April: Elizabeth tried to introduce perspective drawing. Went slowly, with many blunted pencil points. (Details invariably escape attention beforehand.) Invent a system of guards or sleeves to program a lighter touch?

There's a tenseness about the boy when he's not doing well that makes him awkward, which embarrasses, even infuriates him—good for us if wearing for the child. At his most tense he slips his tongue, *Upside Down,* between his teeth. A furious intensity. Once he gets the idea he'll spend hours trying to master it. I sympathize, admire, share the impulse

& predict that this tenacity will make him ours in the end! Every day—it is my obsession—I ask his name. In spite of Bushnell. Elizabeth is with me in this. She can't stand not knowing either.
27 April: Elizabeth found drawing slow. E. also reported that he kept drawing off the page onto the drawing board. She laughed, kept telling him to keep it on the white.
28 April: Presented a slate. Asked his name. The boy clouded over. Over Bushnell's infuriating resistance I insisted until he grew frightened. *It will come!*
The afternoon not lost. He loved erasing the slate.
Experiment: Bushnell and I stayed during the first half hour of E's piano practice. Kept telling him he had nothing to be afraid of—it helped. I believe he is beginning to know an étude. Someday it will pain him when she makes a mistake. (Do not read this to E.) What does he feel now? Is the fabric of mind infinitely stretchable or does each piece of new information displace (erase) some old?
29 April: Elizabeth reported that the slate was filled with markings again this morning! Two times in a row!
30 April: A *Milestone!* He told us his name: Tumbling Hawk! I believe he's been considering telling us awhile now. I asked Bushnell—curious what a deterrent constant opposition can be—to relay my customary opening request. B. balked but did so. They discussed it longer than usual (hopes growing). I heard the child speak, & then Bushnell dubbed him "Tumbling Hawk," which is a translation of the active form of "tumble" in Cheyenne. B. explained that tumble refers to either a hawk in its dive for prey or its dropping like a stone, "Just cuz they like to!"

We are his friends now, Bushnell said. I thanked the boy for trusting us, in a few deeply felt words. Elizabeth glowing; she looked beautiful. I asked him to learn his name in English (odd that it's a gerund) and had the pleasure of hearing him finally pronounce it correctly.

Anxious to start his writing lessons. Am greatly encouraged and very happy this day.

Each one of Tumbling Hawk's enthusiasms accused him. Yet could he lie to himself and say, "I hate learning to draw; hate their fabulous pictures, my watch, the glass?" No.

Then the question was—Did he accept it all too easily? He did not think so, but could not be sure. Why wasn't he sure? Because he resisted all things he understood, yet gave in to their magic.

Because he saw great power in their world, remembered his vision and Rumbling Wings' prophecy, and wondered if he could carry away their power with him.

Because every defiant gesture seemed weak pretend. Because every day, twice a day he asked, "How long before you let me go?" And they patiently explained they weren't holding him; he was too weak and sick to travel. If they moved him, infection would set in. "Bone rot," red beard called it. He might lose his leg. He might hobble like Hard Ground forever. Because—this was ultimately the largest because, though Tumbling Hawk did not like to think of it that way—because there was nothing else to do.

As tortured as that explanation was, it described his situation too simply. For example, he was not totally comfortable believing the whole thing had been preordained. Yet who could ask him to give up his best alibi since it just might be true?

Or, take what happened to his senses. He got used to the way they smelled, their speech, the sounds that came from road, school, church. Yet as familiarity dulled his detectors, he felt spiritually weakened—he could translate his own physical discomfort as betrayal too, if he let himself, if he wanted to.

That was the unfortunate trap—trying to measure the purity of his intentions.

Two days later Hyde delivered his oft-revised, long-awaited lecture on the written word: He told Tumbling Hawk that whites needed only one man, not two, to tell a story. Whites had words—drawn words—much like pictures, and each larger picture was made up of little pictures, each of those little pictures representing a sign for a sound. The sounds made their own noises, but *silently*. They worked like smoke signals, only they held together for years and could be carried far beyond the distance two men could see between them. This drawing, which they called writing, guaranteed that no one could ever change what a man says.

Tumbling Hawk interrupted: "Who would change what a man says?" Bushnell relayed the question with obvious relish. Hyde read the scout like a falling barometer; he rained inspiration.

"Suppose your storyteller isn't with you. Can you carry him in your hand? Tuck him into your pocket? Can you recall every one of his words in order, without mistakes, as many times as you'd like for as long as you'd like? Can your children do that? Your children's children? Can you start at any place in the story any time? Can it be infinitely repeatable?" At that gate he outdistanced his translator, but that did not matter to Hyde. He was fed up with Bushnell's foot dragging and even of Elizabeth's scrupled delicacy. With such an enormous job ahead, they could waste no time on niceties. "Is it possible to be reverent and dutiful and concerned for truth without the ability to be that scrupulous with a man's words?"

Satisfied, though still not calm, Hyde turned back to Tumbling Hawk. "Do your people have stories whispered aloud into their inner ear by their eye? Can they hear a story word for word by seeing it?"

Of course Tumbling Hawk could not understand how you could hear by seeing, but his disposition to believe was upon him.

Time passed quickly after that. Under Hyde's relentless overseeing, Tumbling Hawk painstakingly began to mark his idea of their letters on the slate, wobbling through the straightnesses and uncertainly rounding the curves while hating the gap between what he saw in the primer and what he drew. He felt mocked by the military precision of Hyde's printing, which marched across the slate as if parading on flat ground.

They took him downstairs: past those rippling white balusters, by the dark swirl of wood where the banister ended, into a room swarming with nameless bric-a-brac, portraits, draperies. Bushnell lowered him into his first chair while Hyde stuffed a fat leather cushion under his damaged leg. Elizabeth sat at the unsteady-looking darkwood thing with the flat black and white strips set like teeth along its front. She struck a chord, then sang in vibrant soprano, Hyde crooned along in unswerving baritone, his small chin tucked in smartly. Bushnell did not sing. Tumbling Hawk tracked Hyde's moving fingertip across the page from left to right as it dropped through the verse; he mouthed the words to:

"A-wake our souls; a-way our fears
Let ev-'ry trem-bling thought be gone;
A-wake and run the heav'n-ly race,
And put a cheer-ful cour-age on."

The voluminous bursts of sound rolled over him easily now, the shrill vibrations no longer shook him.

Each room in Elizabeth's house offered more surprises and new materials for his lessons, but his favorite was the kitchen, with its tantalizing smells and its air of habitual industry. The kitchen provided a copious inventory of white invention, with its corers, peelers, scrapers and cleavers, sieves and mincers and mashers; an oven that cradled fire in its belly; pots and fry pans and collanders hung from the freestanding counter Hyde had built for Elizabeth. Tumbling Hawk felt closest to home in the kitchen: there he saw Shell clearly, could almost recall the smell of freshly chopped wood that clung to her.

In one corner of Elizabeth's kitchen stood a large brown pail into which she casually deposited eggshells, scrapings of flour, wadded bits of dough. In it he noticed bones, tops and peels of vegetables, *scraps of meat, meat fat.* He wondered what they used this pail for, but kept the question to himself.

Every day Tumbling Hawk digested new words. He laboriously coupled his eye to the lyrics of "Zion, the City of God," "Rock of Ages," "To the Kingdom of God Within." Before he had a hundred-word vocabulary she began to read from her Bible. ("It is as important as the alphabet.")

So moral ABC's were interwoven with grammatical ones, and Tumbling Hawk's instruction proceeded simultaneously in the paths of reading and righteousness. Each time she read from the Bible, Tumbling Hawk detected that same unyielding set to her chin, those earnest fret lines plied her brow. Whenever she held that black book in her hand, she was solemn, impersonal, preoccupied. Even when Bushnell translated her stories about the great warriors or his new hero, Moses, her strangeness disturbed the boy. Why did it bother him? Because Hyde guessed right in his diary entry for 24 May: "Tumbling Hawk likes Elizabeth, is coming to accept her assumption of intimacy."

One afternoon in late May Tumbling Hawk kept writing his addition tables after the cramp, which turned his fingers vagrant, marched beyond the base of the thumb, crowded through the wrist, and spread to his forearm. The cramp gave an exquisite controlled pain, exactly what he had felt in his forearm when he first learned to draw the bow. The pain remained so specific it allowed him to work on. Which was good, for while he worked he could not dwell on his troubles. He kept writing those unappeasable repetitious forms until, suddenly, his head began to swim. His skin lost all feeling, it became as thick and horny as a turtle's shell—under it his body seemed to die. Tumbling Hawk felt doomed to watch helplessly as his mind ticked on without him, going 123456789, 123456789. His eyes sent Elizabeth this message: "I cannot deal with this. I'm not equipped to understand how my confusion makes you triumphant." She removed the pencil from his hand and got him to lay back. Her cool hand stroked his temple. The only refuge offered was her sympathy; she gave no other promise.

During the day they kept Tumbling Hawk busy, continually bombarded him. Only after they left at night did his absorption with the white world break down. Then he wrestled with his terror of being crippled, then he admitted he'd never let himself return home like Hard Ground. The boy remembered the feel of his body as he ran, the rough bite of dawn air on his way up to pasture to get the ponies, the veined bronze of Mohe's hands as they braided a rope. He wanted to apologize to Lightfoot for not being understanding while his friend suffered his ordeal; he wanted to be back on the surround again, and to do his part, and no more. How he prayed to see his parents again. Often he would dream he was riding south through familiar country toward his village. Just as he picked out Mohe's lodge, the whole village would disappear. Something would tell him to look behind and he'd see the village to the north, in the direction from which he came. So he'd ride back and reach the same point only to see the tribe just disappearing over a range of eastern hills. Nightly he pursued his village to the cardinal points. Each time he rode forward it reappeared somewhere behind him.

In another dream he would be walking in the woods, see something bright and shiny on the ground among the leaves. Stooping to pick it up, he'd find a letter. Then he'd notice hundreds of letters at his feet. The trees, the grasses held letters—numbers too. Looking around he found letters everywhere—F's as petals of flowers, L's on trees.

Hyde swayed slightly on the balls of his feet as he stood at the scrivener's desk to read Jim Coughlin's letter.

DEAR BEN,

You are a rash, precipitate, impolitic fellow, and I heartily applaud your scheme to educate this Shoshoni. Not one sensible man in Washington could imagine taking on an Indian child, so the idea must be proof against charlatans and fools. Officially, however, the Department has to be concerned about your overly evolved sense of responsibility and will so advise in a note drafted by yours truly on Government stationery. (How excited you sound, dear friend; how much I would give to play even a minor role in your "noble experiment.") The child has fallen into our hands (correction, your hands) and he might, if we are blessed lucky, provide impetus for the Indian education policy we discussed. He might become a great leader of his people. He might do everything! What better beginning than Laramie, and who better for his mentor than a crusty old Indian fighter? Undoubtedly there will be rumblings in your community, but I trust you will deal with whatever Christian indignation the local mob can drum up.

My drawling "superior," Mr. Jefferson Davis, publicly negotiates for that strip of desert over which he hungers to route the transcontinental railroad. He's even appropriated your invention and calls it "a military road." It is still too early to fret about the railroad surveys, Ben, for they are mere squawling infants now. Do not work yourself up prematurely, for there will be plenty to rail against once Douglas' august Committee begins to take testimony. Speaking of which: I think Douglas' decision not to survey the Platte route works to your advantage, since it places responsibility for proclaiming the route's virtues where it belongs—squarely in your hands, not in the clutches of a Southern engineer.

Yes, Douglas is furious about the Platte Bill delays. My even more educated guess is that, if the question of Indian lands is not resolved in a month, Douglas will introduce a bill that splits your Platte Territory into two territories. He will do this to keep the railroad from slipping out of our—his, yours, and my—grasp. In the northern sector, which he calls Nebraska, there are no Indian lands. In the southern part, which he calls Kansas, he offers a small sliver of the eastern border with Missouri as Indian lands. Pure tokenism, this allotment, but it is a nod in your direction. If Douglas does introduce this legislation, it would behoove you to withdraw your support, of the sensible, well-drawn Platte Bill and applaud Douglas' scheme. I know how distorted this sounds, Ben, but the Platte Bill is not going to reach the floor. And you must protect your own and Laramie's interests.

On the larger point we are agreed, of course. The country (read legislators) must some day realize that Indians, like other beings, require land to live on; that unless we intend to massacre or starve out the entire bronzed race we must adequately allow for their presence somewhere on this continent. But your clear-headed, forward-looking stand excites animosities. The preference in the Capital City is always for temporizing, for ducking each problem until it becomes a crisis. Or, as Mrs. Hastings puts it: "Your eyesight's too acute. You distort reality by making distant things loom too large. The rest can't see, so they think you are a crackpot or a crank." Or, again, "Cassandra never played to a large audience."

In spite of her jibes, Mrs. Hastings misses you, misses our lengthy talks. As do Dorothea and I. I pray for success in your extraordinary venture.

JIM

"How vital to have a candid friend," Hyde concluded. But he gazed at the maps of the Indian villages with troubled affection. The Platte Bill epitaph had been expected, and pride did not opaque his disappointment. "Douglas will have a new bill by the New Year." That troubled the colonel for he knew that, whichever way Douglas carved up the western territories, there would be no provision for Indian lands.

How vital to have Jim in that post now. As Undersecretary of War, Coughlin could stop the conniving Southerners from tilting all military advantage to their side. Hyde saw the large-boned freckled face, still boyish, the sun-catching sandy hair. On tiptoe, Hyde stretched himself to full height. While his hand lingered near the rafters, he seemed to bear the entire weight of the cabin.

Through the long hot summer, pain remained the boy's nagging companion. Cooped up in bed or anchored to his chair, Tumbling Hawk found himself locked in spots of memory, little isolate islands with graphic indelible topographies but lacking bridges to the mainland. As summer wore on, familiar landmarks suddenly faded—he could not remember Running Bear's face, he forgot the markings on one of his father's favorite ponies. Panic followed. At times a whole existence tottered on the verge of extinction; he was not moved when he thought of Mohe's eagle pit or even of the plateau where he had faced his vision.

At other times quick, quick came the images of his old life, streaming past as richly as they did when he flipped the illustrated pages of one of their books.

The half-shadow man appeared twice. The second time, after another bootless attempt to force the image to clarify, Tumbling Hawk sat up in bed: Rumbling Wings said he would leave home; he had. Perhaps the prophecy would come true. Perhaps he would go east. The word itself fired his soul with fear.

Sometimes his leg hurt so badly, Tumbling Hawk wanted it cut off.

What did Tumbling Hawk like least about the white world? His pain, his confusion, his listless impotence against what they told him; his being there, his ambivalent sense of betrayal, being cooped up, Hyde's injunctions when he felt too tired to resist, the days of spiritual torpor, when the deadness of his soul found relief only in erratic flashes of pain or his own growing guilt. What did Tumbling Hawk like most about the white world? The moments without pain, machines, Bushnell's exaggerated stories, Elizabeth's apple pie, cinnamon buns, sourdough bread, the pale-grained sheen of her lute, her gray-green eyes. Often he would draw after her example or copy as she sewed or ironed, played her lute or piano, cooked or wrote letters. Or he would listen as she read from a storybook, *Uncle Tom's Cabin,* or the old part of the Bible. (In spite of her insistence, he had little patience with the new book.) He always asked for the warriors–Samson, David, Gideon, and, while his luck held out, Jephthah. Or Joshua, who not only blew down those walls but lured thirty thousand men out of Ai with a Cheyenne ploy Big Road had once described to him. Or Moses, his champion, whom he watched grow under his captor's eyes, saw rise from an infant outcast of a despised and humiliated tribe into the man who struck down his people's hated tormentor. (How Tumbling Hawk exulted when that blow fell.) Moses was a chief, Moses was a shaman. Tumbling Hawk walked with Moses as he led his people out of the house of bondage, followed those pillars of cloud until Moses could promise to "bring them out of that land unto a good land and large, unto a land flowing with milk and honey." Tumbling Hawk rejoiced when the Red Sea divided and became "a wall to them on the right hand, and on their left," when "Israel saw the Egyptians dead upon the sea-shore." He trekked in the wilderness, climbed up the great mountain beside Moses. It was Moses the boy revered, Moses against whom he wanted to be able to measure himself. And when the man looked down upon the Promised Land he could never enter, that land of milk and honey, the land to which he had guided them through the strength of his belief and will, it touched the boy more deeply than he understood.

Occasionally Matthew Sherrin visited Tumbling Hawk. Sherrin was the oddest-looking person the boy had ever seen, with that great flat fair face and that wide bow mouth which looked painted on. Perhaps because they had so few words in common, perhaps because only seven years separated them, the two young men remained awkward together. With Bushnell present and Sherrin telling stories about the colonel, things went well. More often a grinning Matthew would stand by Tumbling Hawk's chair, enunciating the primer's vocabulary with exaggerated precision.

Tumbling Hawk felt his body going soft. He spent hours flexing his stomach muscles–emptying his diaphragm of air then sucking his stomach in, snapping it out like Buck's Heart had shown him. He constantly measured his wrist for shrinkage, tested the firmness of his bicep, strained to pull one arm up while holding it down with the other, beat the fat off his belly. One evening faint red pimples surfaced on his left buttock. By morning the itching raged. He called Elizabeth and indicated he wanted her to look at something. Turning over on his side as far as he could, he began to raise his nightshirt. But she blushed, turning away, and said in English, "Bushnell. I'll get Mr. Bushnell."

He said nothing about the incident; it confirmed an old suspicion. Tumbling Hawk had lived with his parents for thirteen years; he couldn't count the number of times he had been sung to sleep by their lovemaking. He had all the normal expectations of a thirteen-year-old and would never have subscribed to Elizabeth's belief that if you didn't think about it, it would go away—having thought about it a lot, he didn't want it to go away. He was sensitive enough to have observed the chilled sliver of distance between Elizabeth and Hyde and now knew enough to guess its cause. But he could not understand why anybody would choose to live with that limitation, and it saddened him for them, especially for her.

In the kitchen Tumbling Hawk kept an eye on that pail. Usually he found it full by dinner. But no matter how early he came down, it was empty. One day, as she dropped scraps of veal fat into it, he asked Bushnell who got to eat it. Bushnell relayed the question. Flustered, Elizabeth explained, "That's garbage—no one eats it. It's thrown away."

Bushnell intervened: "Garbage ain' somethin' a Cheyenne got. They don' have that much they can 'ford to throw it away."

To a Cheyenne waste represented the prime heresy, an offense to life's exact balance. Tumbling Hawk's former existence had been one of humble, sustained economy: each rabbit was petitioned for, each deer demanded a prayer in explanation of the need and in hope that the loss would be tolerated.

Prior to sitting on a stool in Elizabeth's kitchen watching those scraps being cavalierly dispatched, Tumbling Hawk had only one image of waste: thousands of buffalo rotting in piles at the foot of a cliff. Mohe told him the story of this great sacrilege, how his ancestors before the horse, or even the bow, had driven herds of buffalo off that great height just for meat for a few summer days. For each rotting carcass—thousands lay there, perhaps tens of thousands—his people spent a generation atoning, working out the use of the buffalo until not even a single hair was thrown away. Still the Great Spirit demanded retribution, and whenever the supply grew thin the entire tribe saw that same image again, and all wondered if their debt could ever be paid.

The boy found it shattering to live among a people with an established place for waste, in a world where things existed just to be pretty, where pots and skillets and stewpans, corer, parer, mincer and dicer took the place of the bowl and knife of his parents' lodge. A tantalizing forbidden notion seized the child: for a momentary victory over want, for that single instant of freedom, the white man's world just might be worth it.

He tried to shut out the debasing, unnatural idea, but he sensed it would work on him like their words, like the food with which they weaned him away from the taste of deer and elk and buffalo. The thought drummed into him like rain into thirsty ground, made him wonder what soil inside allowed these ideas to germinate.

In late September–Tumbling Hawk had lived in the house for six months–he surprised Elizabeth with this handwritten chart:

b b c b c b b b s b s s b b c b b b c s c s s s s s
a b c d e f g h i j k l m n o p q r s t u v w x y z

s b c b s s b s s b s s s s c b b b c s c s s s s s
A B C D E F G H I J K L M N O P Q R S T U V W X Y Z

Elizabeth studied it but finally gave up and asked him what it meant. Surprised it wasn't self-evident, he explained that "c" stood for curved, "s" for straight, and "b" for both. Hyde's next letter to Coughlin boasted: "This chart convinces me. The boy has natural genius."

Hyde came in stealthily, broadcasting his intention to surprise the boy. Tumbling Hawk would not look up. He hated when Hyde acted like a child–the boy felt it deprived each of them of dignity. Suddenly a round sheet of glass slipped between his eyes and the piece of paper he wrote on.

Under the glass, the letters expanded until their ends splayed out over the disk's edge. The colonel moved the magnifying glass: the solid letters went runny and kept inflating. The boy found it fascinating, but the strange exhilaration unsettled his stomach.

Without explanation, the colonel whisked him to the window and thrust a strange device–two parallel black snouts joined by a black metal bar–into his hand. Hyde guided the two snouts up toward the boy's face–those eyepieces seemed designed to suck out his eyes–and fiddled with the focus.

"Look over there into the schoolroom." Tumbling Hawk saw children seated in rows at their desks–one with pretty blond curls, another with a blotched scarlet face. At the front of the room stood a woman about Elizabeth's age; her mouth moved, he saw the wrinkles at the corners of the mouth, the pink tongue. On a large slate behind her ran a row of familiar white letters. The colonel explained that with these binoculars a man could watch the flight of birds or correct the angle of artillery fire, distinguish movements too far away for the eye to resolve, or spy upon an unwary enemy. They had still more powerful eyes than these, called telescopes. Here Hyde opened a book entitled *Binocular Instruments.* White man turned telescopes to the nighttime sky to stare at the planets and the stars and the moon, and the greatest of these could see six thousand times more powerfully than the human eye.

The book provided drawings of microscopes like swarms of ungainly praying mantises, instruments that enabled men to peer into the minutest mysteries of the universe. Magnification made it all possible, which was done by lenses—glass again.

Only the boy's desperate elation carried him through Hyde's lecture, and he kept this blind grip on himself until Bushnell deposited him on the bed. Then Tumbling Hawk's mind began to shiver—he pictured thousands of those long cool eyes staring up into the sky, a thousand of those frigid praying mantises peering shamelessly into the world's intimacies. He stood with the instruments too, a grotesque creature with one glassy eye thick and wide and round, and one eye stuck far away from his face at the end of a long black snout. How fantastic his grandfather's story had seemed when he heard it all those endless years ago. Suddenly how inescapably, how intolerably real. Muscle spasms convulsed him—he had trouble keeping his injured thigh still. Had he lost his rightful eyes forever? He had been shown how a man could give up his birthright, like Esau in their book. Tumbling Hawk feared he was too far gone to do anything but rush blindly forward with white man.

"Clever piece of legislation," Hyde conceded. He had just finished reading the text of Stephen Douglas' Kansas-Nebraska bill, introduced to the Senate one week before on January 23, 1854. "Two territories, not my one, which means they can concentrate on organizing Nebraska for the railroad if things get bogged down in Kansas. No Indian lands. Clever, very. Douglas sidesteps the Indian problem while wooing southern votes by saying, 'We leave the decision about slavery entirely in the hands of the voters.' How democratic—a referendum on slavery. 'Popular sovereignty,' he calls it. Indeed, very democratic. But then

Douglas needs a fetching title for the bill that wipes out the Missouri Compromise."

In late mid-April 1854, almost a year to the day after his capture, Tumbling Hawk could not wait to get out of the house and on to Cloud, the buckskin pony Hyde had purchased from a Cree for one hundred dollars. Elizabeth dressed in black for the occasion and raked her hair into a severe bun, which stretched the worry across her broad forehead. Her recent concern about whether he'd go or stay had aged her, and Tumbling Hawk despised writing new lines in her face or streaking her hair gray. Still, for the first time in a month, he could look at her without guilt. That made the colonel less cocksure about the boy's future. Sherrin, as usual, looked puppy-dog hopeful, his mouth primed with its all-devouring grin. Tumbling Hawk read Bushnell's eyes and face with interest and found that, like an Indian's, they assumed nothing.

That pleased the boy. His mind grew stronger after that. He refused Hyde's solicitous offer of field glasses, obliged him by taking a last brief glance at the map, then handed it back. He told her, he told them, nothing, even when they walked out onto the porch and she almost faltered coming down the stairs. He really did not know what would happen, and he refused to turn future into past. That was their way. "I'll know soon. That will be soon enough for them." He said his goodbyes, mounted and spun Cloud around. He turned in his saddle, raised his hand in a Cheyenne salute, then rode away from them.

When he did disappear, the colonel pointed to a spot high on a distant ridge and held out the field glasses. Elizabeth brushed them aside so gently it seemed to thank Hyde for the gesture. Her eyes clung to the spot where he had pointed. "What do you think, Mr. Bushnell?"

"Can't tell, ma'am. Don' believe he made up 'is own mind yet. Now he got wings, it's up to him to clip 'em hisself."

She did not question again, just stared at the point as if in her clouded gray eyes she held him there.

Tumbling Hawk felt Elizabeth's eyes on his back long after he passed out of sight. Once he felt tempted to turn around and look, but he fought that off and rode on. He saw no point in torturing himself about what had passed: not after spending months and months in the house of bondage going relentlessly over and over his fears of doubt and betrayal. Before, of course, his leg had imprisoned him. Now all that lay behind; the clarity of the woods lay ahead.

He rode north slowly, looking for that mystical wave of green that lay beneath winter's withering skin. Sometimes Tumbling Hawk saw it clearly—on budding branches, in sprigs, in young tender grasses; but he found it also on the southern slopes of hills, by the river, around watering holes. Yes, he told himself, that saving green still brushed the Plains.

The boy skirted Rawhide Buttes, the jagged red bluffs which incised intricate parallels through the Plains. He pushed on to the Niobrara crossing. Where he could, he stayed on the south bank, following the river's sunny wrigglings on a deer path until he reached the right place—though he hadn't been looking for it. Here the riverbank sloped up from the water. A cluster of feather maples and one burred grandfather oak stood near the crest of the hill, pulling the eye up a series of terraces toward the trees and the cap of pine woods above.

Cloud went at Tumbling Hawk's touch—up the inviting regularity of slope's treads and risers. The boy's lungs filled like sails.

At the edge of the forest Tumbling Hawk quickly stripped off his denim shirt, his boots, those hot brown socks, that clinging underwear and trousers. He threw himself onto the earth, rolled over and over in the soft spring grass. He grabbed daisies and larkspur and wildflowers and stuffed them in his mouth, chomped at the pliant grass. He jumped and danced, ran around in circles, whooped to the sky, looked up at the sun, felt the soft receptive earth with his feet and hands and body. He beat the flab on his belly and did two of Buck's Heart's exercises. Not until he was sweating and breathing heavily did he remember Cloud, who stood less ecstatically, munching grass. Tumbling Hawk uncinched the saddle and threw off the biting metal bridle. He leaped on his pony's back, guided Cloud in three tight circles, then, gripping the mane, turned him to the water. Down the terraces they streaked in a mad race to the water, moving faster and faster until they dove in.

The shock cleansed Tumbling Hawk; its long-denied familiar force scrubbed him inside and out, washed their smells from him, rinsed his mouth clear. Long after Cloud stood dripping by the bank, Tumbling Hawk lolled in the stream, recalling the spring day when he and his friends had plunged together into the water. What seemed so remote yesterday breathed in him now—the swift-moving water brought it back. The boy didn't know when he began talking to the pony in Cheyenne. He floated in gray-green water, and beyond that lay a blue-green pool while farther out, under a rock outcropping, the stream turned blue black, color of ink. Under the water, multicolored pebbles glinted like a tray of jewels; a deep fluent note hummed to him from where the water ran a weir of rocks and boiled through a chute. What a pleasure to feel his body again, to know that the skinny, hairless, blotched leg that barely broke the water's surface would grow strong again, that the flab at his waist would melt away. His skin was as wrinkled as Mohe's when he emerged. He felt so good that, in spite of the doctor's orders, he raced the pony up the last three flats.

At two o'clock by the sun Tumbling Hawk left Cloud grazing on the slope. He entered the woods alone and naked, looked in at a tawny doe and her fawn, and moved off without disturbing them. He spotted a barred owl asleep in his tree. He recognized rabbit fur clinging to a stripling oak, brought squirrels into chattering convocation, saw trees overbrowsed by deer, and felt glad spring had come. Everywhere he walked he noticed marks of passings, meals, baths, fights: welcome notes scattered by old friends. Birds called out to him. He answered the jay's shriek, the sparrow and the finch's song in their own tongue, then in a burst of joy ran through a babel of animal sounds—whose answers rang together through the woods. As he walked, his old way of moving slipped onto him again. His foot felt the tingling jabs of cool pine needles, his ears picked up the lightest whirr and flutter and fall; he drank in smells, chewed grasses and tubers for their taste. Moving up a long slope, he came into a camas meadow edged by a rocky ridge where wild onions grew. There was mustard and peppergrass and, farther on, barley grass and wild rye—in a month the field would be a platter spread before all things, before all men wise enough to know it. He came home in this frolic, a bright sun in his heart.

Not until the sun was dropping did he start back. Through screens of green/black pine needles he watched as clouds on the horizon spread the sun like a lump of butter across the sky. He reached Cloud at sunset, his mind empty. Their ideas had run out of him like water from a tub.

He watched the stars come out one by one, then in clusters—tiny pinpricks of light flung across the blacking sky. He ate nothing, though he had their food beside him. Did he need their bland tastes when underneath all life he heard the force of the Spirit's breathing again? Rumbling Wings' words spoke from inside him: "Remember how you have been." With absence-honed clarity he remembered rocking in his cradleboard as white pieces of gray sky fell, his first snow; he saw Shell smiling in the tepee's finely diffused light, Big Road, Mohe's eyes in their dark, cracking cases of leather, Rumbling Wings' thunder-provoking stare, his friends, the warriors. Underneath a quilt of stars he remembered his vision quest: remembered trying to rush the landscape into him, remembered the half-shadow man with his arrows and coup marks and that unmanning unearthly sound that seemed to issue from the air around him. Perhaps some force of envy or greed inside him had driven him to the white world. As Tumbling Hawk studied his perplexity, looking up into a star-drenched sky, he realized that the white men squinted up into it with their giant eye. He drained himself of this idea and waited.

After seeing with the eye of the ant and the eagle, after looking at invisible things, then counting pockmarks on the moon's cheek, how could the world change back into what it seemed before, if it ever had been what it seemed? He held their implements and his hands changed. How he lusted to visit white man's cities, his factories, to observe omnibuses and steam engines. If he stayed he would go east, Hyde promised, to New York and Washington, to school. His vision guaranteed him honor: if he went east. If he went home now, armed with a few paltry tricks, he had gained nothing. Hyde said: "The choice is clear. To be effective, to help your people, you must continue your education. You have no really effective tools yet." Undeniably, too, the colonel would have rejected him if he wasn't the right brave young man. Giant machines kept smashing down all those bridges back to his old world.

He waited for dawn with increasing impatience. At the first hint of light he took out a piece of beef and bit into it ravenously. Having eaten, he started back.

TUMBLING HAWK IN LARAMIE

HAPPILY FOR TUMBLING HAWK he rode Cloud every day. He worked up to running two miles an outing, and occasionally he went through Buck's Heart's exercises. His muscles, remembering, brought bittersweet recollections of his parents and home, and sometimes he would work himself beyond exhaustion to stupor's refuge. He faced changes, of course—his clothes, his boots, the saddle and bridle, the pistol and the rifle Hyde gave him. The Sharps rifle cut down the need for a stalk, so he substituted his pistol at bow range. When Bushnell drew post assignment they rode out together, the scout entertaining the boy with embroidered recollections "of days mebee a mite better." But Bushnell spent more time with the buffalo herds as the summer wore on. That left Matthew Sherrin, whom Tumbling Hawk still found uncomfortably overeager and who kept enunciating the simplest English as though the boy was deaf.

When alone, Tumbling Hawk filled a corner of his afternoons with discreet vestiges of the life he had once known. He tended that little spark with care, making sure it never burned out but also watching that it didn't flare too high. He never took off the saddle again and never spoke to Cloud in Cheyenne.

The Fort intrigued the boy. He studied the weapons, horses, intricacies of parade, dogs, saddles and tack, the ins and outs of military procedure. Except for the irrepressible Sherrin, the other officers remained reserved with him. The "post Indians" largely avoided him too; this made avoiding them easy, for he despised their slinking manner—with eyes lowered and ragged trade blankets drawn up over their shoulders, they seemed afraid to show their faces to white men. Bushnell cautioned Tumbling Hawk about a rough-looking commanding Pawnee named Speckled Tail, describing him as a "hard 'un." Speckled Tail, the leader of the Pawnee scouts, dressed in breechclout, moccasins, and a deerskin shirt open to the waist. As a concession to the military he wore a pair of crotchless pants, which were split like chaps. The Pawnee and the Cheyenne were blood enemies, but more than that, Tumbling Hawk's presence enraged, even imperiled Speckled Tail, in the manner of an elusive, pestering mosquito. In his dreams Tumbling Hawk kept seeing that wire-thin scar under Speckled Tail's lip, which gave him such a mean second smile.

Hyde received Coughlin's letter in early August. By then, the Kansas-Nebraska Bill had been law for two months, time enough for northern and southern settlers to start killing one another, to have begun to scramble over each other's bodies for the best lands and the honor of making the Territories either free or slave.

Dear Ben,

I do sympathize with what you call "living life as if one stuttered horribly"—the week-old newspapers, the long-delayed letters. But let me assure you that your insights are not posthumous. And let me tell you how I envy your freedom in the woolly West. At best, Washington is too inbred; at worst, as now, it's undergoing one of those periodic reigns of terror caused by an uncertain executive playing out a bad hand. In the attempt to keep the party together, the Democrat idiots turned the Kansas-Nebraska vote into a test of party loyalty; at one stroke they've done their muddleheaded best to found an opposition party.

For ten years now certain loosely allied banking and real estate interests have been sitting vulturelike in the Eastern wings, paring their monied talons and waiting for the golden issue that would turn North against South and provide a chance to make their new party national. What they wanted was one good anti-Slave issue to *impact* all the little and medium-sized sectional grumblings into one potent national cannonball.

Enter Chairman Douglas in haste to lay railroad tracks from Chicago west along what, we hope, is the oft-traveled trail by your door. These interests take the doctrine of popular sovereignty and hokus-pokus, read into Douglas' scheme a plot to spread Slavery into Kansas! Hogswill! But the Democrats, our benighted faction, go one better by demanding party loyalty on Douglas' Bill. In Congress, men stand up and proclaim, "I won't vote for the Bill. It's against my conscience to sanction Slavery!" Presto! The Bill works for the dubious intent of this "new coalition," which is in fact an old coalition of Eastern banking interests, disaffected Whigs, and Free-Soilers searching for a new lease on life.

Four birds downed with one stone, Ben. These Republicans get the Chairman, whom they despise and fear, they stir up the vagaries of Free-Soil democracy while insisting that popular sovereignty's a blind for spreading Slavery; they split the Democrats right along their vulnerable Mason and Dixon; and *lay the foundations for their new national party!* (You would color at the king-making talk in the District of late.) All that from the Kansas-Nebraska settlement! They are inspired publicists who play this shell game without one damn pea!

It's fascinating to watch the Chairman as the attacks grow more vicious. Democrat newspapers dropped the little man overnight. Ward healers who owe him their jobs call him slaveholder (His wife's family owned slaves) on the streets of the city he built. Yet he's absolutely masterful on the floor—it's his swansong, cogent, resourceful, righteous, always righteous. Whatever one's feelings about him, he is a master.

In parting, I offer the wisdom of Mrs. Hastings: she is afraid we underestimate the significance of the Kansas-Nebraska question. Our "intellectual arrogance" causes us to "see too finely." "It's like believing a mirror is penetrable," she says, "and ending up too deeply into it, and getting scratched. The secret of good politics is knowing where the reflection begins." Got that?

Less poetically, it does not matter what the real truth of the affair is. With Greeley's newspaper doing its best to make the extension of slavery into the territories the most important issue of the decade, with the Kansas-Nebraska Act splitting the Democrats, hastening the demise of the Whigs, quite probably creating a new party, and moving to abort the Chairman's career, with estimates of violence escalating in Kansas, with the country being torn apart by this almost entirely invented issue, it *does not matter* that our perspicacity tells us the issue is a manufactured one. "Truth is irrelevant," Mrs. Hastings say sagely. "All you have to know is what *they* believe." Her argument's excellent but depressing. I'm afraid both of us will always be tempted to see beyond the rhetoric. That probably makes us poor politicians, and poor cynics.

Enough dreary philosophizing. My very best wishes to Elizabeth Harter. We await your visit to Washington and the opportunity of meeting your boy.

With fondest thoughts & regards,

JIM

One day a train of supply wagons rolled into Laramie under the escort of Matthew's company and a few Pawnee. Tumbling Hawk happened to be moving Cloud across the Parade toward South Gate and, as the wagons passed under the arch, he drew aside into the shadow of the wall to get out of the way. He had grown so used to the swaying wagons, the loads bowing the beds, that he watched without seeing when suddenly Speckled Tail shoved his pony against Cloud and snarled, "Out of my way, cripple."

Triumph snapped the facial scar taut, triumphant anger blanched it a flickering, ghostly white. He shoved Cloud again, but this time the pony held his ground.

"Lucky you are weak and well protected!" the Pawnee cried. They were side by side, their faces turned to one another, legs almost touching. The older man loomed over Tumbling Hawk, his second smile a livid pulse on copper skin.

Tumbling Hawk felt no fear. In Cheyenne he spat out: "Cowards hunt their own blood."

"You do worse! You wipe off your color!"

By now the wagons had halted, the usual dust had settled, usual sounds had died. The soldiers, straining to understand this sudden unintelligible rage saw the massive Indian towering over a boy. But the boy did not back off. Matthew Sherrin, who had come through the gate yards behind Speckled Tail, drove a pair of pack mules between them and ordered the Pawnee to lead them to the stables.

The scout hesitated a rebellious moment before moving off.

"Don't worry about it, Tumbling Hawk," said the adjutant as Speckled Tail rode stiffly by the stalled wagons, the rows of intent soldiers. "He'll cool off. But, for god's sake, don't make a point of getting in his way."

Banker Avery lowered himself into the ladder-backed chair beside Hyde's desk. On this steamy August day Avery, a spectrally thin man, wore a black worsted suit lightened only by a thin layer of dust. His slicked-back hair carried the furrows of his comb straight down to his scalp. His skin looked flushed and, when agitated, his face and hands blotched.

The banker got down to business: "You know, Colonel Hyde," his tone insinuated that he and Hyde had previously agreed on premises, "under Senator Douglas' legislation, the organization of the, uh, Territory will put some of us in handsome positions."

Hyde indicated Avery could continue.

"Like the bank, for instance. Or, uh, Laramie, I should say. When the Territory is organized, land prices will rise. Also, the railroad just might come through Laramie." Innuendo stuffed each word, gorged every phrase.

"What the eastern public understands about the settlement of the Kansas Territory," Avery said slyly, "is what it reads, and what it reads is the product of—a number of amalgamated interests. It would be shortsighted to dissuade anyone—anyone at all—of the import of this issue."

"Here in this office does the scaly toad of a moneylender dare lecture me?" Hyde hated Avery's tone and, more broadly, he hated the way the deadly North-South antagonisms were being manipulated to whip up settlers to scramble for the territorial lands. All as though the Indians did not exist, as though those lands had never been ceded to them. The colonel despised their using politics and "progress" to camouflage greed.

"It seems pointless to quibble about estimates of violence in Kansas when the conflict voices—correct that—when it anticipates a national need."

Hyde intervened from fatigue, tired of hearing a land grab called "manifest destiny," tired of the inflated rhetoric Greeley's paper lavished on an issue he himself had invented: "There are twelve slaves at Kansas at this moment, not a single solitary slave in Nebraska!"

"They can't count back East!" Avery pitched forward as he shouted, then, settling back, went on in an edgeless monotone as though he had never raised his voice. "There are interests, uh, watching these settlement questions with an eye to something greater than schoolboy arithmetic." Below the desk the banker scratched at his hands; yet even while one hand pulled at the other, he held his upper body absolutely still. "But I note a certain impatience on your part, Colonel, which I take to be not, uh, inattention but rather the habit of a busy man."

Avery's eyes narrowed. "There is a spirit growing in this country, a new sense of interdependency and mutual concern."

"The trick," thought Hyde, "is underlining all those words in a row."

"The self-sufficiency of the pioneer is as out-of-date as wagons in the railroad era. For the first time the country is about to turn in on itself." The banker's mottled right hand tried to get back at his left. "Lines are making their way across it to tie it together. Certain, uh, venerated ways of looking at the world must be relinquished, Colonel. Even the petty antagonisms of personality, fierce as they are, must be rethought in the light of new demands. For the future is coming in such complex ways it will be hard for all but the farsighted to fathom it."

Avery offered this comment cynically, with open disdain. His eyes were nearly shut now. "Oh, politics is so complex these days. Politics is just another name for Fate. Heroism is something used to bring tears to old ladies in the six-penny seats, yesterday's virtue losing ground to today's reality. Virtue is too unwieldy a tool when history is being made minute by minute." His eyes shut completely, as if they preferred to dispense with sight in the face of these manifest truths. He gloated—and didn't care if Hyde knew it. Avery had always hated the colonel's assumption of moral superiority; he thought Hyde's stand on those Indian lands amounted to political suicide, and he enjoyed rubbing Hyde's nose in this string of prophecies.

Avery's eyes sprang open. "This press thing is nothing, Colonel Hyde, a trifle. Even if he wished, no man could stop it; none but a fool would try. Analyze what's happening—those emigration societies herding droves of Free-Soilers to Kansas—you don't imagine they're financed by a few well-meaning old biddies in Boston?"

With that, he insinuated himself out of the chair. Opening the door he added, "It's not hard for an informed man to see the Whigs are dead, that the Democrats have turned their backs on their most treasured principles and will split North-South. Younger, more virile forces are finding popular expression. Of course, this is still a time of negotiation, when anomalies are appreciated. It makes a man more valuable, Colonel Hyde, when he knows his worth. And you have always known your worth. But it is folly to overestimate anything. And, as a well-intentioned caution, I suggest you do not wait too long." He shut the door behind him.

Avery had told Hyde two things. Douglas still needed him to pacify the tribes and keep the trail open; to help with the organization of the Nebraska Territory; and, in the fall, to testify before his committee. In spite of Hyde's stand on Indian lands, Douglas still favored the

Laramie route for the railroad. Which meant there were no other options open to him.

Greeley and the Republican's power were growing, otherwise Avery would not have adopted such a tone with him. Still, it had been an impressive recruiting speech: part chastisement, part admonishment. ("Watch your step, Colonel, or you'll be superannuated"); part back-handed compliments.

Hyde wondered when the animosity had started. Perhaps the previous January when Avery had tried to buy a strip of land along Lodgepole Creek and Hyde had stopped him, or the first time Hyde saw Avery's unctuous smile and hated everything he stood for. Hyde also despised Avery's political party, which was cynical enough to force Kansas to go slave rather than let the state go Democrat. Hyde thought that was a fitting origin for this new Republican "Party of Progress."

Finishing his lessons early one morning, Tumbling Hawk rode over to Hyde's office only to find the colonel out. Sherrin immediately asked him if he could be of help, was there anything at all he could do, would he like to see the new ordnance, and what seemed like five other things at once. Tumbling Hawk was tempted to retreat, but Sherrin eyed him like a well-meaning puppy. The boy gave in and asked to see the ordnance report. The adjutant walked to the colonel's desk; Tumbling Hawk studied him. The lieutenant returned; the boy attended more closely. "Walk back," Tumbling Hawk ordered in English. Sherrin seemed surprised, but he demonstrated his loose, hip-swinging gait once more.

"Matthew," Tumbling Hawk concluded, "white men walk funny." The boy expertly mimicked the lieutenant's walk. "See where your weight comes down? Try it this way." Tumbling Hawk kept all his weight on his back leg and did not shift the weight forward on to the ball of the foot until certain where he wanted to place the foot. "This way you stop before you put the foot in a hole or on a rattlesnake. This way you avoid shaking the ground."

They began Indian-stepping around the office, Tumbling Hawk in the lead, Sherrin trying to watch his tutor and keep his weight off of his advancing foot. So the colonel found them—poised on left legs, their right feet inches off the rug. They laughed so hard even Tumbling Hawk had trouble keeping upright.

After this, Matthew took his walking lessons in the woods or on the prairie. At first Sherrin was inept, but Tumbling Hawk remained patient, glad to have something physical to do, glad to have an oblique manner of celebrating the old ways.

Sherrin told the boy everything he knew about Hyde: Hyde's successful maneuvers in Mexico, where his capture of Monterey won him a colonel's rank; his handling of the Laramie Conference; his political fights to cede lands to the relocated eastern tribes; his part in sponsoring the southwestern Indian Territory; the ongoing and unpopular fight for adequate Indian lands and Indian funds. Tumbling Hawk learned more about the miseries of the relocated Indians, the Creek and Cherokee and Chickasaw and Seminole, the Natchez and the eastern woodland Sioux. Matthew's unaffected adulation and his sense of Hyde's place in white man's history made Tumbling Hawk more at home with his decision to stay.

A clear hot day, the boy out for his daily ride, running his two miles, starting and finishing, as usual, back at the yucca-spiked knoll. The southeast wind dried out his mouth, so Tumbling Hawk decided to detour around to Fish Creek.

He left Cloud where the plain gave way to long grass, sere in the August sun. Beyond that, over a humpbacked ridge, lay a tumble of huge boulders that edged the north side of the stream for a mile. He was not yet clear of those boulders, working his way through the gully when he heard their laughter. The familiarity urged him on: the time he chased shy Small Deer too close to the women's pool and large bare-breasted Gray Flower indulgently shooed them away. Curious now he came round the rocks and took a step into the open before he spied the naked girls. One bent down in the shallows—in profile he had her, framed by reeds. She meticulously washed the length of thigh, up and down. Two half-immersed girls languidly splashed the fourth, the striking blond girl his eyes had pursued in town, in church. His eyes lay pleasurably on the smooth shimmering belly, the aureate thigh, on that startling fullness of golden bush. Pliant young flesh provided the setting, a banquet of breasts and bellies, unguarded laughter, and unhampered movement. The water's sheen drenched her gold, this dazzling nereid whose whole being threatened to deliquesce except for those gem-hard nipples pointed by the cold stream. The sight was beautiful, a vision, and though rocked by lust Tumbling Hawk felt no guilt.

Considerate of the odd way the whites treated these matters, he ordered himself to turn away. His eyes lingered another instant. He realized that she, this yellow girl, her companions too, not one of them would ever be his; realized how alone he was among them; how much his sacrifice or ambition would cost him. Incompletion clutched at his stomach: he longed for home, where such frolic would bear relation to him.

Tumbling Hawk turned away. Turning, he saw the older woman sitting on a rock in a high-necked, elephant gray, long-sleeved frock, dryly overseeing—Mrs. Orton, a fuller version of the slender long-waisted girl who splashed his nereid.

He had his hand raised to touch Cloud's muzzle when the pony neighed its welcome—as loud and clear in that still dry air as a pistol shot. Their laughter died. Mrs. Orton must have reared up indignantly, marched through the crotch of those rocks, and stationed herself there. Tumbling Hawk did not know. He leaped on Cloud's back, struck the pony with his heels, and rode off as fast as he could.

Hyde stood at an angle to Tumbling Hawk, so that he looked at the boy over his right shoulder as if sighting down a rifle barrel.

"Did you—ah—spy on those young women?"

"No," said Tumbling Hawk staunchly. He explained how the laughter led him up through the rocks, and suddenly he found the girls there, bathing in the stream, without any clothes. "I was also surprised. I looked at them for a few seconds. As soon as I understood I should not be there, I turned away. I did not do this on purpose."

"The temptation to lie is great. You must tell me the truth."

That "lie" hit like a slap. Tumbling Hawk felt angry and mortified—angry at the suggestion he could lie, mortified because he had run away as if he was guilty.

"I looked at the girls one second or two too long. I turned away then. I do not lie."

Hyde replied deliberately, his eyes as intense and professional as when inspecting a soldier on parade. "Understand that only if you tell me the truth can I defend you against Essie Orton and the others."

"I understand."

"Why did you run from Essie?"

Tumbling Hawk stood dumbly, recalling his humiliating ride: clinging low against Cloud's neck, praying he would not be recognized. The boy had felt that, whatever he said, they would not believe him; that the very people who corrupted him wanted to believe he lied. How complex the white world seemed then; all the while the image of her body pulled at his groin.

"I felt I had already done wrong. I don't know why I felt this, but I did." At home he could have spoken to Mohe, Big Road; even his mother would have understood what had happened. But he could not speak now because Hyde knew nothing about men and women.

Minutes passed while Hyde's gaze wandered from maps of the Nebraska Territory to his books on warfare, the books out of which Tumbling Hawk had learned military strategy and tactics. Only once before Tumbling Hawk had stood before a man with such absolute faith in his power to determine guilt or innocence: Rumbling Wings, when he had searched for the violator of the sacred hides. He found it odd to think of Lightfoot while his life in the white world hung in the balance, but he felt badly that he had not sympathized with Lightfoot's initiation ordeal.

Hyde's minimal chin pointed at him like a weapon. "Of course I believe you. Considering everything, you didn't behave badly. Not perfectly, but not badly. Now go on."

All morning townspeople stood by hitching posts or on the wide porches in taut conspiratorial knots. Someone called for a citizens' meeting, but that never got off the ground. Rumor had it that Tumbling Hawk had laid a red hand on one of the naked children; he had lured them to that out-of-the-way place and spent the afternoon ogling them, then, under threat, made the girls dance before him. Such filth sickened the colonel: he despised the dark side of these minds, the exaggerations they enjoyed. The intensity of their enmity surprised, even frightened Hyde. How shortsighted of him to underestimate their resentment of the child. It made the colonel wonder, underneath, if perhaps Avery was right. Maybe his political instincts had decamped, maybe he had grown too old.

Hyde assigned Sherrin to stay close to Tumbling Hawk until further orders.

Sitting in his pudgy armchair, Hyde knew Elizabeth had been crying, something she had not done since Lieutenant Rostow's command of nine had been wiped out by renegade Sioux. The colonel wanted to comfort her, but understood they could never refer to Tumbling Hawk's accidental indiscretion. He felt lonely because of the willed silence and a little resentful. There seemed something unfair in Elizabeth's avoiding this crisis and leaving it entirely to him. Hyde kept considering leaving, but stayed on, hoping that something could be said.

"How quickly things change these days." He heaved himself up, feeling his muscles had been wrenched loose from their insertions. "Men age so quickly now, Elizabeth."

"Benjamin, you're not old, you're the most youthful man in Laramie. What you stand for–I don't ever want to see that fineness or our values neglected. This town needs them, even if they don't want to admit it." The subtle gray eyes had a doleful brilliance, a vestige of the long day's sadness. She had never said she loved him, though Benjamin Hyde had known it for many years. He would have given anything, then, to hold her in his arms.

Five hundred copies of the handbill decorated the town. The colonel and Sherrin posted it on every store and building, stuffed it under every doorframe, and wrapped it around the hitching posts.

It read:

Office of the Commander
Fort Laramie
Nebraska Territory

TO THE CITIZENS OF FORT LARAMIE:

I have investigated the incident thoroughly and impartially. To the best of my knowledge, I find the child innocent of any untoward intent, guilty only of an accidental intrusion.

BENJAMIN K. HYDE, Colonel
Army of the United States of America

Elizabeth did not tell the colonel that she had seen the handbill; nor did she say she kept a copy buried deep in her knitting basket.

Matthew and Tumbling Hawk spent all their time outdoors, talking about Tumbling Hawk's life and outlining what lay ahead, hunting or just riding through the parched countryside. Sherrin learned to move as quietly as his tutor. He began to see and hear better. Tumbling Hawk taught him to ride bareback and sidesaddle, taught him how to tell a horse's speed at a glance, know his age, blood, and health with a few casual strokes of the animal's body. They became friends: Tumbling Hawk told Matthew that galloping away from those girls at Fish Creek he kept thinking about something the Bible said: having the thought is as bad as doing the deed. Tumbling Hawk refused to believe that; he certainly was not disposed to think kindly of the idea; but knowing that many whites, including Elizabeth, did, had made him feel tainted.

Calling the child "Tom" had its ironies, of course, but Elizabeth insisted on the name. In a simple ceremony in the first brick building in the Nebraska Territory, a fussy clerk officially titled the boy Thomas Hyde. Hyde and Elizabeth, Bushnell and Sherrin served as witnesses.

One of Banker Avery's tellers handed him into his rig. As he slowly rolled out of town, he nodded or waved or tipped his hat (depending on station or sex) to whomever he saw, and if the citizenry bothered to think about it, they would have believed that Banker Avery was out for a midday drive. Beyond the fort, he made a large loop east, which took him three miles from the main road. He drove in and out of an infrequently used two-track rut through the unchanging landscape. On his way he raised rabbits and attracted the attention of a querulous bird or two. But he heard nothing, being deeply absorbed in his thoughts. Habit took him to the dry streambed. He halted by a clump of cottonwoods, looked around, then drove in among the trees. A quarter of a mile into the woods, he spotted Isaac Straw. The merchant sat a horse which, considering everything, bore his weight nobly.

"You're late, Avery."

"Don't speak to me like that, you swine!" He looked at the obese man as if to say, "Hold your tongue or the deal's off!" Straw glared but said nothing.

"The Pawnee's ready, I take it?" Avery didn't wait for an answer. "Get the other one and get it over!"

Straw seemed to weigh alternatives as he seemed ready to speak. His mouth vaguely hinted at a sneer.

"Don't speak to me of your filthy work!" Avery's face broke into that betraying rash; his hands burned. "The first day that's right, do it! I want the thing over with."

"Same signals?" Straw asked lazily.

Avery screamed: "Did I tell you to change anything?" An instant later, without apparent transition, with a control more threatening for the contrast, he said, "You are, I needn't remind you, exclusive agent in this matter." That had its desired effect. Their roles immediately resettled. "Afterwards I don't want them around town for a month, understand? A full thirty days."

Once free of Straw, Banker Avery gladly faced the dusty ride back. He wanted to flush that scum out of his mind and substitute the other, bigger game. "I'm going to get Hyde, going to get Hyde." He almost sang that. "Bided my time. Soon to be paid in full. With compound interest. For nothing—one dumb Indian and an expendable piece of white trash, whichever one it is. And a little of the ready, marvelously little."

A mile later he shifted into his righteous tone: "An Indian prodigy looks good back East, where they can afford to think it courageous and progressive. Here you can't sell folks on that. Laramie's fed up with being Hyde's flock. Nothing worse than the flock that turns on its prophet."

Hyde, his thoughts continued, had been a god in the old frontier days. Now that he had outlived his era, it was time to erase the myth and get on with the succession. Otherwise, Laramie would remain backward frontier. Certainly they could not afford delay now with the triple spurs of the transcontinental railroad, territorial organization, and the new national party converging on them. Meanwhile, Hyde, blind to change and impervious to the promptings of progress, uttered humane homilies about equitable treatment of the Indian.

Avery felt compelled, quite possibly beyond the limits of reason, to instruct the colonel in the new realities. The peeping episode supplied the right ammunition, for it had turned all respectable citizens against their high-minded founder. Avery would simply bring to pass what they had wanted, what they had prayed for since the boy's arrival. What a fitting way to demonstrate Hyde's obsolescence, he who had built his empire around a principle of protection for all. People would say, "Why he can't even guard his own ward."

Through the binoculars he looked like a child as he rode steadily at them, not over a mile and a half away. Ord Cobb elbowed Speckled Tail. "Well, here he come lickety-split, red. Seem in a hell o' a hurry to get it done with."

Speckled Tail said nothing, not even to the pointed dig in his ribs. He felt relieved this day had come. If he had to lie in the dust beside this white man once more he would've slit Cobb's throat. Even now Cobb's stubbly Adam's apple looked like it waited to be cored. For two days they had lain side by side, so close that the Pawnee was forced to breathe in Cobb's nervous sweat and firewater breath and listen to his incessant chatter. For two days he had heard what a dirty stinking thieving lot Indians were, for two days he had accepted Cobb's curses of his "spooky Injun quiet." All the while the big Pawnee had concentrated on the boy, placing each one of his movements, marking every spot he habitually returned to. Now these unhappy partners lay in heavy buffalo grass on a slight rise about two hundred yards and a little to the left of the spot where the boy started and finished his daily two-mile run.

Speckled Tail was no fool. He knew what getting caught meant. But that didn't matter any more. Under the armband he flexed his bicep, feeling the cool beads against his skin. He wanted the boy dead. The Cheyenne was a force he could not understand. He looked powerless and insignificant, yet somehow he had acquired what Speckled Tail never had, and without giving up anything. That crazed the Pawnee, who could tally every item he had forfeited.

"I don' rightly understan' why yo' want t' kill this boy, Injun." To kill time, Cobb had developed a habit of talking to himself. "I know he's a Cheyenne, but that don' seem 'nough for all the hate you pourin' his way. Ain' the money. Sho ain' 'nough of that to wake up no hell-fire hate." In Speckled Tail's field glasses the boy looked only a few yards away—his full lips rested in an easy smile, his round bronzed face clear. Even as the Pawnee watched, that strange fear of the boy awakened.

Cobb whispered, "Best quit jawin'."

They kept the field glasses on him as he dismounted, stripped off his cotton shirt, folded it neatly, and left Cloud grazing. The boy started away from them, to their right. They watched as he threaded the small hillocks and islands of parched, yellow grass. He moved up and down in their glasses, sometimes dipping as low as his shoulders in the ruts, then rising again, moving quickly through the narrow channels of a dry streambed, and looking no more tired after a mile than when he started.

Speckled Tail knew just how Tumbling Hawk felt—the air entering freely, filling his chest all the way up from the bottom the way water fills. The scar on the Pawnee's chin seemed to chew this bitter delight as Tumbling Hawk made his way through the last lap. About one hundred and fifty yards from the point where the boy started and always finished, the Pawnee carefully set aside the binoculars and picked up his rifle. At one hundred yards he had Tumbling Hawk in his sights, at fifty yards the image grew large, his finger tensed. Speckled Tail wanted to wait until Tumbling Hawk stopped, until he was sucking in those last deep breaths. He continued to track the boy back—thirty yards, twenty, ten.

He jerked the rifle up. The pony had moved toward their little rise in search of grass, unknowingly aligning himself between the knoll and the boy's shirt. The Pawnee stood up quickly to get a line over the pony. He took hurried aim, fired.

The shot rang out; it hit the boy high in the right shoulder; he staggered but kept his feet. The pony had been well trained, for the instant Tumbling Hawk was hit, Cloud started moving back toward him, running directly away from the shot. Reloading, Speckled Tail screamed at Cobb: "The pony! The pony!" But it would have taken a better shot than Cobb to hit Cloud, and his bullet just kicked up dirt a few yards behind the pony's heels.

Tumbling Hawk kept the pony between himself and the rise. He waited until the last instant before slipping just to the right of Cloud, grabbing the pommel with his left hand (the right was useless) and with a combined lunge and jump managed to slip his left foot into the stirrup. He was still hanging on to the stirrup and pommel when the third bullet whizzed by his ear.

They ran straight away from the hill, trying not to present a broadside. Tumbling Hawk held on sidesaddle as long as he could, but he was losing blood, the shoulder hung like a weight, and at one thousand yards he heaved himself up onto the saddle. He thanked white man for his saddle and said in Cheyenne, "Good boy, Cloud. Go." It took effort to talk.

The Pawnee sprinted to a spot a little higher on the knoll trying to gain a broadside shot. The boy was nearly out of range, but he fired anyway, an empty gesture of habit or wishful thinking. He missed by twenty yards.

"We got t' catch him!" Cobb's eyes looked like a startled rabbit's.

They raced for their lives. Their only hope was that he would fall off. Swearing, praying vultures, they galloped after him, hooves pounding, dust flying, whipping and spurring their horses harder and harder until blood coated the animals' dusty flanks. They could not close on him. The two figures remained locked at the same futile range in an unalterable tableau as Cloud carried the boy toward safety. Two miles from the post they stopped.

In the middle of the empty, arid prairie those two desperate men turned to each other. "You dirty stinkin' Injun," snarled the man who was dirt himself and stank. His last words gurgled in his throat; the Pawnee's knife pinned his Adam's apple to his spine. Speckled Tail stripped Cobb of his gun, binoculars, and the advance payment of one hundred dollars. He turned his pony north and rode away as fast as he could.

Banker Avery enjoyed a hugely successful day. In the morning he received a letter of thanks from Stephen Douglas: the chairman had been ecstatic to learn the Lodgepole bypass cut fifty miles off the Platte Trail and saved, at a minimum, thirty thousand dollars in engineering costs. Before lunch Avery had negotiated a sizable loan with a couple of Denver lawyers at excellent rates for the bank, and at precisely one o'clock Straw rode by his window. Now it was just a few minutes before five, the bank was closed, and everyone had gone home. Everyone but the banker himself, who perched on his chair supremely confident, suffering only a minute trace of impatience. A man who turned his wildest wishes into well-plotted operations, he could savor this last short wait, suck every last morsel of honeyed expectation.

As the clock on the church steeple struck the first count of five, Banker Avery sat erect at his desk. He neglected the papers in front of him in favor of the view straight ahead, out of his window. A minute passed, two, and Avery cursed Straw for his inefficiency. "The cost of dealing with that type," he thought. At five-five the Banker felt less confident, and by five-ten his hands tingled, his face kept hinting at his worry. As the clock struck the quarter, his rash popped out on his face. At five-twenty he saw a crowd forming in front of the General Store. He hesitated until the three-quarter hour, then walked through the empty bank past the safe, past the tellers' windows, around the low railing. He locked, double-locked, triple-locked the door, crossed over, and walked down Main Street.

"Have you heard?" asked the town surveyor. "Young Cheyenne boy's been shot." Avery's face felt livid. He could hardly keep from lifting one seething hand to it. "They think that Pawnee's done it and gone renegade, and that fellow Cobb, he was in on it, too. At least that's what I heard; they found Cobb dead, scalped too, a few miles from the Fort."

In spite of his torment, the banker managed to speak with the right amount of concern: "Is the boy all right?"

"Oh, he'll be fine. It's just a flesh wound."

Avery put in the requisite five minutes, then slowly made his way back to the bank. He passed through the locks, through the deserted bank again. In his office he sat down at his desk. He thought about Hyde, thought about Straw and his henchmen. Finally ready, Avery composed a sympathetic note to the colonel with hearty expressions of relief that the boy was not seriously hurt and best wishes for a speedy recovery. He next wrote an indignant letter to the Laramie *Recorder* which demanded that all right-thinking citizens band together to eradicate such behavior from the Territory; the banker also called for a new era of civilized enlightenment.

"You have seen him?" Elizabeth asked as Hyde entered.

"Yes. I spoke to Dr. Symonds. He'll be fine in a week, just fine."

"How did he look?"

"Sleepy," Hyde said gently. "He's going to be all right, Elizabeth. He's just suffered a little shock."

"Like his friends."

"Yes."

Both sat tensely in their chairs, as though ready to start for their destination and only waiting for that initial jolt. They had always wanted to believe the hatred would stay cloaked in civility, that it would never leap out so naked and so vile.

"It seems so soon."

"It would always seem soon, Elizabeth." He thought he might rise from his chair and enfold the woman he loved in his arms, comfort her, embrace her. But he did not do so.

They had been preparing for the boy's going away since they had begun to share him. When Hyde first told her about Douglas' letter asking him to testify in Washington in November, they did not say, "Oh, he'll go too and enter school and complete his education properly." They had agreed long before on such a plan. Though Hyde would be called to Washington again, they knew they could not wait for the next invitation.

"If the boy could stay here." Bitter tears dimmed her eyes. "They could turn up their noses forever. I don't care." Her voice strangled the last words.

"He knows that." Hyde grieved to see Elizabeth distraught. He always felt he had failed her at those moments.

"You must be very disappointed, Ben." Her voice came under control again.

"I am. But it will go away. I think—I think I was wrong. Not about our raising him here. About them—trying to tell them anything is a stupid self-indulgence. They've got this mindless formula that stops them from ever even hearing the first words: 'Lecture us and you violate the rule. Nothing didactic!' They're so divinely stupid. To shoot at a child."

"What about him?"

"He'll learn quickly enough. He's got to. Back East it won't be much better. Only maybe they won't take pot shots at him."

ON THE ROAD

THE OFFICERS' MESS AT Fort Kearney impressed the boy—the long low room with its bowing beams blacked by countless fires, the newly whitewashed fireplace where the initials of all the officers who had served on the post were carved in the stucco; at dinner came the toasts to Hyde, the clink of crystal goblets, and the flash of braid. Tom felt odd surrounded by men who had fought against Indians; yet Indians fought Indians too, he thought.

When spoken to, Tom Hyde answered the officers' questions. Yes, he had enjoyed the trip down the Platte. Yes, it seemed strange to be heading east when all the wagon trains were pushing west, hurrying toward the shelter of the forts. Yes, it had taken time to get used to their food—and a few other things as well. Two men at Tom's end of the table laughed between bites of their steak. That turned more eyes his way. No, he said after dessert, he wanted to help all the Indians, not only the Cheyenne, and the colonel believed he would be able to—with the proper education, discipline, and guidance. At that point a major with a horsey face and an exalted mustache spoke up: "But surely this boy can't—you won't—I mean, you can't think of sending him back to an Indian tribe?"

Tom's jaw went slack, displaying a gob of half-chewed potatoes. Elizabeth had warned there would be people who disliked Indians, who wouldn't understand the principle to which he intended to dedicate his life. But Tom Hyde had not imagined how it would feel to hear someone speak of his people as if they were vermin, an inferior form of life. Tom Hyde wanted to leap up, shout his war cry, and plunge a knife into that horsey major's chest.

The colonel looked at his protégé as if to say: "Relax. Don't be angered by such a stupid attitude." Then Hyde answered for the dumbstruck boy, who had just managed to shut his gaping mouth. "He will go home someday, of course. But at the moment he still has too much to learn about our world to consider anything but school."

That diverted the company to the where and when of the boy's continuing education, which gave Tom time to recover. He handled the rest of his first public showing well enough, though whenever he answered a question he felt like a trained animal. Apparently the colonel enjoyed his performance. This bothered Tom, but he had no opportunity to speak about it before they led him to bed in the adjutant's quarters adjoining the colonel's suite. It was supposed to be quite an honor.

For the next hour Tom Hyde fought the war against the major's contempt for the Indians and his own sense of being betrayed. The most hateful of white man's attributes swarmed through his mind: the fact that they made men slaves, that some of them spent their days making pins; their misunderstanding of men and women; the white man's unending arrogance and unfounded assumption of superiority. All this led again to the riddle of whether he ought to stay in the white world. But Tom Hyde knew he couldn't escape yet, not with his absolute need to know more about them and his belief that, someday, this weird exile would be of use. Finally he got himself thinking about the wooden trusses forty feet above ground in Fort Kearney's massive storeroom, all those sleek greyhound dogs—Bushnell had said, "They ken outstrip a horse." Everything was beginning to swim around and mix over itself as it does just before sleep, when a quiet tap on the door broke the flux; the colonel entered.

Hyde sat down on the edge of the bed as he had done in those early days at Elizabeth's. The boy could feel the colonel looking at him in the dark.

"They're all extremely impressed with you."

Tom Hyde could not bring himself to reply.

"Not all of these men understand what we want to do or what you have to do. This is not going to be easy. That's clearer than ever now. But don't get too upset over one fool's ignorance, Tom. And don't feel betrayed and get angry at me. You have to understand I can't help being proud of you."

They left it at that and said their second round of good nights.

After two hours on board the river steamer, Tom finally took the colonel's word that the boat would not blow up. Because of this he could stand stalwart at the railing as they steamed past towns, settlements, coaling stations, little landings, which stuck a pier like a tentative toe into the water. They passed fingernail farms scratching for a grip on the unyielding wilderness, which laid its indifferent timeless siege everywhere. What awe he felt at finding himself perched ten or twelve feet above the water on an idea, an uncertain idea at that, one that shouldn't work. Around him the whites strolled on the promenade without the slightest interest in the machinery trembling and whining beneath them. The women seemed as casual as the men, twirling their parasols in lustrous silks with all those buoying layers of skirts.

That evening after dinner which, in spite of the captain's urgings, they took in their cabin, Tom and the colonel strolled on the top deck. As they approached a very pale woman in taffeta and her beautiful young daughter, a black man slid by them carrying a tray. Though he had never seen one before, Tom Hyde knew from the way the man walked he was a slave. The boy froze—the black man halted and bowed very slightly to his mistress. Tom ordered himself to look away, but his eyes would not desert that ebony figure, and he stared as if the slave would provide the answer to the fear and horror his own face expressed. With one exact stride Hyde put himself between Tom and the ladies, then pivoted the boy around and started him back up the deck away from them. They did not speak until they had walked halfway around the boat.

They stopped at a railing, their backs to the other promenaders. The colonel looked over the water to the wooded bank. He whispered fiercely, making a stifled sound, afraid to lift his voice lest he shout: "It's hateful, Christ damn hateful to sit and watch human beings abused like that. But there's nothing we can do yet. That's what's so maddening!" Impotence always infuriated the colonel, but this sort sent the muscle chords in his cheeks pulsing erratically, ropes pulled by bellringers who had lost count.

The instant he had seen the black man Tom understood what slavery meant. All Elizabeth's abolitionist lessons struck home, as did the colonel's contempt for slaveholders and Matthew's story about

Hyde helping runaways get to Philadelphia. Tom Hyde didn't even have to watch the women receive the glass as though it was handed to them by the air, he didn't have to hear that choked, high, sugared voice say, "Is'n this all you be wantin', Missie Belle?" The gait itself imprinted indelibly—"It isn't the walk of a man!"

The next evening, at the captain's table, they sat across from the pale woman and her remarkably beautiful daughter. Through the meal the slave hovered near them, a lusterless black moth sometimes almost disappearing against the dark night outside. Always he hovered nearby, bending down to lift a glass or lay a plate, yet they never seemed aware of him. Tom couldn't help peeking too often, now at the black man and the obscenely pink palms, now at the beautiful girl, who already had perfected the mother's fluttering eyelashes, the coquettish tilt of the head, and that thick lisping speech. He couldn't help disliking her and being attracted to her at the same time. Hyde ate very little; he remained rigidly polite until the southern woman, in response to the captain's question about the cost of maintaining the Negroes, said, "Even if it doesn't pay, Captain, Providence put the servants in our care. We couldn't desert them now, could we?"

Hyde spoke softly, just loud enough to be heard, "President Jefferson declared that slavery was more pernicious to the white race than to the black." Minutes later the colonel and Thomas Hyde excused themselves.

"I can't eat with them," the colonel said. "It makes me ill." He straight-armed the upper berth, leaning on his small, manicured right hand. His brown eyes focused intently on nothing. Despite the receding chin, this was not a face in retreat.

Tom shimmied into his berth, the colonel unknotted his cravat. "Either you fight it—which means North-South war on an inconceivable scale—or you insist it must be handled lawfully. Trouble is it's the lawful position that's most hateful and slow. Meanwhile, you pray like an idiot that it'll go away." He sat down on the lower berth, trying to unwind. "Somehow it's more tolerable when you aren't exposed to it, when you don't have it rubbed in your face." His anger halted him. "Tom, do you very much want to dine at the captain's table?"

"It really doesn't matter to me, sir." Tom leaned out to look at him, but Hyde presented his back.

"Let's not. I'll only get disgusted with myself with being civil to them."

The colonel blew out the candles and said good night. Soon the boy heard his regular deep breathing. Tom felt uncomfortable in his cramped, stuffy upper. He liked the way the colonel had asked him about eating at the captain's table.

Tom was reminded of his father telling him that Man-Who-Runs-the-Farthest wanted to hold the banquet. Tom wondered if he really understood why he stayed with the whites. Could it be that his vow to help the Cheyenne was his true reason? Or were there other reasons, reasons he did not quite understand? He told himself to be honest. The command shocked him because his honesty had never been in question before. Suppose it was impossible for him or anyone else to lead the Cheyenne? If he failed, what happened then? In his mind Tom saw the black man's self-abnegating shuffle, that hooded, ashen face. The boy's muscles felt waterlogged, his arms and legs heavy as if their core had rotted soft. He forced two leg lifts. The shaman had promised that he'd journey toward the rising sun. How little that meant then. Now he had to trust that fulfillment waited for him in the East.

They knew the boat's routine so well that when the *Northwest Passage* cut its speed, they hurried to the sun deck. A moment later the captain appeared on the bridge. Hyde and the boy watched as a dingy swamp boat—no larger than a raft—drifted leisurely downstream; they stood at the rail as it pulled alongside. In it sat four men, all carrying rifles. Four men—rubber-booted to the thighs, drawn, lined men who looked like muddier versions of those who squatted in the dust outside every ranch along the Platte Trail. All wore the badge of U. S. Marshal.

The colonel gulped down his breath to whisper, "They're hunting runaways, boy."

The passengers held their places, the marshals moved by them like hunters on stalk. They worked as if they were alone—poking into cabins, scrutinizing the lower decks and the hold, each closet or cubby, even the smokestack. They had to be thorough, they couldn't show their fear, yet the slightest hint of arrogance could have sent the four of them over the side forever without a trace. They moved among the Northerners, these enforcers of the hated Fugitive Slave law; not a word was uttered except to serve their business. Those frozen in place on the upper deck could hear the trunks scraping, the crates being pried open, the muffled "I'll have to check in here." Always answered by "Yes," a reply without graciousness or invitation, always grudging yet apprised of the necessity that demanded it. Everyone seemed entranced—the tall thin man with his hand wrapped around an upright stay, the woman who twirled her rose parasol one way, then the other.

The firemen stoked slowly, the engine idled dreamily, content to hold the boat against the current.

The equipoise stretched through forty-five minutes of unhurried search. For the law still had its magic power then, and perhaps because all knew they sat on something that could be ignited by the smallest gesture, no man would presume to set it off. The spell did not break even when the four armed men climbed over the side and started back upstream. Only after they had disappeared into the swamp did the captain wave to the firemen for steam. He still stood on the bridge looking after the marshals when the colonel and Tom reached him.

"Does this happen every time?" the colonel asked this stubby, bristly man in the blue cap.

"Every time we go North," the captain responded dully, studying the view upstream.

"Is it always like this?" Hyde asked the question with such forceful professional interest that the captain snapped out of his mood. "It gets worse each time, Colonel. There have been a few incidents."

The colonel knew that one of these "incidents" involved the drowning of a federal marshal just south of Peoria. A congressional committee began an investigation, but no charges were ever brought. Whether a slave had been on board or not had not been determined. Hyde also knew that the boat was the *Passage*'s sister ship. But he said nothing else; the captain concluded: "Won't be much grumbling about the search, Colonel Hyde. You watch. Not even the loudmouths will talk about what they might have done."

Hyde had no free time for the boy during their two days in Chicago, for Stephen Douglas' executive secretary occupied the colonel's every waking instant with the chairman's schemes for the development of a mid-American empire. Hyde was supposed to be suitably impressed.

From Cairo, Illinois, they trained east. For three days Tom Hyde stayed awake in wide-eyed wonder. The train didn't move: it held still while the whole world was drawn flashing by him. The train click-clacked away like a giant racing clock; Tom learned to tell their speed by the intensity of the sound. Suddenly the train would burst into a town, raising flocks of chickens, making horses rear and children wave, slicing so close to the backs of houses that once the boy felt he could lift a teacup from a table.

East of Toledo the country had a more settled air. Nature had been ruled into rectangles here, cultivated fields lying end to end or side to side that ran over the contour of the hills and cut down into the valleys as if dealt out by a hand so skilled that it could carelessly let fall the arrangement it desired. In the old Northwest it seemed man and nature had made a pact. Man's hand was partner there, and the lines he drew with his ruler ran over a map of real ground. The earth seemed pleased with the arrangement and would mother and husband for him. The terms of the age-old fight had been changed. Tom Hyde found it impossible to quarrel with such accord.

New York seemed stupendous to the boy, a colossus, all noise and hectic motion, with its thousands of people, wagons, carriages maneuvering by each other, with those unexpected concentrations of colors and forms in all sizes and proportions—from churches and houses and office buildings shoved up against each other to the signs and letters on the storefronts visibly screaming for his attention. Ramshackle saloons stood next to marble palaces, exquisite shops; filthy oxen and horses paraded along with grand draft horses, riding horses, mules with tufted headgear. As they drove from the waterfront to their hotel he felt in two places at once—a poor, rundown town and the grandest city in the world. His eyes lost focus; exhilaration escalated to giddiness. He wanted the jumble and confusion to stop. Finally he sank back into the carriage seat, shut his eyes, and huddled where only the noise could reach him. Tom felt as bad as he had that first time Elizabeth played her piano. The colonel nodded knowingly at Bushnell, then laid a gentle hand on the boy's forehead. "Relax, Tom. You'll get used to it."

In New York they registered in a quiet hotel on a fashionable tree-shaded square. Hyde's original intention was to lodge Bushnell in a boardinghouse a dozen or so blocks away, but the colonel did not want to leave the boy alone in the suite in his unsettled condition. So he asked the manager, with whom he'd done business for many years, to allow Bushnell to remain with the boy until he returned. The manager looked absolutely unperturbed by the unusual request, but the colonel made it quite clear that Bushnell would not stay beyond suppertime.

The colonel was already overdue for his appointment with Horace Greeley, so upstairs he changed quickly. He parted with this admonition to the scout: "I don't want either of you to leave the suite. You are both confined to quarters until I get back."

Tom and Bushnell napped in the spacious green room with the labyrinthian ceiling trim and beds so large that Bushnell's feet tucked neatly under the covers. They woke up at four, and Tom immediately ran gallons of scalding water out of the nickel-plated faucet. The temperature in the suite's three rooms fluctuated as much as twenty degrees during the next few hours. Only occasionally did they work up the courage to look down from the windows, and then only when the one looking had hold of the other, and the other had a firm grip on the bed.

Hyde was late getting back, so it was dark when they started out on their walk. Hyde intended to familiarize the boy with New York a little at a time. They walked until they reached Broadway, where they had to wait for several minutes.

Tom watched the carriages rush by, their swinging lights fanning shadows like ink blots across the large dark volumes. He caught glimpses of fleeting profiles, heard the rhythmic clip of horses' hooves, creaking springs, grunts and shouts of the men on top and, always, those high thin-spoked wheels rolling over and over.

The traffic continued unbroken. Hyde realized there was no point in standing there waiting, since any route would do. But as he reached for Tom's arm, the boy stepped out into the street. Suddenly his boot caught on the hump of a greasy cobblestone. His leg kicked out to one side, splaying like a deer's on frozen ground. He ran forward, desperately trying to place his feet under him, but his boots could not comprehend the cobble or those rough spacings between the stones, and he continued to stumble.

Hyde and Bushnell stood transfixed. A coach whipped by just behind Tom. Another coach rushed by, then from the other direction a large black carriage bore down on him. The boy stopped in his tracks and turned blankly toward the sound. The driver braked and viciously whipped the head of his lead horse, and the carriage veered to the side just in time.

The older men tore into the street, Hyde to the driver, Bushnell to the boy. "I'm sorry, terribly sorry," the colonel shouted through the traffic. "Thank god, you missed him."

The driver's wind-red stubbled face seethed. Hyde could see his brake foot trembling. He shook his fist as he shouted, "Goddamn that wild kid. I could've run him down. I would've been liable. They take away your license!"

"I'm sorry, terribly sorry," the colonel apologized, gripping the carriage boot and turning a concerned face up to the man. "The boy isn't used to cities."

"So you let him run in front of me?" Hyde feared for the driver, whose face was blood color, his foot now pumping wildly on the brake stick.

Meanwhile, Bushnell had worked his way forward and taken hold of the bridle of the leadside horse; he had Tom firmly by the arm, standing in the eddy of the two large animals.

"Hey, get your hands off my horse, you long-haired son of a bitch. I almost ripped my Daisy's mouth out!"

The colonel apologized again and made his way around to Bushnell. In spite of the driver's curses and threats that he'd strangle, stomp, and throttle the scout, Bushnell kept the horse's bridle in hand until the avenue was clear, then quickly ferried Tom back to the sidewalk. The driver shook his whip and poured filthier curses after them, but they didn't listen. They led Tom back to the hotel like a sleepwalker.

One day, to the relief of a handsome woman caught in her brougham and to the cheers of onlookers, Bushnell stopped a runaway horse. The next day they loped behind the fire brigade down the narrow lanes of lower Manhattan where ship masts seemed to shoot up out of the streets and riggings reticulated the sky like branches. They ran past shot towers and churches until they reached Coenties Slip, where spectators milled around and cheered when the second floor of the coffee warehouse caught fire.

That afternoon an anxious-looking, well-dressed man approached them. His mother lay desperately ill in Philadelphia, he explained; he despised the situation he found himself in, but he had just been robbed and left penniless. He lived on Long Island, in Stony Point, in fact, and had to have fifteen dollars for the train trip. Bushnell, who located six dollars in his pocket, gave the man four dollars. The grief-stricken fellow blessed and thanked the scout profusely, then elaborately transcribed the address of Bushnell's boardinghouse and handed the scout a card with his Stony Point address, "in case of any mix-up in the mails." A draft for the exact amount would be sent as soon as he reached Philadelphia.

Two days later they spotted the same anxious-looking fellow pouring out his heart to an elderly gentleman. This time, they soon learned, the man's father faced imminent death in Wilmington.

Bushnell interrupted the woebeset fellow, "Pleased t' hear your dear old ma's improved."

"How dare you accost me. Come one step closer and I'll call the police."

Bushnell grabbed Tom's arm and hustled him off down the street. They turned the corner, the scout said, "Run!" and they dashed down the crowded sidewalk on into the street, dodging people and dogs and horses and not a few pigs. After a block Tom yelled, "Bush, what are we running for?"

Bushnell stopped. "Don't know." They broke out laughing. Passersby looked curiously at the man with the greasy yellow hair and the Indian boy dissolving in laughter in the gutter near the corner of Bowery and Spring streets.

They had less humorous moments. The streetwalkers affected and disturbed Tom Hyde, especially those girls who looked his age. In the poorer section of town they stalked everywhere, exposing their ankles and wiggling their asses, and leering, winking, and pouting. Tom added the streetwalkers to his list of white man's strange practices: women for sale, blacks sold into slavery. How different these women were from the girls he had known. Under their dresses every unmarried Cheyenne girl wore a braided thong, its plainly visible lines running over the thighs and joining at the waist. Once, after a narrow escape from a white-skinned dark-eyed girl from Cork, Bushnell sighed, "Ain' a chastity belt in all o' New York. Not in this part o' town anyway."

One afternoon, as they sat in a dim, low-ceilinged oyster cellar, the big man to their right muttered, "When they start letting Indians in here?"

"Mind your tongue," Bushnell suggested.

"Another word, hick, and I'll slice your tongue off and hand it back to you."

"Might be healthier if yo' shut your own face, hoss."

The man spun on his stool and slowly, his fingers working with exaggerated deliberateness, he pulled out a knife.

Bushnell slid to the floor, took a long step toward the man, and delivered a short rising kick to the knife hand. As the hand shot up, Bushnell slipped under that hand, trapped the man's arm under his armpit, and levered the offending arm down over his own wrist. The knife clattered to the floor. "I'll snap this goddamn thing off if yo' don't 'pologize to my friend here."

In great pain the man slurred, "Sorry, mate. 'Pologize."

After the bartender escorted the man out, he offered the scout a drink on the house. Bushnell kept the knife. Tom told the scout he hadn't seen such a graceful movement since Man-Who-Runs-the-Farthest killed the sentry.

The parade along Broadway was more elegantly attired and less casually visited than that of the Bowery. A certain physical and spiritual dressing up was required. In a way, Tom felt more familiar with the upper world than the other, but he had never seen it function as a whole before. Its smoothness and force surprised him. People of that world shared a sense of obligation to its power, and they communicated with the invisible source of power in visible ways. Stakes ran high here; mistakes could not be afforded, so considerably more had to be agreed upon. These agreements took shape through a range of cues, a secret gestural language which the boy found enticing and curiously accessible. The colonel and Elizabeth's conduct had prepared him well: He saw the proper way to greet, how to take an arm, excuse himself; he observed the correct carriage, the handling of hat and gloves. And, not surprisingly, he absorbed their manners as unselfconsciously as he did their speech. He felt neither superiority nor cynicism in this. He loved to satisfy the demands of form; it struck him no different from an exercise of Buck's Heart's. At the same time he did enjoy that air of knowing style that dominated their hotels, and the mounded creamy delicacies of Taylor's exquisite pastry shoppe, and the twelve enormous plate-glass windows of A. T. Stewart's "marble palace" department store, where the wealth of the world lay arrayed for all to see just beyond their fingertips. He observed how their atmosphere appropriated public places—so Broadway became their promenade between two and five in the afternoon; Third Avenue uptown north of Astor Place was reserved for their racing horses; and the Croton Reservoir on outlying Forty-first Street functioned as their exclusive pleasure ground.

At this stage of Thomas Hyde's development, his enthusiasms tended to overpower his powers of discrimination. He might have been interested in making firmer distinctions between the elevated and the workaday worlds if he had been able to spend more time with the colonel, or if his education had been further advanced. Or if the higher order had been more accommodating to Bushnell, instead of raising such highly arched eyebrows at the scout that Bushnell found it difficult to enter the lobby of Tom's hotel. He would wait for the boy outside in a quiet corner of the street, not daring to enter the park. After two trying days, he retreated to his quarters, and the boy began to pick him up instead. Tom, who had learned some of the rules of polite behavior but few of the reasons for them, thought the whole business unnecessary. But he felt enough pressure to insist to himself that his own attitudes would never change. That made Tom quite a heroic figure to himself.

Even before Tom Hyde became a regular visitor to the brick mansion on Nineteenth Street, Mr. Horace Greeley, editor of the New

York *Tribune*, loomed as the most prominent personality in the higher social world. Ever since Tom could remember, Hyde had instructed him in the game of separating what the editor really meant from what the editor said. A fascinating exercise, and Tom was continually amazed that Greeley could literally speak two ways at the same time.

When for the first time Tom and the colonel entered the smoke-filled drawing room, a white-haired gentleman rose from the far end of a large table. The perfect image of the kindly old man, full-faced and rubicund, he was dressed in a plush frock coat cut rather long. A short but perfectly even fringe of beard outlined the lower half of his face. Heartily he shook the colonel's hand, then turned to his companions to say, "Hyde's come East while others head West. There might be something to it." Though he spoke quietly, his voice seemed used to addressing thousands.

The men at the table laughed. The colonel glanced back at Greeley, then to the table. "To be perfectly frank, gentlemen," he said with the same lightness, "it's easier to book coming this way." The table laughed exactly as loud as before, as though they had a device for calibrating sound.

Only Tom did not laugh. Never before had he heard Hyde called anything but "sir" or "Colonel" except by Elizabeth.

Horace Greeley was a clever man, not one to miss an occasion. "And this is your boy," he said graciously, sticking out his hand for Tom to shake. "I observe he's fiercely loyal to you, Colonel." Greeley smiled. "That's a fine principle. Excellent principle."

The speech sounded charming, the tone pleasant. Tom disliked Greeley immediately, disliked and feared him. Yet the moment he recognized this dislike, the boy felt certain the editor knew it, too. Greeley never altered his tone. "Will you excuse me, Colonel?" Then, "Excuse me, gentlemen." The same glance somehow covered the colonel and the men at the table, yet he did not appear to hurry. The editor gently laid a hand on Tom's shoulder blade and ferried him through a door into the next room, which was solid with books—books on all four walls from floor to fourteen-foot ceiling.

"You like it," Greeley said as presciently as before. The editor seemed gratified. "Here are the newspapers. I understand you've read a few of them." He drew out a thick bound volume of *Tribunes* labeled "1854 Jan-June." Next to it, from right to left, old *Tribunes* jumped back through time in six-month leaps. Greeley explained the library's organization and asked Tom to consider it his own while in New York. He extended borrowing privileges to the boy, saying simply, "Private libraries are greatly underused." He withdrew only after excusing himself with the same apparent ease and absence of hurry. Yet Greeley slipped away before the boy knew it; a copy of *Ivanhoe* had lodged itself in his hand.

While Tom read sometimes Hyde's voice would reach him, sometimes that of the editor. He had been in the study for an hour when the voices in the other room grew louder. He had just ordered himself not to listen when he heard a gentle knock on the door. He waited, the knock came again. So Tom said, "Please come in."

A man dressed in black entered carrying a silver tray on which there was a silver dish. A silver spoon sat beside it on a linen napkin.

"Ice, sir?"

As it was offered, Tom accepted it. The man behaved as though he, Tom, were a caliph's son, arranging the drapes (though the light seemed fine to Tom), offering to fetch another volume down from the shelves. "If you want anything, just ring, Master Hyde." He indicated the gray velvet cord, made a modest bow, and back-pedaled out of the room.

Tom Hyde had never seen men behave like that toward each other, especially in their own homes—it was worse than the hotel in Chicago with all those porters and messenger boys bowing to the guests, to Bushnell, to him. He didn't like being waited on by a man older than himself. The fussy ceremony of the drapes unsettled him—Tom got so lost in these thoughts that the chips of strawberry were thawing when he tasted the ice cream. It melted in his mouth, releasing the tangy sweetness into the cream; he ate greedily, trying to catch each plump half-frozen strawberry before it melted completely.

Later, in the midst of the second tournament at Ashby-de-la-Zouche, just as "Desdichado" meets Brian de Bois-Guilbert, he distinctly heard Greeley shout, "Surely you're joking, Hyde!" The colonel replied—he could hear Hyde's voice but not make sense of the words. He spent the rest of the afternoon in the chair, in the position of someone reading a book. He tried to decipher those voices from the next room, but could only catch fleeting, isolated words. He kept thinking, "Mr. Greeley shouted at the colonel! Actually shouted!" Finally he heard a bell ring, chairs shift, then he thought Greeley bade his guests farewell. A door shut, steps approached the library, and Hyde and Greeley entered like the best of friends. Tom couldn't hide his surprise.

"I see the time's been well spent." The editor spoke with such confident geniality he didn't sound smug. Though Greeley looked at the book, Tom knew he was being examined. He nodded dumbly.

The older men parted congenially after Greeley extracted a promise from Hyde to return the next afternoon at two. "You come too, Tom. If you want to."

Their coach ride passed in silence. The boy would have liked to commiserate with the colonel, but he had enough sense to restrain himself. He felt genuinely upset and concerned for Hyde. And another thought plagued him: he realized, for the very first time, that Hyde was not the most powerful man in the world.

The struggle for Hyde's political soul grew hotter. He kept in daily communication with Washington, both with Coughlin and Stephen Douglas' offices. He also paid his respects to Greeley every afternoon. On Nineteenth Street he joined in days of reasoned compromise, days where "mutual interest" sounded the keynote. Some days Greeley bullied him to join the Republican party: "Your scruple about party loyalty is archaic. Holding out isn't virtue, Hyde, it's obtuse individualism." But the editor never bullied too much. Which confirmed Hyde's estimate of how much big eastern money banked on Laramie in the transcontinental railroad race; their sense of his effectiveness in pacifying the Indians; their faith in the importance of western Nebraska to the nation's growth. Hyde also privately admitted that the Republican program offered many desirables: They would actively encourage river and harbor legislation, which would develop the West's interior; they would raise the tariff to protect the farm markets of the old Northwest, and the manufacturers of the East. While the Democrats, to hold their southern wing, would do none of this and had, in fact, blocked all pro-northern and pro-western legislation, clearly impeding progress and growth. Hyde had one supreme objection to, indeed a terror of, the Republicans. As he put it to Greeley just after the editor bruited, "The Republicans will get the country moving." Hyde: "Yes, to war."

That remained the sticking point, his sufficient objection; but something less obvious also informed the colonel's resistance. Hyde did not approve of the Republicans' "new democracy." He believed that politics should be conducted by reasonable men reasoning together, in the spirit of the founding fathers, in the manner that Jefferson had articulated. The Republicans bade for a new audience; they stooped to rabble-rousing, to exciting the expectations of artisans and farmers and workers and those hordes of city dwellers. They created unreason and misrule with their mob scenes, then labeled them—as they had in Kansas—democracy. All of this stirred a dark subterranean corner of Hyde's gentlemanly soul. Which led Hyde to fear that in this matter of party, emotion might triumph over reason and policy and self-interest.

Near the end of their New York visit Tom smelled something that translated as fear coming from the colonel. By then Hyde was juggling so many things at once that even as he juggled it occurred to him he might not be able to keep them all in the air. Tom took it as a bad sign that Hyde kept nicking his neck while shaving. That raw patch above his Adam's apple declared his uncertainty, and Tom wanted to cover up the badge so that no one else could see it. Another complication: to learn more about Hyde's dilemma, to help support him, the boy asked more than the right number of questions. At other times, in more expansive moods, the colonel would have patiently explained. But Hyde was too unsettled to be the patient pedagogue. Tom became a little abrasive to his mentor.

They began to have taxing arguments about servants, around whom Tom could not relax and with whom the colonel insisted he must be completely at ease and "Turn ease into a command." A few years later Tom might have argued with the colonel's "Watch me," or said such luxury corrupted, or no man could be good enough to be another's master. But he certainly couldn't say it then. He just kept repeating, "Servants make me nervous."

New York was overwhelming, spectacular, New York was as artificial and affecting as the theatre where they sat and watched the greatest actor of the day declaim the virtues of freedom as he stood half-dressed in front of a giant flat of the Roman Forum.

Tom sat spellbound through the play about a slave revolt led by Spartacus, in which the weighty might of imperial Rome towered over the weak but earnest gathering of slaves. The audience followed the underdogs' struggle as though their own freedom were at stake. When the actor announced he would make Rome howl for its denial of human liberty, the freedom-loving leaders of New York, seated in their boxes in the gracious half dark of the Broadway Theatre, fiercely howled their approval. Every instant he occupied the stage Spartacus kept a fierce grip on their attention. The audience became just another one of his regiments, whipped into shape by his commanding, bullying, elevating, insisting on his right and power and obligation to lead. Spartacus, who hurled himself around with fiendish energy, Spartacus springing up the mast of the galley or the steps of the pilastered Forum, bursting his chains and single-handedly fighting off the legions while he declaimed nonstop and resonantly in blank verse. It was an extraordinary pitch to maintain, but he did it.

After the curtain dropped and flew back up a dozen times, and the thunderous hands finally wearied, the editor led the colonel and Tom backstage. The spectacle and the fine sentiment still roused Tom as they walked through a world of one-dimensional castles, city streets, and country fields, past a rack of headless knights, kings, soldiers, and beggars, down a narrow staircase, and threaded a long corridor before stopping at a door decorated with a single gold star. Under the star in gold letters:

NEVIL WOODS

TRAGEDIAN

Woods sat at his dressing table, so Tom's first glimpse showed the actor with three heads. Each of these appeared too large for his three torsos, but each sat on the thickest neck Tom had ever seen. Woods had a theatrical face not meant for close-up. His makeup had just come off so his skin looked like a baby's, which set off his eyebrows. Or rather eyebrow, since it spread uninterrupted between both eyes, pitch black, thick, and tangled, like a narrow fur pelt. His eyebrow matched his hair and that patch of whisker he had grown just under his lower lip to make him look more fierce. The cropped hair had been waxed so that it stood up in a row as sharp as a palisade. Even in repose he conveyed an air of ferocious energy.

The actor came directly to the editor, taking his hand warmly between his own. Woods had giant hands; the veins jumped out as he tensed them slightly. "Good evening. Good evening."

The tragedian's voice originated from the base of the diaphragm, modulated through the sounding board of his chest, then moved to the region where tones were rounded, clipped, or made tensile. He could control his tone with the ease and precision of a musician tuning.

"Remarkable performance tonight. Simply remarkable, Nevil." Woods cocked his head to acknowledge the compliment.

If the editor's voice sounded a whit less dramatic than the actor's, it was more democratic. Not an artificial overtone infected this perfect organ of the people.

Hyde had disliked the play, found Woods' performance unregenerate bombast, and was no more impressed with the little show they were enacting. He remained gentleman enough to restrain himself, but just barely.

"This is my good friend Colonel Benjamin Hyde." Hyde shook hands with the giant-headed actor. "How do you do?"

"And his charge, Thomas Hyde." The boy had never felt such a powerful grip, even among the Cheyenne.

"It's such an extraordinarily moving play, Nevil," Greeley said. "Does it always get this reception?"

The actor said "Yes" with princely assurance. "I mean when I'm at my best it does. I've never *had* anything that's as well suited for me." He spoke a phrase, and suddenly Tom felt the actor stood on the stage, the giant Forum behind him. "There's a new relation with my audience—for me as well as for them. It's something I've never *felt* before, not even with Lear. Lear, that's of another world. It's between me and that magnificent old man. I *become him;* the more I *am* him the greater it is. But the audience isn't there in the same way because it's too majestic. I could play it alone. Here they're *with* me when I howl. At that moment I *become* the *voice* of an entire people's wish for freedom."

In the style, Woods was an accomplished actor. He worked hard at his trade and observed carefully. He didn't address his next question to Greeley or Hyde, but to Tom. "Did you enjoy the performance?"

Tom beamed: "I howled louder than everyone else."

The actor laughed his fullest basso, the editor laughed as if to say, "What a prodigy," and even the colonel shook off his mood and joined in. Tom's enthusiasm set the tone for the evening. While Woods' valet dressed him behind a gold oriental screen figured with long-legged storks, they chatted amiably. Then they went out to dine at Greeley's club. Tom felt quite adult that night and listened spellbound to the actor's tales of the stage. He felt unusually at ease with the editor. Tom's buoyancy carried him halfway through the carriage ride home. As they turned on to Broadway the colonel spotted a hoarding advertising *Spartacus.* "Well, it's good that freedom still packs them in." He touched the boy softly on the shoulder, straightened the creases in his trousers so they fell over the middle of the knee, then settled back into the abstracted mood that had overtaken him on leaving the club.

Two days after Tom's theatrical debut, Hyde and Tom made their farewell calls on the New York magnates, and they climaxed that duty by driving to the editor's mansion. Greeley came out as their carriage scraped the curb. Their good-byes were civil, if not truly friendly. The editor seemed to direct his remarks to Tom. "It takes a strong and willful man to bid me wait after my fires are lit. The colonel's one of the few who can resist my eloquence." Hyde looked vaguely bemused, as if interested only in fulfilling the demands of courtesy. He volunteered little until Greeley claimed, "He gives me reasons when we must have action." Hyde came back quickly: "It's just at these moments that we must have reasons." He spoke as if he had made the point before. Greeley spoke, again to Tom, "You see!" His open palms emptied the air of Hyde's objections. Then Greeley delivered a short editorial to the boy:

"Hyde calls me preacher and showman, which I've always taken to be the same in any case. I tell him he will be left unavoidably behind if he does not affiliate with our new cause. I show him a progressive alliance of business and idealism; I tell him: Make slavery the issue and morality will follow. But your guardian will not, he cannot hear. Perhaps you can reason with him, for you seem to see clearly for one so young."

Greeley's manner couldn't have been more gracious. Greeley had asked Tom to side with him: the boy wondered why he too had been thrust into the intricate maze of conflicting loyalties. Hyde became rigidly formal, a sure sign he was furious. They said good-bye, Greeley pretending he had been abused. Hyde did not turn back to wave as they passed out of the ornamental gates.

THE NATION'S CAPITAL

AT THE FERRY'S RAILING the colonel, Tom, and Bushnell watched the shot towers and the spires rise out of the rows of houses, factories, and warehouses. Slowly the largest buildings lost their features; landmarks submerged or flattened themselves into the pattern until the lower end of Manhattan Island became a screen of contrasted reds and browns, overlaid textures, interrupted geometries. The scene grew flatter and more abstract, and the changing composition might have held the three of them together at the rail if Tom hadn't said, "Even from here, it's frightening." Something in his tone suggested the colonel might agree and made Hyde impatient. The colonel moved away; they were off to another bad start.

A train waited for them on the other side, and they rode it to the crossing of the Delaware. On the way they ate and talked and looked at the sights, which the colonel described with vengeful particularity. Tom would've been happier with all the details of the tour if only the colonel's tone had been warmer. But the guidebook excessiveness made the lecture seem a duty, which hurt the boy. He had never felt like a burden before.

As they approached the Maryland border, Hyde began to tell Tom once again of the evolution of slavery, which led to the Compromise on North/South boundaries and culminated in the dispute over the location of the nation's capital—timed for their arrival in the District. Meanwhile, Tom prepared to ask the question that had been in and out of his mind since they left New York a day and a half before.

"Why did you pretend to be so friendly with Mr. Greeley?" Mentally he drew back, waiting for the rebuff.

The colonel answered with muted, annoyed fatigue: "It helps us believe we want the same thing." Tom's question was crude: it suggested how little the boy understood and, though the colonel knew Tom couldn't be blamed for his ignorance, Hyde felt no desire to explain the complexities of politics or to justify his own actions. He could feel the boy waiting tensely. "The price of parenthood," he thought, "having to explain what you don't want to explain."

"You can't reduce such complex questions to likes or dislikes. Personalities are only one more factor to be considered. Have you ever asked yourself why Mr. Greeley put you in the library?" Tom had not asked himself. "Is there any reason why he would want you to hear what went on in the conference room?" He let the boy consider a moment. "There are many holes in your education. That can't be helped. I've brought you along quickly. But sometimes I feel like I'm plugging up a leaky dam, and I don't enjoy the feeling. You'll have to take some things on faith, boy—like believing how important tone is. It's what lets the world go on for us."

Having said that, Hyde softened. "I'm tough on you because I expect a great deal. Everything, in fact. But don't worry. We'll fill in the blanks." Tom had not heard such a pleasant speech since they had arrived in New York.

Late that afternoon they reached the nation's capital, "The City of Magnificent Distances." Washington's official parlance tended toward overstatement. Distances dominated, to be sure, but the great avenues led nowhere, terminating in nothing. Views existed, but their tendency was to be more potential than actual—muddy tracks encroached upon by tubercular looking grass, past unpromising sandlots, swamps, and irrigation ditches. Nothing was finished—the Capitol dome lay open to the sky, a fretwork of metal joists, the Senate and House wings remained besieged by scaffolding; Washington's Monument was rising slowly; the Mall functioned as a drainage ditch. Plantings had begun—the flowering chestnuts, privet and hedge, cherry and apple and azalea; but everything was drawn up at the same height, as if a congressional edict had started all nature at the same instant. Here and there a great building—the Smithsonian Institution, the White House, the Capitol itself—stood alone like an impassioned senator rehearsing for an audience that hadn't yet materialized. The entire city resounded with empty rhetoric. All public buildings had the proper thoughts inscribed on their pediments, properly intimidating columns lined the porticoes and properly ponderous statuary filled every available niche or public square or circle. The city constantly mounted gestures–opened with great invocations, closed with thundering finalities. But it lacked a middle. There seemed to be few homes, few shops, few inhabited blocks. Mere people living their lives appeared to be hard to find in the capital. The city languished; public men took that as their cue. The utterances grew louder and more insistent in order to disguise the absence of constituents.

The only section willing to admit human needs was known, familiarly enough, as George Town. Tom and the colonel headed there after depositing Bushnell at a boardinghouse at the edge of the slave quarter.

They had entered the quarter through a crude wooden gate whose crossbar balanced uneasily in the crotch of two bald locust trees. A mud track wound between two ragged lines of hovels. All the trees near these hovels had been cut down or girdled, so the gardens grew rotting stumps and scattered root systems along with high straggly grass, weeds, and mud. The track had thick logs beaten down into it, which made their passage jarring and slow. The driver soon stopped to shoo a swarm of black children out of their path.

Neither Elizabeth's lectures, nor Tom's initial exposures to slavery had prepared him for such squalor and unrelieved wretchedness. The abolitionist alphabet Elizabeth had taught him tripped on in his mind:

B is a Brother with a skin
Of somewhat darker hue,
C is the Cottonfield to which
This injured brother's driven.

The carriage bucked and humped over the ruts. The third tarpaper shack had a number 8 scrawled in childlike hand to the right of its doorless entrance. "Someone can write." Hyde shook his head stiffly; the neck seemed to want oil.

Other dubious symbols of status marked their route–a white picket fence accordioned on its side; a rusty cart with a missing wheel; a barrow set like a planter in front of a cabin, a black child trying to ride it as he would a listless pony. Women milled about, colored bandanas piled turbanlike on their heads. A sooty woman wore her skirts reefed up over her thighs with a bit of rope; one coal-black girl had a strawberry inkle which dived down over her shoulder into her loose gray cotton dress. Black children peered at the carriage–toddlers and a few sleek young people about Tom's age, also bad-teethed stringy children, two with grotesquely bloated bellies. Runty pigs foraged in the road; pigs rooted in patchy gardens, wore sharp paths through the grass alongside the open sewage ditch. The air had been fried in cheap cooking fat until it turned rancid, sticky sweet; it coated everything. Tom wanted to wipe his arms on the upholstery.

"Providence put the servants in our care," muttered Hyde. A half-dressed woman leaned her considerable charms out of a window, eyeing the opulent carriage with pleasurable intentions for its occupants. "Massa," she called, "massa, me wish you come in 'ere."

B is a Brother with a skin
Of somewhat darker hue.

The abolitionist verse drummed in Tom Hyde's head. He saw Topsy toeing the ice floe in that illustration from *Uncle Tom's Cabin*, saw that black-moth servant handing the southern lady a pear. The self-denying gait of that black man on the Missouri steamer, that steep tightrope walk of the slaves at the Missouri landing, their mournful wail, this intolerable place—slavery took on form for him now. Tom could see the curse leeching the ground, sapping the energy of this fetid, clammy hell. Most of the cabins, log or tarpaper, were barely twelve feet square, few had windows, and none had doors except for the whore's home, where a sliding shutter assured privacy. Everyone's clothing looked worn out, too big or too small. Their tools, their patched houses, even the fabric next to their skin were white people's castaways. The Negroes lived off the rejects of their masters. All of Elizabeth's training could not prepare Tom for how much he hated it, for how much it terrified him.

"What a spot for democracy's capital, aye? A swamp in slave country, worse than a dungheap. It's a judgment on us, boy," the colonel insisted. Hyde, who had difficulty breathing through his nose in the thick stench, let his jaw hang open. Tom couldn't stand seeing him look so ugly.

The Negroes paraded naked, inescapable reminders of the white man's power to bring men low. Tom wondered if their thoughts no longer had the right paths to follow, if their masters had erased the part of the black man's mind that dealt with volition. Elizabeth's Bible had taught Tom about will. He was startled to see it totally obliterated. These people had lost even the surly underhanded guilt of the post Indians—they seemed total slaves.

George Town brought a devoutly wished-for relief. While the slave quarter pressed its horrendous, terrifying message and the capital raised noisy claims about democracy, the bricks of the heights spoke calmly of domestic order, warmth, and intimacy. It placed the personal in the center, where the mind could contract down to its size again, the eyes take in the proportional agreement between door, window, and wall.

They stopped in front of a freestanding brick building, whose only assertiveness spoke through modest refinements of its trim and the high polish of its brass. A stark white face appeared at an upstairs window, peered down imperiously and nodded. The colonel, on the streetside, did not see the face. Tom did and graciously returned the nod. The face withdrew; a second later a giant man burst into the doorway, seemed to shake off the house, and came charging down the walk. Hyde leaped down. They met at the sidewalk, just under Tom's window. Coughlin was fair, with sandy red hair, broad features, and a solid body. His face kept opening into a larger smile.

"Hello, Ben," Coughlin said, pumping his friend's hand, his eyes pouring over Hyde's face. "I've been waiting a long time."

"Me too," said Hyde with surprising simplicity.

After quick introductions, they walked inside. Coughlin kept up a running narrative: "Dorothea's out doing good somewhere. A committee or something. It's not like we've been expecting you two. Dorothea's been making up the guest rooms and arranging meal schedules with such vengeance that cook says you'll get nothing but hardtack from her. Mrs. Hastings has been peering out of her window for the last week while I–" Coughlin colored, "–I've been the only cool head in the house.

"There are letters from Elizabeth for you and Tom. Some whiskey, I know. But is it cakes? Or something a bit more substantial?"

"I'm starved," said Hyde, patting his stomach and breaking into a broad grin of excitement and relief.

"Good. Tom must be hungry too." A hovering servant carried the message to the kitchen. "Come upstairs now."

The colonel knew the usages of the house well enough to spare his host further explanation. At the landing Coughlin turned and looked at the colonel to assure himself that his friend actually climbed the stairs behind him.

Upstairs they entered a cluttered sitting room divided into four recognizable aisles. Everything–pictures, curios, diaries, papers, books–lay scattered around on tabletops, which gave the room a curiously horizontal orientation. This unique arrangement reflected the dictates of the powdered face Tom spotted at the window, Mrs. Hastings, mother of Coughlin's wife. A strange visage she was—her cracked pip of a head mounted on a bean-pole neck, the line of white powder visible just above the high neck of her dress. She sat in a wheelchair. Eight years earlier—two years after her husband's death—she had ordered it. The day it arrived she sat down in the chair. From then on she lived her life almost entirely in a plane between three and four feet from the floor.

The colonel walked up to Mrs. Hastings and planted a kiss on each of her painted cheeks, which she offered him by turning her head first to the right, then to the left with as much interest as a pendulum. "It's been a very long time, Benjamin," she said in a surprisingly crisp voice. The bony hands resting on the chair looked gray and lusterless, suggesting the skin color under the white dusting.

"Far too long. You know how I've missed you."

"Tell us about Elizabeth and your trip. We just had a letter from her telling us how pleased you were to be coming East."

"Of course, of course."

All this time, Tom remained standing, totally ignored. Only when the colonel settled himself to tell about their journey did she beckon the boy to her and extend the final joint of her first two fingers. Tom shook them. Then she eased her chair toward the cloud made by their cigar smoke, as if she wanted to plant her head in their exhalations. Which, indeed, she did, for it reminded her of her late husband.

The colonel sketched their cross-country tour quickly, pausing in Chicago to comment on its growth and impressive commercial potential. In New York he got down to cases, "You might say they wooed me in Manhattan, though not entirely with a silken hand. The message wasn't new—the Democrats have sold out their traditional alliances, extended slavery to the territories, and so forth. On the other hand, the Republicans are the party of progress, 'the reforming spirit of the decade.' "

Mrs. Hastings positively cackled. "The reforming spirit—what's that mean now? New England cotton spinners and Pennsylvania coal and iron men, New York bankers and real estate. That's rich." Tom thought he heard her teeth clack.

"Once they disposed of the Democrats, next came the inducements. Which, let it be said, were not small potatoes, friends. Finally, the lesson in realism. They gave me a detailed account of how many convention votes are presently stuffed in their pockets, which disaffected Democrats of our acquaintance are at what stage of disaffection, and what Greeley's editorial schedule and those 'accounts from the scene of

Bleeding Kansas' will look like for the next six months." Hyde paused. Tom felt grateful for the pause. Their conversation was going by too fast.

"But hold on, you haven't heard the clincher. Greeley's sure they'll poll between a million and a million and one-half votes in the '56 presidential. Can you imagine any new party getting more than two hundred thousand?"

Mrs. Hastings' low whistle broke the stunned silence. "Are these votes of Greeley's 'moral approval' or the invisible hand of history?" She laughed hard enough to make her chair skitter beneath her. Tom thought it an impressive trick, but found it harder to return Mrs. Hastings' gaze than to sneak glances at her. He somehow knew her approval mattered. But was he supposed to smile, be serious, or pretend not to be there? She looked so odd, the room smelled so stale, like dead skin and old cigars.

"Greeley said, 'A prospering, cooperative industrial system will doom slavery!' True enough. But what I don't like—"

"What you don't like," anticipated Coughlin, "is that it's just too bloody convenient."

"How well they know each other," the boy remarked to himself. In profile Coughlin's face looked slightly flat, with a hint of concavity at the base of the jaw. His smile exposed two eyeteeth set a bit sideways in an otherwise perfect row.

The tap of a servant at the sitting-room door interrupted them. Their meal came garnished with a note from Stephen Douglas welcoming the colonel to Washington and asking for his testimony the next morning. After the servant departed, Hyde declared, "I wish my intelligence moved that quickly." No one smiled.

The boy was beginning to appreciate how difficult New York had been for Hyde. Not just the political pressures, the overbearing intricacies, which truly escaped the boy. The colonel had been lonely since they left Laramie. The loneliness exhausted him as much as the weeks of maneuvering. Now, tired as he was, Hyde looked more alert than he had in weeks. He had a constitutional need for these people; he relaxed into their intelligence. Tom Hyde vowed that, someday, he too would afford such aid and comfort to the colonel.

Along with her meal, Mrs. Hastings kept pursuing thoughts that had occupied her, on and off, for a long time. Coughlin and Hyde, both familiar with the process, left her alone.

"Greeley's too smart for himself," Mrs. Hastings barked out, brandishing a slice of cucumber at the end of her fork. But an ingredient eluded her; dissatisfied, she withdrew again to improve the recipe.

Her comment stirred a drowsy thought in Hyde. "On the night we went to the theatre to see Woods play Spartacus, they put on a little after-the-acts benefit for my young ward."

Mrs. Hastings eyed the boy intently. His mind worked hard as he felt her gaze: he remembered how impressed he had been with Woods, how he howled for his freedom, and then the colonel's mood in the coach afterward.

Coughlin winced. "They have no taste."

Hyde answered, "It did annoy me, I admit." He smiled just a bit stiffly at Tom as if to ask, "You understand more now?"

Mrs. Hastings chased her thought. Suddenly she had it. "Greeley's not really absorbed by politics. It's not politics to use a boy like that. Something else moves our editor. Politics is about as close as he can get."

"God help us if he took it more seriously."

She cackled less at the rejoinder than in appreciation of her own idea.

"Mother," said Coughlin, altering his tone, "we're going to have to excuse ourselves to get to work on some very dull details."

"Yes, yes," she said impatiently, obviously annoyed at being left out. "Have the boy shown to his room. He'll want to rest." It was a command. After the ceremony of kissing her cheeks and cold fingertips for Tom, the men went downstairs to Coughlin's study and the boy was led to his room.

Tom passed the afternoon in exile, putting his clothing into the wardrobe, organizing his desk for study, pondering. Thinking about Greeley made him furious. Yet Tom felt a certain fascination with his own negative power: In this world, so crisscrossed by conflicting allegiances, even he, so totally insignificant, had been turned into a weapon by the editor. Since he had been fooled, Tom felt vulnerable and anxious to apologize to the colonel for what he hadn't understood. His head swam with the complexities of personal and national politics.

At table that evening he met Mrs. Coughlin. She was beautiful, her face a fine oval tracery of bone covered with the palest, softest skin, almost irresistible to touch. Her nose was long and straight, her forehead high, the mouth had a shy succulent fullness. She wore a dress of soft wide stripes, jet and orange and gray, and her arms moved in and out of a gray veiling which reminded Tom of a mist. She seemed only tentatively present in the dim white sea that spread out from her—the spotless damask serviettes, the discreet glints of silverware, the sheen of crystal, those silver stalks supporting white tapers. Fascinated by this fairy-tale beauty, Tom could not take his eyes off her and completely missed Mrs. Hastings' disapproving scowls.

Coughlin and Hyde talked expansively about their West Point days, their travels and campaigns. They edited out the good parts—no gore, no politics, nothing controversial, which left the two men skating on the thin narrative ice of whether they had been reunited in Monterey in May or June of '47. Social anecdote was too brittle for the boy, with too many actors whom Tom didn't know. Curiously enough, Mrs. Hastings joined in the empty chatter and offered none of her unique brand of political notation. Mrs. Coughlin interjected periodic bursts of laughter, often unrelated to what was said.

"There's been a remarkable change since you last came East." Dorothea's voice sounded light and hollow; it might've come from an empty shell.

Hyde's smile offered a brotherly embrace. "There've been great changes in two years, Dorothea. Chicago's developed so rapidly—"

"Chicago. Oh yes, Chicago." Mentally she reached, but a lack of vitality kept her from remembering. Tom hated to see that childlike vacancy fasten on that exquisite face.

"I can remember only a dozen livable houses when I last visited, in '52. Now all but a few of those are gone, new ones—scores of them—have replaced them." The colonel paused, offering her a chance to speak. Then he took it up again. "And New York—New York is a colossus."

"It must be so vulgarized now."

Mrs. Hastings appeared to be restraining herself from thinking. "Everything's more vulgarized, dear." Her face was touched beyond its age with a softening concern. The candlelight turned the powder into a layer of dead skin. Tom didn't know which woman seemed stranger.

"Vulgar as it is, it's the most important city in the world today. The clipper ships bring China to Wall Street in a few weeks." To the boy Hyde sounded like one of Greeley's reporters, mechanically listing New York's virtues.

"I haven't been there for such a very long while." Each word required enormous effort, and her voice kept slipping down into the cracks between her energy. Her husband hung on her words as though he sucked life from them.

"The boy and I saw a dreadful production of *Spartacus* with Nevil Woods."

"Bombast!" she said with unusual force. Her listeners looked sadly cheered. Tom felt he was listening to someone's lessons.

Dorothea spoke, but Tom couldn't tell if she spoke to herself or to them. "I've never much enjoyed the style."

She tinkled a bell to call for the clearing. Later she rang dessert in, then rang the bleeding blue dessert dishes out. She directed the entire meal from memory, her arms fluttering in and out of the ghostly veiling. In that shifting pool of candlelight each practiced gesture appeared disconnected and dreamy. To the boy she seemed absent and sepulchral, an unreachable sleeping beauty attended by her courtiers and that strange witch or fairy godmother.

Long before the Kansas-Nebraska question soaked up the nation's attention, the Senate Committee on Territories had a firm sense of power. Quite a natural assumption, since the committee administered the territories through the laws it wrote and the officers it appointed. With these fiefdoms at its disposal, the committee handed out favors liberally to those of the same party (predominantly Democrat) and similar stripe. Stripes varied according to the great sectional divisions of the country—North/South or Free/Slave and East/West. The attention Kansas and Nebraska received during the first nine months of 1854 made the committee members no less conscious of their power. Nor did the transcontinental railroad surveys, which lent themselves exquisitely to the sectional rivalries—a southern route would transform the backward South into an industrial power, a northern one would bankrupt the South, a central one create the mid-American empire of Stephen Douglas' dreams. Inestimable amounts of influence, power, and money rode on the projected route of those rails—cities to be built, fortunes to be made—American cutthroat expansiveness ran high. Those builders of the future on the committee could not be expected to be completely unbiased; the men who wrote history were not above scribbling in a few lines favorable to themselves.

Colonel Benjamin Hyde stepped into this world on a morning in late October, greeted many committee members by name, and took a place at the far end of a massive mahogany table. Stephen Douglas, chairman of the committee, sat at the opposite end, near the arched double doors. Flanking the chairman sat the committee, not entirely at its ease. The members anxiously awaited Hyde's testimony, since South

Pass had been the front runner for a considerable time. It had the chairman's blessing and remained such a "natural" favorite that the committee had decided against the need for a new mapping survey.

Hyde's testimony began at the eastern terminus of the trail, in Chicago, where he detailed his impressions of the city's remarkable growth and its potential as a mid-continental commercial center. In the colonel's dispensation, Chicago combined the best of two worlds: favored by lake and river (God) as well as canal and rail (man). From that commercial Eden he led them west to Davenport, and from Davenport to Des Moines, Des Moines to Council Bluffs. At Council Bluffs they embarked on "the well-traveled trail of the builders of the West." In those eastern parts of the Territory Hyde followed General Rollwright's maps, which he had been over inch by scale inch. "Emigration is like a ray of light," he said senatorially. "It will always seek the shortest distance between two points." At that, Hyde saw a Connecticut senator scribble a hostile note.

The colonel built a case for continued support of an already large investment; he detailed the work already done at river crossings (ferries, bridges), the improvements in grades, straightening bends, and softening curves. "There are incalculable advantages along a trail every inch of which has been gone over by men, horses, mules, oxen, and every conceivable wheeled conveyance." He carried them to the branching of the Platte, then up the north fork into Laramie, where he paused to speak of his own town's growth. Then he took a deep mental breath. He prefaced his introduction to the high ground by explaining, "This afternoon I propose to cover the ground between Fort Laramie and South Pass inch by inch. The clerk's look informs me it's getting late and I'd like to leave time for your questions while my testimony is still fresh in your minds. Not that I think it will soon stale." He drew a laugh.

"I find South Pass a fitting and a moving place. From there, at the top and in the very middle of the country, a traveler can look back at all that he has traversed, then look onward toward his destination, toward the great western ocean. I propose that the railroad bifurcate at the Pass—at the traditional parting spot for Oregon and California—one trunk line would go north to Puget Sound, another south to San Francisco. But let me stop here."

The chairman had his pick of committee members' hands; he recognized a freshman senator from Pennsylvania, who leveled the charge of bias at Hyde. "The senator from Pennsylvania suggests I'm biased. Of course I am. For a while now I've been aware that the

Nebraska Territory isn't the only section of the country interested in the railroad." That drew scattered legislative smiles. "Now that that news is out, it's fair to suppose that any testimony before this committee will have a sectional lean to it. Given that, what can be done? Assume we're all equally guilty. Call us even on that. Then analyze, dissect, reconstruct the arguments. For me, and for my bias, consider the use of the Platte Trail, the Overland, the Oregon Trail—this thrice-named transcontinental route. Then ask why it has become the major artery to the Pacific Coast? Weigh the costs and the ease and the safety as well as the simple common sense of following the old, natural, proven road west. Is there any other route where labor can be found, fed, housed, and protected while the rails are being laid? What other trail offers military posts from the Missouri to the Rockies? Already along that road we've changed the movements of the Plains Indians—cut off the northern Cheyenne from his southern brother, split the Sioux nation, and totally transformed the use of the Platte forks. Shall we give that up? Shall that loss of life, all that work be reduplicated? That seems unnatural to me, a costly extravagance and an insult to all those who paved the way. But then I may just be biased."

In the sea of waving hands, the chairman focused on a single rigid right arm—the man Hyde counted on to raise the most serious objections to South Pass. Senator Hiram Bender from Missouri was a difficult, brooding, unpopular man who had revived a flagging political career by insisting he'd drag the railroad into St. Louis if he had to do it with his own hands. The people of Missouri may not have believed him, but they were at least willing to give him a chance to try.

"Lives and dollars—sacred couple," mocked Bender. "Follow the good colonel over South Pass. He'll save lives for us. But there's more. There's money too. All those incidental advantages on his 'natural' path—ease of supply, unlimited amounts of labor, military protection; we are to have all this for nothing, of course. Gifts of history we've stopped paying for. Delivered into our hands free of charge. The colonel wants it to seem that on the one hand—his hand—the outlay's superficial and the returns great. On the other, 'naturally,' the outlay's enormous. But then he won't pause to speak about the returns. He skips over that. Recognize the ploy? He balances present cost against past benefits and decides in his own favor. It's bad economics but extremely persuasive politics.

"If our choice was as obvious as the colonel insists, why haven't we all seen the light? Why the investment in costly, time-consuming surveys? Because we're pledged to talk to our constituents about the real cost to the country, not some mystification dreamed up by the military." His sneer piqued Hyde. "I distrust the sort of tactic that looks down its nose to say, 'I'm fair and reasonable,' while at the same time it's snatching bread from your hand. If you want to argue, sir, you might argue that the 'incidental' outlay—forts, ranches, roads, all the jobs the railroad will cause to blossom in its path—would be good for another part of the country, that it might create the movement and settlement that other parts of our country need, not to say deserve. You might argue that if you were capable of getting past the economies of your own—" he just barely caught the words "greed"—"interest."

Hyde thought Bender's speech deformed. He would never permit himself that sort of tone, in public or private.

Bender's deadly natural enemy on the railroad question was Robert Hitchins of Virginia, chairman of the Appropriations Committee and the most powerful Southerner in the Senate. Only a week earlier they had fought a desperate battle over the proposal for the Gila River route. Bender had mounted an impressive show—he screamed of collusion between the Secretary of War and southern interests; demonstrated how the Gadsden Purchase formed an integral part of southern railroad strategy; insisted "A desert wolf wouldn't be caught dead—yet alone alive—anywhere along the proposed route"; and detailed the paper towns and maneuverings about rights-of-way by which the southern supporters planned to make millions out of the Secretary's scheme. A week earlier rumor of a duel ran through the congressional corridors. A week later Hitchins would be flaying Bender for his hopeless (and costly) attempts to find a pass out of the San Luis Valley. But now their common interest lay in keeping the Platte route from winning too much favor.

The chairman recognized Hitchins. He spoke with the soft arrogance of the South: "The colonel rhapsodizes about a land he knows intimately. He gives us a stirring portrait of our forefathers lobbying for his interests. But he forgoes to talk about those forefathers who died cursing his trail, frozen on the high ground of the Pass. The Pass—let the argument dwell there. It will be immensely costly to try to keep it open, and we have only the word of two wet-behind-the-ears second lieutenant engineers that it can be kept open. And even their word is mere conjecture. How do we know an engine can get through a midwinter snowstorm? What guarantees are we given to prove that rails can be laid on those steep mountain grades? How do we haul materials up there? What about those northern aberrations called frost heaves? or snow slides? avalanches? How can we supply the poor unfortunates sitting vigil when in your winters sixteen-foot drifts look like snowflakes? Colonel Hyde," he said with insinuating slowness, "would you yourself enjoy being stationed up there?"

"There are more appealing posts." Hyde's flipness raised a laugh from both his supporters and Hitchins'. Bender didn't crack a smile. "Although I did spend the end of February and a good deal of March vacationing up there, seeing if it was plausible to establish an outpost."

"And of course," Hitchins said with mild contempt, "you found it plausible."

"Difficult but plausible. A great deal more plausible than—"

"I didn't ask—"

"—than the problems other routes pose from start to finish."

Hitchins reconnoitered. "Let me ask another question, Colonel, since you skate by the first. Where do the hardy settlers live in winter? Do they crowd up to the Pass?" His arm made rhetorical arabesques, as if leading a song. "Sleep with bears and timber wolves in snowbanks? Or are they pushing into Omaha, Leavenworth, Fort Kearney? Perhaps you've even seen a few of them around your post?"

The question seemed too absurd to warrant reply. Yet Hyde felt vulnerable, exposed. Why had they taken his testimony so soon? Why no new survey of the Platte Trail? After all that hospitality in Chicago, why hadn't Douglas arranged to see him privately? A moment before, Hyde's thoughts had been marshaled for his testimony; now unanswerable doubts assailed him. But Bender was speaking again.

"It pains me to see this man in the uniform of the United States Army trying to deny our legislative right, our constitutional duty to see what other routes might seriously compete with what he claims to be the untarnished perfection of his own."

"I'm sorry that the senator wishes to put my testimony in that light. What I stated was that I believed South Pass the best route because it's the one people use. Really," Hyde said, his eyebrows arched tensely, "I can't argue against your bias and of course I assumed you will *survey* the other routes." The colonel wasn't angry, but the charade had begun to tire him.

"Would you care to venture a comment on the surveys then?"

Looking at the sober paneling, the portraits of Washington, Adams, Marshall, and Jefferson, he wondered what Tom would make of the room, the proceedings. The notion refreshed Hyde.

"My suspicion is that the surveys will confuse the issue." Bender looked exultant. Hyde abandoned the forced graciousness: "That's not to say you shouldn't have them. You'll have them, and then each partisan will insist that his survey conclusively proves his route is superior. You'll argue about how to justly make comparisons. Perhaps an evaluation committee will be set up. Perhaps you will resurvey the surveys. Nothing will be accomplished, but everything will be even more confused."

The speech was a bold one for a witness, and the committee hung back. Hyde looked at Hitchins. The chairman recognized a livid-looking Bender: "Yet you're the one who comes before us with statistics to support your argument. Are you claiming the exclusive right to address us? It's preposterous."

Hitchins slid in smoothly. "Let us suppose that a single overzealous engineer, eager to please his conscientious superior, altered the angle of one of these many descents ever so slightly—"

"That, sir, is a matter of public record!"

Hitchins sneered. "Not to impugn you."

"You are impugning me!"

"Ah," said Hitchins coolly, breaking into a smile of real triumph, "you are hot and misunderstood. I was speaking about your command."

Hyde shouted, "I'll answer for my command."

"Not entirely. You overstep your rank, Colonel." He underlined Hyde's title. "I'm referring to the entire survey, some of which was originally conducted by General Rollwright as you explained, and all of which, including your portion, is under his jurisdiction."

"All right," the chairman said. "Let's stop right here. This isn't the way to pursue matters of information."

Dressed in his new suit and sitting in the coffered Senate Committee Room with Bushnell at his side, Tom Hyde felt splendid, quite the little man. The colonel stood a few paces in front of them, addressing the senators. As announced, the afternoon testimony involved technical matters, with Hyde presenting measurements of snowfall and manpower estimates for the maintenance of a post in South Pass as well as reams of engineers' reports. Everything went smoothly until Hyde's narrative reached Poison Creek. The colonel wasn't anxious to consult with Bushnell, for the scout looked jittery. But Sherrin's last letter had hinted at an interesting possibility, and Hyde hoped that he could get away with one or two specific questions. He felt he needed the scout's visual memory here. "If you don't object, Mr. Chairman, I'd like to ask my scout something."

"The Chair has no objection."

Bender intervened: "Are you willing to ask him in front of us all?"

"Frankly, I hadn't thought of any other possibility until the senator suggested it."

Hitchins slid in with smooth precision: "I'm sure this gentleman will be pleased to give us any and all the information he can."

Bushnell, who looked anything but pleased, could not return the Southerner's oily smile. He stared again at his hands, which suddenly appeared to have grown too large.

"Mr. Bushnell," Hyde began. The "Mr." startled Tom. He felt sure it sounded as unlikely to the senators as it did to him.

"You know the ferry at the junction of the North Platte River and Poison Creek?" The colonel enunciated too clearly, which reminded Tom Hyde of the way Matthew Sherrin used to speak to him before he learned English. "The one put in by the 7th Ohio Cavalry in the summer of 1851?" It sounded like he was talking to a child.

"Yes," Bushnell answered in a small voice.

"Do you know of any way that crossing could be avoided?"

The scout spent a long moment convincing himself: "Stupid t' be scared. All yo' got t' do is talk." But his words were barely audible: "Used t' be–"

"Please may I have that again?" The clerk of the committee made the request in a flat, disinterested voice.

Bushnell hated to have to repeat what he had a hard time saying in the first place. His voice cracked, "Used t' be–" He awkwardly cleared his throat. "They'd stick to the west bank 'ntil they got real close in by the cliff." The scout looked up along a narrow corridor that led from his hands to the colonel's eyes. "Yo' jus' talkin' in Hyde's office, Hyde's office." But his voice betrayed him: it wanted to patch up the grammar and diction as it went along. "Thar's a limestone wall thar, no more'n twenty foot up. They liked t' skirt it cuz th' bank und' neath fall 'way 'bout like that–" He indicated the angle by tilting his hand.

Bender leaped on it: "The clerk may have difficulty recording the witness' sign language."

Only the meanest partisans honored the remark with low snickers. The colonel quickly flipped through the pages of his testimony. "Originally that was a 12 per cent grade," he glossed exactly. "Three years ago we shaved it to 9 per cent. That's already entered in the record, for the senator's information. But wouldn't you gentlemen say that's just about the right angle?" Hyde tilted his hand like the scout.

"I asked only for the sake of accuracy. Accuracy," Bender said, his hard lip curling sharply, "that's what we're all here for."

"Gentlemen, gentlemen," came Douglas' voice of nonpartisan annoyance, "this is not a court of law and neither of you are conducting a prosecution or a defense."

After Bushnell was dismissed, the colonel's wit led the testimony through South Pass and on to the Pacific. Though Tom continued to feel impressed by the proceedings and ennobled by his surroundings, as the afternoon passed the boy paid less attention to the discussion and more attention to the way Bushnell's legs kept crossing and uncrossing unmanfully as though they had lost their natural positions and hoped by trial and error to find them again. Caught up in the Senate's self-confirming display of its own importance, Tom felt convinced that this great body had judged Bushnell impartially and found him unworthy, ignoble, even laughable. This condemnation meant that Bushnell had let the colonel down, let Laramie down. And when Tom looked to Bushnell to have that judgment denied, if, even then, he had looked with his own eyes and not theirs, he still would've seen an intimidated, ludicrous rustic.

After the hearing, Tom and the scout waited in the hall while Hyde completed what Tom hoped would be a final round of handshakes. But when Hyde joined them, he said, "Tom, you run Bushnell back to his lodgings, then go to George Town. Tell them it went well, everything considered. I'll be home for dinner. I'm sorry that it got ugly in there, Bushnell. Bender's an unspeakable ass."

Bushnell nodded numbly.

Then, boyishly, Hyde asked, "What did you think of it?"

"It was the greatest, sir." Inspired by something, he added, "I howled for you."

The colonel looked surprised and slightly embarrassed, but also quite pleased.

A haughty Tom led Bushnell down the Senate corridor; it didn't take the boy many steps to realize he enjoyed leading. He had an impulse to tell each person who passed he had nothing to do with the shabby fellow who shambled behind him. That rotten thought made Tom even more angry and impatient with the scout for trailing him so dolefully.

It wasn't a long ride from the Capitol to Bushnell's boardinghouse, but on the way the boy reconsidered all the time they had spent together. He remembered those icy stares directed at Bushnell; the smell of liquor rising off the scout each morning on the trail and most mornings in Chicago, New York, and Washington; the scout's boasting and tall stories; his bad grammar and the colonel's disapproval; his until now unfathomable fear of the New York hotel; his perfect inappropriateness on Broadway and in restaurants and in the Senate chamber.

"I wish we hadn't missed the morning session," said Tom as they approached the partially completed memorial to Washington. "He may have been even better then." Bushnell did not reply.

"Bender and Hitchins tried their best, but they couldn't stand up to him. He's probably the greatest in the world at it, don't you think?" Bushnell answered yes without malice.

"The way he tilted his hand—terrific."

Bushnell did not reply.

The drama of the Senate hearing stirred Tom more deeply than a play—with real people making up their own parts as they went along, where real things happened which had real consequences, where those who failed to live up to their chosen parts faced failure and disgrace. Since Tom judged by the arrogant hopefulness of youth, he couldn't help feeling superior to a man who couldn't understand or do any of it. He felt that if he worked hard, he would be able to respond when his turn came. That was his duty.

It wasn't a long ride from the Capitol to the rooming house, but on the way Tom could feel Bushnell slipping away from him. Or being pushed. The scout had been his friend and confidante, the most graceful white he had ever met. At the beginning he had been his voice, often his mind too. They had started together, but Bushnell had fallen woefully behind.

"That's some building, huh? See that building thar, boy?" He pointed to the Smithsonian Institution.

Tom wanted to reach out and take hold of his old dear friend. But he nodded without particular interest at the Doric order on the front of the Post Office. The falling away, painful as it was, also intrigued him. They rode on.

Whatever his weaknesses, and they should not be minimized, Bushnell had never pretended to be what he wasn't, he had never asked to be judged by another set of rules. Bushnell felt annoyed and embarrassed that Tom had recognized their differences as he had in the Senate chamber, but he recognized the inevitability of their separation. He had sensed the unnaturalness that first day they had dragged the child into Laramie. His Senate appearance had been torture. Now, in the carriage, the pain felt less excruciating, only a heavy silence, which he didn't break through again because he didn't like apologies and hated words that got most of their kicks from diddling themselves. The scout's eyes held no blame for the boy and no pity for himself as they swept the half-completed city.

It wasn't a long ride, only long enough to let trust and friendship slip behind.

Dorothea Coughlin remained a mystery to Tom, hovering about the rooms and landings like an alluring flickering spark that could never ignite. She had occasional moments of lucidity—once she came down the stairs in a dove-gray dress, said "Hello," and turned a full-fledged smile on him; once, while she arranged a spray of dried flowers, she demonstrated how she tried "to make them fall softly, entangled in each other." But Tom remembered best the day she was being fitted for a ball dress she'd never wear. Neither Coughlin nor Hyde were at home, so she had called Tom in and asked him, with the beautiful tarlatan dress pinned up around her, "Do you like it?" He said, "I've never seen anything so beautiful." A blush burnished the alabaster skin, which made her beauty at once as fragile yet more breathtaking because more believable. Often he saw that image of her, standing awkwardly pinned up, those long graceful arms raised, thanking him by that blush. He saw Dorothea and the wordless delicacy of her family's concern for her, and his heart went out to all of them.

The Christmas holiday had no special air at the Coughlins'. Visitors still passed through the main part of the house stealthily, as if they were making their way past the room of an invalid. In Coughlin's study they reanimated—smoked, spat into the nickel spittoon, drank brandy, and discoursed on politics. But they retreated down that corridor on tiptoe. The domestic routine remained stringently unvaried. Time around Dorothea was arranged as carefully as a blind man's room.

That is why Tom's course in the matter seemed clear. Coughlin's colleagues had just decamped, but Tom stayed behind in the study to read. Yet something kept nagging at him—that extra chair, the one brought in from the dining room for Representative Mondell. Greeley's eloquence about the pro-southern maneuverings of the Secretary of War intrigued Tom enough to keep him glued to the chaise until he glanced at his watch—"Four-fifteen. Mrs. Coughlin will be coming down for tea." Tom jumped up and grabbed the chair. Moving into the hall he heard her light step on the stairs. Heart racing, he ran as quickly and quietly as he could down the hall, turned into the dining room and slid the chair into place just as she appeared in the doorway. She looked at him without seeing and passed on into the sitting room.

Tom's shudder surprised him. He knew if the chair had not been in place she might have stood frozen on the threshold for hours.

By New Year's, Tom's mid-January entry into Arundel Academy had been arranged. He was to "come up" two weeks before the term's start. That would allow him to "acclimate a bit while being tutored privately." So Headmaster Byron Bovie wrote. He'd start regular classes "after we determine his intellectual standing. If all goes well the young man can summer at Arundel."

Though Tom had chilly apprehensions about the great stone hall that dominated the cover of Arundel's information *Gazette,* he insisted that the colonel accompany him only as far as New York. They had to take Bushnell there anyway so that he could catch his train for Laramie. (Everyone agreed the scout would be better off back home.) Tom would make the train trip to Boston, then to Acton. A rash of fatherly impulses made Hyde less reasonable than usual until Mrs. Hastings pointed out that the colonel would be forced to travel two hundred miles (one way) out of his way at a time when he should be presenting his final decision about party affiliation to Greeley and his crew. Tom felt glad and frightened when Mrs. Hastings' argument prevailed. He knew he had to face the preparatory school on his own, and he wanted to begin that way. At the same time he wondered if he would ever stop stepping off into strange new territories.

At Battery Park they hailed a hansom and raced uptown to the railway station. Unfortunately, Bushnell's train had been delayed, which left them with an hour to kill. A lousy piece of timing, since all parties felt equally anxious to part. Bushnell suggested that the colonel and Tom go on, but Hyde declined with meaningless politeness.

Tom sat sandwiched between the scout and Hyde, who unconcernedly turned back to the columns of the *Tribune.* Bushnell puffed away at a packaged cigarette, the tongue flicking shreds of tobacco off his red mustache. They waited silently on that stiff bench in air supersaturated with time—the huge clock ticked it off as a distant voice rasped out the scheduled arrivals and departures and listed stops on route like so many temporal units to sweep by.

In front of the boy configurations formed and changed. A wedge of people swept left across the main flow to converge on the tiny point marked "Track 2." A dignified man with a long gray scarf aimed for Track 2 at a dogtrot, then slowed to pick his way through the shifting weave of pedestrians. Long strings of those seated on the straight benches heaved up at a common word, hoisted infants, coats, boxes, and bags, dropped a finger or two like ladders to toddlers, then moved in a stringy knot to where they presented their tickets to the trainmen and trudged down the steamy platform to their respective places. Peddlers, newsboys, cabmen, porters jammed the massive waiting room; Tom thought the Bowery had been brought inside.

The station exhaled a musty smell, which the boy assumed came from greatcoats and wet boots—too much outside held captive within. The thought didn't occur to him, but perhaps the air grew stale from too much emotion, the specific gravity of so many giddy reunions and intimate, rushed farewells.

The train finally chugged in on Track 3. With a new wedge of people, they pressed through the funnel of a gate where Bushnell flashed his ticket, and they purchased platform passes. The odd trio stood together uneasily. In his rumpled suit, his cuffs sticking out too far, his belly wrestling a button up, the scout lacked the self-importance of his fellow travelers. To their last instant together, Bushnell looked inappropriate.

Tom dredged his mind for something to say, but it stayed dry. The scout relieved him of the bundle.

"What yo' like me t' tell Mrs. Harter?"

"Tell her I'm fine," Tom shouted above the noise of the locomotive, "and not to worry. I'll write as soon as I get to Arundel. And say hello to Matthew, please. And Cloud."

Bushnell smiled. They shook hands heartily.

"Good-bye," Tom said sincerely. "Thanks for everything." He looked up gratefully into the older eyes that could tell him something but would not presume to.

"Best o' luck t' yo'. Yo' do right good at that school thar. Make us all proud. See yo' back home, li'l beaver."

They hugged briefly, Tom's cheek momentarily squashed against the scout's lapel. Bushnell patted his shoulder.

"G'bye, Colonel, sir. See yo' in Laramie right quick." The smile still came easily, though those bags under his eyes looked permanently embossed.

Bushnell mounted the steps of the train, pulled his case up behind him with a little helping shove from Tom. A moment later they waved at the red beard in the window that began to move away down the platform, and a sense of terrific relief settled over the boy.

Hyde was in a good mood himself. "What would you say, sir, to a drive around the Island?"

Two dandies out for a night on the town, they stepped outside and hailed a carriage. Tom remembered Fourth Avenue well enough to pick out the haberdashery (a word he loved) where he'd bought his cravat. Hyde explained that New York was easy to remember because it impressed itself upon you so forcefully.

"No one has to tell me the difference between New York and Washington," Tom replied. "I can feel them."

Hyde looked at the boy to see if he needed to be reassured. He didn't. The colonel chuckled with appreciation. "That's right, Tom, that's right."

They drove under the open-work skeleton of the cast-iron fire tower, its vertical shafts moving like slats across the coach window. The light pinned Hyde's profile against the plush wall, a perfect, proud silhouette.

"Bushnell would really rather be in Laramie," Tom thought aloud.

"This was really no place for a man like him." Tom, who wanted to say more, decided to shelve the subject.

They arrived at Delmonico's just before midnight. The maitre d'hotel welcomed them in exotic accent and found them a quiet table in the corner. Almost instantly a huge platter of oysters nestled in crushed ice was set before the two squires.

Two courses later, Hyde remarked, "We're behaving like a couple of old habitués."

"What's that?"

Hyde explained while he watched his protégé elegantly dispose of his beef, fork concave in left hand, knife in the right. Yes, Hyde thought, the boy had come far and done well. This product was Hyde's creation, his and Elizabeth's and a few intimate friends—against all odds, against scorn and assassination attempts and pagan intransigence. He remembered his diary entry the day he first believed that the noble experiment would succeed, he remembered saying in way of praise and simultaneous warning, "It's lonely to be unique, Tom, and you'll be unique." Arundel spelled loneliness, challenges of many kinds, high and low. Yet the colonel believed the boy had the potential he'd once barely dared to wish for: intelligence, talent, wit, and the intense seriousness of purpose which Hyde believed was one of the few indispensable ingredients of success. Moreover, the boy had accepted his destiny. This decision to go on to Arundel alone was another indication of the child's strength. And the way Tom had handled the perilous terrain of the Coughlin household—

"You won all the Coughlins' respect."

"Even Mrs. Hastings?"

"Especially Mrs. Hastings. Remember, she's brusque with everyone but Dorothea. And she's in two minds about you. On the one hand she thinks you've been coddled, which you have been till now because we've had no other choice. On the other hand, she's afraid you haven't spent enough time outside the company of sophisticated adults."

"I don't understand," Tom insisted, his dark eyes a deep question.

"Well, so far most of the problems you've had to face have been my problems—like the Greeley matter." They looked squarely at one another. "Naturally, you've been in over your head. Mrs. Hastings sees you about to face people your own age, and from her point of view you don't look ready for it. But I'm not worried. I know you fairly well."

There was one other thing Tom didn't understand. "But if she's worried about me, why does she make it so hard?"

"Because she can't bear to see you spoiled by your doting father." Hyde smiled, his eyes wrapped in laugh wrinkles.

There was an unusual intimacy latent in this moment, but neither wished to dwell upon it. Hyde took a sip of his claret. He realized there was one more thing: "You know we'll provide for you and your education, Tom, just as we've provided for you till now. I want you to understand how this is arranged.

"Elizabeth has a small inheritance from her father and there's Mr. Harter's pension. Then there's the small amount I put away from my own salary. All this doesn't add up to an invitation to profligacy, but it should cover your expenses during the next few years. If it doesn't, you must inform me."

Tom nodded somberly to assure the colonel he understood. But he was surprised to realize he wouldn't be going to Arundel if it wasn't for this money; he was lucky it existed. Privilege was the word; as early as Chicago Tom had been struck by the differences between rich and poor. Now he could see it among the sea of tables, the enormous gilt mirrors, in the certitude of the gentleman's red neck at the next table, in the breath-stilling flash of his companion's long arms as she reached for her glass. In the silver shimmering light of Delmonico's, Tom Hyde felt he understood privilege, and so he accepted the colonel's grant of privilege with the ease that comes from knowing no other choice.

ARUNDEL

THOSE FIRST THREE WEEKS, while Tom Hyde had Arundel to himself, the school was all that Tom expected. He moved into his own room, number 317, which was distinctively marked with a skull and a crossbones and the name BILL W. still visible under three ineffectual coats of whitewash. He met his literature master and "moral tutor," Jordan Cable, a loose-jointed, asymmetrically-jawed young man of formidable intelligence, perfect manners, and unlimited patience. The time passed idyllically for the boy, who, long afterward, would remember wandering through snow-covered fields past the elms, which pointed craggy fingers at the sky as if making ineffectual nets to catch the wind.

After a year and a half in the company of Hyde, Elizabeth, and Bushnell, Tom found solitude delightful and inspiring. He had time to reflect on his whirlwind cross-country tour, to consider his impression of the boat and the train, of burgeoning cities and slavery and politics. He examined the implications of his separation from Hyde and Elizabeth as well as his sudden change of attitude toward Bushnell. He raised all sorts of unanswerable questions about the strange women of the Coughlin household.

Then the others came back—tall boys, short boys, round and thin boys. That first night they rampaged through the halls, shouting and swearing, wrestling and pounding each other on the back. They swarmed all over Tom's room, fingering Elizabeth's daguerreotype and handling his belongings as if convinced the everyday articles had different origins from their own. All the while they fired presumptuous, ridiculous questions. How many wives did his father keep? Did Indians always go naked? Why had he come here? Had he murdered any whites? They called him "Chief" and "Tom-Tom" and "Tomahawk," which unnerved Tom because he had not told them his Indian name.

Walking to the dining hall that first night, Tom felt spied upon, for every boy in the school seemed to be straining to get a glimpse of him. A thin child stuck two fingers up over his head in a signal Tom did not understand. From the faceless double row of boys who lined the courtyard, he heard a war whoop, which set off another. And another. A voice stage-whispered, "Honest Injun." Two smaller boys shrank back as he passed.

During his solitary stay, the dining hall had grown familiar to Tom—paved with Arundel's characteristic gray fieldstone, the walls paneled in smoke-stained hardwood, with portraits that composed a frieze of stern bewhiskered masters. Three rows of refectory tables ran the length of the hall and a huge fireplace lit up one wall. On a raised platform at the far end of the room stood a smaller table covered with a damask tablecloth, silver, and wine goblets. A second fireplace warmed the length of the masters' table.

Tom always sat at the end of the first table by the near wall. His place was occupied now, so he hesitated before picking out an inconspicuous spot on the middle bench. But when he stopped in front of it, a boy slipped in front of him and stuck out his arm like a turnpike bar. "I'm sorry," he said politely, "that's reserved for Harris."

Tom stepped to his left, but the boy solemnly shook his head. "That's Beaver's." He pointed. "Smythson's, and Peabody's, Sargent's, and Parker's, and Mann's." He turned to the end of the table and started up the opposite side. The hall suddenly quieted.

Tom made for the table against the near wall. A second spokesman read him the seating arrangement.

"Where did Bill W. sit?" Tom called loudly. A hand shot up, pointed to the far table.

At the fireplace wall he asked again, "Where did Bill W. sit?" The fellow seated in front of him hunched his shoulders and leaned forward over his plate until his face touched it. Another boy looked up toward the incremental mysteries of the hammer beams. Two older boys stood warming themselves by the fire. The heavier one took his hand out of the pocket of his striped trousers and gestured with unhurried insouciance. "Three to the left from the end—this side, against the wall."

Tom nodded to thank him but he had already turned back to the fire. Tom thought he might be a master, he looked so old.

To the scions of America's ruling families, Tom's presence was either an affront or a joke. To most he seemed backward, for he usually missed the point of their jibes. Tom hadn't learned what a "greenhorn" was, how one could "laugh in his sleeve," what it meant when someone spoke of "hobnobbing with the chief." He was too serious for his classmates. In a few days Tom's rapt lecture-hall attitude became a favorite subject of campus pundits. They labeled him "the pensive savage." And pensive and earnest he remained. According to the colonel's code, study was necessary and edifying—in itself, and as the practical means of getting on to the more important business of life. So Tom was disturbed when the others counted the number of times the Latin teacher said "Ah," or passed notes or tittered among themselves when one of their number floundered in recitation. Tom didn't see why they refused to do their homework; why they laughed at the same stupid nasty things again and again; why they shoved and mauled and humiliated each other. The thought never occurred to Tom that his classmates found the academic fare tedious, irrelevant, arbitrary; that from their point of view, the primary object of interest consisted of their continuing war of wits with the staff. On the contrary, Tom Hyde felt too great a need to digest what was set before him to quibble with the dish.

As he lied to his diary, "It's better to be alone; that way I don't have to do things that are not important. I get much more work done this way."

The young Indian's purposiveness caught the attention of an ad hoc Arundel organization called the Vigilant Vigilantes—VV's for short. The VV's effective leadership was a triumvirate, a curly-haired, dimpled lad named Tyrone, a hulking senior known as Moose, and a scrawny wiseacre called Mouse. They called their newest diversion "Ruffling the Indian's Feathers" and devised entertainments like short-sheeting Tom's bed and stuffing frogs into his dresser. They scrawled VV on his door above the skull and crossbones. One evening after his run Tom opened the door to 317 and an elaborate series of ropes and pulleys and counterweights sent his bureau hurtling into the window frame, smashing two large panes of glass. A few nights later he found a note pinned to his pillow: "The only good Injun is a dead Injun." It was signed in chicken blood by the VV's.

He fought each of the VV's leaders in turn, starting with Mouse and working on up to Moose. He did well, winning two of his three bouts. All three came away impressed with Tom's doggedness, strength, and shin-kicking, even Moose. The VV's couldn't safely escalate beyond that, not after the difficulty Tom had convincing the third-floor proctor that he had fallen into a ditch. An uneasy truce followed. Tom and Tyrone argued publicly about who started scalping, reds or whites. Neither convinced the other, but Tom won a few supporters on the strength of his arguments. Arundel was odd that way—it had its code of ethics too.

The boy/man before the fire with his hand in the pocket of his striped trousers turned out to be Morgan Hall, who had inherited a few million dollars at the tender age of four and who had been trained by relatives' greed to colossal cynicism as soon as he could count. Being a misanthrope, Hall considered befriending Tom Hyde on the principle that "anyone they all hate can't be all bad." The first time he dropped into 317, Tom thanked him for having pointed out the right seat that first night. "That's O.K.," Hall replied. "I enjoy being despised. Made a relatively short but intense study of it in my day. 'Tis a virtue to be cultivated in the midst of these charlatans and thieves." Hall whispered the last part, holding the backside of his hand alongside his mouth like a screen. Tom thought Hall quite funny. Later, Tom made a passing remark about "Headmaster Bovie" and Hall called him "that sanctimonious bastard," a phrase which Tom later tried to track down in Dr. Johnson's Dictionary with only partial success. After their interview Morgan Hall decided the Indian seemed too young for him. Hall, after all, was a man who had gone "straight from swaddling clothes to decadence."

By late May the polish of Tom's idealism had picked up a few nicks. With the exception of Cable's course, the rest of his classroom time consistently bored him. The dean's math course proved intolerable, for he treated his students like captive political prisoners: "You third-rate intellect, let me see if I can shove this through that impenetrable membrane!" (accompanied by a box on the ear). "Dolt! On your feet!" (a cane brought smartly across the knuckles to bring the pupil out of his desk). At first, each imperfection in academic paradise troubled Tom. When he could no longer hold out against the evidence of his senses, he began to absorb the others' disenchantment, though he never became entirely comfortable with his schoolmates' cynical, denigrating tone. And in his letters, Tom never let on to Elizabeth and Hyde, or to the Coughlins and Mrs. Hastings that Arundel did not live up to its advance billing.

Every Saturday night behind a closed door, they gathered in Moose's room to drink. Or, more accurately, to get drunk. That night Tom felt lonelier than usual. Elizabeth's letter harped on his being true to himself and what he believed right, and Hyde's postscript catalogued his political problems and ended with a comment about how small the buffalo herd had been that spring.

The doorman ushered Tom in, through layers of smoke from contraband cigarettes, past bodies lying or leaning in unorthodox positions. Peabody kept patting himself on the shoulder while spilling beer down the front of his school blouse.

Moose proposed, "Look, Tom, I must know. Once and for all let's find out if what they say about Indians is true. Scientific experiment. That ought to appeal to you." He threw a testing arm around Tom's shoulder as he breathed Bushnell breath into Tom's face.

"Stay out of it," Tom cautioned himself. He had grown tired of always staying out of it.

"I'll take a swig," he said jauntily.

"Swig?" One of the grotesquely angled bodies hiccoughed.

Moose turned gracious, spider to fly. "Help yourself. Pass Tom the brew."

The bottle reached Tom. "So I'm going to get drunk."

"Join the club."

His first taste of bourbon stung and burned through its sweetness. Gritting his teeth, he swallowed hard.

The second drink felt thicker than water. It tasted sweeter, smoother. Tom felt the warmth working its slow way down to his stomach. At the same time it surged toward his head. Yet his stomach remained curiously empty. Drinks crowded closer together. He barely cleared his mouth of the stinging fluid before the next compulsory swig was upon him. They were leading him on, and Tom knew it, and he didn't care.

Suddenly it seemed appropriate to speak. "I know . . . I know I've been standoffish." His lips were difficult to move.

"No, no," a voice cried mockingly.

"You're an all-right fellow," Moose drooled. "A trifle solitary, perhaps, but a reasonable mortal, a sport."

Tom couldn't remember when he insisted on showing them how to walk like an Indian, but by then he felt in love with all creation. Only his feet didn't comply with his instructions and his legs grew as heavy as his head got light. The floor tilted and scrambled beneath him; he dimly remembered lurching across a dark, cobble street.

"War dance! War dance!"

"No, scalp!"

He felt hands on him but was too uncoordinated to push them away. He remembered feeling glad to have it over and done with; everyone, including himself, had been waiting a long time. The room spun as they twirled him around and around, around. A pressing hot feeling deep inside, then a rush of bittersweet porridge made Tom gag; it spouted up into his mouth, his nose. The worst thing he had ever tasted.

A rude tap on his instep had awakened Tom, who found himself shivering in his own clotted vomit on the hall floor; the proctor had loomed over him. Yet the full force of the word "expulsion" didn't strike Tom until he stood in the hallway outside Headmaster Bovie's office.

"What do I tell Mr. Bovie?" Tom inwardly wailed. "I wanted to be more like the others, sir. That's why, sir! I'm just an eager beaver."

The imposing oak door with its shining plate–BYRON BOVIE, HEADMASTER–swung open slowly. In his long cleric's robe Bovie looked the Old Testament patriarch. Without looking up, he curtly beckoned Tom in, then crossed to his desk, where he stood flanked by diplomas.

The headmaster gestured toward a backless stool. It was so low Tom had to peek up over the edge of the cherry desk, cleared of paper to let Bovie's fury blow straight at him.

"When Dean Prosser spoke about our practices at Arundel that first day of term, you did understand that drinking was expressly prohibited. There were no–uh–problems of comprehension?"

The boy answered no, his voice stuck low in his throat.

"Then you have no excuse?"

"None, sir," Tom murmured.

"Speak up!" Bovie put his fingertips together like "This is the church, this is the steeple."

"No excuses, sir."

"I don't understand." The church fell apart. "Did you not consider how the colonel would feel? The opinion of your mortal tutor? Not to speak of me. Of what this means to the Academy."

Tom's stomach felt like a distended bladder, rough and horny; his face had been worked over by a rasp. "Failed," he decreed, his hot heart sinking heavily. "I will be kicked out–." Tom stopped there.

Bovie moved to the large Gothic window to the left of his desk. Backlit, he looked still more magisterial. "I believed you would represent so much for us."

Tom squirmed as the headmaster plucked the intended chord. "Do you take us for fools, young man? Do you think we are ignorant of the goings-on in your dormitories?" Tom's heart knotted. "That young man whose room you occupy, Weller, we knew what he was up to long before he was terminated."

Bovie strolled back to his desk, leaned down on his palms; the gown's puffed sleeves ate up his arms. "Laws exist when they're not enforced and the ones who get caught pay for the ones who don't as well as for themselves. That's called interest." Abruptly, then: "You should be expelled. That's clear. But I'm about to consider something I never allow myself–making an exception. I know you're not a ringleader so, in a minimal legal sense, you've been victimized too." Bovie fixed Tom Hyde with a shallow pious eye. Tom felt relieved yet uneasy too.

"I want to know who gave you the liquor. I want to know who ringleads these weekend debauches." The headmaster's stone-hard eyes dug into Tom. His left hand, searching for a rest, came down on a trophy of a lion. It had been presented to him by Arundel's class of 1850–"In Great Appreciation for Unrivalled Guidance and Leadership."

"I know this isn't easy, but I'm giving you one last opportunity to make your loyalties clear. Which, frankly, is considerably more than you deserve." He clipped on a bow-tie smile. "A trade then." He jabbed a finger at Tom. "Now I want you to know this: I do not need the information. I want it from you; I want you to do this for *us.*"

"All wrong, it's all wrong." To give himself time to think, Tom studied the headmaster's reflection in the gleaming dark wood of his desk. "If he knows, why does he ask?" This "trade" exposed Bovie's contempt for Tom, which insulted, disoriented, surprised the boy. He did not expect such behavior from the master of Arundel.

His next words, Tom feared, spelled the end of his career. Moses fell dead, assassinated by an untenable position and an impossible request. "I can't do it, sir. I don't want to be expelled from the Academy, I would like to help, but I can't do it."

Bovie's lip curled, curdling the smile. He hadn't expected this from–

Tom could read his look very clearly, he had seen it often enough by now—a wretched Indian child. "Get out!" His voice sounded frozen. "Out now! You'll know what's to be done with you by ten tomorrow."

For a few hours Tom's popularity surpassed his wildest dreams. At eight-thirty that Sunday evening four proctors entered four rooms. Within an hour they seized eleven bottles of whiskey, two of wine, four quarts of beer. The next day seven boys were expelled, including Mouse Marshall of the VV's.

They called Tom Hyde "bushwhacker" and jumped him in pairs, slammed him up against any wall they caught him near. He fought back wildly, but they could always call on a third ally or a fourth. Once each week they broke his window, once a week he found horseshit in his bed. Tom quickly learned there was something worse than expulsion. Bovie's indifference or malice had engineered it brilliantly—Tom's reprieve was his punishment.

Yet as bad as the Arundelites treated him, there was one thing worse: Jordan Cable—on whom Tom Hyde depended for tutelage, intellectual and spiritual, the only person at Arundel to whom he could talk seriously, the one person to whom he could truly listen—Jordan Cable grew cool and distant, and at times clearly shunned contact with him.

The summer began, Tom worked on. He stayed at Arundel through July, then went south to Washington for a much-needed vacation. It felt good to be near Coughlin, a man he respected, and one who liked him. Tom dragged himself back to school in the fall reluctantly, aware of how small the Academy would feel after all his freedom in Washington, and all those heated discussions in Coughlin's study about the future of the Republicans in the '56 presidential elections.

Arundel was worse than he expected—his classmates now felt vindicated for every nasty prejudice they bore toward the Indian. Backed into his tiny psychic corner, Tom grew more stoic and uncommunicative.

He studied hard and thought of his family and his old life on the Plains. Tom escaped from self-pity because of the double knowledge that he had done nothing dishonorable and that Bovie continued to be a perfidious wretch, if only by omission. That sustained the boy, though it confused him too. The headmaster was the first person of authority he despised, which went against all his instincts and training.

Tom Hyde lived in a clumsy, uncertain light that term, not the sort of illumination he was intended for.

Not until April of Tom's second year did Jordan Cable reach the point where he had to know why Tom Hyde had broken all the unspoken rules of the Academy and turned in the other boys. "Like an old wound that won't heal," he groused as he sat in his study, a volume of Byron in his right hand. His coffee cup perched precariously on the rounded arm of his reading chair, his long legs followed the established angle of the hassock down. "Fact is, it's been almost a year and I've detected none of the usual indications of guilt—he just seems to be waiting. For what?" The tutor absentmindedly turned the page, then turned it back again.

From the beginning Tom's action confused Cable. "Was he tricked? By whom? For what?" He started through his list of mental explanations again. "Would someone in his position commit social suicide? No, only if he didn't understand. But I know he understood. Knew enough not to say anything to me or anyone else when they broke his window with the bureau. Was he tricked? That makes no sense." His eyes skimmed the page, but *Don Juan* offered no answers. Cable hadn't spoken to Tom Hyde since the beginning of spring term.

Tom Hyde stood uneasy before his tutor as the older man sat, frowning slightly, in his armchair.

"You know I've been disappointed in you. That drinking episode and your role in what followed weren't at all what I expected." Cable did not find it easy to say this. He hated overt directives about matters of conscience.

"I could feel that, sir."

"Tom," Cable started solemnly, "I want you to tell me exactly what happened during that interview. Everything. From the beginning."

Tom breathed a soul-cleansing sigh. "I didn't tell Mr. Bovie their names, sir. I didn't tell him anything at all." His dark eyes opened wide with clarity and trust.

"If he's lying," Cable thought, "it's horrible. But if the whole episode—a year of this boy's life—if the whole thing was a fabrication of Bovie's, it would be vile, unspeakable."

Tom told his tutor everything, from the beginning, his eyes resting unflinchingly on the older man. He felt glad to get it all out, glad to get it over, glad that Cable had unlocked his secret.

"Cruel and unusual punishment, cruel and unusual punishment."

Cable kept listening to that phrase. So unnecessary, so cowardly!

At the end of his recitation Tom added, "I feel better now, now that you know." He saw no benefit in tallying up past suffering. He only really gave a damn about Cable anyway.

"I'm sorry, sorry that I didn't press harder, mortified that we've all behaved so badly. But let me ask you one thing: why didn't you tell anyone?" The boy's extended devotion to his own sense of rightness seemed perverse and a little frightening to Cable. Fanatic.

"Nobody asked."

Cable's heart sank. "But you might've said something."

"They believed what they wanted to." Tom stated it as observed fact.

"Then it's your responsibility to set them straight." But Tom Hyde's moral tutor didn't really believe that.

Early afternoon found Jordan Cable ensconced in his reading chair. Earlier he had summoned two of his favorite seniors and had "set a few things straight about Tom Hyde." The two boys assured their teacher that they got the message.

Having acted on Tom's behalf, Cable now strove to act on his own. At first resignation seemed appropriate. But the no's kept tallying higher, primarily because Cable's resignation would do nothing to alter Bovie's behavior.

Cable had long suppressed an aversion to the headmaster on the principle that it was the proper way to do business: you ought to respect your boss. But he disliked the man and his pious sentimentality. Then the question arose: what to do? Public denouncement? Walking in and demanding that Bovie apologize? A manifesto published in the Arundel *Gazette*? Cable felt uncomfortable rehearsing these charges to himself, practicing the loud noises he knew he'd never make.

"Jordan, Jordan, how searingly perceptive you've been, you who pride yourself on humane insight, on moral sensitivity. Tutor seeing student sitting in his rooms each night, an isolated outcast in a brutally alien world, doing his exercises and running two miles every afternoon, waiting for over one year for some dolt to pop the right and obvious question. Finally said student comes before you with that look of abiding respect, of affection and faith in your moral perspicacity, as if your presence alone were edifying!" Cable bounced his knuckles off the lap desk. "Why comes the student before you thus? Because of the way you talk! Talk! Talk! You talk an excellent existence but don't teach one goddamn iota of value!"

The ultimate horror struck him: Bovie could claim he didn't intend to hurt the boy, and all he actually had done was to let a false impression linger. Cable's right calf began to tremble. His stomach burned, heart pumped like he had taken too much coffee; he started to sweat a chill sweat; his life and his work seemed tainted.

Sweetness formed Tom's portion at dinner that evening. After the dean read his nightly announcements, just as the custard tinkled in pewter bowls, Morgan Hall clanged his knife against a glass goblet. Heads snapped around, eyes fixed on the pasty, oddly aged face. Hall lounged impassively, one hand in the pocket of his customary striped trousers.

"I, too, have an announcement this evening." The Academy's most notorious cynic cleared his throat. "It has been assumed for the past year and some few months that Tom Hyde—" With that, Tom's heart commenced to race. "—that Tom Hyde was the snitch who turned in the Alcohol Seven. But I've just had a chat with Headmaster Bovie, who informs me that we've all had our heads threaded incorrectly, our scents confounded, been laboring—as it were—in the wrong vineyards." Bovie's color, which during the preamble had deepened to bold scarlet, now faded to blanched almond. "Hear this, company: Tom Hyde said nothing! Not one dishonorable syllable." Hall's booming voice bounced off the fieldstone up into the intricacies of the hammer beams above, where he let it die away. The founders and past masters watched over the scene. "The headmaster, as usual, was way ahead of those villains; he already knew who was supplying the heinous corrupting brew. Hyde was in the headmaster's chambers that morning simply to discuss the matter of a hangover he was suffering."

They laughed—mainly to relieve their shock at Hall's boldness—Cable, the dean, even the prissy third-floor proctor laughed.

"And so Headmaster Bovie—" Morgan Hall shot a scathing smile toward the high table "—has asked me to propose a toast to Arundel's noble Thomas Hyde, in all too limited recompense for misplaced suspicions and with many good wishes for an acclaimed future."

The hall erupted—half because of their hatred for Bovie and half because of embarrassment for what they had misunderstood for so long—as Hall raised his glass.

Morgan Hall's room surpassed Tom's expectations: a jewel box with a green silk lining studded with an exquisite Turkish rug, pieces of jade and lively, exotic Persian miniatures, including a race between gold and red horses. Tom entered indecisively; Hall feigned surprise.

"Hello," the older boy said, lifting his striped legs off a brocade quilt on the bed and straightening up in his armchair. "To tell the truth, I've been brooding over that last phrase of my toast. Pity it's so timeworn. I rather did want to raise the cheer—and it always seems to get it."

This went by too quickly for Tom, who had come to thank Hall and ask his question. "You didn't speak to the headmaster, did you?"

Morgan Hall sloughed off the question and the thanks, though Tom's earnestness amazed him. He went on as if Tom hadn't spoken. "Know why I cleared your heretofore not completely unblemished name? One, I hate that impotent old buzzard more than I can say." His eyes kept their droopy indifference, but the voice took on a hostile edge. "Two, my guess was that if I left it up to Cable, he'd dawdle too long."

Tom felt loyally upset. "I don't understand."

"Not his style. Cable's too full of the niceties, friend."

"But Mr. Cable started it. He was the only one who knew."

"That's fine as far as it went. But imagine what he would've said to our beloved leader: 'Dear sir, I think you behaved questionably in this matter.' " Hall mimicked Cable's Oxford accent, which infuriated Tom.

"Put it this way—I'm a bad one, Cable's good. It's nice to play Robin Hood for a change—keeps the others on their toes, confuses them."

Tom wondered why Hall worked so hard to spoil the fine thing he had done.

"Tom Hyde, it's my turn to ask you the question. Your debt to me." He laughed, looking younger for his joke. He had a very free laugh. "Why didn't you tell anyone? What possessed you to drag it out for a year?" Hall wasn't often truly confused by another boy's actions.

"Nothing I could have said would have changed their minds. That was always clear to me."

The answer so impressed Morgan Hall it took him a moment to accept it. He remained silent, his eyes examining a tiny Persian dancing girl. "No begging from—excuse the expression—the great white fathers. Is that it?"

Tom offered no reply.

"You knew you hadn't done it—that was good enough?"

Tom nodded.

"Ah, great satisfaction," Hall archly intoned. But he knew no one else in the school had the courage or the integrity to do it. For a passing moment he even wondered if he would have behaved as nobly before ruling in his own favor. "Christ, what a class you're in," he thought. "Only you and one red Indian."

They didn't have much more to say, but when they parted they did so with an uncommon sense of incompletion. As long as they had been at Arundel, neither had felt as much respect for a schoolmate.

They didn't rush things at first, but slowly Tom and Morgan Hall grew friendlier. An odd pair—innocence and decadence, optimism and cynicism, impressionability and virtual imperviousness. Initially, the only thing they truly shared was the lack of a childhood.

Tom's celebrity threatened to last through term, in spite of Hall's repeated prognoses about the date on which Tom's newly won admirers would drop him.

"You're so disgustingly popular you're getting corrupt. Bad for your sense of proportion, not to say your political future."

Out for a walk on a beautiful afternoon in late May, they had stopped to throw pebbles into the river. Rather Tom had, for Hall couldn't stand to get grit under his fingernails.

"From my astute observation of your life, Thomas, I'd say that around here people approach you in three ways—the museum approach, where you're addressed in third person and examined as though you're dead."

Tom managed that slightly hurt grin which Hall coaxed out of him too often, and skimmed another pebble sidearm on top of the water. He counted five bounces. "Five," he said.

"No," Hall replied, "two. Or second—the best-friend approach, or there-are-no-barriers-in-this-world-as-long-as-we-work-mutually-to-make-it so. Characteristic: claims to know you perfectly well, understands after looking into the depths of your fathomable dark eyes the incorruptible (though unsalvageable) nature of your pagan soul. To which the answer to the unasked question is, 'Then how come you missed it last term, Buster?'

"Three. The backslapping, you're-a-regular-fellow attitude. Used by those without the interest or wit to invent or observe something else. Rather more generalized than particular, like a suit from the rack. In this you're one of the boys but still a pre-initiate, almost ready for club membership. Invited to parties, wined, dined, but never, never invited to the palatial home or asked to call upon his sister."

"Hall, you're so unregenerate." Tom smiled, trying not to let it get to him. "How can you come up with such thoughts on such a day? I'm surprised you haven't driven away the sun."

Hall crammed a hand further into his trouser pocket, bowing the stripes. He kicked at the dirt and sent a shower of pebbles down toward the water. "Because I'm a realist, you dolt!" He looked at his friend seriously—for him. "Thomas Hyde alias Tumbling Hawk, you'll never be an ordinary citizen. They'll either over- or underadore you. School has contracted with you unfairly, understand, and is now—and forever more—paying off its debt. Ah, it's a long winding uphill trail for you, me lad. But you'll tire of them. Unless you've got the patience of a red saint—which, blessedly, I know you don't—you'll end up like Hall, a bad-tempered ill-speaking old pisspot."

"Listen, Hall, I'm having a perfectly fine time."

"But for how long? How long can any righteous soul take all this camaraderie?" The stream flowed by, the willow bent in the wind, not answering.

Back at school in the fall of 1857, Tom found the work easier. He added a ruffled shirt, a touch of cologne, a full gray cape, and walking stick, as well as a rakish swagger. Tom and Morgan Hall would stride about like Paris dandies, bemused by their schoolmates' bumptiousness. They took up positions at the fireplace side by side. They were united by their mutual aversion to the foul-mouthed excesses with which the others tried to hoodwink their peers into believing them sexually competent. "It's like an auction," Morgan used to say, "with the bidding going higher and higher—a dozen entries of an evening, thirteen inches."

Meanwhile, Tom and Morgan often slipped off to an elegant Boston whorehouse where Tom sat and drank and hardly noticed the moment when social intercourse became sexual, or who initiated it, but he found himself on silk sheets under a canopy with beautiful blond Edith or Caroline, who seemed to enjoy his youth. He told Hall that the only thing bothering him was he couldn't afford to patronize the lovely Caroline often enough.

Tom argued with Morgan Hall about Cable, Hall insisting, "I can't see how you can respect anyone who at thirty-three years of age knows what he's going to do for the rest of his life." Or, another time, "It's too easy to sit there and tell us how things ought to be done. I should think he'd tire of playing ethical god." Tom defended his tutor vigorously, but Hall's arguments imperceptibly altered the boy's vision of Cable.

Hall had a genius for Tom's tenderest spots. One day he noticed Tom rapidly beating his stomach with his knuckles.

"What are you doing? Pummeling off the fat?"

Tom's hands dropped. "No. It's just a nervous habit I picked up." Only Hall had caught him; Tom lied.

An odd pair, these two–Hall with his shallow breathing, his bad circulation, a hatred of cold so extreme he wore a scarf around his neck into May. Hall, who asked in utter disbelief, "Do you actually do exercises? I mean in cold blood?

"Savages are the most religious folk," Hall took to saying. "I despair of turning a believer into a proper dandy."

One very late-night conversation in his room, Hall blurted out: "You believe in good intentions. Worse, you still think that your goodness excuses you. That's putrefying hogwash, unrealistic twaddle, and what's more, boyo, it reeks of self-love."

At that moment Tom hated the big boy, those jowls; that underhanded kind of hatred made him feel very small.

Hall insulted Cable once too often; then Tom challenged him to arm-wrestle. He was surprised by the strength under Morgan's layers of fat.

BACK HOME AGAIN

"HOME," TOM THOUGHT AS the roan cleared the first low hill and dropped the Platte ferry out of sight. The first time he had been alone in weeks—not sitting rigidly upright with elbows tucked, not rolling with the spine-shattering bounces of the cramped stagecoach, or riding a whirring train. No more of those sixteen-hour days spent trying to avoid the others' eyes.

The dry predatory air scoured his lungs, lifting his long hair off the neck and trellising it out behind; it rose and fell, fanning his back. Hyde's last letter said that the Laramie Pawnee were in worse straits than when he last saw them. "And there are others, now, sharing their fate." Tom would soon know what other tribes had prostrated themselves, soon know when he would go back to the Cheyenne to see his parents, Mohe, and his friends.

Hyde's letter also laid out a grandiose scheme for irrigating the entire Platte Valley with windmills. This intrigued Tom, but he wondered if the windmill venture offered the colonel a way of sidestepping the still unsettled railroad question.

South of the Platte the country had more roll, which relieved the regularity and made Tom feel he was getting somewhere. Like the ferryman said, the roan lathered quickly, though that seemed to help her get her wind. He galloped through the patchily bald terrain, the mare's hooves beating that fast familiar roll on the hard-packed ground just under the loose dust.

He came up over a virtually hairless hill and below him, baking in the middle of that enormous skillet of a valley, lay Laramie. Main Street had thickened some, but the town looked smaller than he remembered. He looked beyond the single street to where the Laramie River made its cinch loop around the fort. "Flagpole, Old Bedlam, the jail." Three, no four new whitewashed buildings stood in a straight row. The earthworks now made a semicircle, the raised surface of a smile running southwest to southeast. The remnants of the original Pawnee village sat at the base of the grin, but the outline of the old camp circle had been obliterated and now tepees were strewn haphazardly to the south, as though forced by hunger to eat up more of the valley floor. On the eastern outskirts near the Laramie River, a second spire caught his eye—Hyde's windmill.

Scanning the town again, he located Elizabeth's house. "Have they aged? Will they be there? What will I say?" Two and one-half years had passed.

Tom reined up smartly in front of the house, swung out of the saddle and dropped to the ground. He took the steps in two strides and ran straight into Elizabeth's arms. She smelled dry and warm, of talc and a faint familiar perfume. At arms' length he inspected her. Her hair had turned a bit grayer, her eyebrows still dark but touched with gray now, too. "You look wonderful. Absolutely radiant!"

His familiarity—and the unfamiliarity of his tall good looks, his confident charm—Tom seemed so different from the child Elizabeth remembered. She suddenly felt shy and a little hesitant.

"But I've gotten dust all over you."

"Take more than that to dampen her spirits." The colonel stepped forward, grinning, and took Tom by the shoulders. They stood head to head. Hyde tried to picture the bewildered child he had left on a train platform in New York. "Welcome home," he said softly.

Elizabeth had thought his face might be thinner, but she hadn't imagined how this would emphasize the cheekbones, lending the face an exotic, almost austere quality; those full lips were not a child's.

"Why you're a perfect young gentleman!" she concluded.

"Hardly perfect. I'm saddlesore from doing nothing but sitting where one sits for the past two weeks. Can't wait to stretch my legs and scrape the dust out of my throat."

"Did you see the town?" the colonel asked.

"Yes. And your windmill too. From a distance." Tom suddenly regretted he hadn't stopped there. "I'm sure it hasn't been easy—I mean, convincing the town they needed it."

Hyde's smile momentarily faltered at this allusion to the difficulty he had had financing the project. He felt annoyed Elizabeth had written about it.

"What are we doing standing out here?" She opened the door. "Come in."

"Where is your luggage?"

"Coming on with the stage. Don't give it a thought, Colonel."

Hyde's jaw muscles set. "I think I'll run over and check."

"Don't bother, sir. The driver told me he'd bring them along."

"Come inside, Ben," Elizabeth urged. "Don't run off now."

Hyde insisted on clearing up the matter of Tom's luggage. Looking sheepish, he quickly mounted and rode off with: "Only take a minute."

Suddenly alone on the quiet sun-dowsed porch, Tom and Elizabeth exchanged a long smile—it started as affectionate indulgence toward the colonel, but as it melted away Elizabeth's reserve it spread to blanket the entire occasion.

"It's good to be home," Tom said gloriously.

Inside, everything was as he remembered: the lace-covered tables still held the porcelain ballerinas, the little rose quartz birds with amethyst eyes, the bowing Limoges shepherdess whose snowy skin now reminded him of Dorothea. His eyes roamed the room like a scout, checking for changes. Only the draperies were new, a bright floral damask. He said, and he meant it, "Elizabeth, this is the most beautiful, elegant room in the whole country."

"You're marvelous, Thomas! You've grown so."

"Same package, different size and shape. Will you excuse me a moment, I just want to run up to my room."

He was still upstairs, testing the rope springs of the bed, drinking in the dry sandalwood fragrance he had tried to remember for so long, when the colonel rode up. Tom tapped on the windowpane and waved with delight to the man below. The colonel pantomimed what Tom assumed to be a report on the successful dispatch of his luggage.

Tea awaited Tom when he came down. "How's Mr. Bushnell?" he asked. The huckleberry tarts made their loving way to him.

"Fine. You'll see him in a day or two."

"And Matthew—what do you hear from him?"

Sherrin had been transferred from a post in Charleston, South Carolina, to western Pennsylvania, primarily to get him out of the South. "He should be made a captain soon. Jim is working on that; I write periodic endorsements. But the South has such a stranglehold on the chain of command, it's hard to push a Northerner up the ladder, no matter how good."

"There's so much I want, we want, to ask you, Thomas. But are you tired? You look a little tired."

"More like excited and tired at the same time."

Tom savored the sugary lightness of the pastry and its tart berries. In mid-swallow he remembered and had trouble forcing down the pie. "About the Pawnee, Colonel—your last letter left me up in the air."

"I'd almost rather show you than talk about it."

"What other tribes are out there now?" Tom skirted the direct question.

"Sioux, mostly Santee with a scattering of Lakota, a few Cree—The buffalo are disappearing fast. That's one of the problems; actually, it's all a problem." The voice sounded soothing, sympathetic.

"There will be a great deal to do this summer. A new treaty has to be drafted. Perhaps you can help me."

Tom didn't want to hear any more; all those days of riding concentrated in the small of his back.

"I'm not trying to get rid of you," Hyde said, "but you look exhausted."

Tom forced another bite before he laid down his fork, too tired to go on.

"You're right. I'd love to sit here all day with you, but I can't."

"Don't be silly," Elizabeth scolded. "Go on up to bed."

Up he went, undressed, and fell asleep in seconds.

So familiar for him to stagger into the kitchen barely awake, pull up his stool, watch Elizabeth's intent movements as she shifted pans, spilled off grease, shook the eggs so they wouldn't get that papery crust he hated and had spent his time East forcing down. How he loved her square-cut face, its broad brow, the generous frame of bone that set off her smoky eyes. They made him think of the Cheyenne rule that demanded a man avoid looking at his mother-in-law's eyes. Cheyenne. He could go home to his family now—if he wanted to.

"The colonel looks very well."

"Ben's so happy to have you home. I can't tell you how much he's missed you. He's been saving up all his summer projects for your return."

"I thought I'd ride over to the fort after breakfast, unless there's something you want done here."

"No, it would be nice for you to be together."

"Elizabeth," he asked, contemplating the egg's perfect white with the edge of his fork, "what about the train surveys? Are they going better?"

She frowned. "Yes and no. It's unpredictable, always up and down. They just can't seem to resolve it."

"Did Mr. Coughlin's becoming a Republican upset the colonel?"

"Yes, it did. Ben's accepted the move, but he isn't used to not having Jim in the Democratic power councils."

"The mare!" Tom exclaimed, sliding off his stool. "I'm supposed to return the ferryman's mare by noon!"

She smiled. "Ben sent one of his men over this morning."

"Oh." Tom felt half-impressed, half-annoyed at Hyde's formidable efficiency. "I'll ride over tomorrow and thank the ferryman."

She nodded. "By the way, Private Downing returned Cloud last night—he's up the street at the livery."

Tom's heart began pumping alarms at the first sight of the stockade, even before he saw forty or so ragged tepees sprawled over the bottomland, a mile south of the fort on the far side of the Laramie River. To the east, near a bald ridge, Hyde's windmill tilted at the sky.

The tribe lived in lodges patched with worn army slickers and other scraps of U.S. issue. "Better to build cabins than live like this!" In his field glasses he spotted a painted tepee—its coyote peeling off, leaving a black smear of nose and a scabrous tail. Another painted lodge bore the ensign of the 3rd Nebraska Cavalry, a pair of crossed Springfield rifles.

Without actually thinking, he rode toward the straggling settlement. He stopped fifty yards away from a lodge, near a half-burnt mound of rubbish—paper, garbage, what might've been human excrement, and the remains of a rusted rifle. Dogs half-heartedly scavenged there while three naked boys performed a parody of a war dance. A bent-backed old man in a cavalry hat moved aimlessly along the perimeter. Though the afternoon was warm, six blanket-draped men sat before a fire, passing two whiskey bottles.

At first they eyed Tom suspiciously, sneaking glances at the dark, well-dressed stranger, uncertain whether they could afford to be surly. Even that vague hostility quickly subsided. They seemed more interested in the two amber bottles.

Tom didn't draw any closer. He saw no women in the camp. Did they hide in shame? In one of those dilapidated lodges did a woman sit stitching deerskin or fleshing hides? It seemed unlikely. Tom had come back to the Plains fully intending to rededicate himself to his mission. But now that he had arrived, now that he saw Indians, he felt fearful, unwonted flutters deep in the pit of his stomach. He had been away longer than he knew.

Tom did not know how long he sat on Cloud watching the listless camp while trying to remember the pleasurable bustle of his Cheyenne home. Eventually a round-faced woman with beautiful black hair emerged from the lodge marked with the crossed rifles. Her army shirt was parted to reveal the cleavage between her breasts. Tom grew aroused even before she cupped those breasts and began to rub them in slow hard circles. The red snake of her tongue ran over the upper lip, intimating he'd be wild for the taste. "Soldier's whore," he reproved without noticeable effect on his genitals.

Not satisfied with the young stranger's response, she slowly unbuttoned her shirt. Mouth open, tongue working the lip, she rolled the nipples between her fingers, stretching the tips longer and longer until they stood erect and pointed right at him.

Suddenly the men at the fire got louder and a sallow young man pitched over backward. Two laughed riotously, another jumped up and shoved the brave next to him. Tom swung around to watch them fight over the last swig, relieved to get his eyes off the woman. He had never seen grown Indians strike one another before.

He turned in the saddle again. The new three-story officers' barracks loomed above the plain, its breeze-cooled porch wrapped all the way around the second floor. Tom could see the gravel paths that ran up to the steps of the barracks from the whitewashed outbuildings, scoring the dusty ground in orderly fashion. New corral, carpenter shop, the rebuilt timber shed—all ran in a line east. "A man can't live in the shadow of another man's power, on rejected scraps from his table, and not lose heart. Red man has a vision, but he's lost the strength to support it. A vision without strength," Tom proposed, Cable-like. "And the whites—all strength and absolutely no vision!"

He remained transfixed, unwilling to look again at the camp or the woman. He might have stayed there all day if he hadn't heard light steps running toward him—three children roughly eight or nine years old, all scrawny with tight little bellies and rib cages of chicken bones. The biggest one screamed, "Penny! Penny!" The others picked it up, "Penny! Penny!" With these shrill shouts they began to dance around the pony. Cloud backed nervously.

"She-it! She-it!" their leader chanted, dancing near the pony's hooves. "Penny! Penny! Penny!"

Sick to his stomach, Tom reached into his waistcoat pocket, took all his change and flung it down. They dove for it, the biggest boy sinking a knee into the back of a smaller one and pinning him while he stretched out over the body and groped for the half dollar. "Sheet! Sheet!" cried the little one as he spat out a mouthful of dust. "I kill you sheet!"

Tom spun his pony around and rode off a couple of hundred yards. On a rise by a cluster of dwarf pines he bent down over Cloud's side and threw up.

Light-headed and shaky Tom stepped from the colonel's front porch into the anteroom. He paused there, trying to order the crazy patchwork of his thoughts, but the scene offered only a strange, hallucinatory familiarity. He wondered how it could remain so much the same when he and those Indians outside had become so utterly different.

The colonel sat behind his desk. Everything else had been pegged in its old place—the familiar maps with their pins, the books lining the wall, even Matthew's upright desk. Only the quill medallion near Hyde's hand looked new. "Sioux," thought Tom. He remembered when all white men's knowledge, when all their terrible new power seemed lodged in this rough board room.

"Did you rest?" Hyde asked anxiously.

Though Tom had finger-combed his hair and rinsed his mouth, his eyes were watery and he looked awful.

"I slept well enough."

"You've seen the camp."

Tom nodded unhappily.

"These last few years have been difficult out here. The buffalo are disappearing like snow in springtime. It's brought despair and panic and these, of course, are impossible to reason with." The colonel had to explain the process already underway which, like all historical processes, was not simply the result of white man's greed or politics in Washington. If the boy placed too much blame on policy, he would misunderstand the very thin margin on which a man could work effectively.

Tom had just come from a broken, humiliated people—his people. He didn't want wisdom or sweeping prophecies now.

"Let me try to put it clearly and simply," Hyde went on. "The tribes have to be domesticated. I see no other way. They are *functionally* defenseless."

Tom's jaw muscles locked, his finger traced the diamond outline on the medallion. Hyde had used that phrase in his last letter. Did he suppose that Tom had grown used to the idea by now? No, there had to be other options: some way to retain their dignity and some part of the old ways. The place he had just come from—a dungheap, a graveyard, where the Indians' omnipotent enemy had sunk a bottomless well shaft through the center of all forms of ceremony and tradition. Tom felt he had already heard the colonel's overbearing preachments. He did not care to listen to them on this day from this man.

"The younger braves talk war. But that's no answer. We've got to keep them off the warpath."

Blood incarnadined the boy's face. Sympathy and comfort were his needs now, not insults. "Isn't it better to die with honor?" The automatic litany seemed spoken by an old part of himself.

For an instant Hyde looked at him as though his question raised doubts about all they had accomplished together; the look took them back to their first clashes—the day the boy refused to speak, the day the colonel dazzled the child with the simple magic of the glass. The colonel's eyes tried to drop the charge of treason, but the muscles around his mouth upheld the conviction. "Indians shoot and dance around the fire and get themselves worked up and ride out to kill 3 white men. Newspapers nationwide scream massacre and that mobilizes political support. Generals eager to make reputations push through requests for more troops, and 2 battalions of cavalry wipe out a village of 112 women, children, and old people." His voice calmed to a low growl: "You and I have got to protect red men from their own senseless and outmoded idea of honor!"

"He's right, you know," Tom's brain hissed to his abject heart, to his roiling viscera. "We have work to do! work to do!" While that phrase rolled through his mind he saw an image of eastern schoolboys in blazers and knee socks, laughing and shouting mingled with quiet conversations in paneled drawing rooms, and those mingled images spread like a snowy blanket over the turmoil. School seemed so easy, so manageable now.

Believing he had made his point, the colonel said, "Let's go see the windmill."

The windmill tower was a tapered lattice truss of pine, supporting the iron shaft which ran from the gear on which the blades turned down to the pump. The blades were slightly scooped, slender paddles roughly six feet long and skewered by a rod which extended through to the other side of the tower and flattened into a fifth stabilizing paddle that stuck straight out through the back. The tower stood thirty-three feet high.

In its shadow, Hyde explained he changed the blades to wood because the cloth kept tearing. He could raise another three hundred to four hundred gallons a day, he figured, for the Greeks drew treble that amount at places where the water table was not twice Laramie's. However, Avery had balked at giving the colonel loans for excavation, pipe, construction of a second mill, and he had to pay for part of the cedar water tank out of pocket. Hyde would not use army material or personnel until he got the department's approval. Which had been delayed because the southern-dominated command insisted on other priorities. The colonel kicked up dust with his boot heel. "I know I could turn this place into a blooming garden." In his mind, Hyde saw miles and miles of wheat, corn, potatoes stretching in every direction to the horizon. But Tom hadn't been listening well enough to dredge up the proper response.

They climbed up, the tower swaying under their weight, the whistling wind untouched all the way from Laramie Peak to the eastern rim of the bowl. The blades creaked; they had to be oiled constantly because the wind dried them out so quickly.

Bent double, Hyde poked his oil can into the parched bearings. That intense pip of a man, whose own covering seemed to be dying out as he aged, this leathery crusader out there battling with as much success as those bladed fingers outstretched to catch a wind to draw up a pitiful dribble. And below, to show for it—a postage-stamp garden of drooping lettuce, limp cabbage, dusty turnips.

The wind whistled hollow, the dry plain stretched out forever.

"Enough wind up here, aye?" Hyde shouted, a landlocked sea captain. The words got stretched by the wind, the sound blown away.

"The railroad and the windmill, they're the same thing," Tom thought. "He has a penchant for gestures like that. What did Hall say of Cable? 'If he can't handle that spineless backbiter Bovie, how can he tell us how to live?' " The colonel faced an epidemic of problems: a reluctant bank, an uncooperative water table, a skeptical town. How old, how betrayed had he felt when Coughlin wrote that he had decided to turn Republican? On top of that, the route of the railroad, on which he had staked everything, remained unsettled. Had Hyde lost his touch? Out of the corner of his eye Tom examined the crusty old weasel, his hair whipped flat back by the wind. The words slipped out: "Are the surveys any more promising, sir?"

Hyde blinked into the wind. Did he detect a sardonic note? Both of them had put in a difficult day. He yelled, "No, not yet. But I live in hope!" The wind stretched the last word to many syllables.

By nature an interventionist, the colonel could not keep his nose out of Tom's business. He could not resist telling his protégé to hold the hammer at the far end when the boy tried to hang up Elizabeth's new etching. He also told Thomas to carry the carving knife with the point down, to which Tom almost replied, "Indians never trip." Elizabeth, who couldn't help observing Tom's testiness with these fatherly directives, waited until after lunch when they sat in the rockers: "Ben can't do enough for you, you know."

Tom studied her face for signs of partisanship, wondering if he ought to say it. "He treats me like an infant!" It came out harsher than he wanted.

She looked wounded. "Indulge him," she counseled. "It can't hurt you, Thomas. He's had so little time with you and seeing you now, he knows you haven't much childhood left."

He rode away from the frame house feeling happier, promising himself he would hold still the next time Hyde reknotted his cravat. The pony took him along the southern edge of town, within sight of the fort. He tried not to pick up the Pawnee village out of the corner of his eye.

The hard-packed turf sang under Cloud's hooves, the enormous blanket of sky stretched over Tom. The world didn't pinch here like the East; no directional arrows pointed toward this or that; he felt free to ride and ride toward that thin blue line that ringed the horizon.

How much Elizabeth knew about that delicate, mutually understanding trade by which one person comes to live with another's virtues and foibles. Could Elizabeth's love for the colonel and him make him feel so alive and responsive? Or was it simply being home again? Home—how strongly he had felt the pull in the East, where the Plains worked like a giant magnet drawing him back to his parents and Mohe. How much Shell and Big Road cared for one another: he could remember only that single serious fight, after the battle. He remembered their delight at being near each other. His foster parents never touched. He doubted that Coughlin and Dorothea ever made love. Some strange, ugly reserve stepped in between men and women in the white world.

Tom found Cloud heading in a familiar direction.

The knoll looked exactly as he remembered it, the same stunted pines, the same straggly outcroppings of bunchgrass; the large indifferent sky seemed to have sucked everything vivid up into it. Cautious, he studied the site from the pony's back. Finally he dismounted. Tom stood a few moments eyeing the spot—they had lain in wait just behind that scythelike ridge. A shiver passed down his spine, articulating his vertebrae like piano keys. "Strange, how strange!" From that spot he had always started his run.

He could picture himself moving through the hot frictionless air, down those slight inclines, up the rises, his limbs lubricating as he ran. His breathing quickened, deepened. The edges of sluggish memory sharpened—he was back there, ready to hear a shot ring out. For the first time in years he felt real fear, physical fear. "I could have been killed!" he yelled to the hills. "Me! Dead!"

Sweat poured off him when he pressed the top of his thighs, drummed harder than usual on his stomach. He began to run in place until he felt more like himself. His father told him about a warrior being granted a vision of his death; the warrior had died in battle just as he had foreseen it. Remounting, finally, Tom blessed the place. He had been to his death site and met the boy he had once been.

Hyde had excellent reasons for sending Tom to the Pawnee camp: to find out what the Indian thought about the things happening around him; to sound the red man on his desires; to spell out the options to him. Tom's interpreter in these polling sessions, a stock clerk at the General Store, knew little beyond dry-goods English. He behaved with unwavering unctuousness while he hinted at a complicity between them, which made Tom wonder if they were partners in the sad business of betraying their people.

For a week Tom's eyes moved from lusterless eye to scabby face to toothless maw to slack belly. He asked: "What job would you like?" Meaning, white job. Almost to a man they said, "Scout"—the only available work involved spying on other Indians. When asked if learning English would help them, a few told Tom what they thought he wanted to hear. One drunk, queried about career plans, said, "I get drunk." Tom thought another said: "Kiss women."

In his black notebook he scribbled:

> Three born, 1 alive, age 11. Tell Dr. Wester to treat High Bear's abscessed elbow.
> Five born, one gone renegade, daughter in Indian Territory; 3 deceased, 2 of the cholera. Dirty bandage to be changed (White Buck). No boots; also need buffalo robes for fall.

He lectured captive red men about the possibility of raising cattle; the government might be persuaded to provide two or three head per family. There would be milk. They looked back blankly, sensing that this white Indian didn't believe it himself. Tom knew that buffalo needed more grass than they could get on the remaining open range, yet he ran through the government-issue arguments for buffalo breeding. To almost all his suggestions the Indians—Pawnee, the few Cree, the all too many Sioux—remained impersonally polite and generally disinterested. To schools, the colonel's newest hope, an old man replied, "You ask to put our people inside the log squares, learn about the lines that crawl like yours." Tom kept busy by scribbling in front of them, scribbling in his black notebook. "It is hard to feed ourselves now without losing hunters." Tom saw a ten-year-old Pawnee boy struggling to nock an arrow.

Tom took two leisurely days to reach the junction of Frenchman's Creek and the Republican River, two days of riding along roads and rough cart tracks, past more farms and cattle than he imagined the prairie could support. Everywhere the grass had been burned out or overcropped. Tom waited one full day at the rendezvous site, a sandbar under an overhanging wooded bank. He sat and thought of his parents and whether he would go home as buffalo with patchy coats came to drink from the turgid stream and nibble at the dry grass.

The second evening two Pawnee rode in. After examining Tom's store-bought "Western style" gabardine outfit with its fancy stitching, one deferentially said Bushnell would be along by nightfall.

"How is the herd?"

The scout softly clicked his tongue. "Not good. Bad."

They commiserated silently until the same one asked, "O.K. We swim?"

Tom felt hurt by the question. "Of course. Go right ahead."

"You swim too?"

"No thanks."

Off came their brimless cavalry hats, the chaps, and army jackets, and the two bronzed figures went down to the water naked. They bathed while three buffalo slurped the creek water, only occasionally bothering to raise their shaggy heads. Tom wondered why he hadn't accepted their invitation.

Bushnell made it under an hour. Crashing out of the brush along the riverbank he yelled, "Gawd, pup, yo' shot up into a full growed."

The boy felt happy to see him. "What did you expect?"

"Nothin'. I just din't know when I wuz goin' t' git a gander at yo'!" Bushnell gently pounded Tom's shoulder.

The Pawnee crouched near the cooking fire, viewing the reunion at a considerate distance.

Tom told his old friend that he had missed him, that the East still seemed strange in many ways, and that he had only a few friends at school, but that they were important to him. He never got too specific, but Bushnell listened sympathetically, as though he understood something about the strangeness of it all.

"Yo' stickin' with my outfit a day or two?"

"Yes. I'd like to help with the buffalo count."

"Glad yo' stayin' on, boy, but ah don' need all that much help. Damn few bulls, fewer bearin' cow, and only a slim number o' pups."

"What's said in council now?"

"Let's go fetch us a stick o' firewood o' two." He said it loud enough to be overheard.

They crossed the sandbar and made their way toward the wooded bank. Bushnell bent down and picked up a willow limb, then banged it on the ground, testing for rot. "Don' like talkin' 'bout it near them Pawnee."

A high pile of limbs lay under the overhanging bank, and they scrounged for good wood in among the deadfalls. "Older braves say white man don't know how to live this land. Say he'll go away. But mos' o' them know better. Jus' whistlin' in the dark to kill the fear. Young bucks want t' fight. Always do." He looked sharply at Tom. "Old uns know fightin' jus' means more dead Injuns."

Tom's stomach sank; the sentiment sounded too much like Hyde's.

"Sioux always ask if more whites is on the way. Great White Father tell 'em a hunnert soldiers stand behind every single white settler. Reckon from what I seen it's true too."

"Do you get near Cheyenne camps?" Tom's heart leapt into his throat.

"Now and then," Bushnell answered guardedly.

All those long months at Arundel Tom had dreamed of walking into his village and throwing his arms around his parents, his grandfather, his friends. At school when the students' callousness made him feel most alone, he thought of the kindness of the Cheyenne. But one week in the Pawnee camp dramatized how far he had grown away from his people. And just this evening two Indians had treated him like a white. Maybe that's why Hyde's question had stunned and enraged him;

maybe that's why Tom could not tell the colonel if he intended to go home. "However bad it is for them not knowing how I am or what I'm doing, that might be worse," he thought. Worse for what? Tom felt afraid his people would not know him; he could not stand to carry the same message of doom to the Cheyenne that he carried among the Pawnee. He had a desperate longing to see Mohe, to make certain that his grandfather lived.

Meanwhile Bushnell waited, expressionless. That blankness brought Tom a certain relief.

The Pawnee pair joined them for a supper of dried buffalo hump and Bushnell's celebrated broth. It tasted gluier than Tom remembered.

"What do you think of the colonel's windmill?"

"Don' reckon it matte' much what I think. But it ain' the town's favorite project, I ken tell yo' that."

They sat feeling the endless prairie shrink up toward them; underneath their feet the sandbar became a broad gray paint stroke. The dark of the wooded bank leaned over them.

"In the morning I'll teach you to ride eastern style."

Bushnell sent a questioning hand into the intricacies of his beard. "Eastern?" he asked, as if it was a dirty word.

Tom pulled out his diary and quickly sketched an eastern saddle.

"Whar's the horn?"

As the scout leaned over the book Tom smelled the old Bushnell; it had been a long time. Bushnell scrutinized the drawing. "I think I seen one once. Yup, German gent over in Dodge."

Tom didn't know how, but he knew Bushnell lied. Later, settling his head on his saddle, Tom let the wave of disappointment settle. He felt deeply sad, horribly sad. His people's way of life was dying, he knew that now. And all the men he loved, the men he counted on, had insupportable limitations.

After chasing down the grease with Bushnell's coffee and spitting out the grounds, they rode off to catch the buffalo herd. The Sioux camp lay four miles down the Republic River. On the way Tom showed Bushnell how to post. The scout played the Englishman well—elbows out, back straight. They both laughed at the incongruity.

Approaching a bend in the river, they felt the earth dancing in light staccato; a huge dust cloud floated east.

"She-it!" Bushnell swung a clenched fist in the air. "They're off." He kicked his pony forward; Tom raced after him.

The Sioux's first charge had stampeded the herd. "Mistake," Tom thought. The main bunch still held together, a dark brown blanket drawing rapidly across the prairie. But more and more of those brown dots kept shooting off in all directions as though spun out of a centrifuge. They raced for the broken-backed ridge and spotted themselves there. The scout obligingly passed Tom the binoculars.

Four buffalo had been felled by arrows, two mature bulls, a cow, and a calf. The calf surprised Tom; only children took them, and then only after the bulls on the final cleanup runs. One bull lay on its side, one leg helplessly flaying the air; another had crumpled up over its legs and sat there as if resting. Tom scanned the prairie—a thick-shouldered brave drew alongside a bull and struck his lance into the hump, a perfect hit. Then, to Tom's amazement, the man ripped out the lance with a corkscrew motion of his wrist. The buffalo veered at the warrior, who whipped his pony's head aside; the animal jumped sideways, or seemed pulled, a puppet on a string. He repeated the same clean thrust, the same wrenching withdrawal of the lance till thin parallels of blood ran like red beads along the heaving flanks, till the animal's eyes grew crazed from the anguish and blood spewed out of the mouth. Tom had never seen such cruelty before. Food was not to be tortured.

The bull fell. Tom's binoculars skimmed over the stampeding mounds. He watched for as long as he could, seeing several fine kills—a Sioux drilling a deadly arrow into the chest, a perfect lance thrust through the hump. But he also witnessed winded ponies who could not close on lumbering bulls, and ponies who would not cling to the buffalo's flank; he saw one pony gored and a man's leg broken as the animal fell. One brave took three point-blank pistol shots at a bull's head before bringing it down.

Afterward Tom said in a shaky voice, "I'm sorry I didn't offer you the glasses."

"That's O.K. I seen it all befo'. Too many time."

Tom didn't have the heart to count the kill.

"Don't fret yo'self too much, boy," Bushnell offered, trying to touch his young friend in the right spot. "Some places ain' as sorry as this un."

"Just be patient," Elizabeth instructed the colonel one blazing afternoon in late July. They sat in their usual places, barely able to move for the heat. Elizabeth's light cotton frock bore dark semicircles under the arms; Hyde dabbed at his forehead with his handkerchief. They sipped lemonade.

"I've given him half the summer."

Her voice sounded soothing in the darkened room. "Ben, don't be too demanding of him. It's so very hard for Tom; his life is so unusually complicated."

"But he doesn't even like Indians." Hyde sat up, freeing his sticky back. He paid a price for it—a rash of exasperated sweat beads popped out on his face. "Can't stand to be around them."

"How could he?" She spoke authoritatively. "Tom's trying to dig up the Indian part of him and separate it from what is white. No Indians here resemble what he once knew, and he certainly doesn't care to remember himself or his family like that. Imagine how confusing it is! Imagine coming back to a world so utterly changed. Mr. Bushnell made it clear how sick he was with the buffalo hunt."

"It's not only that—it's those striped trousers, the way he lounges around like an insouciant nobleman. Do you know the Pawnee laugh at him? Elizabeth, he'd rather read Byron or go posting on that Connecticut saddle of his than work on Sioux or teach the scouts English."

"Ben, Ben, maybe that's what he wants right now—but that's no indication he'll want it tomorrow or next year."

"He wants it both ways full-blooded red man to feed his blind pride—white man when it suits him."

"What rivals they've become," Elizabeth thought. Hyde's attitude seemed ridiculous to her. If only Ben had a little more imagination. "You can't ask this poor confused child for consistency now. That's one thing he can't provide." She shifted in her rocker. "How can he understand what should be done—or what his role should be, as you say—when neither he nor you nor anyone else has the vaguest idea what the answer to this intolerable problem is. That's true, isn't it?"

Stiffly Hyde agreed.

"You once said—years ago—that Tom learned by imitating us. Well, he can't imitate those Indians at the fort." She was moving closer to it, formulating as she went along. "So of course he behaves like an Arundelite." She paused. "Especially around you. You with your demands and programs."

"Don't haunt me with my old prophecies." He said it gently, acknowledging her insight. "I get enough of that from my political enemies."

"He'll learn from this confusion, Ben. He'll straighten it out for himself. But we must be gentle." She was fervent. And to Hyde, in the hot dark, she looked very beautiful, very appealing.

"Got any more of this stuff?" he conceded with a tired smile and the offer of his empty glass.

The summer sped by. Elizabeth remained solicitous of Tom's confusion, which Tom appreciated up to a point. Beyond that, his emotional reliance on her made him feel soft. He wondered if it had been worthwhile to come to the white world. But one look at the post Indians answered that—they desperately needed leadership. To become their leader, that's why he stayed with the whites. He thought about going home and put it off, and put it off.

Meanwhile, the colonel tried to convince Tom of the urgency of the red man's problem. Tom got the message, but that only depressed and further confused him. The colonel impatiently pushed more responsibilities at him. Tom and Hyde broke, as much as they ever broke, over Indian policy. The older man insisted on hustling red man out of his old life and into a new, unfamiliar system of formal education and animal husbandry. Tom hated their present condition, but clung to a nostalgic, even irrational hope that vestiges of their old life could be retained. To himself he insisted that after his education ended, then, an answer would appear.

Elizabeth and the colonel and Bushnell saw him off—their parting was pleasant enough. Really the summer had passed pleasantly, though their emotional cloud had lost the silver lining of those early days.

Back at school Tom brooded over the state of Indians and thought up things he should've said to Hyde. He smiled even less, talked more and too loud. The others, never slow to pick up on a classmate's foibles, let him run on to amuse themselves. Tom Hyde became nearly as unpopular as he had been after the Alcohol Seven incident, almost as quickly.

And so he came, a few weeks after his return, to be inspecting his nude body in front of the full-length mirror in the deserted bathroom. He found a passable crop of hair gracing his crotch, but the chest offered only a few scant strands. The face was beardless. His copper skin looked hatefully dark to him. He chafed the left forearm with his right hand, wanting to scrape it down to the pink. He pinched the nostrils together till they hurt, wondering if he could straighten them by sleeping with a clothespin on his nose. He pulled the straight black hair up, then let it fall. Perhaps a curling iron would give it curl.

That evening Arundelites learned that Tom Hyde didn't understand the meaning of garbage until he lived with whites for three months. Next came the stories about drunken Indians; then the confession that he had lived all his life with fleas until the soldiers disinfected him.

They flocked to his room to hear that Indians were filthy, stupid, savage, and bestial, that red men lived like beasts—grubbing roots and cooking worms over buffalo turd fires. Soon the best turned away, including, most notably, Morgan Hall. That left only the dregs, who giddily buzzed around the corpse of Tom's integrity. As often as he could he drank as much as he could, threw up virtually every weekend night of fall term, and often woke to find himself in chilly cellars or lying in mud puddles not knowing how he got there. His work suffered, but he kept on drinking. In sober moments, he read everything he could get about Indians—from explorers' diaries to official reports of expeditions, from bogus "scientific" accounts to trashy popular reporting. What he read confirmed his theory—red men were filthy unregenerate savages and doomed. Twice Cable called him in for conferences. But lectures didn't touch Tom.

For the better part of the school year, Tom embarrassed himself by living like a cur. Aside from his letters to Laramie and Washington, in which vestiges of his dignity survived, he took pleasure only in icy baths and trouncing his classmates in foot races—not particularly civilized virtues. For the first time in his life, Tom reveled in despising himself.

Three days before the end of spring term, Morgan Hall walked into 317. Surprised, Tom spun a chair around for his old friend.

"Don't point that thing at me! I don't want any hostly cheer while I'm in here."

This caught Tom off guard—precisely Morgan's intention. He had come with a singular purpose, like a swimmer who knows the precise number of breaths required, with only enough energy to finish: "I address you as a graduating senior which, as you may recall from your less loathsome days, is not my customary role." Hall's pudgy face soured in disgust.

"This year—this year I haven't seen much of you. Why then? Because your behavior has been revolting, that's why!"

Tom glared at him; he could've strangled Hall.

"Anyone can make excuses for you. Your position's difficult, whatever you faced out there wasn't pleasing— But to self-respect that's absolute nonsense, and you know it.

"I hardly know what to say—I'm appalled by this moral cowardice; I'm astounded that you enjoy being a laughingstock, that your pride can tolerate this. You put me in an untoward position, as sermonizing is expressly against all Hall principles. But I will, this once, because I can't leave without insisting that you stop this hateful behavior." Under the puffiness Tom saw a determined, serious face—like the muscles under the fat the day they arm-wrestled.

They stared at each other. Tom's heart raced as he listened to Hall's shallow breathing. Morgan Hall looked like he wanted to speak again, but he spun on his heel and marched out of the room. The knowledge that he'd never see Hall again broke Tom. But it was for much, much more than that that he leaned over his chair and sobbed.

Yale seemed too easy, too easy and all too familiar. Tom Hyde had wanted the college to be startlingly different, as different in its way as Arundel had been from Laramie and his lessons with the colonel. Yet within a month Yale College seemed merely an inflated Arundel. The same schoolmaster's tone prevailed, the same schoolboys' evasions were practiced. Tom met the scions of great families and found most of them as superficial, dissolute, and unengaging as the Arundelites. His classmates were young men now, with straggly fringes of whisker and struggling mustaches limply draped on undisguisably pink faces. These youths dressed well and were meticulously observant of changes in fashion; a few were attentive to politics. They brought along more servants, reserved, austere men who fussed and primped around their young masters. The town itself offered more variety than Arundel's village—restaurants, saloons, a few fashionable shops. Yet none of these small gains seemed grand enough to Tom. Even his studies were too easy, which suggested what an exceptional tutor he'd had. But the excellence of Cable's instruction provided little compensation during Tom's long hours in the classrooms.

The streets of New Haven, the mild dissipations, and the layout of his rooms had all settled into his life when, on October 16, 1859, John Brown's band struck at Harper's Ferry Arsenal. In a few hours the skirmish ended: Brown severely wounded and captured; sentenced to be hanged by "his vicious blasphemous Abolitionist neck until dead." For a week the campus came alive—northern youths held torchlight processions for Brown, southerners picketed with placards. Fistfights quickly gave way to secret duels at dawn. Two days after Brown's raid a man from Savannah who lived on Tom's floor failed to appear at breakfast. By noon the campus raged with the news: Hollings was in the hospital, shot in the shoulder by Hiram Woods. The wound was not fatal. For a month Hollings carried his arm in a blue sling.

In the Tribune, Greeley canonized Brown as a martyr, a saint. The southern press screamed back: "INVASION!"; asked editorially the size and extent of this plot, who financed it, and concluded that it would stop only "with the country streaming in blood and dishonor." Tom, who despised being stuck in New Haven while the country threatened to burst apart, wrote Coughlin, begging to come to Washington. A telegram arrived: STAY THERE! MARK TIME. LETTER TO FOLLOW.

In the letter Coughlin explained that Brown's raid represented only the first wave of hysteria, that it would take months before the southern legislatures organized their militias, before the threatened Secessionist Conferences could be convened. "New Haven should be large enough for you until summer. Meanwhile, learn something useful and keep your eyes open. Nothing will happen before the presidential election. I thought you understood that." Coughlin added that Mrs. Hastings concurred with his analysis.

Through a stormy winter which threatened national political disaster, Tom doggedly trudged to his classes. For diversion, he attended concerts, plays, and lectures. A few of the men who spoke at Yale did so as if they cared about the opinion of their audience, as if those who listened might some day have something to say to others. Tom Hyde placed the men who treated him as an adult in his private pantheon along with Hyde, Cable, and Coughlin. Thus he heard Henry Ward Beecher preach about the evils of slavery; thus he listened in awe as Emerson himself movingly spoke about Transcendentalism.

At a lecture about a Protestant mission in China, he heard a tall, thin, ascetic-looking minister effuse about "the joyous light that transfigured the spiritually blank eyes of the heathen." While the Christian condescension repelled Tom, the missionary's zeal excited him. He, too, would become a missionary. His message would be a secular one, no alien imposition. For he alone would be able to transform the lives of his people. When war came, he would fight against slavery. He'd persuade all Indians to oppose that odious crime. After the war, with his help, Indians would be able to seize the initiative in their own lives.

Tom wrote Hyde, proclaiming his joy at his "renewed sense of mission." He did not apologize to the colonel for the disastrous Laramie summer. In retrospect, that horrible summer somehow seemed necessary. Tom hated his cowardly shrinking away from the Pawnee; he hated his self-pity at Arundel and his painful parting with Hall. Yet he saw these failings with more equanimity than he had ever been able to bring to his own humiliations before. And he knew he'd never behave like that again.

After the China lecture, Tom became more patient with New Haven.

His fixed sense of purpose made most of his classmates seem unfocused and immature. He lived apart from them, but he did so without the formerly self-satisfying poses of martyrdom or superiority. Since he had no close friends, he did not feel fully engaged. At the same time he felt a growing confidence in his judgment, his character, his sense of himself. Once, the Arundelites had sensed his weakness and quickly taken advantage of it. Now a number of Yalies instinctively recognized, even appreciated, Tom's new sense of certainty. Tom Hyde created a place for himself. Classmates asked his opinion; some occasionally requested his company. Often that spring, Tom considered something Mrs. Hastings had said: "You've had no childhood." Tom felt her remark was wrong. He'd had one childhood; one was enough. Now he had to get on with the business of being an adult.

CHARLOTTE

Tom had been in the capital for two weeks when he received an invitation to a party at the home of Markham Harris, a good friend of the Coughlins, who had the bearing of a Roman noble and the admiration of all Washington. This powerful civil servant held an unassailable position beyond even the reach of politics. It couldn't be said, however, that politics lay beyond the reach of Markham Harris. Tom admired Harris at least as much for his daughter Charlotte, whom he had met at a ball the summer before. He had spent an unusually pleasurable, if temperate, evening dancing with her every third dance. Both seemed surprised to like each other as much as they did, Tom because she had a reputation for being chilly and as Roman as her father; she because she had heard the young Indian was unduly somber. Both had nice-enough feelings about the evening not to want them spoiled and they made no attempt to see each other again.

The Harris home conveyed an air of uncommon importance. A broad-columned portico overlooked a rigorously cropped lawn that swept right up to the house and dropped beyond it in a series of ample terraces down toward the Potomac. Beds of dahlias lined the carriage drive and in the fading light their edges became dark curves inscribed by a giant compass.

Tom stepped down lightly from Coughlin's carriage and made his way into the house among the other guests. In the main salon he said his good evening to Markham Harris, his wife, their son Stuyvesant, who also attended Yale but was three years his senior, and finally to

Charlotte. She looked very pretty, Tom thought, in a rose taffeta gown which opened in a modest yoke to reveal the smooth intricacies of her collarbone. As was proper, Tom asked Charlotte for a dance. She said, "Yes. The third." Tom didn't get the point.

He went on into the ballroom, hesitating inside the doorway before one of a group of young officers, all with drinks in hand, picked him out. "Over here, Hyde." Not that he could've missed them. They stood in the absolute middle of the dance floor.

They interrupted their heated talk about the tariff to welcome him back. Through the hellos and the do-you-knows, Tom's mind wandered. He smiled to himself and promptly switched his attention to the tariff question.

Tom offered the pro-western argument: encouraging the free farmer would help the country grow. As he stood there discoursing with them, Tom noticed something unusual. From one side of the room drifted the soft indolent southern sounds, from the other the sharper, more varied accents of the North. It felt curiously intimate, oddly sensual, to hear the split slowly made audible. Everyone began to notice. The servants who offered the drinks and hors d'oeuvres kept to the side they were on, not daring to upset the balance. Sentences broke off abruptly, and the ballroom grew quieter when a single Northerner ran on loudly about postal rates, his voice hollow in the large space. Surprised, he cut himself off in mid-syllable.

The young men in the middle of the floor, roughly divided into North and South, felt extraordinarily vulnerable. None knew where to look; they avoided each other's eyes. Then the music started.

Through the first two dances Tom conversed with a dowager who asked about Mrs. Hastings' health, then bore in on Dorothea, "the poor thing." Finally he excused himself and went to Charlotte, who looked as glad as he that their dance had come. She had been dancing with her podgy uncle.

As pleasantly as he could, Tom said, "So nice to see you again."

She nodded, expecting him to say something more. He didn't. That made it her turn to ask the dumb question. "You're at the Bureau?"

"I guess so—every morning I go to work."

"My father says you're indispensable." Markham Harris spoke with precision about important—meaning political—matters, and his daughter spoke precisely too. These questions aroused her most intense family feelings.

Since Charlotte looked interested, he said, "Oh, I do have some perspectives that the others lack."

They smiled together now, Charlotte a trace sheepishly, just as the music started.

The music carried them on to the floor and they waltzed in sweeping bows. As they wheeled toward the far end of the room, she was surprised how well he danced, this Indian who went to Arundel and Yale, Stuyvie's school. How odd, she thought, yet so pleasant. As she danced she closed her eyes a little so that the gas lamps glowed rainbows through her lashes.

To him she seemed very vivid. The word kept coming to him. Her body seemed weightless, almost translucent. Charlotte was blond, her aura golden, her eyes a startling blue. The first time Tom looked at her bodice, he thought something he had thought before: it was hard to tell the shape of a woman's breasts in a gown, from that angle. Then he imagined them clearly: firm and longer than they were round, full for her size, and lifting off her chest in rich crescents.

As the dance ended, Tom dabbed his forehead with his handkerchief. Charlotte had been promised to one of her father's secretaries for the next dance, but she excused herself and asked Tom to take her outside. He felt pleased, of course. Through the large french doors that opened on to the garden, they walked arm in arm and stood before one of the stone benches that lined the terrace.

"So you're glad to be in Washington?"

"Yes. It's good to leave school behind."

"Oh?" She tried to disguise her expression, but he knew she found it surprising.

The garden offered its lavish perfume of mimosa and honeysuckle, sweet and thick in the dark.

"I went to Yale carrying freshman baggage. I had my own idea of what it ought to be, so of course I was disappointed when it didn't turn out that way."

"What did you expect? Thrills? Adventure?"

"No, I had enough of that in other places."

She let it pass. "What *did* you expect?"

"Men of high virtue and integrity, men to look up to." Tom overstated this only enough to suggest he expected too much, but not enough to mock his own seriousness.

"And they weren't there?"

"I found men who spoke about everything but did not do anything, men who'd rather feel good about what they said than anything else. There were pedants, bores, drunks. I had one man who spent his life teaching ethics, yet was afraid he wouldn't look like a genius in front of a handful of freshmen unless he invented stories about things he had done in places he had never seen. We used to bait him—was that the trip to Tangiers, sir, or was it Morocco? I had a government professor who couldn't fathom the importance of the railroad surveys, who kept insisting war wouldn't come—men of good will would never let it. He knew less about politics than the file clerk at the Bureau. One professor told my class he hated to read—he woke up one day eight years ago and realized he never wanted to pick up another book as long as he lived. I could never go back there now."

"But you have to go back."

"I can't now that I'm actually getting a little done. Those professors at Yale are so insulated, Charlotte. The realities they're supposed to instruct us about don't penetrate the ivy on the walls."

"Washington's a little like that."

"At least some work gets done here."

"My father's always saying nothing ever gets done."

"Your father's right." Tom agreed without showing any embarrassment at the contradiction. "He's talking about what should be done and what actually gets done. But he hasn't visited New Haven lately." She smiled. "Here at least there's a sense of crisis. You can smell it here. Even a young bureaucrat may find a few interesting things to do soon."

"Oh, from what I gather, you already have."

Charlotte sat down on the bench and Tom joined her.

"No," he said disarmingly, "really I do very little. I tell them where a band of Sioux will be on June fifth or how many tribespeople can move together in early March, or what they'll need in the way of supplies—nothing of ultimate significance. Oh, and I'm the author of a few resounding phrases. 'As long as the grass shall grow and the rivers flow.' That's one of my most quoted."

She thought it touchingly beautiful, which made her gay. "You haven't lived in Washington long enough. You'll see, it's always the same—Presidents come and go, administrations switch places, a tidal wave could strike it, and after they cleaned up the debris it would be exactly the same."

Her intelligence impressed him, as did that hint of weariness. He demurred, "I do feel like I never left it."

Footsteps on the terrace interrupted their conversation. Stuyvesant Harris appeared, obviously come to fetch Charlotte. "Mother would like you to help Aunt Sarah arrange the interlude." He did not offer his hand to Tom. Charlotte rose and had already taken a step away from him when she turned back and touched Tom's hand. "You won't forget tea then, Monday at four." Then brother and sister disappeared into the gaily lit ballroom.

Tom sat down again, weighing this first mention of tea. Ten minutes later he reappeared in the ballroom, talked politics through two quadrilles; then he excused himself and went home.

Charlotte danced every dance the rest of the night; she danced with a number of officers, including Roger Whipple, an old beau and a friend of Stuyvie's. She was vibrant and gay—vivid, to use Tom's word. But she didn't say another word to her brother that evening. Aunt Sarah looked unusually vacant when Charlotte offered her help.

Upon retiring, Charlotte dismissed her maid, telling Carolyn to go to sleep in her own room. Then, in her nightgown, Charlotte took a place on the window seat and peered out into the garden.

Its smells rose to her, rich and familiar. Rain had not come. As the air touched her it felt turbulent; she wondered if it held its breath. Her head felt full of Tom Hyde. He had been rumored to be too earnest. That seemed wrong, stupid. He was charming, even witty; and he had that way of being aware of his seriousness without deprecating it. Intense, yes, but richly so. Not a solemn idealist and certainly not a fool.

And he happened to be an Indian, he made that perfectly clear. If he had pretended to be white, or toadied to whites, or tried to flatter her father, she would've dismissed him. If he had been belligerent, he would have bored her. Instead he struck a middle ground she never knew existed. Though she couldn't articulate it, she admired people who worked out problems that seemed insuperable to her. Charlotte was clever, but lazy. Yes, he was charming; surprisingly endearing, this strange red man. And handsome—she couldn't help giggling as she climbed into bed—for an Indian.

Two days later Tom received sufficient reason to change his mind about the importance of his work at the Indian Bureau. Coughlin's valet woke him and told Tom to hurry to the study. Coughlin had been up all night, his sandy hair rumpled, his shirt collar unbuttoned, but he looked young and fervent. As Tom shut the door, the older man began: the Secretary of the Army, that delightfully loyal gent from Macon, had a clandestine plan for reorganizing the territorial forts. This plan now circulated among the powerful Southerners who controlled the War Department. It called for the elimination of all small posts west of the Mississippi and their absorption into larger forts. In the name of economy, all weapons, ammunition, and ordnance would be stockpiled centrally. Did that sound reasonable? Certainly, once you understood that all the western garrisons, with the exception of Laramie, were commanded by Southerners.

"We need a countermove, Tom, one that will keep the Secretary and his cronies protecting their flanks for the next three months—until the election." Coughlin glanced up to make certain the boy understood. "I have in mind a letter that describes a bluff of sorts that anticipates the shenanigans they'd be up to if they'd thought of it first. Point is, the action it describes must be a plausible one, altogether in line with their present behavior. But I can't have the letter come out of my office."

Coughlin's smile dazzled the boy.

"I want this note in the summer dispatch to all post commanders. And, Tom, I'd like you to write it for us—in your own words."

Coughlin let the message sink in. After a pause, he added, "One final thing. This will be the first overt mention of a hostile act in a government document. Don't be surprised if someday some scholar accuses you of firing the first shot."

Using every spare moment, Tom was able to hand the Undersecretary this draft the next morning:

MEMORANDUM TO: Post Commanders

FROM: Thom. Hyde for the Bureau of Indian Affairs

Confirmation has just been received of a rumor that has been circulating for the past month among our informants in the Western Nebraska Territory. There is an agitator moving among the northern Plains Indians, and it is possible he will move South, to the Indian Territory. His purpose is not yet definitively known, though his activities are now under investigation. It is reported by John Bushnell, a scout attached to the Ohio Cavalry at Fort Laramie, that around the 5th of August this person, identified only as a tall dark man from Mobile, offered the Oglala headman 100 muzzle-loading and 25 breech-loading rifles, 5000 rounds of ammunition, and 2 light artillery pieces (not further identified) if the Sioux would repudiate the 1848 Laramie Treaty by refusing to appear at the fall gathering. Apparently there was a promise of more rifles in October if these Sioux also disputed certain access routes into the Black Hills along the proposed line of the new forts. It is still unclear whether this man is an adventitious renegade intent on profiteering or whether his activities are part of a larger network with hostile intentions toward the federal government.

In any event, this constitutes a clear threat to our present peaceful relations with the Sioux. We suggest you contact your superiors in the

War Department and inform the Bureau of Indian Affairs in the event of any repetition of this problem.

We feel it is our duty to alert you to possible sources of conflict in your command, and thank you in advance for your assistance in helping to preserve the peace and promote welfare among the tribes.

Verbatim copies forwarded to:
Secretary of the Army of the United States
Undersecretary of the Army of the United States
Adjutant General of the Army of the United States
Bureau chiefs of the Army of the United States

"This is perfect," the big man clucked to himself as he finished the draft.

Just before lunch Tom Hyde slipped the letter into the sheaf of orders and directives that made up the fall dispatch. That afternoon it went off to the printer. On the sixteenth of July, four days before its mailing date, the proofs came back and were sent into Smythe's office. From midmorning until lunchtime Tom doodled vacantly; he had difficulty digesting his cold chicken. At 1:17 the door at the front of the room burst open, banging against the wall so hard it almost shattered the pebbled glass. White-faced and trembling, Smythe, Tom's immediate superior, stalked stiffly down the aisle and turned into Tom's cubicle. "Who told you to write this?"

At their desks the others could hear each word plainly.

Tom took the paper thrust into his face. "I did. The information came from a scouting report from Fort Laramie. I knew you'd want to make the Bureau's position clear."

"I don't give a damn who—" Smythe stopped. He couldn't say what he wanted to about Coughlin or Hyde or this little Indian whelp and the plot they had cooked up. Not with everyone listening.

Tom looked hurt. "I just thought the commanding officers and our agency personnel ought to be alerted to this problem. That's all, sir."

"This is not our domain!" his boss shouted, slamming his fist on Tom's desk.

"Oh, but it is, Mr. Smythe. We're responsible for any threats to the treaties. That was the Bureau's position on the settlers who started the trouble with the Seminole. Then there was the Sauk-Fox conflict about the railroad right-of-way. You remember." Tom had prepared to quote precedent all day.

Smythe took his final stand. "What makes you think this letter"—he shook the paper until it rattled—"will ever get out of this office?"

"It's our duty to send it, sir. Besides, I've already mailed copies to the Secretary and the Undersecretary, the War Department and the other Bureau chiefs—the list is on the draft."

Smythe knew he had been beaten, but Tom couldn't resist rubbing it in. "Why it might even be helpful for us—it might mean bigger allowances..."

His boss didn't wait to hear the finish, but turned and stomped past all the desks pointed toward his office.

Tom shouted at his retreating back: "To keep the tribes from being lured away by those outlaws."

Tom left the office early, excited and happy. "Perhaps Coughlin's right," he thought as his carriage drew up to the Harris home at twenty minutes past four. "The war's started. I had a hand in it." A maid ushered Tom into a low-ceilinged alcove off the drawing room; Charlotte sat behind a low table spread with tea apparatus. He felt surprised to find her alone, unchaperoned, but then he had heard that the Harrises were very unusual people. And Charlotte had a reputation for having a mind of her own.

"So glad you could come." A trace of annoyance cooled her voice as she offered him her hand.

Too pleased with himself to apologize for being late, Tom said, "Things have picked up a bit since I saw you."

She dropped her pique in favor of her real question. "Father tells me interesting things are happening at your office." She looked at him closely.

"Could she have any idea?" he thought. "Harris is a genius, but no one but Mr. Coughlin, the colonel, and I knew until a few hours ago. Can't be. Unless he's in on it."

"Oh, to be sure," he answered expansively. "We're working on a new way to settle rustling charges—telling the ranchers that Indians prefer buffalo to steer because they don't find beef tasty. Then there's the Northeast Trading Company of Harrisburg. I was skimming their catalogue and came across these hollow cylinders of bone—or what looked like bone but turned out to be wood. They're about the diameter of packaged cigarettes—" He measured the imaginary width with his thumb and index finger "—and perhaps a bit longer. If they're as good as they look, we'll include them in our fall annuity along with all the gay new trade beads."

"My father says you've made changes in the treaty—who was it with—the Omaha?" She seemed pleased to have remembered.

"I ought to ask your father what else is happening at my office."

They laughed together. Within her family there was such a complex and fierce loyalty, it wasn't easy to speak to Charlotte about her father. She liked the way Tom handled it.

After tea Charlotte suggested a walk in the garden, and they went out onto the terrace. Leaning on the low stone railing she explained, "Father designed it, dug a good part of it, and planted almost every living thing in it. It's his way of relaxing." She smiled at the family joke.

The magnificent garden stepped down to the Potomac in three broad tiers. The first tier was formal, an extension of the promenade from the ballroom. From the middle of the terrace wall a spring-fed rectangular reflecting pool extended perhaps seventy-five feet; near each end, the pool was crossed by a narrow stone catwalk that stretched into semicircular gravel paths lined with barbered box and privet, enclosing beds of roses and lilies, lupines, delphinia. The classical urns and spheres of topiary which paralleled the pool were subtly spaced in a forced perspective that lengthened the view toward the river.

The far corners of the reflecting pool ran down into tiled basins that distributed water evenly throughout the second tier; for the second tier was devoted to husbandry. Neat beds of vegetables and flowers were separated by grassy paths and punctuated by an amazing variety of fruit-bearing trees—plum, apple, cherry, fig, and pear. Nut trees—pecan, almond, butternut—stood next to sunflowers that by August would grow almost as tall. Everything bloomed and flowered, presaging the bounty that another month would bring.

At the edge of the second tier, the water collected into a great stone shell and from there cascaded into a shallow brook that wound through and disappeared into the wilds of the third tier. No visible restraint was imposed on the azalea and rhododendron that narrowed the winding paths through this level of the garden. Off these paths at discreetly spaced intervals were romantic nooks set with wooden benches. A fieldstone gate framed a turn in the path as the stream meandered past honeysuckle and wisteria; past pinks, alyssa, clematis, and bellflowers hanging in profuse abandon. Set like a jewel in the midst of this bottom tier lay a brilliant green meadow, hedged on three sides by the garden's oaks and maples, and on the south by the river itself.

Tom and Charlotte reached that beautiful meadow and walked noiselessly over the sod. It felt cooler here.

Charlotte had wanted to see Tom as soon as possible, if only to make sure his appeal was genuine. But she had delayed inviting him to tea until her brother had left for the family cottage on the Chesapeake Bay.

They sat down on a weathered wooden bench. "Stuyvesant is going off to the Army in a month." The idea absorbed her; she might have been talking to herself.

With all his heart Tom wanted to go to war. But he had his instructions from Coughlin and the colonel: he would be needed to work with the tribes. "It's a fine time to go into the Army. Stuyvesant is a lucky man. I won't be able to; they tell me I'll have other duties when the time comes."

"Whatever's most important is your duty." She spoke passionately, stating one of her oldest beliefs.

"But I have a hard time picturing myself at a desk, reading accounts of battles in newspapers. Even knowing it's the right thing, I'll hate it."

She examined the wide face, his coal-black eyes. For the first time she understood Tom's being an Indian made him different.

"Did you see Stuyvesant much at Yale?"

"Not much. I was a freshman and he a senior. There's not much contact."

"But his rooms were near yours, weren't they?"

"Not too far."

"But you didn't see him?"

"Not a great deal." He tried to make this statement sound final, but it fell flat—not at all like what the colonel or Coughlin would have been able to do.

Charlotte became impatient: "Did you know my brother was the head of Spoon and Bowl?"

"I heard rumors. Around college, you never know what's true."

"Did you believe this particular rumor?"

"It wouldn't have surprised me."

Charlotte had wanted to know more about this unusual young man. Now his attitude exasperated her. Either he didn't understand, which indicated stupidity, or he had no ambition. "That didn't mean anything to you?"

"I'm not sure I understand what you mean."

Annoyance thinned her lips and pinched her mouth. Charlotte offered no mediating veneer, which left Tom standing at the top of the mineshaft looking down at her tremendous commitment to her own will.

"Did you not see what sort of influence such a position meant at Yale?" She put the question preemptorily, convinced he had missed the point.

Tom replied calmly, "To whoever's interested, Spoon and Bowl must be very important."

Tom knew he had to explain his position to Charlotte, for if he didn't she would not respect him. This was not a woman to appreciate her inferiors. And, today of all days, Tom didn't feel inferior to anyone. "If you're asking whether I understand how the prestigious societies work, yes, I've heard of the old boy network, the old school ties. I know how much that can help. But I also know the antics that go on in the goat rooms of the societies, and I've got very particular objections to them."

Charlotte glared disdainfully. "It's not even so much being able to crawl on your knees up two flights of steps with a mouthful of alum, though that's not something I'm anxious to experience since I've been through what I consider a much more authentic version. I just can't imagine asking someone else to do it, let alone making his membership depend on it." The impassioned tone gave way to irony. "Let's say I'm not their type. It's my prejudice, not theirs."

"He's a prig!" she thought. Anger and wounded family pride made her forget that she knew better. She wasn't prepared to hear this from Tom. Not because he was an Indian. Charlotte never would have allowed herself such an excuse. She rejected his answer because she believed this cocky young man overestimated his worth. After all, all those other Yalies—even her own brother—found the society important. How could he reject it and imply that he'd make his own way?

A cooling period followed and they talked amicably enough—for a short time. After a second silent interlude, Charlotte indicated she had to go in. They walked back up to the house and said good-bye. She did not issue another invitation. Tom left her jauntily, but he spent the ride home making second guesses and after-the-fact formulations. He found defeat hard to swallow on the day of his greatest political triumph.

One week later when Charlotte came down to breakfast, a copy of the New York *Tribune* lay next to her napkin. Her father had left a note:

"See what your young warrior friend is up to."

The front-page headline read, "SOUTHERN PLOT UNMASKED. Indian Uprising Checked."

The story paraphrased Tom's letter, citing Thomas Hyde and the Bureau of Indian Affairs as the source of the story, and quoted the commander at Fort Robinson, a Mississippian, who insisted that the story of the shadowy agitator was "trumped up, a bold-faced lie."

Charlotte read the front-page story twice, then scribbled: "EXTRA! EXTRA! READ ALL ABOUT IT!" She put the note and the paper on the remaining undisturbed place setting. Stuyvesant rarely ever got down to breakfast before noon.

Charlotte pulled a few sheets of dove-gray writing paper from its compartment in the Chippendale secretary where she sat. She smoothed it as she started to write, feeling happily obligated and not a little excited. She was writing to a man who had become, after all, something of a national hero.

Charlotte felt not only fascinated by power; she also assumed that, since it always had been, it would always remain easily accessible to her. Her father said that power gave a man the chance to work in a scale commensurate with his own capacity. Anything less than that, she felt, meant diminishing oneself. Her father had created both his position and the need for it, made it exemplary, then moved above suspicion, audit, party politics, and now even budgetary control. In its last three sessions Congress had voted Markham Harris more money than he asked for. She had been reared to respect the instinct for power just as she had been reared to judge the fabric, cut, and fit of a dress, and she felt the family ethic more deeply than thought.

The twin clerks greeted Tom cordially when he arrived at the Indian Bureau office. Other co-workers, who usually had little to say to Tom, wished him good morning. The opaque glass door at the front of the room stayed shut. Mr. Smythe was writing a letter of resignation. Just before lunch Charlotte's note arrived.

> If I can say so, I feel very proud of what you've done. Congratulations. I'll never trust a word you say about politics again. If you're not too busy, please come for tea at 4 this afternoon.
>
> CHARLOTTE

Ah yes, Tom thought, a perfect day.

Charlotte sat at a high tapestry loom near an open sunny casement that overlooked the garden. She wore a cream-colored dress, high-necked and patterned with tiny gold and red flowers. The gold and red seemed part of the tapestry, her golden skin a background finer than the flowered weave she worked on. Her pale blue eyes lit the field.

He caught her in an unusual mood. But she wouldn't be rushed out of it, and came back slowly. Now that Charlotte had discovered her taste for the romantic, she didn't mind indulging it.

"I've been outwitted by a wily politician," she said sweetly, offering her hand. "It was a little unfair to let me make a fool of myself like that. I was running on about schoolboy societies, while you were working out your intrigues for the good of the whole country. It's not proper to hold a lady at a disadvantage."

Tom's pulse rate jumped.

"I won't ever trust you about politics. I mean that."

They chatted about Tom's new celebrity. They had tea sent in to them, which increased the intimacy of the small room. He felt pleased and surprised to be in her sitting room, but then Washington talk suggested Charlotte Harris always did things her way. Her eyes reminded him of the wash-blue horizon line at the edge of the Plains.

His full soft mouth intrigued her—the way his lips were pinched at the corners accentuated their fullness. She first had noticed his hands in the garden that day. They would never be elegantly kept hands: strong, with wide strong fingers; she loved the way his muscles gathered just above the wrists and ran up the backs of his hands to his knuckles. Charlotte had started to sense the slim strength under his clothes, but was too modest to pursue it. Up to this moment, she'd had only a giggly fascination with such things.

Hesitantly, he took her hand. She did not withdraw it. He ran his fingertips lightly over her palm. Her hand moved dreamlly against his. His clasped tightly, then loosed to let the fingers entwine. Too shy to look at each other now, they watched the ardent movements of their hands; fingertips gently caressed, tightened till the bone ached pleasantly, then released to explore new delight. Her skin had the softness of flower petals, as soft as it was pale.

Tom didn't work up the courage to kiss her until just before leaving. He left her quite unmistakably in love.

Tom Hyde's run on the front page lasted two days, enough time to incense all of the Southern press. Charlotte called him "the two-day wonder." Tom said two days wasn't bad in an election year. He got two invitations to speak, one from an abolitionist group in Baltimore, the other from a ladies' literary society.

Washington, much in need of a bright spot, seized on Tom's speaking success. Within a week Tom Hyde became a fashionable outing, with crowds of the capital's elite flocking to hear this passionate young red man say: if the Union did not want a two-front war on its western extremities, Indians had to be enlisted on the government's side in the coming crisis. White and red men must be partners in a nation where justice and freedom reign. "This is a land we share," Tom concluded one night while Charlotte and her mother looked on, "and we must learn to share it in accord. Too long now has the government manipulated the Indian's guilelessness. Let us make the coming crisis a means for reinvesting the red man with his natural dignity and self-respect, and let the Indian remain as important to us in the future as he is now as we call upon him in the Union's hour of need."

Tom continued to be toasted by Washington society, northern society, that is. Hostesses led him around dinner parties, and one smitten older woman made her amorous intentions clear. Headwaiters greeted him; people recognized him everywhere. Which led Mrs. Hastings to growl, "Don't let them pet you too much, boy, or the next thing you know they'll be asking you to jump up on their laps." He smiled awkwardly; his conscience wasn't as spotless as his linen. But Tom was having too much fun to care.

In spite of his public-speaking coups and the dull flat beat of national war drums, Tom's summer revolved around Charlotte. Her independence never ceased to please and surprise him, for Tom had grown used to white women without minds of their own who slavishly conformed to the most idiotic dictates of conventional wisdom. They went for walks, took rides; he had tea with her, listened to her play the harpsichord; he visited her workroom where he watched the unicorn gently place his hooves in his lady's lap as the tapestry's design emerged. One day Charlotte told Tom no other man had ever been in her workroom, except for her father and Stuyvesant, of course. Their kisses grew longer; it became, sometimes, difficult to breathe normally.

On that humid August afternoon the air clung like moist sheets to Charlotte and Tom as they sat sipping melon punch in her workroom. The dense, hazy sun pushed in through the great south window.

"It's so hot I can hardly breathe," she said.

"Maybe it's cooler in the garden." She nodded but made no move. He pressed the glass of cool liquid to his wrist, then leaned over and pressed his wrist to her forehead.

"It's always cooler in my room," she said slowly, as though asking a shy question.

"The servants . . . ?" His pulse raced hopefully.

"All downstairs. And everyone else is gone."

They stood and, holding tightly to each other's hands, tiptoed into the hall. Charlotte's room was on the far side of the hall in the southeast corner of the house. They paused there on the threshold.

"No man has ever been in here before," she said with breathless virgin wit.

A cool green counterpane covered her four-poster bed; the pillows beneath made inviting mounds. One narrow casement opened onto the garden, the view shaded by a tulip tree. A light breeze graced the organdy over the larger window on the east wall.

Inside the room they kissed, his lips playing on hers. Light suggestive pressures passed back and forth between them. Warmth sanctioned now, Tom's hands moved to her shoulders, then down to her breasts. Charlotte caught her breath, which pushed her breasts up against his hands. Tom felt their firmness, learned their shape; her nipples lifted toward him.

She liked to feel his hands moving on her. Charlotte realized with a shock that she wanted to feel his fingers on her flesh.

Their ardor rose like a great warm wall around them. Tom moved to the bed and gently pulled her down to the counterpane. His hand awkwardly tried the clasp at the back of her dress, then the buttons. Fingers got in the way; Tom felt he was wearing gloves. The dress got stuck as they tried to pull it over her head. Underneath the canopy Charlotte let out a tense hot giggle.

Finally the lovely rose and cream dress slipped off, lifting up her crinolines and revealing her slender legs in white silk stockings. Tom, who had determined not to look at her too lustfully lest he frighten her, felt like a mad old ram as his eyes ran over the slim bow of her calves to the fuller swell of her thighs. But there were crinolines to remove—so many layers that Tom felt amazed he had been able to sense her body through them. Layer by stiff layer they made their way down to her center. Her smell rose up to him—pungent, rich, a kind of mysterious confection—essence of Charlotte, a fulfillment, an enlargement of that distinctive taste he'd taken from her lips, breathed from her hair.

The exciting garters came away, then her stockings. She lay in her chemise—last layer—when Tom took off his own clothes. Now Charlotte watched and shyly examined. Then, flushed, she turned away to remove her chemise. She turned back to him slowly—her small liquid breasts were free. The triangle of golden hair below had thicker tighter curls than her head, as though it grew more luxuriantly in that damp, productive soil.

Trembling, Charlotte slid down into the covers. "It's a tepee," she exclaimed in a little voice. Tom hardly heard. Under his hand her breast turned silk, the nipple firmed and rose above its textured galaxy of bumps. Then Tom sent his fingers through the matted hair and into the mouth of her vulva. She knew this would feel good, for she had done it herself, but she hadn't known quite how good. "So very good," she thought, but his probing finger melted away all thought.

His finger chased the spot around in a slow circle. That much he knew—his grandmother had once called it "the button that makes a woman smile." He watched the skin go taut across the stomach. Her eyes, his eyes grew heavy-lidded.

As he rose above her, suddenly the blue eyes unsettled, caught between a moment of fear and her curiosity about this strange new feeling. His movement broke her body's concentration, lifted her out of that stream of pleasure, left her stateless, a little confused.

"Slow," Tom instructed himself. He eased the head of his cock down into the intricate folds of skin. She lay still, wondering what she should do to help, and intrigued by the mechanics of this act. He pushed through to the resisting membrane and began rocking gently against it. He nudged forward a little roughly and she jerked back, suddenly wary. She felt little pain, only the sense of muscles straining to accommodate this vibrant thing. "Good riddance, good riddance," she sang to herself of the girl she was moments before. She could feel the passage easing for him. His presence in her body seemed awesome, almost puzzling; she found it hard to understand what made him fit so well, why he filled her so completely. She saw his parted mouth, his eyes bulging out a little, the tensed forearm, and that body stretching all the way down over hers.

At first they were awkward together. He hung back, trying not to come too soon. She moved uncertainly, perplexed that he did not take the lead.

She found a sliding movement and began to ride up over his cock in a way that threatened to drain him. Yet how good it felt to have her opening and closing around him, calling his pleasure closer and closer to the surface. At the last moment he pulled out: "I've got to stop."

The abruptness jangled her. She felt no real discomfort, but she couldn't understand why he stopped when he hadn't been doing all that much. He smiled down at her and swept his hand down over her body and back between her legs. She squeezed his wrist, moving her body to place that concentrate of her pleasure under the moving tip of his finger. The finger pursued, it danced for her.

When he came back into her, her breath came deeply. They moved together now, in time, those long slides soon pulling his semen up from the sacks. He tried to distract himself, thought about leaves, grass blowing in the wind, even the Washington Monument—anything neutral. But the sound of them moving together excited him too much, her breasts were too hot and pointed and alive.

Nothing could stop the undeniable rising and, finally, just as her feeling mounted, Tom picked up the pace. He thrust hard, taking her breath away. Charlotte responded. They thrust together—hard, tantalizing, all too short, with Tom breathing so heavily she thought he shouted at the end. He clung to her afterward, trying to hold his softening cock inside her. Her thighs opened and closed, trying to keep him. But her movements only worked him back down the channel, and finally he slipped out of her.

She felt tense; a dull, drawing sensation—as though that network of muscles and nerves, which had been working together, carrying, pulling, driving her closer to some extraordinary new place, had suddenly been blocked.

He leaned over her again and brushed his lips over her breasts, her shoulder, her neck. His fingers burrowed into her crotch and dallied there until she started to move her loins up into empty air. He lay and watched the gold patch wave forward and back, calling for him.

Entering went easily this time, a smooth fluid slide. Now Tom rode freely, without cagey delay. At first he worked with long hard strokes strong enough to last forever, it seemed. Her eyes opened slowly, surprised by her pleasure. Mutual mirrors, they watched each other's feeling intensify. Charlotte's breath shallowed; her nipples scraped his chest.

His thrusts began to lift her off the bed a little. She found it funny and very intense—bellies began to slap; the sound paced them, drove them faster. She felt him enlarging in her and arched her back to spread the sensation through every crevice.

She lay stretched on that pleasurable rack when Tom came. Her tension never quite broke, there was a moment of physical dismay, but slowly, in degrees, the tension retreated. She felt better on the outside than the inside, but she had no real expectations about lovemaking and didn't truly understand the question her body posed. She did know she liked having his hot, lithe body on top of her.

They lay there, quietly roasting in this profound new heat.

Later she asked, "Why did you leave me that time?"

"To slow myself down."

"I don't understand."

"I think men are in a greater hurry than women."

"Really?"

"Yes. I think so."

"Why?"

"I don't know—because of the way they're made, something like that."

"You mean this lovely..." She stroked the sticky limp penis, then leaned down to examine it. Tom laughed. Suddenly her head snapped up. "How do you know about that?" The question announced a fishing expedition.

"That's what the Cheyenne say. Honest, my grandfather told me."

"Your grandfather!" All she could think of was the prim old man who told her German fairy tales, as if to scare her. Grandfather Harris she could not remember at all.

"That is my father's father." Enjoying her surprise, he then surprised himself by saying, "His name is Mohe. The last time I saw him was almost six years ago. I miss him as much as I miss my parents." He told Charlotte about Coyote's famous strategies with women, about the time Coyote masturbated before an appointment with one of his favorite concubines so he wouldn't be too quick. "My grandfather told me that story too."

His amazing frankness made Charlotte all the more appreciative. How womanly she felt learning all these things. "It's extraordinary—I mean, no one here—"

"There are so many differences, Charlotte." He told her how his parents met, how his father won Shell from the old chief of the southern Cheyenne in a brutal slugging match—all day they beat each other with clubs. For the first time in six years Tom felt the need to talk about the world he came from. Of course he had spoken about his old life, but never had he really begun to remember himself. Now his open receptive body spoke; in that afterglow of intimacy he felt whole; that part of him long gone felt as if it had been restored.

Later, when Tom had left and her mother returned, Mrs. Harris asked, "Did you get much done today, dear?"

"No, Mother. I spent most of the afternoon talking to Tom." She said it matter-of-factly because she felt absolutely no guilt at all.

Any amount of time apart would have been too long for them, but evenings were out of the question because the Harrises entertained then. Meanwhile, Tom's work conspired against their being alone during the day. The young bureaucrat faced difficult problems now, the most ticklish coming straight out of the Indian Territory, a place impossible to police.

Many of the better-off Indians were slaveholders. The leadership of the Five Nations remained southern in sympathy. To make things worse, the superintendent of Indians at Fort Smith—the principal post in the Territory—was a Southerner; his agents were pro-slave. For two years spoilage of foodstuffs at Smith had run unnaturally high; thefts of guns and ammunition outstripped reason. The Bureau put Tom in charge of separating fact from rumor, collecting proof, and drawing up a formal complaint. A familiar story by now, Tom concluded–Indians being courted by Southerners with goods stolen from the federal government.

So Tom was unable to see Charlotte immediately. Dorothea and Tom often rode about in her carriage–quiet trips for the most part, with neither speaking much. Once, however, Tom had been beside Dorothea on the Capitol steps when she froze in place–a pile of dog shit lay two risers below. Tom had quickly led her back into the Senate wing and sat her down. Grabbing a newspaper from a guard, Tom went back out, wiped up the dog shit and deposited it and the day's news in a refuse can. Then he led Dorothea down to the carriage. A few days later, a drunken beggar approached their carriage at a busy intersection on Pennsylvania Avenue. When the drunk screamed, "You rich bunch of bastards!" Tom grabbed the driver's horsewhip and the drunk retreated sullenly. Dorothea had said, "I'm glad you responded for me, Thomas. I'll tell you something–I do not believe that man was up to resisting you." It was the most cogent remark he would hear from her that month.

Tom realized that Mrs. Hastings, in spite of her gruffness, had grown fond of him. One day he overheard her saying that she felt badly for him because he had never had a real childhood. Another time she called him into her room and explained that, since he had become a trusted member of the household, he should understand that her daughter's nervous condition had been brought on by the death of her son in childbirth. Tom wanted to offer his sympathy and ask other questions, but Mrs. Hastings started to sniffle and abruptly shooed him out of the room. The subject was never mentioned again.

Two weeks passed before Tom and Charlotte had a chance to be alone together. Tom, who had been anticipating the moment all too vividly, came almost immediately. Which startled Charlotte, who had barely gotten underway. Fortunately her lover was young and vigorous. After some nervous fumbling, that soft wet internal mouth surrounded him, the soft clam mouth began to suck and pull on him. He imagined himself moving through a multichambered shell of great beauty. There were exquisite chambers, great halls, countless rooms and alcoves to importune. His mind drifted into poetry.

Later, Tom said mischievously, "My father once told me it gets better as you get older."

"If it gets any better," she exclaimed, "I won't be able to live through a day without you."

"It's hard being apart even for a few hours."

"It's the uncertainty that's so dreadful." She looked positively glum.

They were stumped, absolutely blocked. Then Charlotte erupted: "Here! We'll do it here! At night!"

She took his breath away.

"Now, when? Which night can you tear yourself away from the pressing problems of the nation? On which night will you take your pleasure?"

He managed to utter, "Every night."

Charlotte turned businesslike. "Tuesday and Thursday."

"Monday and Thursday," he decided. That made it real. "What about your maid?"

"I'll order her to sleep outside. Banish her to the stables." Charlotte imperiously waved the notion of Carolyn away. Nothing stood in the way of her resolve.

"We'll need a signal. Something romantic—a candle. No, a taper." She clapped her hands like a child, the lucid eyes sparkling.

"One if by land," Tom suggested.

The walk across George Town offered few perils; nevertheless Tom ducked into shadow or doorway whenever a carriage approached. Heat lightning broke up the sky, illuminating the undersides of dense clouds—the faces of buildings glowed darkly. His body felt charged like those lightning bolts.

Outside the Harrises' grounds, he took out his watch. Twelve twenty-three. "Half hour early," Tom cursed. No light shone in Charlotte's window. Should he keep walking or hide? But walking meant being out in the open.

Quietly as possible, he slipped off his boots and crept down into the garden. He walked on the trimmed grass at the edge of the gravel and moved silently enough to satisfy himself. "Still a tolerable Indian," he thought when suddenly he came upon Charlotte from behind. She sat on their bench looking out toward the river.

With his hand he softly stifled her cry. She spun around. In the flash of heat lightning he saw her nipples through the sheer cotton nightdress. They kissed and, holding hands tightly, walked down to the lawn below, where they made love on the soft grass at the edge of the meadow. The moonlight cooled him.

"Oh, how wonderful I feel, I feel," Charlotte whispered in his ear.

She made him feel like a prince, a fabulously happy and fortunate prince.

Every sacred Monday and Thursday of September, Tom slipped out of Coughlin's and stayed with Charlotte until dawn. He needed sleep less than he needed her. On the evenings he didn't climb up the trellis to the tulip tree to the window of her room, they went down to their meadow. There they lay—they joked that they were invisible—in changing light and felt the clouds race by the moon; or were enveloped by the succulent dark; or sprinkled by gentle rain. As Big Road predicted, it got better.

Mouths strayed where hands had been. Mouths became greedy, searched high and low for new tastes. They found new ways to please each other. She lay on her side, squeezing him with her thighs; laving him with the rivers that flowed into her center; Tom became, for those few moments, her new center.

In between, in the passion-drenched lulls, Charlotte surprised a need to talk seriously; it amazed her they didn't run out of things to say. Lying on her four-poster bed or in their meadow, the breeze lapping them softly, he told her about his family, the Cheyenne world. One night, finding a strong note of longing there, Charlotte asked him why he had stayed in the white world. He described how overwhelmed he had been by glass, by Moses, by binoculars and electricity, by the promise the white world made available to him, by his own ambition and the colonel's insistence that he might become the leader his people so desperately needed. He also told Charlotte he had a genius for forgetting; he felt both proud and suspicious of this.

A few times Tom told her that, for all his good intentions, he accomplished very little that actually helped the Indians. Charlotte always objected. But her psychic pats on the back helped little. As Tom read the newspapers' proud rhetoric about settlers conquering the West, as bridges spanned more rivers and railroads linked more cities, he felt a spreading hopelessness and a strange feeling of jealousy.

One night Tom suggested they move from their spot on the lawn; he feared they might wear a brown patch in the grass. Charlotte felt lazy and told Tom that next time they could move. But she didn't like her tone and suddenly confessed, "You wouldn't have liked me a few years ago. I was too spoiled then." Tom admitted that as a youth he too had been obnoxious, that at his lowest point he had a habit of telling stories about how backward and dirty Indians were.

They were right—in the old days they wouldn't have liked each other. Certainly Charlotte would have recoiled from the least hint of moral weakness in a man she loved. But now Tom could show her a minute part of the process by which he had become that man. Without apology or plea for sympathy, he explained how he had grown up, how he had learned. Like the horrible story about the Cheyenne war party splitting up late one night because one group insisted that the coyotes they heard howling were not coyotes, but Pawnee. The skittish ones went off downstream while the others laughed. In the morning when those downstream awoke, they noticed the dogs would not go near the stream. But the men drank and bathed and then made their way back. They found the camp site ravaged; everyone had been massacred—their blood still seeped into the water.

Charlotte had been horrified. But when she thought about her reaction, she saw herself as a horrid little girl in a short frock stamping her feet and shouting, "No! No! I won't hear of it!" His presence complicated things. Without intending to, Tom showed Charlotte how protected she had been, and how much she could come to know about life. And as her feeling for its complexity grew, her beauty awakened.

Meanwhile, around them, the nation readied for the coming presidential election. The most ordinary activities went on at a feverish pace—there were more traffic accidents, more crimes, more parties as the frantic citizenry tried to milk the last sweetness out of the world they knew before it disappeared forever. The election crisis produced a stagey madness which made the young lovers suspect that the urgency of their passion had spread everywhere.

One night, in the midst of the political din, Charlotte and Tom met in the garden. They reached the meadow arm in arm and were about to lie down when Tom heard footsteps coming toward them. He squeezed her hand tightly to get her attention and whispered, "Don't worry. I'll hide. Go back to the stone bench." Suddenly Tom vanished into the night; Charlotte didn't hear him go. Startled, not quite comprehending, she turned around. Then she heard the steps.

She trembled as she made her way up the path. "Be calm," she commanded. "Stop shaking." But she couldn't. She was almost to the bench when she recognized Stuyvesant.

He walked quickly, as though heading for a specific destination. "Charl, is that you?" His voice told her nothing; she couldn't be sure if he sounded surprised or reproving.

Her tongue stuck to her palate; try as she might she couldn't speak. Stuyvesant stopped in front of her, his face set for the explanation. Finally, after a damning, oppressive silence, she forced out: "I slipped down to get some air." "Slipped" sounded horribly underhanded to her.

Fortunately the night had stayed muggy, though for all Charlotte knew it might've been snowing. Stuyvesant looked at her as though she hadn't answered his question.

"You'd better come back inside with me." His words hung loud in the thick damp as though printed on a marquee. He took Charlotte's arm and they started up the path toward the house. Tom heard them crunch up one level, the next, and, finally, the french doors shut.

Stuyvesant stopped under the hall lamp and looked his sister over carefully. She could not disguise her trembling. "Is anything wrong, Charlie?" Not expecting kindness, Charlotte had a moment of absolute panic. She had no idea what would come out of her mouth. She was afraid she'd start to cry. "Have you taken a chill?"

"No." Then, "It's just that you frightened me out there." The excuse seemed hopelessly transparent, thinner than her sheer nightdress. But he said nothing further until they halted outside her bedroom door.

"Do you often go out for midnight walks?"

"Not very often," she replied, her smile a bit too fixed but otherwise recovered now. "Only when it's very muggy."

Stuyvesant looked at her like a stranger. "Good night," he said and went off down the hall.

She got inside, then shut the door before the trembling became uncontrollable. She crawled exhausted to her bed and pulled the linen sheet up over her head. "I've given us away, given myself away," she moaned, the tears streaming down her face. The excuse looked worse and worse—of course she knew her brother's step; of course she should've felt safer with him there—who else could be there? She felt terrified, godawful.

Would Stuyvesant go out and comb the garden, find her lover there? Oh, they had been so clever, she and Tom. Charlotte went round and round and over and over her mistake until she fell into a strained thin fitful sleep.

The note that arrived the next morning did nothing to relieve Tom.

DEAREST,

I really have no idea what last night means. I wasn't in any condition to guess what Stuyvesant did or didn't understand. He may have overheard us, or maybe—I pray so—not. I'm terrified and bewildered and only wish there was some way to talk to you, my dearest. All I know is that we must be very, very careful. I miss you more than I can say. Last night was the worst night of my life. I don't see how I will survive today, but I'm afraid for you to come this afternoon. Stuyvie doesn't leave for another week and if he does know anything I think I'll go mad.

Can you wait until tea tomorrow? I can't but think it's best. All my love.

Your distressed, CHARLOTTE

Tom's reply suggested that, if possible, she meet him at the Smithsonian after five. He'd wait an hour. And pray that she would come.

But she didn't come. Tom pounded the pavement as though he had a grudge against it and the half-finished city around him. He waited until six-thirty, then left. That night he got out of bed twice. But he knew he couldn't go to the Harrises.

The next morning Tom had a bad moment when Coughlin called him into his study. Tom felt certain the Undersecretary knew about him and Charlotte. If Coughlin had issued the suitably discreet injunction to stay away from Markham Harris' daughter, Tom had prepared himself to say, "No, sir. I cannot. I love her and must go on seeing her." That drama did not materialize; instead Coughlin explained that if Lincoln won the election, which seemed likely, war would follow. Tom would be chief field man for Indian pacification, which meant that in less than a month he would be sent west, certainly to the Indian Territory, and probably to St. Louis as well. Coughlin added, "You're the best possible man for the job."

Tom thought, "I'll do it, but what about Charlotte?"

On November 4, two days before the election, fall suddenly overtook the District, catching late buds and blooms. Colors looked artificial and took on that high, rusty dullness that comes from being wrenched out of summer. Washington quieted too, the city whose heart was about to break. While the candidates cranked out their final perorations, while the press hoarsely shouted, and the priests of both sects raised and plunged their rhetorical daggers, a fatigue settled over the citizenry. Northerners and Southerners who had not spoken for months passed each other with a like yearning for old times.

Lincoln polled 1,870,000 votes, less than 40 per cent of the total ballots cast. His opponents got 2,800,000, but they had to split them three ways. Thus the United States elected its first minority President, the result of its first truly sectional election. The nation reeled, stunned and punch-drunk. Many who voted Republican couldn't believe their candidate had actually won. Many of those Republicans wanted to change their vote as soon as the results were in. But the Constitution contained no provision for that. A jittery, head-burying uncertainty descended on a nation run by one exceedingly lame Democratic duck.

November turned treacherous, full of the apostate's false faith in the healing power of reason. Moderates in the North, in the Border States, and in the South all chimed in, extolling the virtues of the Union. Compromises abandoned years before were exhumed. Reasonable men met endlessly to see if they could forge a route to sanity. The Senate Committee on the Crisis—blunt name—met and met. They always seemed poised on the brink of a breakthrough. All those hours of tedium, all that quibbling over procedure, and those collective decisions about phrasings, all the talk, talk, talk came to nothing, less than nothing. For the nation had already stepped over the edge, and it grabbed at these straws as it fell through uncharted space toward civil war.

During the first two weeks of November, the young lovers had no chance to be alone together. On the fifteenth, unable to stand it any longer, Tom climbed up her trellis—a risky undertaking but absolutely necessary at that moment. They came together like a husband and wife who had been apart for years—their bodies remembered what their minds couldn't have possibly recalled.

Afterward she said, "I love you."

"You only tell me that when we make love."

On the last day in November Charlotte and Stuyvesant went walking in the garden. She felt they were examining the skeleton of a dinosaur, or rather they were in the skeleton itself, moving down the spine from head to tail. The garden seemed nothing but bare bones and outline—the dead flower stalks, the unproductive beds, the half-leaved trees slowly divesting themselves. Stuyvesant had on his lieutenant's uniform, the first time he had worn it at home. He began talking about his regiment, the fine soldiers he would soon command.

Fortunately, Charlotte enjoyed her brother's heroic moods and admired his dashing appearance in dark blue. They reached the meadow and stopped near an old oak she and Tom favored. Charlotte had grown uncomfortable when Stuyvesant reached into his pocket and pulled out a handful of coins. He juggled them once and seemed about to speak when he absentmindedly flipped them up again—a couple slipped out of his hand and rolled toward the mound of grass where Charlotte had often lain with her lover.

As Stuyvesant bent to pick up the coins, Charlotte blurted out: "You don't like him!"

Stuyvesant, down in a crouch, looked up at her from that angle. She had dark rings under her eyes, and the eyes, usually so clear, looked milky. "Who?" he asked with bland innocence.

Her stomach sank; she cursed herself for starting it in the first place. "Oh, never mind," she said weakly.

But Stuyvesant stayed right there, soothing, silky. "No, Charlie, who?"

If he had been cynical or mean, Charlotte could've resisted. But he met her with a caress. For a moment Charlotte felt she might give way to hysteria; worse, she might confess. Instead she said the first thing that came into her mind. "Your new gelding. What's his name—Division?" Her laugh leapt out as a shrill bark. As soon as she heard it, Charlotte cut it short.

Stuyvesant didn't get the crazy joke. He replaced his warmth with cool formality. "His name is Arbiter," he replied, speaking of the horse. "And you're right, I don't like him. I'm not sure he can be trusted."

In the final month of 1860, most of the nation wanted an end to the colossal uncertainty. Not to settle the argument between North and South—almost all knew better than that—but to provide a means by which the argument itself could be obliterated. The horror that lay ahead would wipe out all capacity for reason. One side, having slaughtered hundreds of thousands and watched hundreds of thousands of its own die, would raise a bloodied hand and proclaim, "It's over," knowing, even as the victor made that gesture, that nothing had been solved. Men go to war madly, but with the intolerable understanding that the problems they face are too complex to be solved, that this horrible bloody carnage is the only way of dodging the problems themselves. In this spirit, North and South went about their senseless, murderous preparations.

A week before Christmas, Mrs. Hastings delivered a lunchtime harangue about the idiocy of locating the capital in the South in the first place. She implied that her son-in-law was responsible for the original mistake. Not that she would move for safety, mind you, but she didn't think they—or the old home they lived in—could stand the hubbub. Clearly, she worried about Dorothea, who hadn't spoken a word for a week.

Christmas Eve the four of them gathered at table. Conversation lagged. Coughlin had too many things on his mind, Tom felt unspeakably lonely; even Mrs. Hastings finally gave up. No one spoke during the meat course. Tom was chewing a hot potato when Mrs. Hastings asked, "Have you seen Miss Harris recently?"

He sucked in his breath sharply; the potato came with it. A hot chunk lodged in his windpipe. Tom coughed, spraying an atomized mess back on to his plate and onto the tablecloth. He coughed again, trying to dislodge the scorching chunk before he strangled. Dorothea turned green. Coughlin jumped up and began to pound Tom smartly on the back. The boy's face turned vermillion. He sputtered, trying to catch his breath; he gagged, then finally the piece slipped down. Coughlin continued to pound him rhythmically, slowly easing off.

"Are you all right?"

Unable to talk, Tom nodded yes.

Mrs. Hastings said, "I didn't realize it was such a violent question."

Tom apologized and excused himself. Upstairs, he lay in bed thinking of his last conversation with Charlotte. She told him how solicitous her family kept being; they couldn't do enough for her.

"The more attentive they get, the less freedom we have. You're in jail, darling."

Weakly she said, "We don't have proof they're trying to keep us apart."

"Proof!" Tom exploded. "Who needs more proof? We used to have every Monday and Thursday night together. Now we're lucky if we can walk alone for an hour once a fortnight."

The Harris family had its own set of unspoken rules: from the age of ten, you were treated like an adult. Others could be called on for advice, but once you claimed responsibility for an action, you were on your own. Never before had Charlotte's judgment been so at odds with the family's. The Harrises simply showed their daughter the chasm that might open if she pursued the logic of her pleasure. They suggested that this particular joy had become a seesaw: when one side flew up, the other came down. They had made this clear without uttering a single word and without violating their formal libertarian code. Tom didn't know all this, but he sensed the force and direction of the pressure. And he could see the pressure taking its toll on Charlotte as she rode the seesaw up and down.

Three days before Christmas Tom stood in the hallway of a shabby suburban hotel. He punched the desk bell sharply, greeted the fat woman in faded calico a little too effusively, and paid for a room. By way of explanation he said, "I'll be back in a half hour."

"No bags, sir?" the woman inquired.

"No," Tom replied uneasily. "None." He asked for his key but she shook her head. "Keys stay on the board on the way out. Pick 'em up coming in."

"Very good," Tom said ponderously.

She looked at him as if he had spoken in foreign dialect.

Six blocks from the hotel, he stopped and peered through the steamy window of a seedy coffee shop. At a table in the corner, dressed in black and thickly veiled, Charlotte appeared tiny, quite absurd.

Tom felt so relieved to see her, so glad that she had come, that he couldn't resist teasing as he approached her table. "Good afternoon, my dear," he said in his best espionage voice.

She didn't think it funny. She found nothing amusing about waiting ten minutes in such a squalid place, and certainly nothing funny in the way the slatternly waitress kept squinting through the veil when she took the order.

Tom could see little chips of her pale blue eyes through the dark mesh. "Shall we go," he said, still standing.

"Let me finish my coffee." Until then she had not put her lips to the cup. In this dreary setting, Tom seemed like a stranger to her.

Outside, his hand wrapped the inside of her arm; his knuckle brushed her breast. "I've missed you terribly. More than I can say." She liked feeling his fingers again.

"I'm only glad nobody can see me, Tom. I'm positively scarlet under this ridiculous thing."

In the carriage, Charlotte lifted the veil. He kissed her and told her again how much he had missed her. She kissed him, her lips softer now.

The hotel didn't have much élan, Tom explained, but they would be safe there. He couldn't take the chance of being seen with a veiled lady. Might be bad for his career. He intended his bad joke to shift the burden off her.

"Can you see me?" she asked sharply as they pulled up in front of the hotel. For the second time in a block Tom answered no.

He handed her down, then moved ahead to the door. The hotel had no lobby, just a dingy passageway. The parlor lay on the left, halfway down the hall, the desk just beyond to the right. Charlotte noticed the worn divan with the blue horse blanket thrown over it, the paint peeling off the ceiling in the far corner of the parlor.

Tom was reaching for his key when the woman who had taken his money bustled out of the door marked "PRIVATE." "Oh, it's you, Mr. Cooper. Back so fast?"

Tom only nodded.

"Does Mrs. Cooper care to sign?" She pushed the greasy register around toward them.

"No. I signed for both earlier." Tom jabbed in the direction of the open page.

The woman pivoted the book back toward her and ran her finger down the column. Then she tried to penetrate the veil–she stared at Charlotte. Failing that, her eyes went to the gloved hands, then on up to the edge of her sleeves. Charlotte knew the old crone was trying to determine the color of her skin.

"If you'll excuse us," Tom demanded.

Charlotte went up the stair nobly, feeling those prying eyes on her back, knowing the filthy creature was studying her. She wondered if this dreadful woman's room lay right below theirs; if the woman would sneak down the hall to listen to their sounds. The hotel couldn't have been more dreary and grotesque, she thought. Quite grotesque.

The room looked exactly as she had pictured it: drab, gray, shabby, bare, anonymous, with a faded rose-colored throw rug, a nighttable with a smelly oil lamp. And a lumpy bed, covered with an overlaundered pink spread.

She stripped off her veil, relieved to see the world without its dark speckles. The room was hot, the stale air thick. "Fleas!" Charlotte shuddered as she thought, "We might catch fleas!" Involuntarily she remembered that Tom had lived with fleas for thirteen years. For the first time in her life Charlotte felt unclean.

Tom watched carefully. "Charlotte." He found this difficult to say. "We don't have to stay here."

Having survived the humiliation of the veil, Charlotte found this altogether unfair. She looked at Tom a long time before marching to the head of the bed and turning down the blanched spread; then she inspected carefully for wildlife. With the top sheet rolled down, she sat on the edge of the bed, unbuttoned her blouse and took it off. Next she removed the top of her chemise.

"If you think we should leave, then we'll leave," Tom said, almost pleading. Her breasts were beautiful. They hadn't made love in a month. Her blue eyes would not answer.

Charlotte took off her skirt and her undergarments. Then came the first silk stocking, which she rolled down deliberately from the top. She took off her shoe to remove the stocking, but immediately slipped her foot back into it, never letting the bare foot touch the floor. Then she rolled down the other stocking. Tom saw her golden hair, the slender legs. Naked, she crossed the room in her shoes and hung everything carefully on the provided hooks.

She crossed to the bed, dropped the shoes on the floor and swung her legs up. Then she lay back stiffly, like a painting of the Virgin Mary floating impossibly just above the spot where ordinary mortals are obliged to lie. Her body touched the bed in three places, no more.

No, she didn't act fairly. But had Tom acted fairly in subjecting her to the filthy presumptions of that awful waitress and this monster downstairs?

Tom realized he had made a mistake. He took her wrist. "Come on, Charlotte. Not like this."

"We're here, aren't we?" It sounded like a curse.

Since Charlotte seemed to insist, and since Tom hoped that their passion, their joy at being together again, might obliterate the squalor—they made love. Her pale skin, the color of the waning moon, did arouse him. But he could not impart his passion, try as he might. Her body was only intermittently with him—she examined the cracks in the walls, the dull gray paint, she read the ceiling's rippled texture. Tom suffered the mental version. They—he—tried two more times. For Charlotte too many things had been disconnected. Nothing happened for her.

Later Charlotte lay in her bath scrubbing the sponge roughly over every reachable part of her body. She wondered why she had gone through with it. "Because he wanted you?" No, the melodramatics of that didn't satisfy. She remembered feeling distant and condescending, she who had never lagged in interest before. She shuddered again, tears starting, thinking of the way that woman had looked at her—as if she were a prostitute. She slapped her arms against the water, spilling it all over the floor. Then she lowered her body into the tub until only her chin remained exposed.

Tom had taken her too far away from that very special world she inhabited, beyond the perimeter of good taste. All those forgotten deficiencies which had been waiting like bad spirits in the wings rushed at her now—his walking into the privy after she told him not to, catching her with that disgusting embarrassing strain on her face, seeing her so ugly; that brutal joke he made then about bears shitting together, to make her more open about these things. Times when his enthusiasms were pitched too high; when he begged for her approval; when he seemed too foreign. That tea when he had been so surly and aloof in front of Stuyvie, after she had built him up so. She let these and every little awkwardness and flaw—even his slightly stiff accent, once so endearing—flood through her body, too tender and sore, too exhausted to be fair. She opened to him because of his sensitivity, his eagerness to draw himself and her through new experience. She opened to him because he seemed different, more sensitive. Now—ultimately—he had misunderstood her nature, blundered and badly abused her. Bitter, bitter tears dropped into the scented bath; her own petals—so splendid in their recent opening—folded in on themselves.

For Tom Hyde, the New Year couldn't have been bleaker. The penetrating gray chill provided suitable accompaniment for his endless second-guessing of the disastrous day at the hotel. What an ogre he became to himself.

Three days after the incident, a note arrived saying she was going away for a few days and that she would think about him.

On the sixth day of January Florida joined South Carolina in secession, the day after that, Alabama. "An epidemic," the *Tribune* quipped. In one week plus one day Georgia seceded; Louisiana followed a week later, on January 26. Then on February 1, Texas dissolved its ties to the Union, or so it claimed.

Meanwhile, Charlotte's notes kept arriving—frustratingly cheerful, pleasant, but bland and coolly impersonal. Tom wrote religiously, limiting himself to one letter every other day. He kept his tone guarded, for he did not want to presume too much.

On February 6, Tom learned he'd have to leave Washington within two weeks. He wrote Charlotte a wildly injudicious note, pledging undying love and explaining—"My call to duty has sounded." He could not tell her why he had to leave, but assumed she understood the implications of the front-page story in the *Tribune*—the Choctaw council meeting scheduled for the seventh was expected to approve a resolution favoring secession of the Indian Territory if war came. One of Hyde's major strategic emphases in the event of war was to enlist as many Indians as possible on the northern side, thus minimizing the number of military actions west of the Mississippi. All available troops could then be used for the major offensives, to isolate and quickly defeat the South. Tom's job involved keeping the Civilized Tribes in the Union camp.

Charlotte wrote she would be back by the tenth. On the ninth the rebels seized the federal arsenal at Little Rock, Arkansas. Charlotte didn't return until the twelfth. Only his work saved Tom from going stark raving mad.

He found her in the downstairs sitting room leaning against the back of the settee, looking out into the garden. She turned to him slowly, as though reluctant to break away from the view. She wore the full dark blue skirt, the white blouse that demurely buttoned up to her throat with a ladder of mother-of-pearl buttons. Tom's eyes greedily lingered on their shining surfaces.

"Hello, Charlotte."

"Hello, Tom." Her smile seemed less than wholehearted.

"How have you been?"

"Fine. It was very pleasant on the Bay."

"Good," he replied, thinking of Stuyvesant's officer friends. Just four feet of settee separated them. The blouse looked so austere, those mother-of-pearl buttons seemed like miniature locks. She had never seemed more of a Harris to him. Tom wanted to reach for her, to cry, I missed you more than I could tell you even if we had a whole lifetime together. But he only said: "Is it too cold for a walk?" He regretted it immediately; a walk would lead down to the meadow. But Charlotte had already thrown a wool shawl over her shoulders and was moving toward the french doors. They converged there.

"Kiss her? Shall I, can I kiss her?" Uncertainty made his heart thump. He couldn't presume on their former intimacy when it seemed so obviously in question.

Charlotte gave Tom her arm without really looking at him. As they wound down the garden path through the dead garden, each silent step became a void he felt he should have filled with the right sentiment. He seemed to hear Stuyvesant's footsteps on that dark night.

Charlotte didn't like the way Tom combed his hair down over one side of his forehead. More important things occupied her, of course, but she had never really noticed how it shortened his brow. She felt impossibly sad. The man next to her had been her catalyst. He awakened a beauty inside her—one day, one night it came; suddenly her girlhood lay behind her. But Charlotte sensed that what he started could sustain itself now, that a man could pass out of that blessed state with a woman.

"Charlotte," Tom said authoritatively, disgusted with his hesitancy and desperate to have it out, "I wrote you how I felt about that afternoon in the hotel." She whitened till the skin around her mouth looked like a bleached sail; her oddly distracted smile became a sieve through which too many painful memories flowed. "I'll apologize again if you think that'll help, but there's really nothing more I can say because I've said it all before. You—and that horrible hotel—are all I've been able to think of for the last month."

Her smile stiffened. "I took you there because I missed you too much, because I felt desperate about our not being together. I wanted to make love because I love making love with you. It turned out to be awful, a terrible ordeal for you, I know. So now it's entirely up to you if you want to turn it into something tragic—if you want to hate me for it. But I think it would be an incalculable shame."

The corners of Charlotte's mouth hooked down, the lips hardened as something fiercely unmoving gripped her face. Her anger struck him like a shotgun blast. "Did your skin crawl when it touched those sheets? Were you afraid to lie down for fear of fleas or some awful disease? Did you feel so dirty you had to scrub yourself until your skin was raw all over and started to bleed?" Her voice quivered; she shook her head to control the trembling.

"Of course I hated it." He found it impossible to plead his own case and calm her at the same time. They had reached the wooden bench and Charlotte sank down.

Tom had been over the hotel episode a thousand, thousand times. Yet, ugly as it had been, he didn't believe it sufficient reason for her to stop loving him. "Oh, Charlotte, dearest, the thought of hurting you at all tears me apart inside. I hate it more than anything I know in the world. No, I didn't understand how much it would hurt you. That was unfeeling, stupid, I admit it. I wanted you too much to think clearly."

"So I was the human sacrifice? You'd do it all over again." She hissed at Tom, surprised by her own ferocity. The pale eyes turned ice blue.

"No," he replied sadly. "Not at this price."

She didn't answer.

"Charlotte, two days away from you makes me totally obsessed. Just standing here, I can't keep my mind off your body. We keep ending up in bed." She wanted to say: in a filthy hotel. But she let him go on. "Once, twice, three times a day I can almost feel us together." For the first time that afternoon, she fastened on his glistening eyes. "I'm haunted by exquisite images of you. They crop up in the bath, in the middle of a conversation—'Yes, Mr. Secretary, I'll see to that,' I say, seeing your legs sprawled across the sheet. You show up when I take walks, go for rides, sit down to table. I'm obsessed by visions of you, of us making love."

She warmed a little, remembering her pleasure.

"I love to make you happy. There's nothing in the world I'd rather do—I could live for that." He reached for her hand; Charlotte gave it to him. Underneath all her crinolines, she was wet. "If only there was some place to go."

"You'd have to be invited." She pulled her fingers away, which shocked him.

"I hate that!" Tom took two restless steps, then sprayed up gravel with an angry boot. He spun back to face her: "I won't bargain for your body! I won't treat you that way. We make love because we want to, not because somebody begs or tricks somebody into it, or wins it."

"You must understand I'm sore inside, Tom." She spoke quietly, eyes dim now. "The look that woman gave me—I've never hated anything so much in my entire life. It was—like being raped." She did not like to say that word. "It shook my confidence in everything, even you." The fine line of Charlotte's jaw wavered. "I'm not finished with it yet, that's what you don't understand. It won't let go of me."

Tom's eyes restlessly scoured the stripped trees, not knowing how to look at her. "When *will* it let go of you?"

"I don't know."

"You know I'm leaving in two weeks?"

She nodded dumbly. They were beached at the spot they started from.

"To me what's happened between us is more important than one wretched afternoon. You can spread your feeling about that afternoon back over the whole summer, but that would be a lie—that would mean lying about what it's meant to both of us."

"Tom," she wailed, "it's not a question of *wanting* to do anything. I'm sore, I ache, I'm devastated inside, I feel all alone. Right now I feel I can't trust you. Someday, probably, I'll get over that."

"In the meantime," he spat derisively, "I'm to restrict my behavior—and my affections—then, maybe . . . it's like an infernal test!"

"It's not a test," she insisted. Then, without contradiction: "Besides, we never get a chance to see each other anyway."

Tom kicked the relic of a bench as hard as he could; he wanted to destroy it. He wanted to strip each tier of garden, rip out the rows of careful planting, destroy the tyrannous order that surrounded them. He remembered what Hall said about his "friends" at Arundel, how they would not introduce him to their sisters. The entire history of his conversion leaned on him; he felt the colossal weight of all he had given up—"For this! Fooled myself, lied to myself, played the buffoon to learn their graces and manners. A lapdog. If it hadn't been the hotel it would have been something else." Tom had the feeling their conflict was inevitable. Never had they spoken a single word about their future, about marriage. As he stood there, encased in his suit, sunk on the second tier of the Harrises' dormant garden, Tom had a vision of Charlotte going off with an officer from Stuyvesant's regiment, or some approved Yalie.

Tom knew it would require perfect attention to Mrs. Hastings' orders to squeeze her and her wheelchair into the carriage, so he hurried through the final inventory of his bags and papers that last afternoon. Outside, to his pleasant surprise, he found Dorothea bustling around giving orders to the footmen while Mrs. Hastings, a dry but happy cork, floated above it all.

As they rode through the George Town streets, Dorothea pointed out the interesting houses and noted the family or families who had lived there. Her talent for genealogy and the preciseness of her local history amazed the boy, who found himself taking the most impressive tour he could remember. Dorothea urged him to write regularly; they'd miss him too much as it was. He was not to become such an important man of affairs to let them languish without word. This could be the problem with family—she laid her hand on Tom's arm—you spent all that lovely time together, time that could never be recaptured or reduplicated, then circumstances pushed the family apart. An effort had to be made to keep that time alive and fresh. Not that it could ever be lost, but if you renewed it regularly it stayed fresher, and that much closer to you.

In front of the War Department offices, Dorothea moved to the door, opened it, leapt lightly down. The footman never had a chance to get off his box.

Tom turned to Mrs. Hastings for an answer, but she replied by leaning forward in her seat and watching her daughter dance up the low marble steps. Could all this be for him, Tom wondered. Had his going away awakened her? Did such moments of life burst on them unexpectedly, and did they afterward cling to the memory to keep their hope alive? Was he now seeing what she'd been like before the death of their child? Coughlin and Dorothea felt like lovers to Tom now; he found them all so heroic and moving.

In a few minutes the Coughlins came down arm in arm. Or rather they floated down the stairs in step, gazing at each other like a couple reunited after years of separation.

Radiant, Dorothea reentered the carriage. The strain had lifted from her brow; the green eyes were clear. She looked only a few years older than Charlotte.

"How wonderful our rolling carriage is," she offered once they got underway. "It's our portable apartment where no one enters except by invitation. For as long as we want we're sealed in." Her voice threw sparkling notes into the air.

"Thomas, I can't tell you how wonderful it has been to have you with us. You have been our son. That's something we'll always thank you for." Tom flushed.

"Don't be embarrassed now." She looked at him steadfastly. Coughlin and Mrs. Hastings tendered her words like currency. "You see, you came to us as a grown boy. For us, Thomas, that was a great advantage." The boy wanted her to elaborate. She did not. "While we were together you grew into a man, and now you're ready to go off and do the important business of the world. We are proud of you. And proud to have helped in our way."

No tears at the station, none. Coughlin supervised Mrs. Hastings' extrication while Tom and Dorothea strolled down the platform, arm in arm. Tom noticed how many eyes followed them. Alongside his compartment, they stood in the steamy noise. Dorothea kissed him. "Good-bye, my dear Thomas. I'll miss you." Tom felt enormously happy for her, happy for all of them.

Coughlin came down the platform, wheeling Mrs. Hastings through the crowd. The Secretary let his mother-in-law set the brake, then shook hands with Tom.

"Good-bye, sir."

"Good-bye, Tom. You'll do very well for us. I'm glad it's you."

Mrs. Hastings was more pointed: "I trust I'll see you again, boy."

Tom dismissed that note as lightly as he could. "Of course."

"Stranger things have happened," the powdered visage persisted. He kissed the air close to the cracked cheeks, hugged Dorothea's slim body, reshook Coughlin's hand, and boarded.

THE INDIAN TERRITORY

TOM'S BRIEFING PAPERS FOR the Indian Territory couldn't have been more helpful. But one note annoyed him—the curious condescension with which the whites had bestowed the title "The Civilized Tribes" on those Indians whom they had taught to plant orchards and keep cattle. These Civilized Tribes were split into two factions: Chickasaw and Choctaw remained fanatically pro-South, the Creek and Seminole vaguely pro-Union. But the Chickasaw were a powerful tribe while the Creeks and Seminole were poor and weak. The real key—the real uncertainty as Tom saw it—lay with the Cherokee. So far this largest and most influential tribe had resisted southern entreaties, including the seductive cajolings of one Albert Pike, slave agent extraordinaire. Tom knew that Pike was being entertained by the Cherokee headman, Chief John Ross, and that Pike packed an estimated $100,000 worth of cash persuasion with him.

Tom Hyde felt intrigued by the idea of facing the smooth, well-educated Ross and convincing him to remain loyal to the Union. Ross—exactly one-eighth Cherokee through a quarter-blood mother, like many of the tribe's mixed blood—owned slaves, a fact Tom would never be able to digest entirely. Ross's rise to power had begun over twenty years before with the simple act of persuading the Cherokee mixed-blood chiefs to sign the dispossession order giving up the tribal lands in Tennessee. Ross, however, never put his name on the document. Next he convinced the full bloods that the mixed bloods had sold their sacred birthright. He said, look right here, and waved the dispossession order in their faces. One by one the mixed-blood chiefs disappeared until only one—Stand Waite—remained. Ross then wangled his way into the trusteeship of the $100,000 repatriation money the federal government gave the Cherokee. And he got himself chosen executor of the $5,000,000 in annuities the tribe received for losing their homelands.

Ross's most powerful opponent, Stand Waite, had spent years scheming to seize the old chief's power. Enter the Great Slavery issue. Waite organized a violently secessionist "Border Police," which also served as Waite's personal army. This split the mixed bloods from the full bloods on the slavery issue. Ross responded by taking the Keetoowah, the secret Cherokee society of full bloods, and getting them to revive the old customs. They started bewailing the loss of the old ways and blaming it on the mixed bloods. In the same breath they pledged their loyalty to the Union—the collision course was set.

The gospel according to his briefing papers provided one more useful bit of information: a group of white, "desperate gentlemen" had banded together for the purpose of protecting the Union; they called their organization the Union League. So far the League remained a closely guarded secret, its activities largely confined to the Border States. But, the briefing papers said, the League would soon "grow like wildfire." Tom had to memorize the signs and passwords. Essentially, all the signals came in pairs of two: he held up four fingers, splitting them into two and two; he hooked two fingers in his waistcoat, leaving two hanging out. Similarly, the handshake was a two and two grip. After a while, all those twos and twos got to seem a little silly.

Two days later Tom Hyde stood in the great hall of John Ross's River Slope mansion. At seventy plus, Ross remained vigorous and self-important, with a stony manner that insisted that all those poorer and weaker than he were fools. His skin had a dull milky cast to it, though it had flushed slightly when his man announced Tom's arrival. The chief felt annoyed they had sent him a boy, he who had entertained senators at River Slope about less significant matters. Nonetheless, he gave Tom the customary tour with an itemized rundown of the cost of its furnishings for good measure.

"Come, let us be frank," Ross said as the tour came full circle in his mahogany and green damask study. He gestured Tom to an armchair upholstered in silk brocade. An enormous gilt mirror was hung between two high windows which were ornamented by looped and corded drapes. A rosewood fire screen set off the marble fireplace. "I know what you're here for. You want to keep us on the northern side. Am I right?" His upper teeth came to sharp points where they met the lower.

"In general, yes."

"You come to my house to ask for my loyalty. But, you see, in truth, the tables should be turned." For the first time, the boy looked puzzled, which was the first thing Ross liked about him. "The real question is what your Union government can guarantee *me*. By treaty, you see, I'm promised food, dry goods, ammunition. By treaty, again, we're entitled to protection. What happens, young friend, if your troops cannot supply; if so, they cannot protect either. Am I to stuff my people's bellies with paper promises?" Tom wondered if this represented a mere exercise, as customary as the house tour, or if Ross actually believed what he said. "You see, I'm the one who must ask for guarantees."

Rational Tom Hyde recognized Ross's dilemma, for rational Tom Hyde had brooded about it all the way up the Arkansas River. But Unionist Tom thought, "After all these years, all the food you've ripped out of their mouths and the money you've secreted away, after all the killings, you still want to be bribed." The boy responded too candidly for a good diplomat: "You put me in an embarrassing position, Chief Ross. I came here convinced of the loyalty of the Cherokee, hoping to offer what assistance I could. Now I wonder if there isn't some question about your support for the government that has been your benefactor for almost twenty years."

Experience and wit told Ross the boy's arguments came with his job; but he felt offended by the way in which the young emissary personalized such a complex question: this seemed sentimental, self-deceiving, unfair to the enormous burden history makes a man shoulder. Did this half-baked, unrealized child regard himself as Ross's equal, perhaps even as his replacement? With fine irony, the old chief repeated the formula he had delivered six days before to the southern agent Pike: "The Cherokee will remain neutral in whatever fight ensues. This is the only position I can responsibly take because it is the only one we can hold.

"Understand," the chief continued, "the Union has already lost Little Rock and its arsenal to the Southerners. Within the month the South could take Fort Smith, Fort Washita, Arbuckle and Cobb, maybe Fort Gibson too. What are your not-so-United States going to do for me then, way out here in Indian Territory?"

The chief's logic produced that queasiness Tom invariably got when he embarked on a murky bit of arguing. "The white settlers and their legislators are looking for any excuse to take away Indian lands. Already the Cherokee claims in Kansas are being threatened. You know that anyone who goes with the rebels will never see another acre of government land." The chief recognized a lot of sides to that argument, most of them not pro-Union.

"The government has always paid your annuities. In fact, the Cherokee has been one of the best paid tribes. Now the South promises you trinkets and the unlikely dream of statehood. Isn't bread in the mouth better than words you can't chew? Suppose the government cannot reach you for a month or two? Isn't it better to hold out? Don't you owe the Union something?"

Wrinkling a milky cheek, Ross spoke with a fatigued sense of political possibility: "To me there are just two questions: Can you offer guarantees when the fighting starts? And, second, when the South does take this territory, how can I hold them off? Any other questions are foolish and a waste of my time."

"But the North's cause is just!" Tom insisted on this with all the moral force he could muster. But he knew he was out of his depth. "And what's even more important, the South will lose. Eventually it has to lose. We're too strong, too rich."

"It's an awkward position, you know, to be a slaveholder on the Union side. Can you see what I stand to lose if the North wins?" His hand described a full circle corresponding to the cotton that surrounded River Slope as far as the eye could see.

"There's no honor left in him," Tom thought. "No Indian either. He took their land, money, everything. Whoever wins the war, Ross won't lose—he'll get either his cotton or the annuities."

Ross said, "I take no sides yet. Both are bad, both are after what I've created here." Eight columns supported the roof over the Park Slope portico; portraits from France lined the walls of the salon; he had ninety-seven slaves in his employ, sixteen hundred planted acres.

Ross got up from his chair. "Now that you've catechized me about the righteousness of the North, let me say a word." The old chief's tight nut of a face tilted down toward Tom. "I'm not at all sure the North will treat my people better, and I've thought about that a good deal longer and more carefully than you. The South at least has some feeling for our way of life. Also they need us more, which in this world is always a prime incentive to virtue. But we won't argue that, because I don't think we'll resolve it.

"You think this war will be fought to free slaves, in the name of sacred principles which make you feel bold and warm inside when you utter them. But this war is not a crusade for Free Soil or the dignity of the yeoman farmer. It will be fought for the only things whites ever fight for—power and profit. Those terms which stir you so—freedom, emancipation—they're drags which politicians and journalists pull behind them to cover their paths of influence and greed. The rest is fodder for fools. Forget about crusades, Mister Hyde. People are not destroyed because they're wrong, only because they're weak."

Ross's mind skimmed back over the scarred terrain of his life, the series of decisions which had brought him to this moment; the subterfuge, the lies, even the murders, all the things Tom Hyde hated and feared were to Ross less the result of his character than simply his adaptation to the intractable rules dictated by the world of white men. He felt no guilt.

"If you wish," the older man continued, "you can take at their word a people whose single greatest talent is the lie, whose only law is the breaking of law. You—" The cunning old man stopped there, surprised he had let it become so personal. He thought, but did not say, "You have much to learn, Mister Hyde."

Tom felt fascinated and teased and stung by Ross's speech. Silent doubts found voice here—all too much of what the chief said rang true. But Tom only questioned: "May I ask what Pike offered you?"

Annoyed at having made the effort, Ross thought, "What can this child understand about a lifetime, about a will that engineered all I've done." His thoughts leapt to the living ghost of Stand Waite, the one mixed-blood chief he had not killed, his personal haunting for more than twenty years. Ross's smile lifted the left side of his face.

"Offers, offers?" Ross said aloud, determined to end their interview. "I will stay neutral as long as I can. That's all I can say. But I have no idea how long that will be."

Tom took that for a concession. Chief Ross had intended to tell him that all along.

Following his orders, Tom contacted Henri Denbelle, a black man who lived with the Cherokee. Denbelle knew more about the Civilized Tribes than any living man. A solitary, closed person and a staunch Catholic, Denbelle had spent a decade converting Indians to the Roman Church. Though Tom disagreed with Denbelle about the usefulness of Christianity to the Indians, he appreciated the man's stern integrity. That such a strong man leaned so heavily on such obvious absurdities never ceased to surprise and disappoint Tom.

Ross, Denbelle explained, remained widely trusted and admired among his people; full bloods and half bloods viewed his wealth proudly, as a sign he had matched white man at his own game. Ross had been courted by Pike, but when Ross refused to pledge loyalty to the South, Pike threatened to help Stand Waite take over. Ross laughed in the man's face, exclaiming, "I've been through much worse." Then Pike rode south in a huff to conclude his treaties with the Choctaw and Chickasaw.

Tom felt relieved that his southern rival hadn't made any more progress with the tough old chief than he had.

Under Denbelle's informed guidance, Tom began to make speeches to the Indians. His basic text adhered to the standard abolitionist line, using quotations from *Uncle Tom's Cabin,* semilurid accounts of slave mistreatment, and the inference that men who enslaved blacks might, someday, try to enslave others. He also quoted biblical injunctions against slavery—many of the Seminole, Creek, and Cherokee attended Denbelle's services.

In spite of what the slave men said, Tom would often insist, the Union will never die. The Great White Father—a phrase he detested—will never go back across the Big Water. "Good red men must turn a deaf ear to promises from the slave men; it is wrong to listen to men whose words make a dry wind that returns nothing but their own sound."

Finally, the warning: when war came, the North would win, even if it took time, "even if there are dark days without sun. In the end the sun will shine again on all who help the great cause of free men, the cause of the Great Father. And those who disobey will be sorely punished."

Without moccasins or shoes, in rags or patchwork clothes they came to listen to him. Tom's glance would skim the crowd and alight on a child who reminded him of Small Deer, a woman who resembled Takes-the-Pipe's mother. Around him memories lay scattered—a deerskin robe, a pipe decorated with a sunburst, a pile of simple wooden jacks. His eyes would scan and touch and hold their familiar coal eyes; so many of those eyes now registered confusion—men and women who didn't know what they had done wrong or what had gone wrong in the universe. He sat in their rough log cabins and chewed their corn or an occasional rasher from a Sunday hog and listened to the words of a people with no promise or story to lead them forward, whose homeland lay two thousand miles behind them, those who now scratched out a bare subsistence living from the parched Oklahoma soil. Tom himself barely could find reasons for it, but most of those people—even the aimless ones, the ones who drank and fought among themselves—seemed determined not to desert the Union whatever the cost.

For ten days Tom gave the speech twice, often three times a day.

Maybe the repetition made it go stale. Surely those long tedious arguments with Denbelle about the urgent need to improve the Indians' lot in this world did not help. (How Tom loathed Christianity and its treacly promises for the future; how he hated playing the secular preacher to the resolute black man's otherworldliness.) Speaking became odious to him. Whichever way he phrased and rephrased his text, silent doubts pried into the gaps between the words—"What does happen when the garrisons pull out? If the tribes suffer so under federal protection, what will happen when the troops go? What tortures will those southern jackals invent for redskinned loyalists? Slavery—what does it mean to a poor starving Cherokee? Or Creek? Or Seminole?"

One night a drunken Creek called out, "You red white man, what do you want with us? Leave us alone." Tom Hyde stopped. Away from the fire the darkness grew preternaturally still. Tom Hyde had nothing to say. The silence dragged on, demanding a reply. Tom studied the dark; he watched the fire-thrown shadows dance across embarrassed uncertain faces until a village elder bustled over and begged his indulgence. Interrupting a guest as he spoke, insulting a guest, these were not true marks of a Creek. Alcohol had stolen this man's reason. While the elder apologized, Tom wanted to scream: "This man's right. Absolutely right! Show him up here and praise him. You should despise me for I've come to betray you!" The elder discredited the drunken soothsayer without hearing what he said. Hardly a man among them would listen to the complaint, regardless of its justice, for the truth had been offered at the wrong time, in the wrong way, in violation of sacrosanct rules of decorum. Sick at heart, Tom mumbled obligingly to the old man, then went back to his text.

He found the air sweeter on the western frontier. Dodging a party of southern agents allegedly out gunning for him, he reached the Comanche. Among them lived a handful of Cherokee trying to grope their way back to an unremembered wildness. Tom felt relieved to be among them—yet the last night at campfire he found himself telling Mohe's story about the Cheyenne warrior who tried to fight the cholera.

In full war dress, the warrior rode up and down through a village decimated by the white man's disease, shouting, "Come out. Come out and fight! If only I could see the enemy I would kill him!" He galloped up and down, up and down, shouting his challenge until he fell from his horse, dead.

Tom reached Fort Gibson on April 7, 1861, and found the garrison in an uproar. Two days earlier the rebels had captured Fort Smith.

Arbuckle, Cobb, and Washita would fall next, which would leave Gibson cut off. Everyone believed war would break out any day. Tom went straight to the commandant, a Bostonian with known abolitionist leanings, asked if the commandant wanted any dispatches carried to St. Louis, wished the gentleman good luck, then left. For fifty dollars and his worn-out horse, Tom got a long winded three-year-old mare.

He rode the animal mercilessly all day and all night, trying to concentrate on the ride, the slope of the land, ruts or breaks in the hard-packed turf. He tried not to think about the Indians, the struggle for Missouri that lay ahead, or about Chief John Ross; he tried not to think at all. Yet all the long ride to St. Louis Tom kept filling in the sentence that Ross never finished: "You–

"–have been working for the North when you should be working for the Indian."

"–are a fool."

"–have betrayed your own flesh and blood."

"–have forgotten who you are."

ST. LOUIS

TOM REACHED ST. LOUIS on April 10, at 6 P.M. He left his horse at a Union livery stable in a poor part of town and walked to the quarters of his contact, a Major Greene, who lived a block away from the St. Louis Arsenal. He entered by a prearranged alley and back door. Tom spent an hour browsing military pamphlets and read the most offensive one—"The Cavalry and Indian Warfare on the Plains"—from cover to cover.

At exactly 8 P.M. a tall, gangly figure strode through the doorway—Matthew Sherrin. Sherrin pumped Tom's arm as though to assure them both that the apparition existed. "Major Greene," he announced. "Secretary Coughlin moves in strange and mysterious ways. Over the past six months we've had quite a turnover in Major Greenes. I've been the designate for three weeks now—just in time for you, old friend." The plate face broke into a wide smile.

"It's you, Matthew," Tom said redundantly. "You. I can't believe it. Why didn't someone let me know?"

"They weren't sure if they could move me here in time. And once they got me to St. Louis, they didn't know how long I'd last. God, it's good to see you. You must be exhausted. Do you want to rest?"

"I am exhausted but I don't want to rest."

"You've been out in the Territory, yes?"

Tom nodded. Clearly he had no wish to talk about it. But since Matthew seemed to appreciate his reluctance, Tom told him a little about his speeches and Chief John Ross and his ongoing argument with Denbelle. Tom felt most impressed with the tenacity of the Indians' opposition to slavery. "Morally, most of them simply cannot stand the institution." Tom did not mention how disturbing his experience in the Territory had been; he figured his old friend could see that.

"I read about you," said Matthew, trying to shift the mood.

"More of Greeley's muckraking, that's all. They wanted a new color for their weekly hero."

Sherrin did not pursue it, for which Tom silently thanked him.

"You want to hear a little about St. Louis?" Tom nodded yes. "The city, like the state, is virtually split in half. The fighting could start today, tomorrow. Rebels are massing in the North and they intend to take the capital. St. Louis, as you know, is of utmost importance." They moved to the map. "Two spots you've heard of–Camp Jackson, where the secessionist militia is marshaling–that's here–and this is the Bertholde mansion–you've heard of that, yes?" Tom indicated he had been briefed. The map bore clusters of blue and gray stars: often blue and gray stood next door to each other or across the street. Matthew described each of the southern meeting halls and watering places, estimated the number of men gathered there, named the leaders. "War comes soon!" Tom thought with glee. Action would drive away all those dark uncertainties that pursued him from the Indian Territory.

"You ought to understand one thing more. Ah–I'm not sure how to break this to you; but, ah, they tried to courtmartial me last Thursday."

"Courtmartial?"

"The commandant, like Missouri's governor, is a Southerner. He brought charges for 'Unauthorized Initiatives' and 'Acting Without Orders.' Which means, I tried to fortify the arsenal against the attack they're sure to mount, and tried drilling my volunteer troops. That's the charge they had a chance with, my working overtime. But there were enough Northerners on the court . . ."

"You mean to tell me that you had no orders?"

"Not officially. My only chance is to respond to whatever they spring on me." Matthew's mouth springboarded into the broadest smile. "I know they'd never make it stick."

"So we're on our own, huh?"

"You're right."

As Tom strolled past the Bertholde mansion, he eyed the turrets and upper stories for the best sniper positions. Nearby trees and buildings carried handbills announcing the formation of:

A MILITIA FOR THE PROTECTION OF THE RIGHTS
AND PROPERTY OF THE CITIZENS OF ST. LOUIS,
STATE OF MISSOURI
ALL VOLUNTEERS TO CONVENE AT CAMP JACKSON

A large crowd had gathered in the square and in its midst stood a black man on a keg, his hands and face dusted with flour. He wore a top hat and frayed frock coat which had been slit into strips behind, in rough imitation of a circuit abolitionist. In his right hand he held a large black Bible.

"Ree-poo-lick-ans mean to force whites to marry the black," the slave harangued, thumping his Bible. "John Brown, he gettin' ready to come stompin' 'cross the South. Link-coon—" That drew a monstrous laugh. "—mean to wipe out the slave everywhar, like the boot aim to do to the cockroach. Link-coon gonna let the fugitive slave go all to hell till niggers be trompin' all over the fields. Link-coon burn the cotton down to the stump. He dry up the river and spread the weevil, he . . ."

Tom retreated to the shade of a dusty magnolia tree. "A black puppet jigging on white man's string." The speaker drawled on in mushy singsong until it became a somnolent drone, like the buzzing of many mosquitoes. The air beneath the budding tree lay heavy, saccharine. Under limbs about to burst into bulbous flower he waited for his head to clear and his sense of revulsion and outrage to clear out as well.

Two days later Tom took over the drilling of Matthew's troops. He also served as peripatetic ambassador, ferrying telegrams across the river and organizing squads of volunteers to man strategic locations in the very likely event of fighting in the streets.

Tom fired off a note to the colonel that explained how busy he and Matthew were "here in the city that has such a commanding prospect of the Mississippi." He also managed a long letter to Charlotte filled with picturesque anecdotes about his adventures to date. He said nothing about the condition of the Indians in the Territory, nor did he suggest what pained, contradictory feelings the tour had aroused in him. He thoroughly resented this letter and, when he finished, grew furious with her for forcing him to write of real events in such trivial ways. Tom felt cheated and betrayed. And he despised the imaginative conversion he felt he was undergoing in her mind.

Night had fallen when Tom Hyde took his walk that evening. He felt uneasy. Their plans to rescue St. Louis for the Union seemed stalled: both Matthew and he were waiting for something, but neither knew just what it was. Halfway down the block he realized someone was following him. Another block, still those footsteps on the wooden sidewalk. Tom strolled slowly. Third block, Tom ducked into the livery stable where he boarded his horse.

The empty stable was semidark. Tom placed himself behind the single lit lantern, using the wall of his horse's stall as a barricade, a pitchfork within reach of his right hand. He waited tensely, in air grown palpably thick, wondering if danger packed the molecules more tightly. "Maybe that's just horseshit!" he thought, enjoying the exhilarating feeling of danger. He hadn't felt so alive in a long time.

His pursuer swung open the door, peeked in guardedly. In the dim light Tom could make out only an enormous head; the tiny body came after, unafraid. "A dwarf!" Tom thought as the interlocutor tipped his cap toward him stiffly, holding two fingers out from the brim, the other two distinctly curved over it. Tom casually scratched his nose, two and two. They exchanged cordial good evenings. Then the little man, an aging leprechaun in plaid waistcoat, checked vest, and matching pants, shuffled closer to Tom's stall.

"Nice horse, mister. She yours?" He touched Tom's mount lightly on the flank. His hand lingered—thumb tucked under, the fingers forked into unmistakable pairs.

Tom reached for the little man's hand. They exchanged the Union League handshake. Tom gave thanks to Coughlin's briefing papers.

"I've got nothing to tell you you probably don't already know. At least I think you know." Apparently delighted with this mysterious opening, the dwarf suddenly broke away and scuttled around to check the stalls, retreated back to the door where he listened a moment, then flung it open with impressive agility. Satisfied that the night offered no threat, he shut the door that towered over him and came back to Tom Hyde.

From the way the little man carried himself, Tom could see he had a strong upper body. It went wrong in the legs.

"You must have figured the arsenal commandant a dyed-in-the-wool—I should say, cotton—secessionist." He laughed at his joke. "But what you might not figure is that they plan to pinch the guns in the arsenal. Steal every last one of them and plop them into the hands of the state militia, the Johnny Rebs." He laughed again before raising his eyebrows, which splashed waves of wrinkles over his brow. "They get those guns and they'll take the whole state of Missou." Tom ogled the little man. "Nothing else to say, but you better move quick. And look sharp, mark me."

The delivery had its eccentricities, but Tom got the message.

Suddenly the little man seemed in a hurry. "I wish you luck," he said, casting an anxious eye toward the door. Tom thanked him with as much force as he could muster. They shook hands two and two, then the little man slipped off stiffly, holding his torso like a rigid board. At the door he stopped and called softly across the stable, "Getting pretty good at spotting Leaguers, I'd say." Tom nodded. "You Injun, ain't you?"

Tom's heart fluttered as it always did when asked that question. "Yes."

The little man's smile unveiled rows of teeth. "Well, friend Injun, I wish you the very best of luck." With that he disappeared.

At 7:30 sharp a drover walked up to a couple of men lounging at the intersection of Buchanan and Rose, one block north of the arsenal. Within two and a half minutes the same approach, the same whispered passwords were exchanged by three men at each of the other three intersections one block away from the arsenal.

Sixty seconds later a wagon rumbled through the narrow streets. Wagon, wagon, wagon rolled in from the three other compass points at precise five-minute intervals, and each wagon came accompanied by two men on foot.

As soon as a wagon reached the forecourt of the arsenal, the huge gate swung open. The moment the wagon passed inside, the gate closed again. So the metal-studded fifteen-foot moving wall opened and closed for the next fifty-eight minutes, swallowing the heavily sprung wagons and the men who followed them in.

At precisely 8:30 the wagons had drawn up into three columns, four wagons deep. Three squads of ten men each formed human conveyor belts from the storehouse to the wagons. By 8:33 Matthew Sherrin had opened the arsenal doors, and the first case of rifles shot out of the storehouse and was hefted down the line.

The men took up production-line rhythm. The only breaks in rhythm came at the wagon ends, where the 125-pound cases had to be handed up, then laid lengthwise in the large coffinlike boxes which Matthew had custom-made for the occasion.

Each layer was padded with felt to prevent damage. The artillery pieces and siege guns fitted into somewhat larger crates, and they were stacked in the back at the top. The sidearms came in small boxes. Steady as a metronome, Tom kept time while the German-born citizens filled the night with ferocious silent loyalty; they grunted softly as the moving weight passed down the line; wordlessly they cursed each snag as an insult to their patriotism. How oddly thrilling for Tom to watch in the soft darkness as each pair, in turn, hunched over as they took the weight. How happy Tom felt in moments of such intensity.

By 9:45, sixty thousand rifles and small arms and fifty artillery pieces had been stacked into the mitred boxes with the legend "BIBLES" stenciled on the tops and sides.

"Good work. Good work, men," Matthew stage-whispered. "We should make it."

Sherrin's three wagons left the arsenal first, and a half minute later the first segment of the convoy passed the three regular army men still posted at the corner of Buchanan and Rose. Those men would now become the rearguard on the north ferry to Venice, Illinois.

Tom took the second three wagons east and reached the southern ferry at 10:15. He flashed his papers at the captain, opened one crate to show the mate his top two layers of Bibles, then supervised the work of getting his wagons on board. At 10:43 the ferry shoved off for the Illinois shore with Tom, his three drivers, and ten of Sherrin's shabbily attired soldiers—just in case. All the way across Tom stayed close to the captain, a loaded, but hidden, revolver leveled at the man's intestines.

They reached East St. Louis just before 11:30. Tom drove the wagons north to Venice, where he found ten of Matthew's regulars lolling in the vicinity of a deserted pier a quarter mile from the landing. "Anderson?" he queried.

The sergeant replied, "Sumter. 12 April. 4:30 A.M."

"Guard it well, Sergeant."

"With my life, sir."

A few minutes later Matthew's ferry maneuvered into the wharf. "Perfect," Tom thought, allowing himself a brief moment of elation. He watched the three wagons roll off, his loaded pistol cocked under his waistcoat, knowing that all those indigent-looking fellows behind him also had the boat covered. Going up the gangplank, Tom brushed by Matthew without a sign of recognition. His partner would now ride south and take the southern ferry from East St. Louis back to the Missouri side for his second column of wagons.

As his boat nudged the Missouri shore, Tom saw the next three wagons neatly in line along the pier. A half hour later he watched his final load of BIBLES roll down the reenforced planks.

"Lot o' Bible tonight, aye," a crewman offered aloud.

Fourteen men turned unmistakably hostile attention toward him. The captain, not a stupid man, told the crewman to shut his goddamn face. Later a drunk made the mistake of staggering into Tom. Two soldiers took the man by his elbows, suggesting he be more careful next time about bumping into that particular gentleman. Drunk as he was, the man got the point.

Tom got back to Illinois at 3:15. His instructions told him to wait until 4. If Matthew hadn't reached the landing by then, Tom would drive the wagons they had north to their destination. Copperheads abounded in the area, and Sherrin wanted the wagons well on their way to Springfield before dawn. Tom spent an uneasy half hour under a clear noncommittal sky, not bothering to say much to the soldiers. At 3:50 he readied the teams. He fretted away the last few minutes when he heard a horse approaching at a gallop. They all waited anxiously until the rider reined up and said to Tom, "Everything's fine, sir. They're behind schedule. Ferry got off late and halfway across a boiler kicked up."

Twenty-three minutes later Matthew arrived. They shook hands greedily.

"Clockwork with a leaky boiler," Sherrin joked, yet the tension didn't ease until he had walked among the wagons and counted them, counted every one of his picturesque drovers. "You're all here," he concluded with a wide grin. "And you look fine, mighty fine."

At 4:45 the friends said goodnight—Matthew headed the escort back, Tom rumbled on into the night. At 8:30 Tom's twelve wagons drew up at the gates of the government arsenal in Springfield, Illinois. He told his men that their evening would soon end; then he walked into the brevet colonel's office, saluted and announced, "Sir, I know you're going to find this difficult to believe, but I've got fifty thousand rifles and sidearms and fifty artillery pieces and twelve siege guns from the St. Louis arsenal parked outside your gates. Could you put them into safekeeping for us?"

Even after reading the inventory and the orders, the brevet colonel thought this Indian mad, or joking, or both. But, outside, he looked convinced as Tom stripped off the top layers of Bibles and cracked open a crate of Sharps rifles. Remembering his role as host, the brevet colonel asked, "Is there anything I can do for you and your men, Mr. Hyde?"

"Just coffee and a bite of breakfast, sir. If it isn't too much bother."

St. Louis meant one thing—sleep. Tom could think of nothing else—eiderdowns, smooth sheets, soft down pillows, a sensitive breeze licking his tired aching eyelids. He wanted to lay his aching body down on its stomach, push the right knee out a bit, balance that with the left elbow's thrust, and sleep for two days—a percale fantasy. But when he reached Sherrin's rooms, Matthew sat in his reading chair, feet up on the desk, puffing away at a fat uncharacteristic cigar. "Would you care to partake of a stogie, old comrade?" Tom declined. Matthew cleared his throat, pointed the butt at Tom. "The commandant discovered something amiss when he got back from Jeff City this morning. Summoned me to his office, he did, but fortunately I was out on a tour of duty upriver—

"Then it took me time to dress when I got back because I supposed he'd want me fully regaled for our conference. Got to his office, but had to wait because a runner slipped in just ahead of me. The runner came out; I went in. The commandant was staring in blue-faced apopletic rage at the telegram in his hands. His expression turned less than loving and he passed me the wire."

"Come on, Matt, what did it say?"

"It said he was RECALLED!"

"Really?"

"Yes. Then he called me ingrate and traitor. Ingrate he said twice. Even had the gall to insist I'd arranged for the 'theft of his guns' and his recall at the same time."

"Not true," Tom said. "It just worked out that way." Both wore grand smiles now. "Tell me, what was your beloved colonel recalled for?"

The tip of Sherrin's cigar glowed; his mouth coiled like one of his smoke rings. "A trifle, a tut—something about failure to exercise his duty to safeguard the contents of the arsenal."

Next day the twosome began enlisting volunteers, countering the southern's Camp Jackson recruitments, into the service of the United States of America. Matthew Sherrin, acting commandant of the St. Louis Arsenal, gave civilian Tom a title—Chief Recruiting Officer. Within days, three regiments had been enlisted and, most importantly, armed. That left the arsenal virtually depleted.

Tom's orders were to leave St. Louis by the fifteenth so he could reach the Niobrara country before June when the Sioux held their great summer gathering. He never actually considered giving up the trip, which would have meant depriving the Sioux of the trade goods and weapons he was entrusted to deliver, let alone the speeches that were supposed to deliver them. Yet to perform one duty meant to neglect another. War in Missouri would come any day now, and Matthew sat in a divided city with only a skeleton force of men he could count on. Tom's orders would shift him away from battle again, off to the side where he would be compelled to be a spectator, not a warrior. An old fear of his awakened, which had a most disquieting effect on Tom.

Early on May tenth Tom stood in Matthew's office. The letter in his hand was addressed to the Commanding Officer, Missouri State Militia, mustered at Lindell Grove, Camp Jackson, Missouri. "Civil war begins at home," Tom thought mindlessly. The letter charged the commander with actions hostile to the interests of the United States Government; it ordered him to surrender his forces and arms to the Army of the United States.

As they made their final preparations to deliver the letter, Tom and Matthew exchanged few words, and those they did felt heavy like stone blocks difficult to maneuver. The slightest gestures seemed exaggerated, like oversized garments put on to obscure their fear that the decisions made and still to be executed would actually succeed. These decisions, which might injure people and tilt the country over the brink into the horrors of fratricidal war, lay beyond reconsideration now.

Starting at 8:45 and for the next two hours, the four German companies, three small volunteer regiments, and the single company of regulars assembled at the arsenal. Such a gathering could not be kept secret. By 10:30 the citizens of St. Louis had lined the route to Camp Jackson—they leaned out of windows, stood in door frames, crowded the few existing sidewalks, and clogged the streets. All along the way the rooftops were thronged with people.

At 11 the federal troops marched out of the arsenal. They were greeted by cheers and an equal measure of jeers, a few shouted pledges, and a scattering of threats. But most of the citizens stood quietly, watching the grim, hypnotic rows of soldiers file past, hearing for the first time the amplified echo of feet marching through their streets.

Seven blocks from Camp Jackson a galloping courier rode straight at Matthew and Tom at the head of the column. A fine cavalier with ascot and cape, the rebel reined up sharply, saluted, and handed Sherrin a note. The Commander of the Militia of the State of Missouri demanded to know why troops of the United States were marching against him.

Matthew nodded to Tom, who handed the courier the letter he carried. "If you wish, Major," Tom said, "I'll ride with this gentleman back to his ranks."

Matthew almost smiled at the title. "No, thank you. I think this gentleman will take care to deliver our message into the proper hands."

The courier spun his horse around and rode off briskly. Sherrin shouted to a lieutenant. Double time, he moved his troops forward. In five minutes they reached Lindell Grove.

The spectacle awaiting them did not please the acting commandant. Though most of the onlookers who swarmed the area had the sense to stay on the far side of the street, many fashionable young people had taken up positions on the grassy edges of the Grove itself. Some sat astride horses, others lounged in carriages, and one woman twirled a vibrant yellow parasol and waved vehemently at Matthew.

Sherrin muttered: "They think they're going to a ball," then ordered a lieutenant to clear the field.

The troops could only herd the fashionables back across the street into the crowds who stood behind the military lines. One young blade argued heatedly with a sergeant, indignant at being deprived of his front-row seat. None of this confusion helped Matthew's undertrained, skittish men.

With the crowds shoved back closer to safety, Sherrin deployed his volunteers in battle lines along the river edge, and on the east and north sides of the rebel camp. He split the German company into thirds, each third stationed behind a regiment where they could move to reenforce any breaks in the line. The regulars had already moved off at double time to cover the southern hills, which provided the rebels with their most obvious escape route.

The volunteers stood in position when the rebel courier returned with a second note. The general of the Missouri militia requested time to consider Major Sherrin's proposal.

Matthew coolly glanced at his watch, lifted his right foot out of the stirrup, shifted enough to slip his leg up onto the saddle. With his knee for a table, with three thousand civilians looking on, Sherrin scribbled his reply. "We open fire at 11:28. That gives you precisely 7 minutes to surrender your men and arms." His regulars would be in position in the hills by 11:26.

To impress the courier with the urgency of the message, Sherrin repeated it aloud. The young man took the note, tore his horse's head around, and galloped back. They watched him dismount while the horse was still moving and rush into the general's tent, cape flying.

Three minutes later Matthew Sherrin focused his field glasses on a central hill south of the camp. He caught his lieutenant's signal at 11:25. "Check your primings!" he roared. The order went down the lines, first in English, then in German. The long files of soldiers snapped into a straighter line.

A long minute ticked by. Matthew stared at the entrance to the general's tent until suddenly the courier dashed out, mounted, and rode furiously back at them.

"Let's hope, Matt," Tom offered under his breath.

Sherrin grimly grinned back. "Let's hope they use their heads."

Tom wondered why he didn't feel more excited, sitting there waiting for the shot that might start it all. Yet this didn't seem like war, surrounding the enemy in broad daylight in the middle of a city, pushing the crowd back to the other side of the street, and asking parasol-twirling beauties to please fold them up because their adornments made too good a target.

The crowd hushed as the courier saluted crisply and handed Matthew an envelope. Sherrin opened the note, glanced at it and handed it across to Tom. It read: "I find my troops surrounded. Given the proximity of noncombatants and not knowing what law the State militia is accused of breaking, I surrender under strongest protest. Much more will be said of this."

Matthew raised his right arm above his head and shouted, "They surrender. Disarm the rebels."

His four regiments cheered wildly. As did approximately half the crowd.

"One thousand rebels and their arms," Tom thought. "Not a shot fired. Not one civilian scratched. If we can get through this day—one thousand prisoners, all their arms—the mental advantage, the momentum are ours, which Colonel Hyde says is never to be underestimated. Maybe we can hold Missouri!" Their only remaining problem was the long march back to the arsenal.

For an hour the volunteers collected the rebel guns while Matthew headed the exchange of dignities, wrote out receipts and orders. Sherrin patiently explained to the enraged general that his troops would be held overnight and released the next morning. No, their arms would not be returned. They would be kept in the arsenal in custody of the federal government. Yes, that was the general's as well as everyone else's legal government. Tom thought Matthew acted with impressive control.

At 1:15, his official work completed, Matthew turned to his friend. "Well, here goes." Sherrin led his prisoners four abreast onto the parade ground, then deployed his troops in single file on every side of the column of prisoners. He ordered them forward. The crowd seemed disappointed to see the troops start, as though they hadn't gotten all that they had come for.

In the narrow St. Louis streets, with aroused crowds lining the route, progress came slowly, especially as the unwieldy column stretched out for nine blocks and nearly filled the width of the street. The arsenal seemed miles away.

In the first two blocks spectators cheered the federal troops. In the third, southern sympathizers hooted, shook their fists and jeered, "America for Americans!" "Kill a Kraut today!" The din was terrific, enough to make any man dizzy.

The column slowed like a caterpillar, bunching up in places, thinning out behind. Caught in this human box, both troops and prisoners shared the terrifying feeling that they had absolutely no control over where they would step next.

Tom's section, a block behind the lead section, stopped entirely. "Move it!" he shouted, knowing their only hope was to keep moving steadily. "Move it up in front!"

As they stalled there, flowers rained down. Jubilant faces pushed at the soldiers, holding up children, pawing or pounding their backs. They started again. In the next block someone hurled buckets of garbage down off a roof. The recruits reeled. "Don't worry, men, we'll soon be there. Soon." Only those a few paces from Tom caught his frail encouragement.

One block ahead of Tom, near the intersection of Third and Jefferson, a rock struck a soldier in the forehead. He went down, screaming and bleeding. The crowd cheered and surged forward. A recruit, pushed by a bystander who had been pushed by someone behind him, hit the man in the stomach with his rifle butt. He slumped, gasping for breath. Louder shouting, more pushing. Angry faces closed in on unseasoned troops as more troops shoved in from behind. From the walls resounded the cry: "Kill the Kraut! Kill the goddamn Kraut-eating bastards!"

Five recruits began to swing their rifles to give themselves more air, more room. One rifle went off. The thin report of a pistol answered. A soldier went down. The sweaty, harassed lieutenant saw his man fall, felt the suffocating crush of violent distorted faces, and bellowed "FIRE!" A moment of relative stillness followed, then whoever could or wanted to leveled his rifle and fired point-blank into the crowd. The crowd groaned and surged and screamed and tried to flee. But they had no place to go. People fell on bloody, falling bodies. Doors clanged and bolts slid shut; children rushed underfoot; heads pulled back from windows; windows slammed. Madness and blood and screaming reigned.

By the time Tom reached the next block, twelve people lay dead, another four were dying, ten others critically injured. He got there three minutes after the massacre but he knew, nonetheless, he'd never understand what happened. Who fired the shots, who provoked whom–useless questions in the face of the noise, the blood, the panicked attempt to escape the deadly chute of the street. Tom could only yell to the others to move on as sanely as possible. Others were already tending to the dying and wounded. He saw Matthew lift an infant whose side was half-blown away out of the arms of a hysterical woman, probably the mother. Someone else picked up the body of a frail young soldier who had been trampled to death.

By late afternoon, almost one thousand men were crammed into the arsenal. Their guns had been tagged and stacked away. But thirty-one people lay dead, scores wounded and maimed.

At the hospital Matthew held hands with a bereaved couple whose twenty-two-year-old son died as they looked on. Later Tom watched a soldier and a father of two die. All night they soaked up the accusations of parent and family and friend and lover of those maimed or dead or dying. All night angry crowds carried placards around the giant bonfires in front of the hospital, shouting hatred to the thick night air.

Back in his quarters, Matthew's strength deserted him. He sat on the edge of his cot fully clothed, head drooping over his chest, hands slung listlessly between his knees.

Tom tried: "Matthew, it was inevitable. Something had to give way. We're on the brink of war."

Matthew didn't move: not a flicker, not a nod. Tom could almost see the box of despair that encased his friend. But he could not enter it. After what may have been hours, Sherrin lifted his head and whispered hoarsely, "Get some sleep." It was an order.

By noon, a menacing crowd gathered outside the walls of the arsenal to jeer at the federal soldiers. All day southern sympathizers boisterously roamed the streets; they organized a committee to put up plaques at spots where civilians had fallen. At five the crowd outside the arsenal learned that the legislature had voted Governor Jackson powers of martial law and rammed through a bill which appropriated two million dollars "to raise an Army of the State of Missouri." For an hour Tom and Matthew feared they might have another civilian massacre on their hands. But the crowd dispersed at suppertime.

Tom would soon proceed to Sioux country to resume his speeches. The friends spent their last night talking. Around midnight, Matthew said, "Before you go, I could deliver the colonel's sermon on the difficulty of duty. But only if you like." A reflective smile weighted the broad mouth. "Of course, that would put you one up on me, since you held off the other day."

Tom smiled back, half happy.

They said good-bye at the wharf the next morning, shaking hands with a sense of great loss, but with the perfect assurance of close friends that they'd meet by late summer.

The riverboat pumped languidly up the Missouri. Tom spent his time on deck looking down into the turbid water as if seeking a prophecy. What kind of man could he be, profoundly troubled by the Cherokee one day, passionately committed to the white man's war the next? Playing soldier in St. Louis, where did he hide Chief John Ross's words: "People are not destroyed because they're wrong, only because they're weak." "This war is fought for the only things white man ever fights for, power and profit." Tom's most sacred beliefs, had they simply become opposing poles to shuttle between? What defect of character made his mind so capable of always presenting him with the opposing irony? The Cree drunk had shouted it—"A red white man." Speckled Tail had known it too, that's why the Pawnee demanded his life; even his dear friend Bushnell had sensed Tom's convenient ambivalence, and hated it, and pitied him. Moses—what sort of Moses would he be, propped behind a desk shuffling papers while somewhere out there his people—whose people?—saw their way of life vanish. Meanwhile, he would dwell comfortably in the white world, the exemplary member of his race, the nation's foremost Indian. Foremost because the most white, least red; foremost because a docile lapdog and charlatan, an occasional exotic titillation for their women. Would he fill the slot Hyde had created for him, he who hadn't even the guts to go home to his parents that summer he moped around Laramie? How ashamed Tom felt about his insensitivity to their needs, about his inability to go and see them. Those speeches in the Indian Territory—

shameful condescending lies. Would he dutifully utter the same damnable lies to the Sioux? "Repeat after me—Sioux Indians: a native tribe of the Great Plains, known for their horsemanship—" The murky river only gave back his distorted image drowning among the upside-down trees.

Tom drove his supply wagon northward up the ladder of rivers, Dismal Creek, the Loup's middle fork, the Snake, Niobrara, over the Keya Paha at Rosebud, then east across the Little White River. The summer prairie remained a constant unpromising yellow/brown, with hardly a hint of green. The rivers ran low and alkalai, game seemed scarce. The dryness left the country quieter than he remembered, or so he thought, this stranger in his own land.

He was coming from the southeast, moving into the setting sun when he first sighted the Sioux camp. The light struck the tepees from behind, turning the skins translucent, and, for an instant, he believed he could look into the heart of the Sioux.

Tom felt the wagon bouncing beneath him, heard the rig creaking and the horses' breathing, but he did not seem to be moving toward the camp. The white tepees hung there, crowned by dark smoke rings, a mirage he would never reach. Ever since his capture he had been driving toward those lodges in this dream. The state of suspension hung over him for an indeterminate time. Then the sun bumped the horizon. Suddenly it fell dark. Tom found himself four hundred yards from the Hunkpapa circle.

A Hunkpapa chief led the delegation of warriors out to the wagon. "We welcome you, brother," he said in measured tones, his cheeks streaked red with sun-dance signs, "and offer the friendship of our people." He held out his arms as though handing Tom a package.

Tom beheld a massive camp, with at least one thousand lodges. Hundreds of polite, quizzical people lined the route to the council lodge to see the famous red man sent by the Great Father. He returned their greetings, though his heart felt lead-heavy.

The Sioux draped Tom in a buffalo robe and installed him in the place of honor at the feast. The Hunkpapa saw that their visitor was troubled; then they gauged their attention to his feelings as precisely as an engineer gauges material stress. All night the warriors ate and sang and told of their deeds. All night the drum beat and Tom watched their dances. The ritual perfection struck him like a lash. Here he sat in the reciprocity of a truly civilized people where a host knows what a guest wants, the guest knows exactly what is available, and, for a time, no other questions exist. Tom told himself that their circle bought perfection at the price of scale—it was only because their reach or inventiveness or power remained so circumscribed that everyone knew what was available; their world remained small; it risked little. But he felt like an ingrate. Once again his traitorous seesaw mind presented him with the opposing irony, with that other way of looking at the world. He found himself tired of running back and forth between the white and red worlds, for that night Tom realized that his suppleness provided him with a way of evading both worlds.

By force of will he held their monotonous drumbeat at arms length until noon of the second day when, without warning, his legs ached to push off, he longed to feel the ground come up under him and smack his soles. "Like that time after the battle when Big Road and the warriors danced—how much self-control it took to keep from joining them."

They asked him to speak but Tom declined, saying the Spirit did not move him. They looked at their guest and understood. Even with their discreet unprobing eyes and their politeness, Tom felt they understood too much. He wandered through the colorful crowd as if at a carnival, a grown man admiring the dark handsome women, greeting the braves, looking at the children and trying to remember. Truly the Sioux were brothers of the Cheyenne—they wore the same masks, painted the same yellow stripes on forehead and thighs, shook the same eagle-feathered sticks. Even their faces looked similar—ample chins, broad noses that anchored and centered the face, strong mouths with overhanging upper lips.

That evening Tom gave away all the trade goods—coffee, tobacco, smoked oysters, and candied fruits, powder, ball and primings, twelve old flintlocks. To the chiefs he handed calico shirts, a pair of cotton pants for Old Man Who Rides Sideways, and beads, bone, needles, and cotton flax for the women. The gifts felt tawdry to him, a bribe the Sioux couldn't understand because they had no method for pricing themselves. Stones, toads, horsehair, pebbles—whatever the universe produced they accepted with unperturbable good will. A number of headmen wore a cross among their feathers, stones, beads, and quills. "Too polite to refuse it," he thought at first. But later he realized—remembered would be more accurate—that they'd never consider refusing a gift and were always willing to pile on one more amulet.

The drum struck deeper into his bones. Tom's mind wandered restlessly, not really knowing what it sought. The third day he isolated the problem: the Sioux insisted on fulfilling the immediate demands of their lives; they paid strict attention to the nature that surrounded them; they did not bother to look out and observe what happened outside their circle. That made them vulnerable to threat from the outside. "That's why the white world seemed so unlimited, so magically large to me." The drumbeat pressed his memories upon him: he saw Shell's vibrant face, and Big Road's, and, most persistently, the seamed face of his grandfather. Mohe appeared to him constantly.

Again they asked Tom if he wanted to speak. He said yes. They led him to a flat stretch of prairie that could've been Buck's Heart's training field. He stood on the wagon boot. Eight hundred people came.

He began his usual speech, longing to speak about the questions burning up his soul. He told them that slavery was wrong; no man should be another man's master. He told them about the threat coming their way, said his wisdom told him that three Oglala chiefs had already taken fifteen rifles and ten bolts of cloth and two hundred dollars a piece from the men who wrapped black men in chains. A repentant whisper stirred the crowd.

"Such tawdry, simple magic," the orator thought, watching that sea of proud faces tilt up to him like flowers to the sun. Once again he found it hard to look at that field of faces constructed and colored like his own while knowing that they remained blind to all he saw. Like an Old Testament prophet, no, one older than that, one who could deliver the original and final and enduring testament, Tom wanted to tell them what lay written in the dust just outside their perfect circle—your world is doomed, your lives are about to become as extinct as Dr. Darwin's mastodons. "Develop tools to fight white man!"—that should have been his text. He could show them how; he understood how they made their machines. But how to explain that to a people whose minds had no slot for the idea; how to tell his audience that accident and history and policy had combined to guarantee their extinction, that the benevolent healing nature they had built their lives within had been attacked from without and was dying.

Tom wanted to say, "It tears my heart as a mountain lion tears his kill to be here with you." He wanted to hear them suck in a single collective breath in response to that. Then he would quote Ross, that red white man, more red than the speaker even though he was one-eighth Cherokee and kept one hundred slaves: "People are not destroyed because they're wrong, only because they're weak." But Tom went on with the old text, his mouth forming words his heart did not speak, a madman reciting a grocery list to an audience who understood too much, yet all too little.

When he finished, Tall Bull came over to thank Tom, of course. But the others kept their distance. Tom felt they looked at him sideways, with the kind of puzzled reverence they reserved for a man in the vision trance.

That night he slept soundly. The next morning he thanked everyone and said good-bye to Tall Bull and the chiefs, then turned his empty wagon east.

At Fort Randall Tom presented himself to the commanding officer and explained that he had been robbed of his supplies by a marauding band of Brule Sioux. The inconvenience did not matter, Tom said winningly, but he had to get on his way quickly to get to the Sun Dance before it ended. The captain seemed impressed by Tom Hyde's account of the attack, especially by the declaration that he never would've escaped with his life if he didn't speak Sioux. The captain seemed even more impressed by Tom's letter of introduction from the Secretary of War. He said to the young Indian: "Just take what you want from the storehouse and leave my quartermaster the list."

Tom did just that, taking as many rifles and bullets as he thought he could without arousing suspicion. He added flints, priming, cap and ball, three bullet molds, and a number of dies and forms as well, bar steel, and lead. Then he returned to the captain's office, thanked him for the courtesy, and inquired about news of the war. The captain relayed these details of the Missouri campaign: Major Sherrin had moved men by rail and steamboat up to Jefferson City, only to find the capital deserted. Now rumor had it that Matthew was preparing to attack Boonville, where the rebels had fled. "Matt's about to see action," Tom thought. "There's a good chance this Indian won't be far behind." He thanked the captain again and set off for Fort Sully.

The next day Tom repeated his performance at Fort Sully and drove away with three dozen more rifles, ammunition, another bullet mold, more steel, and a number of other materials which would have surprised the young major who offered Tom Hyde carte blanche. He drove his overstuffed wagon west, along the Cheyenne River, upstream, toward the Black Hills.

BOOK THREE

HOME

A LOOSE RING OF lodges climbed the hillside. It was much like any other small camp, except that he could look at this circle and say, "I'm here. I'm home." He could look up the slope and think, "Parents, grandfather, old friends are all up there, just up that hill."

Six days before he'd thought their camp would be larger—that was before he'd started south to the summer hunting grounds, where he'd expected to find them. On the way he'd run into a party of Sioux who told him that Rumbling Wings' band was farther north, following a smaller herd. His family's party, he was told, was one of the few that clung to the old ways and refused white man's annuities.

Near the edge of the camp circle two round-faced copper-skinned women stopped pounding buffalo steaks and watched. This was the dried meat that would keep them through the winter; it took two or three days in the sun for the meat to get that dark crust. Details from a time like prehistory washed soothingly over his scrambled emotions.

As he climbed down from his wagon, a tiny spot at the back of Tom's throat felt bone-dry. The women looked at him uncertainly. Suddenly he was conscious of his new moccasins and buckskins, his cropped hair just beginning to grow out. Did he embarrass them? Frighten them? Or was their greeting that new mixture of instinctive hospitality and learned suspicion he found everywhere among Indians now?

He took in the camp—the ponies tethered in the usual places, toddlers at games he'd once played, women fleshing yesterday's kill for tonight's dinner; fresh buffalo hung from the drying racks, blood red; white sheets of buck fat. The camp looked like a dripping red and white flag.

Tom didn't want to drive his wagon through the camp, so he left it at the edge of the circle and started up the hill past the first lodges. These were families who'd joined Rumbling Wings after Tom had been captured; families he'd perhaps seen as a boy at the Sun Dance or Massaum Ceremony. One tall woman at her army-issue kettle eyed him as though trying to remember something. A young girl sneaked a quick glance Tom's way, then buried her eyes in her work. The day was hot, and many lodge skins were rolled up to admit the steady prairie breeze.

Dogs lay in the dust, two boys lethargically tossed miniature arrows at a post. Details, details from a life once his. As three boys looked up from the clay figures they were moving about in the dust in mock battle, Tom felt a surge of confidence; he was ready to slip on the old way like a tailored shirt.

He nodded pleasantly as he stepped out of the way of a long-haired woman carrying two water buckets on a yoke. She looked back at him as if not quite understanding his expression.

"Remember!" Tom ordered, slowing as he approached the lodges of the families whose children he'd played with, lodges he could name—Able-to-Reach-the-Cloud's, with that yellow moon and the elk above the entrance. "Stop there later," he told himself. "Moat," he thought involuntarily, looking at the runoff ditch around Two Children's home. He tried to wet that patch at the back of his throat, but it stayed dry.

A new lodge stood next to the Contrary's and next to that stood Man-Who-Runs-the-Farthest's; Island's tepee was missing. Tom shook his head as if apologizing for what he'd missed and walked on into the space cleared for Rumbling Wings' lodge.

He stopped there, tempted to reach out and touch the white skins. He wondered if the sacred hides would ring out again or whether, like the Hebrew soldier who caught the falling arc, he'd be struck dead in his tracks.

Across the clearing, a small girl strung chokecherries on a sinew string; a younger girl was playing the Cheyenne equivalent of jacks with a buffalo hide ball and some stones. Near them White Sage, Takes-the-Pipe's mother, was flaying the long steak off the backbone of a bull. "She's much older," Tom noticed. His eyes intently scanned the round face, knowing that many clues to that lost history were a few feet away from him. It was maddening to have become a total stranger to a woman who had seen him born, at whose breast he'd suckled.

White Sage looked up, then quickly averted her eyes. Tom wanted to run over, take her hands and say, "Remember? Remember me? I'm Tumbling Hawk." But he gave her only a cramped wave, put on a stiff smile, and stole by her like a thief, feeling her eyes and the eyes of the small girls on his back. A few more paces and it occurred to Tom that the two little girls might be Takes-the-Pipe's children.

He came alongside Horn's lodge, with its unusually large smoke hole. "Small Deer might be inside, sitting in there–" He was about to yell to his dear old friend when something urged, "No. Home first."

In a little crease of the hill, suddenly Tom froze–Mohe's tepee was not beside Big Road's. "Perhaps he's living with them now," he said desperately. Tears blanked his vision. He knew Mohe would never have given up his lodge. The signs were clear–his grandfather was dead. Standing on the gentle slope in front of his parents' home, facing that gaping hole in the camp circle, Tom tried to reinvent that slender cone with the blue eagle on the south side. After being gone so long, that did not seem so much to ask. Just one small lodge . . .

The entrance to the most familiar tepee was open, the double thickness of hides laid neatly back, making a clean *O*. In spite of the heat, the skins around the base were not rolled up, so he couldn't see inside. Tom took those last few steps cautiously, aware of the time he traversed now. "So many things to set in order," he breathed, staring into the tepee's dark interior for a long moment. "How does a man do what I'm about to do?" There was no answer. He stepped inside.

Shell was sitting on a buffalo robe, poking a steel needle into a newly cured skin. She kept her eyes on her work until she finished the stitch, then looked up. She knew him instantly; Tom walked into the place she'd always held open for him. The steel needle began to jab lightly at the buffalo skin.

Time pressed the instant wafer thin, too thin to hold all her accumulated pain, her fear, the eight years' daily portion of guilt and reproof. Their feelings shuttled between them, forming a weave too tangled for words or thought to slip through.

Each day of those eight uncertain years, she hated what Tumbling Hawk had done to Big Road, to Mohe, to herself. She hated the destruction his selfishness had caused. And although Shell could have accepted Tumbling Hawk at that very moment, as he was, even though she was overjoyed beyond anger or pain to see her handsome son standing there, his eyes searching hers for a welcome, she felt a grim rigid loyalty to all the time that had passed.

"You drop down on us like a sudden thunderstorm," she said, her black child-starved eyes warning him to keep his distance. The point of the needle poked the thick skin, while the end she held turned in a tight circle. "For all these long years Big Road and I have asked why our son stays with white man, away from us? We have not spoken your name aloud for a full year now—since Mohe's death."

Tom had been so sure of that, the tremor was lighter than he expected.

"But every morning we rise with the same question. And we end our days with it silently pressing on our hearts. When Mohe was with us, he carried it too.

"Can you understand what it has been like for us, hiding our shame from one another though the pain rose over this lodge like a high mesa over the plain? Can you feel my wound as I skinned hides alongside the other mothers? Do you see what your father sees staring into the face of the warriors' pity and contempt, standing beside other men's sons on the hunt?

"Their pity is much worse than contempt, worse even than the talk of our twisted seed."

Tom wanted to cry. He wanted to throw himself before her like a white infant who could bawl and bawl until he cried himself to sleep. Instead he stood there dumbly. Shell was not much older than the eight years that had passed. She was more sad than old.

"It's best you come back without apology since apologies would not answer. But you have always had a feeling for what others wish to hear."

How long Tom had lived among those who did not really know him. After all those years, under all his sophisticated guises, Tom felt naked before her.

"You walk into a home eight years deadened by your absence, and without a word ask us to forget what has happened and receive you again. Only you could put the question that way, you with your way of forgetting in order to begin again."

In that moment Tom was afraid his mother would reject the relation manifest in the shape of her face, the slight slant of her eyes. She did not continue; he stood there looking into that partial mirror of himself—a hint of blue vein colored her forehead, fret lines had gripped the corners of her eyes. She had put on weight, so she seemed to sit in a little pool of herself.

Having said her piece, Shell would say no more. Frantic with impatience, Tom was wise enough to give her time—time for the eyes to calm and soften, time to realize that Tumbling Hawk actually stood before her. Besides, there was nothing to say to undeniable guilt; no repayment to offer for eight lost years, no way to make up for an old man's lonely death.

Her eyes were moist when she told him to sit. He took his old place and waited. Guardedly they let each other seep in.

"When did Mohe die?" he finally asked.

Her head whipped around accusingly, the bitterness flared: "Last year—at the end of the summer hunt." She held her jaw as if it was wired shut.

"A year ago—I was in Washington, with Charlotte," Tom thought. He said: "And how, how did he die?"

"He died like an old man—with eyelids too heavy to lift, very thin in the shank."

After that neither said much. Talk was a bottleneck through which feeling flowed too slowly; behind each word lay a deeper reservoir, untappable yet. They sat together two hours, sharing their sadness while letting the recognition of being together again slowly penetrate. Mother and child were slightly awkward with each other, as if, after having been apart so long, they were embarrassed at having once been so close. The world of the tepee, where he'd been born and grown to early manhood, that seeped in too, as did the skins and robes Shell had fleshed and stitched, the backrests she'd woven out of willow reeds, the floor she'd cleared. He did not bother to crush the fleas that bit him. By late afternoon, the bear grease on her hair smelled like perfume.

At sunset Big Road returned to camp lugging an antelope. Already he'd killed three buffalo, so that afternoon he'd gone after a lighter taste. No one said a word to Big Road about the stranger who waited in his lodge, but from the way the others watched him, standing by the drying racks or grouped around their kettles, Big Road knew something important had happened. He broke into a trot and ran all the way to his lodge. They heard the thunk as Big Road slipped the stiff animal off his shoulder; then he stepped inside.

He caught Shell's eyes first, which explained just how much she could be wounded if he was not kind. She argued for great control, great delicacy.

Three years before Big Road had given up all thought of ever seeing his son again. No one walked out of his parents' and his tribe's life and then, one day eight torturous years later, stepped back in again. After people suffered so much on one's account, no one could presume that much. Nonetheless, it was Tumbling Hawk—their son—who sat there.

Tom was will-less, a blotter soaking up his father's reactions and his mother's mediation. He couldn't speak—still no soothing words came, no sufficient apologies. The pain he'd caused was no sum to be tallied up; he was no moral banker who could measure out the requisite remuneration and hand his parents the correct amount.

Big Road watched his son like an enemy warrior. At the same time, the father considered what Shell carried inside her, remembering how he'd stood by and watched her joy drip out of the hole this boy had drilled in the vessel of their life. How could a husband be asked to forgive that theft? Yet, in one short afternoon, Shell was willing to forget years of heartbreak and humiliation. Shell, right then, was asking him to welcome his son back. "How attached a man grows to his own suffering," the father thought while a part of him vowed never to forgive the boy. Still he greeted Tumbling Hawk, the boy who Lightfoot had mourned as dead. "You have come back." The words were ponderous, the sound rusty.

Big Road's face had gone fleshy yet it held on to enough of its form to remain handsome. A look of false prosperity had loosened the skin on his cheeks and mouth. The lips looked bloated. Tom wondered how this face might've looked if he hadn't stayed away.

Big Road's mood was not so unforgiving that he could let his arms leave his sides. He longed to reach out to his only son and crush the lithe, long-muscled body to his chest. Like the time after the battle with the soldiers when he'd lifted his child off the pony, like those numberless times.

"Father! My words want to rush out to you, to wash away the time which can never be washed away. I would like to take you back to the time when I was captured and did not return—" Big Road's lips, almost obscenely full, bunched impatiently. Tom went on quickly, his eyes shuttling from father to mother and back again: "—to take you through each of the decisions and accidents and inducements that kept me there. I was captured and held; while I made plans to escape my capture became a destiny. I would like you to see how it was for me far from here, the reasons I gave myself to stay and those I took to my heart. I stayed all those years with a purpose. I stayed all those years because I knew someday I would be sitting here with you."

Big Road's eyes would not reply, but Tom could feel his mother leaning with him, as though his explanation were a sled and she could give it momentum.

"Learning about their power took too long and, as time passed, I became more like them than I knew. You find this surprising, but that is one of white man's greatest powers. I want to show you how each step of my time with them passed, but not now, for the story demands too many new paths; it will be confusing and I am not up to it.

"I am come back," he said with that strange quirk of Cheyenne syntax, "if you will let me. I have not come to live with you, for that privilege seems unthinkable. But I would like to set up a lodge next to yours, in the place where my grandfather's home always stood."

The muscle chords in Big Road's neck strung knots under his skin. Mohe died brokenhearted because of the boy's desertion, Big Road was certain of that. Yet—it was so wildly unjust, as chance or magic often is—the boy now repeated Mohe's last request, a request Big Road never believed would be fulfilled. Then, too, by asking for Mohe's lodge, the boy went straight to the heart of the matter. He said, either let me stay, with all the rights that staying grants; or send me away immediately, without condition, forever. Big Road couldn't help appreciating the courage of that. And in the face of Shell's mother hunger, what choice was there? He could not brush away the few thin filaments of hope she flung out in a belated desire to find happiness. Not honor, nor his idea of consistency, nor even the bitter pleasure of living with his uninterrupted pain allowed for that.

"If Mohe's lodge is still in the world," Tom continued, "if his skins can hold breath and fire again, let me live inside the old man's world. There, in my grandfather's shadow, I may meet myself again."

The father studied this wiry stranger who spoke with too much precision, who looked like he'd been newly daubed with red paint, whose hair lay so close to the scalp it revealed its contours.

There was dinner to be made, an antelope to hang, and the men, even if they didn't want to, had to be left alone; Shell smiled encouragement at her son as she got up and went out.

They sat there, acutely awkward at being alone. Tom shifted a cramped leg. All Big Road had to do was say his son's name. But his mouth would not accept the sounds, would not form the words yet. Tom, out of practice at being an Indian, spoke first, confessing he'd seen too much of his brothers' suffering to be happy with his life as a red white man. Or a white red man. Big Road didn't respond at all. Tom tried to tell his father about the slaveholding tribes—that there really were Indians who kept slaves—but there were too many new paths, and he bogged down in the complexities of southern traditions. They lapsed into an embarrassed, highly charged silence.

Fortunately Shell came in for a bucket. It was cedarwood, with metal bands, and hung high on the central lodgepole and she had to stretch to reach it. Tom was tempted to get it down for her, but remembered he could not interfere with woman's work. That seemed arbitrary and stupid to him, which made him impatient.

The two men eyed the white man's bucket.

"It makes some work easier," she said sheepishly.

That brought Big Road to his feet—Tom's heart leapt with the familiar agility. "So the old spring hasn't deserted him."

"I must announce your return to the tribe," Big Road said with fine formality. Outwardly he looked calm as he left the lodge, but down in the submerged contours of his feelings an inferno roared. Steel needles and metal-ringed buckets always reminded him of his father's injunctions about white goods.

Shell kept her head down, eyes on her sewing, refusing comment. The needle snaked through the soft hide. She finished her row, then said, "I must tend to those ribs."

She could hide her weight sitting, but when she stood, her breadth was evident from behind. Her body filled the entrance, darkening the lodge.

"A strange homecoming," Tom thought in English. But what else could he expect after eight years? He couldn't walk into her open arms, and Big Road didn't seem ready to tousle his hair. Underneath all reason, Big Road's coolness hurt Tom. "They don't know me—not to say don't trust me." He doubted that they would ever understand where he had been or the number of names that he could call his own—Tom, Thomas Hyde, Tumbling Hawk, Tom-Tom, Tomahawk. The ironies ate at his gut. He tried to reconnoiter, aware that his father ran off to call a council meeting because Big Road couldn't stand being near him.

Mohe's lodge seemed vital to Tom. He had to live in it. "A few years ago this was my home, these skins my sky—they say it all comes back. But where's it hiding now? Why can't I move any closer to them? Whose fault?"

Tom jumped up, though not with his father's quickness. He walked over to Shell's place and picked up her sewing—she was making a shirt for herself, that familiar sleeveless pullover. An oblong piece of deerskin doubled over, the neck and armholes cut out—Shell left a lot of room under the armpits so it wouldn't chafe. His fingers tested the sinew stitching up the side. "The same, exactly the same, always the same." A great lady of Indian fashion could wear this on Broadway promenade in any season. "I'd like you to meet my Indian princess mother, dressed in the ubiquitously fashionable—

"Forgotten how many things hang from the lodgepole—quivers, his ropes, rawhide sinew, quill sewing bag. Tepee would get more light if they didn't hang so much–" Tom thought. He touched the painted sun that adorned his father's shield. His index and middle fingers walked the painted path of stars. "Were there two eagle feathers before?" He strained for the answer, feeling rotten that he could not remember how many feathers his own father wore.

He pictured Mohe as he had looked the day Tom had gone in search of his vision–the deep wrinkles working down toward the bone, those coal eyes sunk in that dark bed. The yellow breechclout was stretched out in front and behind, his hair braided. But he could not recall which braid was red and which one white and red? Suddenly Tom felt contaminated, a bird who had flown so long in the white sky he couldn't find his way home. He shut his eyes to hold back tears.

Tom did not hear Shell come in, so he started when she began humming. The song was one of his favorites, about a warrior returned home to his woman. She turned around as Tom put his hand on her shoulder, momentarily surprised to have to look up to see his eyes. She rose on tiptoe and kissed him. He pulled her into a gentle bear hug and they rocked from side to side, sad to be this close as the ghost of their time apart intimated about all those lost years.

"Mother," he said. "Mother," he said again, the meaning filling his throat. They held on to each other, familiarizing themselves again. Then Tom took her hand. "I know how hard this is for you; I'll never be able to thank you enough for your..."

She reached out with her free hand and touched his cheek; her fingers wandered over the youthful face. It was good to have him with them, good to hear him speak so.

Outside, Big Road was surprised to find so many people quietly waiting. He volunteered nothing and, seeing he was perplexed, no one asked further. Big Road went straight to the council lodge, which, fortunately, was empty. He'd already decided to give his son Mohe's lodge skins, but he would not feel like a proper father while that stone of resentment lodged in his heart. In the presence of the ancestors, Big Road considered what the boy would suffer from those who had cursed him, from Lightfoot, his boyhood playmate, who had pronounced him dead. "Mohe," he called aloud, "I know you want me to forgive him. I will do my best. You too must be patient with me."

Big Road felt strengthened as he walked toward the lodge of Able-to-Reach-the-Cloud, who was now headman. The father could not deny his son's request. Only by a prideful lie could Big Road disclaim his fatherhood. The boy was his, him. How long ago had Tumbling Hawk taken that white soldier and helped the Dog soldiers in battle. How often in his last year Mohe had said, "The boy does not find the world as clear as you and I do."

Big Road took comfort in knowing how to proceed. Resolute, he asked Able-to-Reach-the-Cloud to call a council meeting, saying simply, "My son has returned."

Able-to-Reach-the-Cloud managed to suppress his surprise. "I will call the council," he replied. Both men understood that Tumbling Hawk's return would not be a simple matter.

His son's needs were on the father's mind when he reentered the lodge, marched up to the boy and said: "Welcome home, my son. I am happy you are here."

Over their dinner of antelope flank, his father told Tom what had happened in the intervening years, a quickly drawn history of deaths, raids, and hunts, of the skirmishes with settlers and soldiers. Game was often scarce; the range kept shrinking as more and more settlers tracked into the Cheyenne lands.

The opposition to Tom had started three summers before, when the tribe learned of his return to Fort Laramie. But it wasn't until they heard about his working among the southern tribes that Lightfoot accused Tumbling Hawk of being a traitor, "a man who drowns red men's thoughts as others flood the nations with white man's goods." When Tom came north to the Sioux, Lightfoot had declared him dead. "It has been, it is a hard time," Big Road continued, eyeing his son seriously. "The world is changing and many look for ways to stop what time brings with it. But none has found the way."

Big Road was shy about putting on his ceremonial clothes in front of Tom, and retired to a dark edge of the lodge. The boy was tempted to peek at his father to see just how fat the old man had grown, but put that pettiness away. He reflected instead on the meticulous good will with which Big Road had laid out the opposition to him just before he faced them in council. Big Road's concern shamed Tom—eight years' indifference to the agony of those he said he loved, now there was the nail to split his heart.

The large crowd of women and children gave a little start as the two men emerged. One whispered, "See, see, it is him!" Another bolder girl said, "Hello, young man who has come back." She giggled as Tom nodded at her. White Sage looked skeptical and would not answer his eyes. Tom greeted all graciously as he walked beside his father down the hill. His eyes scanned the curious gauntlet for familiar faces, trying to pick out his friends' children.

Tom had never been inside the Cheyenne council lodge before, though he'd sat in council with Cherokee, Seminole, Creek, and Sioux. The two center poles were hung with ceremonial objects and various magic devices. Along the rain liner ran yellow zigzag stripes, the sign of thunder; there were also blue wavy lines (water), a number of five-pointed stars, and at the eastern cardinal point, the Circle of All Beginnings. It looked no more auspicious than the Sioux council lodge.

Two men were there ahead of them, men Tom did not know. While Big Road made the introductions, Tom looked past them to the Dream Shields hung from the northern supporting pole. Mohe had explained the significance long ago; all he had to do was remember. "Everything I need is right here in front of me—clues hidden in the buffalo skull by the entrance, in the otter skin, in that pair of antelope feet—" He thought an instant. "—used by the shaman to call antelope and assure a successful hunt." The Thunder Bow of the Contrary was slung over a knot on the southern pole. Bits and pieces were coming back now, but the puzzle was not ready to fall into place.

Suddenly a broad face, one of the last he'd seen in this world, broke in on Tom—Two Children. The scout's hand dropped warmly onto his forearm. "Too long since the last time. I am glad you are here." Two Children's cheekbones tilted up so sharply, his eyes were slotted at a steep angle. Tom remembered how flat Two Children's eyes were, but he did not recall how elusive they seemed.

Three more men came in. As Big Road introduced them, Tom thought, "The otter points east, the turtle, north, frog, south, fish, west—animals with traits of their cardinal points." He shot a glance over the second man's shoulder. The turtle and the fish were in place.

Running Bear entered, looking back over his shoulder, and after him came Horn and Small Deer. They cut off their heated discussion. Running Bear cast a scathing look at Tom and, without joining the reception line, went straight to his place—a shocking gesture in the council lodge. Tom did not want to put Small Deer or Horn in a difficult position, but Small Deer rushed over and threw his arms around Tom's neck, hugging him hard. "How I've waited for this day," he said, loud enough for all to hear. "Now welcome home, Tumbling Hawk."

Tom felt saved. "Small Deer, my eyes have ached to see you." Small Deer hadn't grown much and still looked frail. A bowmaker's squint was settling into place, narrowing the eyes, while his fine mouth hadn't hardened and the tawny skin was flawless. Tom thought, "I'd like to walk out of here with him and talk for days." But Horn stood before him.

"It has been a long time since you sat by my fire."

"Too long," Tom replied.

"It is very good to see old friends beside my son again." Big Road felt encouraged that Tumbling Hawk still commanded respect. Many had opposed Lightfoot's declaration, though that had less to do with enthusiasm for his son than the feeling the young shaman had gone too far by declaring the living dead. "Will you sit?"

Small Deer thanked him, shaking his head. "I'd prefer to stand beside Tumbling Hawk." He took a half step backward, which put him just behind Tom's right shoulder—in the position of his second sponsor.

Just then Takes-the-Pipe strode in, followed by three younger braves. He moved stiffly and, from the way he held his arms out from his sides, it was clear his muscles kept him from locking his elbows. He greeted Tom with commanding civility, as though suggesting he was above taking sides in the debate about Tom's fate.

This posture annoyed Tom, who wasn't one to be intimidated by rank. After the formal greeting he continued, excessively cordial, "It's such a pleasure to see an old friend again. Takes-the-Pipe, you look exceedingly at home in the world."

Takes-the-Pipe didn't know what to make of Tom's words and moved off to his place to the right of the entrance, an honor reserved for the bravest warrior, who was also third chief. However, Tom's remark did not sit well with the chief's young partisans. "Everyone has a following but me," Tom concluded to himself.

The line grew longer as other men, familiar and unknown, crowded into the lodge. His history began to file by: Buck's Heart hugged him, tested for the degree of moistness in his palm, felt his pulse. Then he gripped Tom's index and middle fingers and shook them up and down, one of the traditional methods Buck's Heart used to determine a student's health. The tests finished, he turned with a smile to the others, tapped Tom approvingly on the shoulder and sat down. Hankering Horse greeted Tom as if he'd just got back from a successful raid. That was heartening; Tom was afraid the Horse would side with Lightfoot. On they came—Short Body, Hard Rain, Strong Left Hand, Cries-for-Perch. Tom was caught in this living dream, his father at the left, Small Deer standing as though for support by his other shoulder.

The two tribal chiefs came in together, looking solemn and intent, for neither could be expected to take sides. Able-to-Reach-the-Cloud, the headman, wore the full eagle feather headdress; around his neck hung various stone and bone and tooth necklaces as well as a large iron crucifix. His hair was gray at the temples and his torso was hard and dense like a polished oak bole. Plenty Crows, the second chief, wore his scalp shirt. "White wigs and black robes—white justice. The great men of this nation half-naked before each other." Tom tried to picture the chairman and Markham Harris, the colonel and Coughlin sitting thigh to naked thigh.

Someone announced Rumbling Wings. The lodge, which had been buzzing, immediately quieted. Lightfoot entered first, leading the shaman, who was almost blind. "How thin," thought Tom, looking at another old playmate. Lightfoot cupped his left hand under the old man's forearm; his right hand held Rumbling Wings' stringy bicep. They seemed attached through hand and elbow, Lightfoot the parasite, sucking off the old man's secrets before he died.

Rumbling Wings moved tentatively, his legs reluctant to venture into new space, his feet touching down with brittle uncertainty. The old man was stooped and cataracts clouded both his eyes. A bright yellow growth, like a piece of yellow fat, tied the right eye to its lid, which made it very hard to look at him. Tom suppressed a shudder; at that moment Lightfoot caught his eye.

When Rumbling Wings was lowered into place, everyone expected Lightfoot to cross the lodge to greet the guest. Instead he raised his head imperiously and stared at the Thunder Bow.

All those faces from his past against a backdrop of the strange two-headed beasts of the Dream Shields and the Contrary Bow—Tom found it hard to keep his head clear. The lodge grew still, but Big Road did not move. He wanted Lightfoot to greet his son. Tom only wanted them to get on with it. After a long pause, Big Road stepped forward, faced east and began:

"I come before you, a father, to ask your blessing on the return of my son, Tumbling Hawk, who has been gone—" Big Road's lips seemed weighted, they moved so much slower than usual. "—eight long summers. Today this man called me 'Father,' a word I did not expect to hear again as long as I lived." His voice rose. "It is strange to have a son who many have called dead, strange to hear this son speak to me.

"You all know the accusations which had been laid before his name. You also know, my friends, in spite of all the talk, I have said nothing to deny what was said, nothing even when the death of my father was charged to my son by those who never sheathe their tongues. Not one man in this lodge can claim to know my thoughts, for I have held my judgment under choke rein until I knew what I felt." They nodded their agreement or grunted softly, for the moment his chorus.

"It has not been sunny during the past eight years; I did not make an easy decision today. I realize my son has been far away." The hot constricting cramp in Tom's chest told him he could not bluff this man; the image of his own face moved, mere inches away. "Even after looking into the son's eyes, the father has not seen all his reasons for coming back. The father knows, too, that, if any disgrace attach to his son, it will skewer the father's soul.

"Now I will tell you a strange thing. Tumbling Hawk's first request was Mohe's last request, his dying wish." The men caught their breath; and with that gasp Tom's past broke in on their deliberations like early dawn. Great things had been expected of him. Twice he'd defeated white soldiers; and there was the unresolved mystery of his vision. Except for his father and Rumbling Wings, no one had ever learned the secret of what Tom had seen.

"Tumbling Hawk has asked to live in Mohe's lodge. That was my father's last request—if the boy returns, he said, let him take my lodge skins.

"There is something too mysterious here for me to see, but I cannot deny it. I request his right as a Cheyenne—to live beside me, honoring my old age, honoring my father's dying wish." Big Road looked squarely at the chiefs, then at the bowed head of Rumbling Wings. He moved to his seat slowly and sat down.

Lightfoot rose, still keeping hold of Rumbling Wings' arm. "I see a traitor in our lodge." Slowly his head turned toward Tom; other eyes followed. "I see the man who asked red man to turn their arrows into plows, their buffalo and antelope and bear into thin milk cows, who asked men to scratch in the dirt like the Pawnee. He arranged the word treaties that broke up the great hunting range, gave Indian lands to the wagon settlers, forced red man to retreat and retreat and retreat until they have only a few rocks or grains of sand which the white man does not want. I am not certain if he has killed Indians, but he has disarmed and disgraced them, corrupted them with white man's goods, stolen running waters and green valleys for coffee beans, courted proud nations with firewater as he might woo a public white woman." His hand came off the old man's arm grudgingly, then he flicked an accusing finger at Tom. "Now he comes here, all arrogance and spotted heart, forcing his way into council to claim the rights of a Cheyenne, he who has sold his heart to white man, who looks at us even now and can only see with white man's eyes. Perhaps they have sent him back to conquer us as he would the Sioux; or they have grown tired of him and cast off his rotting carcass."

Furious and shaken, Tom saw Lightfoot as a double image, the thin new face set inside what he remembered as the old one. He saw himself as the perfect scapegoat, serving them simultaneously as traitor and curse. Of course with the buffalo thinning and the white man multiplying, it wasn't hard to imagine how a man got villified.

The light was dying, turning everyone dull gray. At a sign from Able-to-Reach-the-Cloud a young man got up to light the fire. Tom seized the moment to ask if he could reply; the chiefs agreed.

"My friends and brothers, I have been gone a long time. I have walked on paths that no one else has ever taken. Much has been said about my life away from you and, to speak the truth, I have made mistakes that have deeply bruised my soul—how could that not occur so far away from my roots?" His audience sat unmoved; he had not blown on them and made the reed sway. "Lightfoot is right to despise what he thinks I've done. I despise many of the things I actually did, which were mild weather next to what he accuses me of. I did not do what he says, yet it is not hard to see how this might come to be believed. Much wrong is being done the Indian; I was in white man's hands a long time; no other red man had such power in his world. Yet nothing I did was done to harm an Indian. I gave red man more land, not less; I gave him more annuities, more guns and ammunition, always I fought for more, never less. What was wrong was thinking I could help my brothers—my flesh—by working among white man and gaining power in his place. That was my mistake, and a grave one. But now that is over.

"I was not driven out of their world. I come back because I am a Cheyenne, and I wish to live my days with you." The way Two Children sat up and the way Buck's Heart leaned forward told Tom they were listening now, following him as they followed their own, thought for thought, as if, in the interim, they lost their own dispositions and gave themselves over to the speaker's feelings. "My old friend Lightfoot believes I come to spread white man's word. That is not true. I have seen how little goodness there is in white man, how he makes his best people powerless before the worst. You see, I come to offer what I have learned at the price of great suffering and confusion, at the loss of great beauty and peace in my soul." Tom's eyes misted; he glanced up at the smoke just beginning to rise through the brown-ringed smoke hole. When he looked down, he thought Rumbling Wings' head had tilted toward him, as if the old man was trying to hear better.

"I do not want my people to retreat from white man any longer. I do not want the men who cannot stand in the sun to shoo us aside like summer flies. I could not watch your women strip the lodges, our children rush to move out of white man's way while the old ones stood by, adding one more humiliation to their memories." The air of the council lodge was thick with the blood of the summer hunt, the smoke of the new fire; but Tom felt he stood on a mountain top, his head in crystal-thin air. "I have learned this man's cunning, for I knew I would someday be standing here–" He paused to let them take that in, but they were already there, living in his moment. "You see, my vision promised I would return."

Their sigh filled the lodge skins like sails.

"Do not deny the promise of my vision, men of the Cheyenne. Do not do that to me. For I have taken many things out of the white man's camp that he would not part with, and the greatest of these are his weapons of war!"

They stared at Tom, wanting to believe what he said. Of course they did not think that he might be their Laughing Child, their redeemer, they hadn't even formulated it yet. But the wish was there, the need was there.

The red tip of Lightfoot's tongue worked his lip disdainfully: "I cannot quarrel with this vision–if what he says is true. But I can tell what I have seen–" He paused to draw inspiration from the Thunder Bow. "He comes here accompanied by death, destruction, and confusion like none the Cheyenne have ever known, greater even than white man brings. For I, too, have my visions."

Tom was shaken by the bobbing head, the darting red tongue which underlined each syllable of the denunciation.

Rumbling Wings shifted; everyone attended the slight movement. "I have been waiting for Tumbling Hawk." His voice, escaping from a deep crack in his being, barely reached across the lodge. He trailed off into a hacking cough which threatened to shake him apart. All the while Lightfoot's hand did not desert the shaman's arm.

Rumbling Wings set the seal of approval; there was nothing left to say. The warriors came up to welcome Tom, and he thanked each of them graciously until Lightfoot stood before him.

"I hope we can be friends again."

Blood fired the drawn cheeks. "This is no question of friendship. Rumbling Wings only said he expected you, no more!" He clipped his words sharply, eliminating the echo–a chilling effect in the tight space. "He did not say your return will be a blessing. I distrust your smooth-sliding tongue, man who we once called Tumbling Hawk. Soon I will see into the gap between your tongue and your heart."

"I have come back to help against white man."

"We will see." Lightfoot spun around and stalked out of the lodge.

The line stalled. Fortunately Takes-the-Pipe was nearby. As Tom took hold of his thick forearm, he saw that two finger joints were missing from his friend's right hand. "Mutilated himself for the Elk Horn initiation. Cut them off at the knuckle." The livid copper stumps bellowed out their message of how much he'd forgotten. His eyes careened around the lodge—other warriors had missing finger joints; there were thin lateral scars above the nipples where they'd been hung up for two days on skewers over the purifying fire for the Dog soldiers' initiation; the Kit Foxes had deeper, more jagged lines on their chests from dragging the buffalo skull. Tom fought back another shudder, and met Takes-the-Pipe's eyes with a look that seemed to ask if he would ever really find home.

Later, sitting in his father's lodge, Tom explained to his parents and Small Deer why he kept delaying his return—first there was the extended problem with his leg, and by the time it healed he'd vaguely conceived of his plan to use white man's power to help the Cheyenne. That summer in Laramie he'd wanted to come home, he'd almost come home, but the terrible state of the Pawnee and that Sioux buffalo hunt had scared him away. Three summers before, he knew nothing of what he knew now; at that time he hadn't learned how to turn white man's power back against him. He was afraid to come home, afraid he'd never leave again. Shell found it unnatural to hear her son insisting so totally on his own terms—that seemed a white man's affliction. Tumbling Hawk should have considered the pain caused his family before being a hero or anything else. When the men began to talk of war, she curled up in her buffalo robe, feeling miserable.

For the next few hours Tom detailed the extent of white man's military strength and manufacturing capabilities, and projected his own educated guesses about what was ahead for the Indian. He regaled Small Deer and Big Road with his strategies for revolutionizing Cheyenne warfare. He promised to cut casualties to a bare minimum and guaranteed ways to isolate white settlements and hack at overextended supply lines, which were where, he said, they were most vulnerable. Of course he expected difficulty in persuading the warriors to help him produce the new long-talking rifles. But Tom had to make them see that their desperate situation demanded radical changes. Small Deer threw up obstacles to Tom's enthusiasms whenever they conflicted with the Cheyenne way of doing things. Which was often. They even debated the superiority of rifle to bow.

Big Road said little. All night he studied the stranger who was his son, this man in such frantic haste to change the Cheyenne world. He went to sleep troubled, trying to persuade himself that it was only natural for the boy to be a bit mad, having so lately returned from the whites. But Big Road was afraid Lightfoot spoke too much truth about Tumbling Hawk's slippery tongue.

The younger pair adjourned to Small Deer's lodge, where Tom peeked at his friend's three sleeping children, two girls and, the youngest, a boy. Over Tom's objections Small Deer woke his wife, Gray Star, and asked her to make new coffee. She did so without any sense of inconvenience, though she could not help sneaking glances at the stranger about whom she'd heard so many conflicting things.

In that domestic peace, Tom felt as conspicuous as he had in the stagecoach heading west toward Laramie. To calm himself he politely asked about Hard Ground. Gray Star blushed, Small Deer acted like Tom hadn't spoken and asked his own question back—about the repeating rifles, something he'd shown little enough interest in before. Tom felt confused, but left it at that.

Tumbling Hawk left just before dawn. Small Deer woke Gray Star to report, "Tumbling Hawk is groping through madness back to our sanity. All the time he runs ahead of himself. I get the sense of what he's saying, but only a twisted imagination could see the world as he does. It makes me sad. I doubt that any will listen to him."

Sleepily she said, "Except you."

Small Deer nudged her gently and she slipped over for him.

MOHE'S LODGE AND THE REPEATERS

Next morning early Tom and Big Road dug the moat with a spade fashioned from a buffalo's shoulder blade. Then, using the seven-foot digging iron, they drilled the holes for the lodgepoles and cleared and leveled the lodge floor. Tom's fingers felt soothed by the dogwood ground pegs, the worn and the new rawhide thongs. As they unfurled his grandfather's lodge skins, with the red owl on what would be the north side and the twin deer in flight on the south, Tom wondered if the old life would enter him through his fingertips.

Inside, the boy immersed himself in the diffused light of his new home. Here, he thought, he might remember who he had been.

To start the blessing, father and son brushed the floor with sage, then came outside. A sizable crowd had gathered. While the villagers looked on, they singed the entrance flap with a brand from the first fire. Inside, alone again, Tom watched while his father sang to the cardinal points, asking for their direction. The rhythm did not catch up to him till they were turning from north to south to east to west a second time, moving with the fall and rise of Big Road's voice. Tom could almost hear Mohe's voice above his father's calling the cardinal points into agreement. It felt good to be back in a dwelling that narrowed at the top.

As the ceremony ended, Small Deer drove up with Tom's wagon, looking proud and silly with the reins looped awkwardly over his wrists. While Tom, Small Deer, Buck's Heart, and another man tipped the anvil down, children swarmed all over the wagon. One woman touched the wheel spokes while another kept pushing against the frame, as if testing the springs for sway. Others peered over the siderails at the crates and barrels. One old man, fascinated by the grease bucket, got it all over his legs and moccasins. There were many questions, which Tom answered as graciously as possible, trying to convince them he was still the same Tumbling Hawk. Whenever Tom caught the eye of one of the young women in the crowd, she and all her girl friends giggled.

When the hunters got back to camp that evening, they found a huge fire blazing outside Tom's lodge. Anything the notorious stranger did would've attracted attention, but the night was hot and, up close, the men realized that this fire was made by shiny black rocks. Few had seen coal before, so there was mystified talk about the-black-rocks-that-burned-with-much-heat.

Most of the tribe looked on as Tom hacked a chunk of lead off the thick bar he'd stolen from Fort Sully. He dropped the lead into a cast-iron pot, slipped a pole through the pot's handle, and maneuvered it into position over the fire. It was hot work stirring the kettle; the sweat ran freely down Tom's chest.

When the lead was molten, he pulled out the cast-iron ladle and poured the liquid lead into the bullet mold. He then took twelve empty cartridges and metered gunpowder into them; they were the new kind with primers already set in them. When the mold was cool enough, Tom opened it and slipped out the bullets. He filed off the rough edges and seated each one in a cartridge until he had his dozen. Then he picked up the new brass-frame Henry rifle and, one by one, slid the bullets down the tube under the barrel.

When Tom led the whole troupe to the western end of the village, the sun was fingerpainting the sky, running pinks through oranges, undercoating reds with violets. To the Cheyenne eye, the Henry rifle looked too slender, too reedlike to be a weapon of destruction. "It's almost cheating," Tom thought as he raised it to his shoulder. They did not understand the simple logic of how trigger raised hammer and lever pushed carrier block; they did not know why that thin metal loop lay under the stock. Then Tom squinted and squeezed off twelve shots in a row, without reloading, one every five seconds on through an entire minute until the tribespeople could not believe their ears, could not believe their eyes as they watched the earth volcano up at the foot of that clump of bushberries, one hundred fifty yards away.

"Instant heroes, instant gods vanish just as fast." Tom tried to mute his excitement, but there was no denying Plenty Crows touched Able-to-Reach-the-Cloud's arm to convince himself it was true, that all of their faces paid homage to his miracle. Hankering Horse pointed to the rifle: "How can it speak so long without stopping?" Two Children asked: "What magic is in this?" Tom did not answer yet, but pushed the barrel of the Henry toward Takes-the-Pipe, who gripped the gun, pumped the lever as Tom had done, peered down the barrel, and ran his fingers up the loading tube. Tom picked up some ready-made bullets and showed his friend how to load; then Takes-the-Pipe squeezed off fifteen rounds. That convinced the skeptical the magic resided in the slim metal frame.

"How things fall together," thought Tom. "Lucky they've never seen a repeater before." The rifle passed through the warriors' hands, each cradling it as a pilgrim might handle a saint's relics, delicately yet with an urgent need to prove it real.

"This is the new gun white man has made to fight the Indian," Tom began. "It gives him fifteen shots without reloading—as many bullets as the fingers on both hands and the toes on one foot—like fifteen soldiers armed with the old single shots. Soon he will come against us with hundreds of these sticks, the coward who is too weak to take us on in a fair fight." The crowd, which had tightened its knot around Tom, made an angry wounded noise. He had never felt so much like a preacher. "I have come back to warn you of the evil white man intends for us. With this rifle he can make us bleed, he can pick off red man like he does buffalo."

Tom would've liked to shove the men in the front row back a little, to nudge Two Children away. But no matter how cramped he felt, he could not break the spell—they were feeding off the horror he'd shown them. The dying light washed out features until faces grew spectral. Tom saw bones without flesh, hairless skulls—a vision of his people's death which only he had the power to prevent.

"You have seen this weapon work. Are we to launch arrows against its deadly hail?" This time their wounded noise sounded will-less, a dry wind which blew away all hope. Icy sweat peppered his skin, needle pricks moving with the speed of a sewing machine up and down his arm. Tom's job, he realized, was to present a painting to a blind man, to etch the lines inside their eyeballs so that, even if they did not care to see it, they'd know white man demanded their annihilation.

"You have seen me make bullets. You think this is a wondrous thing, yet it is simpler than following deer tracks over rock. I have suffered much to learn what you've just seen. You know that, you who can look into Tumbling Hawk's eyes and see what he has given up. Someday, I promise you, brothers, we will not only make bullets but rifles too, rifles that can speak as long as the one I hold."

Feeling the cue, Takes-the-Pipe let the stock slide out of his hands. Tom raised the Henry brass-frame repeater into the air.

"But you must trust me, be patient with me." He ended in a whisper, sweating and exhausted. Takes-the-Pipe laid a comforting hand on Tom's forearm. In the morning Tom knew he would have to start all over again. But, for the moment, he and his people were reunited.

Next morning Tom overslept—the sun caught him in bed, something Mohe had always warned against. He felt still less Indian when he found a crowd standing patiently outside. But he had a reason for dallying that morning. He had dreamt about a firelit cave in which enormous warriors hammered on scores of anvils, banging out the pieces of his repeaters.

Tom restaged the bulletmaking for the warriors, offering Able-to-Reach-the-Cloud and Plenty Crows a dozen shots each. Everything went smoothly. He would've felt altogether elated except for that bothersome detail of oversleeping and his curiosity as to Takes-the-Pipe's whereabouts. The night before Takes-the-Pipe had come to his lodge and talked till late about how to make the long-speaking rifles. Last night Tom was sure he'd won the young chief's support. But Takes-the-Pipe's absence this morning made Tom nervous. He felt Lightfoot was behind it.

That afternoon Tom began making bullets in earnest. By sunset he'd drafted four apprentices—an old man named Crow Wing who'd been a good friend of Mohe's, and three twelve-year-old boys. One boy was very tall, one short and slender, the other thick; they wore loincloths and unworked moccasins. All three suffered the same itchy uncertainty that Tom and his friends had shared as they were about to come of age. "I look one way and see what I once was; look the other way and there's the image of what I'm supposed to become—an honorable old man like Crow Wing . . . like Mohe."

The coal crunched as Tom tossed a few more chunks onto the fire. Dorothea Coughlin had a little silver bell which she kept by her left hand at table. Cheyenne life was the note that bell struck—"All Cheyenne lives strike the same note—pure yet extremely fragile. The whites cannot hear it above the roar of steamship and train; they can't hear it in cities. That's why they think Indians are savage, when in fact they're absurdly civilized, too civilized for their own good.

"Here when that note's struck it rings forever. These boys play the war games we played; they use our lures, the same circling tactics my father showed me and their fathers still use against soldiers. I drew my bow as Big Road showed me, as Mohe had shown him." He could see the same string of muscles along the right forearm of his father. "They don't know how to change that sound. They will go on repeating themselves in the face of a transformed world until the sound is lost and the world they know vanishes."

Time was inestimably important to him, yet Tom had to build their faith in the part he'd play without appearing to rush. "That's done by sleight-of-hand, Tom-Tom. Simple. It's like being in a sprint but not being allowed to break out of a trot."

To keep up with the buffalo herd, the tribe moved every second or third day, which forced Tom to work out a way to pack quickly. By the end of the first week he could get his equipment into the wagon in the same time it took a Cheyenne family to move their lodge. Although mere mechanics, it built another small bridge to the tribe. He needed even the tiniest boosts, for often he felt on probation. Takes-the-Pipe was politely cordial to him, nothing more. Lightfoot he hardly saw, which was understandable since Rumbling Wings was sick; twice, when camp moved, the shaman stayed behind a few days before being brought up to their second camp. Shell was unpredictable. There were hours of lucidity when they felt happy and natural together—while Tom boiled some potion or banged away at his anvil she would sew or flesh hides or cook at her fire a few paces away. Too often, though, unannounced, a thick depression would envelop her. Tom never knew if she was afraid of him, or paying accounts from time past, or was lost in the impenetrable labyrinth of his reasons for staying away. He knew he'd never explain that adequately. Once, when she was working on his new moccasins, he found her staring down at them, tears just at the point of spilling over. As for Big Road, Tom could never convince him that the necessities of the new weapons demanded that the Cheyenne give up counting coup and start fighting at night. All these challenges to the old ways made the father wonder if his son had forgotten the true meaning of honor.

On July tenth, the day he was expected back in Laramie, Tom insisted on making his quota of bullets. He was very precise about the number—one hundred fifty. In the first place, Tom insisted on keeping his workers fascinated; in the second, he didn't want to run out of materials before the end of August. That morning his work force was down to five, including himself, which was good since it would take most of the day to make the one hundred fifty.

It was hot by the coal fire, and Tom was glad his helpers understood enough so that he didn't have to say much. He fretted away the morning, unable to sink the image of Elizabeth in her blue cotton frock with the puffed sleeves, her hair coiled to keep it off her neck, the dark eyebrows under the graying hair. Hyde stood stiffly in his uniform, that chip of a chin thrust forward. In the white house with the crisp black-trimmed windows they waited anxiously for Tom's stage. They would wait and wait and wait.

Tom squeezed the precious lead bar as hard as he could, trying to crush that vision out of his head. He would've liked to write to tell them how much he appreciated all they'd done. He would've liked to say: "I'm sorry, dreadfully sorry, my dearest and most beloved guardians, to be the cause of your pain. But this is the only way I can see to truly help my people." If only there was some true and honest way to relieve them of the pain, the disappointment, and the unwarranted responsibility they'd load on themselves. Till noon Tom debated whether or not to write, knowing beforehand he could not send a letter, afraid that, whatever he said, it would reveal too much to the colonel.

Sick at heart, Tom finished the last bullets at three-thirty. He thought about abandoning Hyde and Elizabeth without so much as an apologetic nod toward Laramie. He wondered bitterly if that evened the score—if, after eight years on their side, it was their turn to suffer. Tom was weary of being brutal to those he loved.

He recounted his bullets, picked up a cartridge case that someone had dropped, swept up the spilled powder with his hand, and dumped the few grains back into the powder keg. Not for one instant during the long day did Tom's belief in his mission falter. But belief held no consolation.

That night he confided to his diary:

> Odd to leave it all and step free and clear. Never will I feel so free of them as now, on the evening of the day I did not appear. How free and clear then? Do I step out of what I've been for 8 years, leaving no shadow, no corpse, carrying no part of it—of those two—inside?
>
> Sometimes as I sit here in my grandfather's lodge, I *know* I'm more white than red. Each day now I ought to put my soul in a scale and weigh the elements to see if there's more red. When that's lacking, out

to the streambed to pick up clay to tint my pasty soul. Or use blood. No, blood's not enough. How about cutting off a knuckle–

Tom laid his head on the writing table–the lid of a keg of iron nails–and, gripping the edges, he rocked the squat tub back and forth until he wore out a little of his pain.

The chiefs and warriors each held a part of the Henry brass-frame repeating rifle. After they smoked the pipe, Tom asked Takes-the-Pipe, seated in the leading warriors' place just north of the entrance, to pass the rifle stock to Two Children, who had the metal butt plate. Two Children had to drop the metal screws into the holes and turn them with his fingers till they held. Island got it next and passed the stock and its loose butt plate to Hankering Horse, who slipped on the trigger housing, dropped in the two top screws which held the housing to the stock and tightened them as Tom indicated. The rest of the warriors watched each turn of each screw.

Buck's Heart fitted the trigger assembly, which Tom had left intact. Plenty Crows got the hammer, Able-to-Reach-the-Cloud, the trigger guard lever, a difficult maneuver for someone not familiar with the procedure. The lever forced the carrier block forward, cocking the hammer and extracting and ejecting the empty shell. Fortunately, there was only one place for it to go, and at last the chief slipped it into place. Strong Left Hand tried to fit the barrel, only he got it upside down. "That's turned the wrong way," Tom volunteered, wanting to jump up and help the Henry around his lodge. "I mean lift your right hand up toward the smoke hole. Yes, that's it." The growing rifle reached Big Road, who had a long tubular rod. Tom's father eyed the rod deliberately, rolled it through his hand, then, without further hesitation, pushed the magazine in until it housed snugly under the barrel. Pleased, he passed it on.

The Cheyenne had good eyes, good hands, and the rifle went smoothly all the way around, until Cries-for-Perch handed Tom the completed rifle. Tom quickly checked the assembly, then produced his screwdriver. He explained that the thin bar allowed him to turn the screw further in than by hand, thus making a tighter fit. Then Tom secured all the screws.

"It is as simple as that, my friends. What you have done here you can do in your own tepees. We too can make these long-speaking rifles."

He paused to let them take hold of that, in no hurry. "We could strike terror into the heart of the white coward if we were armed with the sticks that talk so much death. Suppose we rode at him carrying a hundred of these rifles, with bullets for each white soldier?" Tom shook the weapon like a battle lance. The lodge was roofed and walled and floored with their desire to believe.

He led them out of the lodge and through the camp. The milling, expectant crowd of warriors brought out others. The whole tribe—men, women, children, and old people—looked on as Tom shot a few test rounds. Then the Cheyenne watched their chiefs and warriors fire and fire and fire until it grew too dark to see.

Tom came out of sleep slowly, trying to hold on to the sensation of floating above the camp on an intricately woven reed mattress. The view was magnificent—the river channeling deep canyons across the foreground, a purple range of glacier-capped peaks shading to dark foothills. His friends stood below, looking up and smiling, waving to him. "There will be problems," he admitted, feeling strong enough to face things realistically now. "No one's going to enjoy spending half the day on a production line. Lightfoot will never let up. But my role here is not like Hyde's with me—I'm not playing magic tricks on a thirteen-year-old!"

He stayed aloft all morning, though in another mood the chill drizzle might have gotten him down. Noon came and went. He was concentrating so intently on the trigger assembly, Tom did not notice the shadow fall across his lodge entrance; nor did he see the sinewy hand trace circles in the air, then rapidly flick his wrist at him.

Tom looked up. The drizzle had fused Lightfoot's hair to his head, a tight black cap framing gaunt cheeks, lurid glowing eyes. "Rumbling Wings must see you."

"When?" Tom stuttered.

His former friend stood in the entrance, blocking the light, the only way out. "Angel or devil? Which one of us is right?" At that instant their roles seemed perfectly reversible. Certainly Tom believed he was right to come back, right to try to rescue them. But Lightfoot took it beyond questions of right and wrong. Tom's plummeting heart told him he had no resource to match this single-minded fanaticism.

In lockstep they marched down the hill through a silence which blotted up the women's usual chatter, the children's game. "Are the days we wrestled in the stream less real than this?" Tom cursed memory's contrariness, wondering why he couldn't reproduce their intimacy now, feeling weak beside Lightfoot's intensity. Rumbling

Wings had prophesied: "You were born with the rising sun, with the hawk and its kind, in the cool clear light of morning. But you will have to travel toward the sun back toward yourself, in order to come west again, to the dark cardinal point where the heart knows itself from inside out."

Not thirty yards from the shaman's lodge he got his cue. "Lightfoot knows himself from the inside out. Me, I've only understood what others wanted of me, the outside in." The sacred white skins rose before him. Tom's loincloth flapped against his right thigh, rubbing a chafed spot. He would've liked to hold the loincloth away so it wouldn't keep rubbing. His heels were still tender.

"I'll enter and stand before Rumbling Wings, their master of self-knowledge, without knowing myself," Tom thought. "I'll tell their wisest man that it all has to be changed, the sooner the..."

Lightfoot reached the entrance first, drew back the flap, and curtly signaled Tom in. Tom knew Lightfoot would stand guard until he came out again.

He'd been in the shaman's lodge only once for that short interview eight years before. But Tom remembered everything—the horizontal bands of day and night running across the roof, the legends decorating the liner. Rumbling Wings sat in the same place: behind the fire, facing east. In the dancing light he looked insubstantial, so scored by responsibility and time it was hard to make out the face anymore. All his joints sagged, which turned the shoulders and wrists and knuckles and knees into dark pools of skin.

"Why have you returned?" asked the shaman in a whisper.

"To help."

"Help?" Skepticism strengthened the voice.

Feeling those cloudy half-blind eyes was unnerving. The skull was excessively prominent, the skin the color and texture of a dried fruit, the unsupported strut of a nose looked brittle and vulnerable.

Tom began by describing the evils of the white world—sordid vignettes of city life, a lurid abolitionist rendering of slavery. He was graphic about the Cherokee relocation and the disastrous cross-country trek which killed one of every four of those who started. The plight of all red men was marching that way, Tom said, as surely as the arrow in the shaman's sky curved into the last night of the West. As white man pushed west, the Indian would be crowded onto an evershrinking island.

Tom did not understand that Rumbling Wings was one of those who'd obligingly allowed white man access through the Cheyenne hunting lands on a trail to be only as wide as the wheels of a wagon. Rumbling Wings, too, had watched the game thin as the endless stream of settlers spilled into their world. For years the shaman had seen the signs. More times than he could count now he had prayed for a change in the magic. But, so far, nothing had come. In the meantime, he'd grown too old.

Tom explained that the whites were now at war among themselves. That was why he'd been sent among the Sioux—to keep the Plains tribes from fighting with the slave men. "Rumbling Wings," Tom announced passionately, "white man will never be weaker. He cannot fight us at the same time he fights the slave men. I have come back with a new weapon, the new rifle that speaks fifteen shots without stopping. This rifle is not yet spread among the soldiers, for many among them are too used to the old to see what the new can do."

Rumbling Wings sat still as a rock, yet he had no weight, no substance. He might've been an old papier-mâché construction, the color almost faded from it.

"If I am not mistaken, we can make this rifle for ourselves. If we can, the Cheyenne will never have to beg from unreliable white man who trickles out bullets like a dry spring in summer, hands us rusty muskets, and demands praise for his generosity."

Tom was tempted to stop there, but he had his momentum up and didn't want to be accused later of holding anything back. So he laid out his plans—the military argument for night attack, which the Cheyenne had always avoided for fear of dead souls getting lost in the dark and not finding their way into the sky. Tom insisted on the need for continuous pursuit, which would take advantage of Cheyenne horsemanship and mobility and the fact that the Indian warrior could ride for days without rest. The old lures needed to be altered; warriors would have to stop circling wagon trains—a questionable tactic against a single shot but virtual suicide against the repeater. Pages of his diary flowed out of Tom—he even argued that after the Cheyenne formed alliances with the Sioux and other friendly tribes, it would be wise to band together with traditional enemies—Pawnee, Crow, Blackfoot, Shoshoni, in fact all the Plains tribes in a giant holy alliance against the greatest evil—white man.

Rumbling Wings was patient, and he listened to the excited young man a very long time. "You have forgotten much, more than I would have believed possible before I heard you speak. Had you remembered, your talk would find a more welcome home in my ear." Tom almost believed speech was the last form of motion left to the medicine man, but Rumbling Wings shook his head sadly. "You ask the Cheyenne to change as quickly as you speak. But we cannot abandon ourselves and become like white man."

Incautiously, Tom argued, "To act otherwise is to let ourselves be slaughtered. To be wiped off the face of the earth by this vicious mocking vermin who calls us inferior yet knows nothing of his place in the significance of things, this creature without brothers or relations."

A troubled and angry man proposing the terms of salvation—morally, Rumbling Wings thought the young man came up short. "You have too little respect for the ways of your people because you have forgotten so much. It is possible you dislike the Cheyenne. It is white man's habit to dislike what he does not understand."

"I love the Cheyenne," Tom protested, realizing why this blind man was their spiritual leader. "I have been away, forgotten much, but I want the Cheyenne to be my life forever. Perhaps I am in too much of a hurry—"

"Hurry leaves a man poor, without time to see what lies along his way as he rushes by. Hurry points to a whirlpool in the soul." The shaman delivered this impersonally, simply stating fact. His scales held weightier things than pity.

The old man fell into a paroxysm of coughing that shook his brittle body until Tom thought the dry ligaments would snap. He had an impulse to grab Rumbling Wings and try to hold the bundle of bones together. Then he heard a movement outside; Lightfoot's shadow hovered at the entrance—it hung there until the fit slowly subsided, turning the shaman's parchment skin the color of cold ashes.

Tom did not speak again until Rumbling Wings raised his head. "I am like a stranger with an urgent message who returns to a land remembered only as a vague dream. He cannot yet speak the language of his own people, yet each day he waits is agony because each day he sees things getting worse. He does not intend to criticize how they have lived. In fact, what calls him home is his memory of their life together, their fellowship and good will. His only concern is to keep that goodness alive—in the face of all threats."

"This person you speak of," Rumbling Wings began in a whisper, "is like a frog who jumps over many of the steps a man is obliged to take, yet when he gets to his destination and finds that man beside him, insists that the man got there by the same leaps.

"What you would do, Tumbling Hawk, and what must be done are as different as east and west. Our life is a body. You cannot rip out the heart and put in a new one, any more than you can cut off one leg and substitute another. We have been as we are since the beginning of time. Now you ask us to become someone else."

"But something must be done!" Tom knew it was a stupid thing to say. But he had a hateful vision of generation after generation blindly following the footsteps of those before until, with each step, they thrust their feet into deep pits—the traps of custom.

"Only a man without honor abandons the things he loves when it is hardest. That is the time when a man must cling to them, when he thanks them for having carried him as far as he has come." With every few words the old man expelled a wheezy inadequate breath. Death was everywhere—in the caved-in face, in the fetid smell of the lodge, in the fading paint. A huge cliff of fatalism soared above Tom's head, up beyond his sight. He scoured it for footholds but from below it looked sheer, an impassive, faceless wall. Bewildered, he forgot his arguments: "It is horrible to just sit and die."

Rumbling Wings said a silent prayer, hoping that Tumbling Hawk's return to the Cheyenne would straighten his heart. "We will not sit and die. Death has long been a matter of importance to us."

Tom confronted a tradition, not a person. He thought, "Not one of them understands—not Big Road or Small Deer or Shell or Buck's Heart. They listen politely to what I say but they can't see it." Outside he heard Lightfoot move—the dark smear of shadow shut out more light.

"What you speak of, Tumbling Hawk, are all questions about how a man lives. A man who lives well will want to die well."

The shaman was all Tom was not, his obverse image, like the white between the letters to the black. The shaman presented Tom his long overdue bill. It read: your crimes are great; you have forgotten too much, lost too many years; it is unlikely you will enter the Promised Land. But Moses, the boy thought, had brought his people through to the end. And Tom Hyde/Tumbling Hawk, he hadn't even begun.

"What is death?" Rumbling Wings asked in the lifeless tone of a man who knew. He looked at Tom like an adult questioning a bothersome child. "If our lives are over, if our place in the order of things is gone, how can we oppose ourselves to that wisdom, since it is the wisdom we have always lived by?"

"A man could fight back, leave scars on white man so he will never forget he has been in a fight."

Rumbling Wings grew unnaturally calm. The face wrinkles smoothed as though time itself had, momentarily, relaxed its grip. "Perhaps we erred. Perhaps it is better not to live in the world that comes after us.

The Cheyenne may be destroyed by white man, but the white will also pass. We came in a wave and will be pushed out by a wave. And another wave will follow in time. We will be gone, but the hills will stand, the trees too, and they will take our revenge. The ground will open under this man, the skies grow black, the water poison his breed. Birds will not sing, they will shit on his face and peck at his eyes. I DO NOT WISH to be here for that."

Something was concluded there, and they would have broken off if Rumbling Wings hadn't asked Tom to tell him more about his life with white man. With a heavy heart Tom turned wizard, ferrying the shaman through scores of exotic worlds, making wonders burgeon before his eyes.

The night passed as Tom talked—the birds were beginning to sing up the sun—when Tom finally asked the question that had been on his mind for eight years. "How did you know I would go away?"

For the first time in their long night, Rumbling Wings smiled. "I knew the sound you heard could not enter our world. In those days," he continued without affectation, "my senses were sharp. I knew every sound and sight, every breeze and spirit in our range."

In his vision, of course, Tom had heard sounds like those he later heard in the white world. He knew the possible explanations—a four-day fast and a suggestible imagination had been known to play tricks before. But Tom didn't care to explain; it was one of the wisdoms he ungrudgingly attributed to the Cheyenne.

"What is the noise?" the old man asked.

"I think it's the sound made by white man's machines—metal moving on metal over and over again. When they make metal things—like steel needles or rifles—the sound is always there. Strangely enough, that is the same music I wish to bring the tribe, for those small sounds offer unlimited power." That was the greatest miracle: the sound he'd heard eight years before in an exhausted expectant dream was now poised at the edge of their world—and he was the one who carried it back.

The shaman brushed his miracle aside: "You believe a man can do much. That is all illusion, the white's way of falsely boasting he rules a world that rules him. It is one form of his license, and it allows him to see what is whole in pieces. But what can a man expect from another who sees with eyes that do not agree? A man can do nothing," said the greatest living shaman of the Cheyenne, "less than nothing. You do not yet think of yourself as Tumbling Hawk. That is very grave. Perhaps among us you will learn who you once were."

Tom was tempted to try to explain further, but that was impossible because the old man had signaled the end of the interview. Tom felt balked: he understood Rumbling Wings' insights into his character but he could not understand why the shaman refused to recognize white man's threat. The Cheyenne were still stuck where he had left them; only now their intransigence amounted to suicide.

He whispered a polite good-bye to the shaman, not certain that the old man heard him. As Tom came out, Lightfoot was rigidly planted at the entrance. For a moment, Tom was tempted to push him out of the way, but instead politely stepped around the young shaman. Lightfoot did not even glance his way.

That morning Tom built up the fire in front of his lodge until it was ready for the coal. The two sets of dies were in his lodge, and back inside he nervously counted twelve trigger blanks, picked up his forging hammer, and went back out again. The fire was hot enough by then.

"This is like a woman's maul," he said to Crow Wing, his five young apprentices, and scattered women and children who stood by. "But it has a handle and its head is narrow so that you can hit things with force in the right place." Tom clanged the hammer on his anvil a few times, then, setting the die on the anvil, he asked one of the boys to pump the bellows. The fire quickened with a healthy swoosh.

Tom heated the first metal blank for the trigger until it turned red orange. "Metal gets soft when it's very hot." His youngest apprentice nudged the one at the bellows, asking for his turn. "I'm going to pound the hot metal until it takes the shape of the inside of this form. It's like a footprint, only I have to push harder." The ringing hammer drew more spectators.

As he pounded the blank into the rougher of the two molds he would use to shape the trigger, Tom thought of the first blacksmith shop he'd seen—in Laramie. That brought back the colonel's face. With it came the usual parade—Charlotte, Elizabeth, Cable, Sherrin, Hall, Bushnell. It was moral cowardice to pretend the undertow wasn't there. He was lonely for them and their world, and wildly lonely for her—Charlotte, whose image he tried to keep alive through erotic memory's inadequate rites. Always the climax felt good, it relieved him; but each time was farcically brief, hopelessly incomplete.

For another kind of inspiration he thought of the Colt factory he had visited when he was at Yale, where great overhead flywheels turned hundreds of lathes and drill presses, which turned out thousands of rifles. His blows rang thicker. Tom pounded and pounded in the hot sun until his blank was rough shaped, until the indentation for the trigger pin was halfway through both sides of the blank. He removed it from the die, told one boy to throw on more coal and another to pump the bellows, then he repeated the forging process, this time in the finishing mold. All morning as he heated, pounded, reheated, and pounded, he explained, explained until his words became as heavy as the hammer. All morning their eager, curious, vulnerable faces tilted up at him. With a thousand strokes on his anvil he told them he'd do his best to keep the Cheyenne alive. His audience understood almost nothing.

That day he turned out twelve triggers, and the next day a dozen more. He worked hard, talked patiently, and by the third day Tom could tell they anticipated most of the steps—that was the beauty of mechanics, it was so simple.

He took eight days to stockpile twenty-four sets of triggers, trigger guards, firing pins, and hammers. Two of the hammers developed cracks in annealing and had to be redone, and Tom had a hard time getting the right tolerances on the nipples, but patience and his calipers finally made them true. His miniature production line worked so efficiently he made time to join his father and Takes-the-Pipe on the day's hunt. He took his first shot broadside at five hundred yards. They heard the crack of the Henry and the bull fell heavily, raising a puff of dust. The buffalo closest to it moved off a few steps; but the rest of the herd didn't even look up. All agreed that was much better than stampeding them.

THE CAVE

NOTHING WAS SIMPLE FOR Tom. When crossing White Clay Creek with the hunting party he'd sat patiently for over an hour in his wagon, watching the young braves splash across and back, promoting whatever route they happened on while cooler, drier heads planted sticks to see if the water was rising or falling, and one old man suggested taking a bucket and filling it with water—if it was clear, the stream was down. Many times in the past month they'd forded similar rivers and streams, yet always there was the same polite round of considerations, always the same characters advancing the same positions. So Tom really wasn't paying attention when Running Brave Bull called to him, "It's firm here. Come on."

Halfway across, the wagon's front wheel dropped off into a sinkhole. Trapped broadside in the middle of the channel, the water swirling inches below his irreplaceable powder and iron bar and those kegs of nails, Tom almost jumped up and screamed: "Look! Look what you've done, Running Brave Bull, you idiot, and the rest of you fools with all your tedious protocol . . . !" A month's work, more—perhaps the chance to save all that his people held sacred—hung quivering in midstream as the load slowly shifted and the weighty wagon, now balanced on one wheel, began an agonizingly slow shimmy, an impossible rippling contortion that threatened to tear the frame apart.

"Get over on this side! All your weight over here!" Tom watched helplessly as the men splashed over to the light side, big kids at play. His life with them seemed over as he raised the bullwhip and lashed off a fiendish crack just between the army horses' ears. The wagon quivered, then lurched forward; the wheel ripped free.

On the safety of the other bank he thanked them for getting him out, even Running Brave Bull. But in the privacy of his wagon, as Tom reorganized the load, his hands trembled uncontrollably. His patience was shredded, and he had no idea how much longer it would hold.

Early in July, as they trailed the buffalo herd along the Cheyenne River, a thunderstorm exploded directly over their camp. Tom measured three inches of rain in thirteen hours. For two days the ponies whinnied and blew like shrill winds; one got so badly twisted up in his hobbles that he broke his leg and had to be shot. The buffalo stampeded all over the Plain. The two-day storm gave Tom a captive audience. As he swaged the lock parts and the trigger assembly, he explained and reexplained the method by which the separate pieces of metal could be joined. While the storm raged outside, the warriors saw the rifles growing in the dim gray light of Tom's lodge.

On the third day they woke to low growls—Thunder was clearing his throat. By noon the ground was dry. So they laid their clothes on rocks, spread the linings of the tepees out on the ground, let the bowstrings contract in the shade while the women regreased and retanned the hides before they dried and cracked. Whatever meat had been on the racks had to be thrown away. Lightfoot went through camp in shredded buffalo skins touching all the ruined meat and wailing, "Rack-dead. It's dead on the rack. Throw it to the wolves."

The Plains dried out almost overnight. As the buffalo moved, they seemed to trample the color out of the grass. The hot July wind blew relentlessly. It scorched Tom's throat, dessicated his lungs, dabbed the vital moisture out of his eyes. His lips cracked. On the day they moved camp, he rode on top of his wagon sucking a piece of buffalo fat and occasionally rubbing it on his lips. Along the way he picked up some of the old people who went on ahead of the hunt in order to reach the next camp by nightfall. When Tom asked, they told him stories. One man spoke at length about Mohe. But Tom soon realized that the old people felt more comfortable walking than riding up on the wagon seat beside him.

As the fall hunt came to a close, the tribespeople knew it had been the best in five years. They felt cheered. They could spare him a few days, Tom reckoned, so he could go off and hunt for the cave he'd seen again and again in fantasies, in dreams. High Tree, Tom's most able assistant, could be trusted with the wagon on the trip back.

It was also vital for Tom to get away. For the past two weeks he'd oscillated between euphoric optimism and blank, impregnable despair. Asleep or awake, his mind groped for the proper strategy, the most effective tone to use with the tribe, which only increased his feeling of distance. He noticed that he frequently talked aloud to himself, and the Contrary seemed to notice it too, for he followed Tom around and honed in on him with his every backward gesture. It was unnerving to see the Contrary striking up into the air as Tom banged down on his anvil, unnerving to have this redundant yet inverted mirror image of himself. "Freaks stick together," was Tom's recurrent gloss. And Tom certainly considered himself a freak. Except that, for him, there wasn't any slot in the ordered Cheyenne world. Which brought him around to Hard Ground again. Small Deer's father had done something inexcusable, it seemed, for he was gone and no one ever spoke of him, not even his son. How vividly Tom remembered the little man's chilling remarks at the banquet in honor of their white soldier, how he'd sprung up—a little knight of righteousness—to defend Small Deer's honor. But now he questioned how the warriors—and he—could have demanded that Hard Ground pretend to be part of the camaraderie from which they always excluded him. Tangled stuff this, when customs which looked like voluntary agreements were unmasked as a kind of collective violence, when now even his own shining boyhood heroics were seen as bullying. Tom often imagined Hard Ground wandering through the sand hills, a few poor belongings balanced on his heavy hump.

Two days later, Tom rode off on his father's buckskin mare. It liked to run so he gave her all the rein she wanted. She covered four quick miles before Tom slowed her to a canter, then to a trot, then a walk. Ahead of them stretched more tableland, the same tawny gold broken only by the shadow lines of the mesas and a light vein of red—iron, thought Tom—which ran north along a sheered-off ridge. As the mare labored up the ravine, he dismounted and walked beside her, occasionally stroking her muzzle. He'd always like these ponies better than the white man's cumbersome horses.

Alternately he walked and rode, wondering if Rumbling Wings would last till he got back. Till his death the shaman would oppose Tom's plan; till the end he'd fail to see the gorgeous colossal irony of red men turning white man's most sophisticated weapon back on him. It would be less lonely, Tom thought, if someone understood this.

He had delayed writing Hyde and Elizabeth until he finished every single one of the handmade parts—except the carrier block, which he couldn't manage yet. He couldn't take a chance on Hyde's figuring out what he was up to. He knew that the colonel was one of the few men capable of a truly effective response. Tom guessed—and was right—that Hyde had an itemized list of everything taken from Forts Randall and Sully, that the colonel would consider every missing piece of army equipment as much his personal responsibility as he would if he'd signed them out of the storehouse. Already, because of a lingering fear of Hyde's military genius but also because of the boy's sense of how well they knew one another, Tom had passed up a chance to attack an army supply wagon loaded with ammunition, powder, and rifle parts which had left Omaha on the seventh of July. He'd also refused to steal the lathe and the drill press when they'd been sitting under his nose in that machine shop in Fort Randall. Hyde would be leaving for the Kentucky campaign at the end of August. By then the enormous storehouse at Fort Kearney would have received its fall supplies, and all the equipment Tom needed would be sitting there waiting for him. In his dreams Tom had waltzed around the storehouse many many times. One hundred repeating rifles—that's all he needed to start, thirty for his raiding parties, those assault groups of five to ten men. That would leave seventy repeaters to defend the enclave—70 x 15 = 1150 rounds. With the Union fighting a desperate war, they could never release one thousand men—not even eight hundred—and move them to an inaccessible corner of the Black Hills. And if confronted with a thousand soldiers, as long as he could make his rifles, Tom would have a bullet for each of them.

So the cave was his next step. In the dream it was beautiful—high chambers lit by blazing coal fires where strong, proud warriors stood, pounding on anvils with their forging hammers. It was like an illustration from a book of poems Cable had shown him, but the air in Tom's cave was thick with sweat and the cutting musk of gunpowder; metal filings crunched under foot.

Hours later the dark outline of the Hills broke his trance.

It was many degrees cooler in the spruces, as though the drooping green boughs had soaked up the heat. Tom pushed on across a marshy meadow to a stand of sandbar willows growing along a fast stream. He led the buckskin into the stream and washed her down. Touched by the spray of a tall flume, he masturbated half in, half out of the water, hearing Charlotte's voice in the sound of the falls. A lovely Cheyenne body got mixed in with his image of his love, but Tom didn't object.

He rested awhile, then worked his way north along the edge of the Hills. He led the pony over slope after slope, his left foot almost always higher than the right. But he did not tire. For he loved the rich fabric of the conifers, their soft overlapping edges like a curtain waiting to be parted. At sunset Tom spotted a pair of Cooper's hawks working the edge of the Hills, peering down from the sky with their hard specific eyes in search of unwary field mice. They did not dive, but hovered and took their currents up and down, closing their wings only to lift themselves back up into the invisible stream they rode.

At dawn Tom started into the interior without a clue as to where he was going. All morning he threaded between the symmetrical Hills, clambering up to inspect every promising opening in their sides. About noon, he saw what he guessed was a cave about ten paces above a tilted shelf of bisalt, the cracked columns thrusting out keglike bellies. The mouth was screened by an unlikely cluster of laurel bushes which looked like someone had planted them. Again he scrambled up. The rock tilted up enough to give adequate cover against attack from below. The spot, as he looked down, was fairly high, over halfway up the hill.

"So far so good," thought Tom with guarded enthusiasm. He stripped a laurel limb clean and got it lit. Then he started in. The mouth of the cave was just under five feet high and went back at that height six paces. Then Tom entered what seemed to be a gallery, perhaps fifteen feet high and roughly circular—maybe thirty feet in diameter. The limestone looked wet in places, and as the unsteady light played hide and seek in among the stalactites, it stretched one and shortened another until the ceiling seemed a swaying, brilliantly colored chandelier.

Leaning against a damp wall, Tom softly murmured, "I'm here." The echo welcomed him. Sometime later he poked into the back of the chamber and found that it branched into two more rooms. In the second room he felt the draft he'd hoped for. He tracked the current of air to a corner, where he found a funnel-like cut which framed a small patch of sky—his flue. Here, he thought, the great coal fires of his forges would light up the cave while Cheyenne warriors hammered out the parts of a hundred repeaters. Right here, under his feet.

The brand had burned down when he said to himself, "Now I'm ready." Outside the cave, he wrote Elizabeth and the colonel with his legs dangling over the buddhalike belly of a column of bisalt.

Dearest Elizabeth and Colonel Hyde,

I'm writing to ask you to please stop worrying. I am fine, perfectly whole and altogether well. But I have gone back to the Cheyenne. I know this must sound strange to you, but it is true. Please don't look shocked or disbelieving–I am an Indian and this is my home. My greatest pain is my sense of loss at leaving you, the debt of gratitude I leave unpaid, and my horror at having been the cause of your pain. But I had to come back. And I must–I will–stay here. Forever. I can no longer pretend to be my people's keeper, guide, and prophet. I no longer want to be an exception. And I abhor beyond words being the half-white redskinned rationalizer for the series of decisions which are rushing my people to captivity. So I have left that and come home, to live again with my blood mother and father, to learn who the Cheyenne are and understand why their lives–and those of other Indians–are being destroyed.

As I write my heart is full of you. There is no smugness or triumph or reproof in me, only a great sadness. I love and respect you both deeply even while I sense the pain I'm causing, and that makes it that much harder. You were wonderful to me always. You failed in nothing. I will always think of you as the very best parents in the world. You may say this is gratuitous. To me it is not. You may think my decision to leave came suddenly. It did not. It is the result of who I am and, in large part, of who you helped me become–a person who does this because he believes it to be right. I think I always knew someday I would have to decide.

My life in Washington with the Indian Bureau was a life for a child. On my trip to the Indian Territory, day after day I saw the ravages of the Civilized Tribes. I walked among their death throes. Now I am a man with a man's responsibilities. and I cannot be employed by a government which beguiles and cheats a people less vicious and more trusting than it. In good conscience, I cannot support that bully, not after I have learned by heart and catalogued and documented all the slaughters wrought by the old policy, not while I can predict all the horrors just ahead. The destruction of my people–of my family and friends–moves closer every day, just as it once crept up on the Seminole and the Creek and the Cherokee and the Delaware, the Mohawk and the Leni Lenape and the Osage and Huron and Penobscot and every other Eastern and Southern tribe on and on westward relentlessly forever. I cannot support that. I have had enough of the rationalizer's way, of trying to do something bad just a little bit better. It is no longer enough.

Please accept my inadequate apologies for the hurt I've caused you both. I write not to excuse myself but to say goodbye and relieve your immediate fears about my safety. Your disappointment, your anger, your justified feelings about my ingratitude, I cannot presume to relieve them.

I am sorry if the goodness of the past must be undone now, if it must be undone. But that is the price I must pay. Please do not come to see me. It would only cause unnecessary pain for us both. You both are a great part of me, more than I will ever comprehend. That probably sounds cavalier now, but it is nonetheless true. Dear Elizabeth, thank you for everything. You are the finest mother a boy could have. I will miss you, I do miss you constantly. Thank you again, Colonel. Please say goodbye to my old friends.

Yours with as much love as ever.

Always,
Tom

In great sadness, he rode southeast out of the Hills to the Little White River, where the Cheyenne scouts had told him he'd find the Lakota band who were going into Laramie to pick up their winter rations. He gave his letter to the headman, asking him to deliver it into the hands of Colonel Hyde.

BEAR CHILD AND A VISITOR

BACK AT THE CHEYENNE camp, Tom took up a more normal life than before. With his supplies running low there was no point in driving the workers; besides, he preferred not to move until Hyde left Laramie at the end of August. So he passed the hot rich days of the Scarlet Plums Moon banqueting with the warriors and listening to tales of their triumphs.

Before he'd gone off to find his cave, Tom had been reluctant to approach any of the Cheyenne women. Charlotte had been powerfully present then, and since his status with the tribe was so unsettled, it seemed unfair to share the burden, even casually, with someone else. But now there came times when Tom had difficulty picturing Charlotte. And the less he thought of Charlotte, the more Indian he felt. The more Indian he felt, the greater his interest in Bear Child, with her beautiful thick hair, her shy sweet face, and strong lovely legs. Tom soon realized he showed all the signs of a man falling in love—the constant state of anticipation as he moved around camp, hoping to see her; and, as soon as she was gone, the overwhelming desire to see her again.

A half mile east of camp a narrow trail wiggled up a hill then cut a steep diagonal down the other side. The top of that hill seemed to rise above Tom's head as the trail led him down. He picked his way between and over rocks to the middle of the dry creek bed, where he stopped and placed his buttocks against a convenient boulder. Faint noises from camp wafted over his shoulder; ahead in the woods where they gathered firewood he heard the girls' laughing, the snap of tree limbs, and someone yelling, "Watch out. Here it comes." He tried to pick out her laugh, wondering if she'd pulled those lovely legs up into a tree, if she was one of the girls breaking off the dead branches and showering them down with that leafy swoosh.

As the late afternoon's changing light remodeled those immobile boulders, Tom waited patiently for Bear Child, listening to the birds' accelerated twilight songs blend with the camp noises, the sounds of the young women in the grove.

A half hour passed before Small Deer's cousin, Gray Feather, emerged from the woods. Spotting Tom, she smiled and swung her hips coquettishly, pretending that he was waiting for her. But as she came up to him, Gray Feather said, "She'll be along soon enough." With that she giggled and scampered up the path over the hill. "Cheyenne girls run beautifully," Tom concluded.

A pair of married women passed more sedately. Then Bear Child came out of the grove—she was laughing, but as soon as she saw him she caught herself, as if her laugh was an act of intimacy to which he could not yet be admitted. The branches on her back made her stoop, which pushed her breasts forward so that, with each step, the soft doeskin confessed their shape. After her came her sisters, two cygnets behind the swan.

Tom's pulse raced. "Hello, Bear Child. May I walk with you?"

The younger girls giggled. She smiled, a little surprised by his stiffness. Her thick black hair was parted in the middle and pulled back over her ears into two long braids which hung to her waist. Her eyes were rich brown.

They walked a few steps before Tom said, "I keep wanting to do things that aren't done, like help you carry the wood. My intention is to help, but I have not found the right ways."

She looked up at him from under her load. "You are much closer to us already, Tumbling Hawk."

A few yards on he was ready to say good-bye. He did not want them to be seen in sight of camp, for then their names would surely be linked.

"Will I see you in line?" she asked.

So Tom took up his place in line in front of Bear Child's lodge. He held her hands and they stood there face to face, sometimes with her two sisters hanging on every word, usually with Takes-the-Pipe and an older brave, Mountain, politely half listening. On the nights Tom arrived ahead of the other two, he got the spot closest to the lodge, as custom dictated. Then he had more time to speak with her before the others took their turn. He carved a six-fingered flute from a juniper branch, tied it with sinew, wrapped it in porcupine quills, and scratched a red-tailed hawk on the stem. He practiced deep in the woods until he was ready, then, each night as she was falling asleep, he played his plaintive love song to a tune much like "Sewanee River." She grew to know his note.

Takes-the-Pipe was also in love with Bear Child, which might have been expected to cause trouble between them. But Takes-the-Pipe was a chief, and it was considered a sign of considerable merit for a chief to be indifferent to jealousy. Thus the story of the Cheyenne headman who, when informed of the kidnapping of his beloved wife of fifteen years by a man she'd refused countless times, was said to have merely grunted and got on with preparations for a raid on the Crow. Privately, Tom wondered why the men did not ask the lady's preference in these matters. But he'd long given up voicing objections to the Cheyenne social ways. At the same time, Tom didn't want to take advantage of Takes-the-Pipe. Impressed with each other's scruples, they began to be seen around camp; when Tom had time, they hunted together. Some said the Henry rifle belonged to the young chief, he used it so often.

By mid-August the villagers were satisfied that Tumbling Hawk had come to stay. After all, he was courting Cries-for-Perch's daughter, one of the Elk Horn maids of honor. As Shell watched her son walking the long deliberate path of Cheyenne courtship, she felt like a mother again.

Coming back from a solitary morning ride, Tom looped around to the south side of camp. He suspected that Bear Child was out picking sand cherries with the other young women, but decided to ride by on the off chance. As he passed High Back Wolf's lodge, he glanced across the camp—three army horses and an unfamiliar pony were hobbled in front of the council lodge. The horses were gigantic, it seemed, blown out of all proportion.

Tom dropped off his pony and sprinted toward the lodge, his eyes riveted on the vivid saddle stamp—US ARMY. It was Hyde's bay. Tom was excited about seeing the colonel one last time. But he was terrified that Hyde had gotten into his lodge and seen the supplies. Fortunately, a thunderstorm had threatened last night and he had thrown a tarpaulin over his anvil and wagon.

"If only they kept him out of there." Entering the lodge, he caught

Big Road out of the corner of his eye just as the colonel's leathery head jerked up at him. There were other men in the council lodge too, though Tom scarcely noticed them. In the presence of his two fathers, the tension was sublime.

Hyde got up stiffly and came toward Tom. He looked older–the folds alongside his mouth were now thick creases, the spots of frost in his hair were spreading over the temples and up the sideburns. But the eyes were sharp and clear. And he carried himself with no less authority.

The colonel raised his arms as though to hug Tom, but simply took his hand instead and shook it up and down.

Big Road watched them measure each other. The other men–Able-to-Reach-the-Cloud, Plenty Crows, the two young army lieutenants, and a Pawnee scout–got up to go. Not a word was spoken as they filed out.

"Let us sit together," Tom said in English. He felt ashamed to tell this man how things should be done, but vowed to stick to principle.

Hyde looked at Tom sternly, but he gave up the boy's hand and moved back to his place.

Tom took up his point of the triangle opposite Big Road, with the colonel on his right, in profile, which gave him a more intimate view of his two lives than he'd ever wanted. Big Road and Hyde were his two distinct heartbeats and, until this minute, he'd always managed to keep them apart.

"Are you really serious about this?"

"Yes. Absolutely serious."

"Why–what will be gained . . ." The colonel faltered ". . . by staying here?"

"I tried my best to tell you in my letter."

"Whatever your reasons–and I take it they're admirable–there are a host of more pressing ones in Washington at this moment. The war in the Southwest will dislocate thousands of Indians–"

"Is that a reason for my going or staying, sir?"

Tom's heart tom-tommed as he watched the colonel take the cheap shot. "Better this way," Tom told himself, feeling rotten and low. Yet he kept up his end of it, eyes fixed on the colonel's face.

Hyde did not answer. He hunched his shoulders a little, shortening his neck. For weeks Elizabeth and he had worried. They imagined Tom drowned or butchered or lying out on an alkaline plain roasting to death. Over the course of three weeks they'd suffered vivid horrors, gone numb, revived to suffer again. Then rumors began to trickle in–he'd been sighted south of the Platte; two days later Tom had definitely been seen near Kearney, with a band of Oglala, then on a ranch near the Sweet Water. Finally, after twenty-eight days, Hyde's Pawnee scout came in to say that he was living with a Cheyenne band, following the buffalo. Hyde figured the boy had gone back to his family. Six days later, Tom's letter arrived.

The colonel had prepared for a last-ditch battle, but he'd come with the tactician's determination to get a better idea of what stood against him. As they talked and the morning dragged on, as Tom kept evading his questions or denying the truth of what the colonel believed self-evident, Hyde felt as he had when he'd read and reread that hateful letter—it was as though, under all the elaborate argumentation, the boy was cheating, as though some basic term of Tom's equation had been left out. Although that infuriated Hyde, he was willing to sacrifice pride to woo Tom and win him back.

"Tom," Hyde said in desperation after the boy categorically refused to return and take up his vital duties, "Tom, I can sympathize with your desire to avoid disappointment. But the question is larger than that." The small chin tilted up at him, the eyes equal parts appeal and demand. "I'm afraid disappointment haunts all mature men."

Tom said the disappointment Hyde spoke of belonged to the white world, not to the Indian's. Hyde insisted for the thousandth time that Tom was the only one equipped to help his people—it was unfair to other red men to throw away all that time and training. Tom said he would not again be party to the cynical gentlemen's agreement which let him live like a white while pretending to care about Indians. Beside himself with frustration, Hyde asked Tom just what he could possibly do in the Cheyenne world. Tom answered: in the morning he'd swim in the cold stream, in the afternoon he'd hunt, in the evening he'd sit by the fire and listen to the others talk until he had something of his own to say. Hyde sensed that missing term again—power had played too large a part in the boy's upbringing for the colonel to believe he could renounce it for this primitive monastery—at least not for long.

Later Tom delivered a short lecture about virtue in the white world—it turns the men who hate greed and envy and bullying into weaklings before the rich and powerful. It mocks the flower of its manhood, calls them childlike idealists, and sentences them to a lifelong struggle against those who prefer to sell too little for too much. "The good and great among you spend your lives that way, as you have done, as Mr. Coughlin has done, as Matthew will do." Tom's eyes misted as they always did when he spoke of heroism. "But I am not bound by that obligation." He saw his old mentor through two lenses—one was composed of their lives together; the other was ground from the bitter impersonal history that had landed the Indian in his present dilemma.

Big Road sat listening to words he didn't understand and observing the similar curve of their fingers as they reached to make a point, the set of their hands as they emptied the air of objections.

Finally, after Tom had joylessly won each round or danced around Hyde's attempts to back him into a straight answer, he said, "Colonel, I'm glad we've had the chance to see each other again, even if it is like this. I wish—I only wish there was some way to make it easier for both of us. But it doesn't make sense to go on any longer. I'm not going back."

Hyde's stomach, which had grown increasingly capricious during the long interview, felt as though some alien creature got loose inside it, as though a piece of his own flesh had torn off and was trying to get out.

"Is Elizabeth well?"

"She's quite well," replied Hyde with as much surface emotion as he'd put into a drill order.

"I'm glad."

They sat awkwardly silent, having lost access to words. But there was one final announcement: "Elizabeth and I are going to be married in August. We both wanted you to be there."

The shock plunged Tom into deep water—the extraordinary irony was that this blessing should come now, when he'd cut his ties forever. Tom realized how much he loved them. He realized he would've given anything for the impossible privilege of having it both ways. When his head came clear of the water, he was glad to find himself so happy for them. "Colonel, this is wonderful news. It makes me very happy."

Hyde gave Tom his hard smile.

"You've ridden a long way. Would you care to dine with us?" "Dine" had such an unfortunate ring, but Tom wanted it over.

"No. Thank you, no." Hyde commanded himself not to dawdle now. He felt an overwhelming revulsion for those moccasins marked with the red quill star, the unseemly breechclout on his own boy. He tried to pin something on the pagan shabbiness, the flea-infested misery of the fetid lodge. But it wasn't substantial enough to hold it.

Hyde rose. Big Road got up with his characteristic leap, and Tom stood too. There was a confused moment when each wanted someone else to go ahead, then their guest resolutely led. After all those hours in the tepee's half light, the sun was blinding. Villagers stood off at a respectful distance. The oversized army horses were only a few yards away.

"Colonel," Tom said softly, stopping his hand inches short of Hyde's uniformed elbow. The boy's fear of being a hypocrite made him afraid to touch him. "Good luck with your new command. I hope all goes well in the campaign. And please send all my love and best wishes—and congratulations—to Elizabeth."

Hyde took that with the same stiff rigor with which he'd bare his knuckles for the schoolmaster's ruler. Good will was hard to take; the boy had become so callous. "We'll miss you," the colonel said hoarsely, his heart frantic with loss, the insufferable passivity of defeat. The bridge he'd tried to build was tumbling down—no, it was already down. He didn't know what was worse, losing the boy or his hopes for the red men's future. Yes, he knew. "I wish you all the luck in the world." He meant it, but the underpinning emotions had all been blown away.

Hyde walked the few paces with his shoulders hunched slightly, eating up his neck. The adjutant scurried ahead and made a cup of his hands for the colonel's polished boot. Back straight, Hyde went up on the bay. The others flung themselves on their animals. Then, looking straight ahead, Hyde signaled with his left hand, something Tom had never seen before. The four riders jumped off in step.

As the gap between them widened, Tom saw Elizabeth's face as it looked the day he'd left. Only he placed her strained expression under a bridal veil, encased in white tiers of lace. He saw them both perched on a tall white wedding cake—her ample figure next to the colonel's terse form . . . while straight ahead of him, the colonel rode out of his life.

He heard Big Road say: "I've often thought of him, though I never expected to see him. How much he wanted to take you away."

They stood side by side as they'd done so many years before. Tom was grateful Big Road had been in the lodge with them, that he understood so much. Tom watched the forms on horseback diminish to small distant figures, till his vision misted and the horizon broke up into a wavering shaft of light.

Big Road stared straight ahead. "He is a man of strength and integrity. Sometimes you move your hand as he does."

"He didn't see my supplies?"

"No. They rode in from the south and Takes-the-Pipe made sure he came straight here."

FORT RANDALL

TOM FINISHED HIS WORK early and took a well-traveled path out of camp. As he approached the circle where the women had gathered to help Bear Child's cousin sew her wedding lodge, the wind was sweetened by a familiar ripe musk. Tom saw himself as a very small boy, barely five, climbing a trampled path up an icy hill toward a circle of buffalo skins. The morning was cold, clear, very bright, but when he pulled aside one of the buffalo skins to enter the ring where Shell worked with the other women, he was met by that same ripe sweetness, though it was richer for being warmed by the fire. All kinds of comforts and strange enticements lay embedded in that fragrance.

This time it was summer, so there was no high circular screen of hides to keep out the cold, only the bride's lodge skins spread out on the ground like a puzzle just pieced together. Tom saw the others as though they were a setting for Bear Child, and she was alone in the midst of the chattering women, on her knees, feet tucked under, waiting for him. She was pushing a needle through a double thickness of hides, her lustrous hair pulled back from her face; a slight film of perspiration highlighted her copper brow.

"Are you working hard?" he asked her. The younger women answered with giggles.

"Not very hard," Bear Child said. "My friends are helping me."

The older women laughed now, adding a wryer note to the virgins' expectant strain. Their laughter legitimized his courtship, said, "You are no different from any other man." Tom wanted to cry out: "Thank you, ladies! Thank you." Instead he said to her, "Let me see your hands."

Bear Child hesitated. The others waited anxiously, sensitive to these moments of drama in another woman's life. Then slowly she held out her hands, palms up. Tom took them and ran an appraising finger across each palm. He turned the hands over, checked the back sides with the same finger. Mouth pursed, he shook his head.

She looked quickly down at her hands, trying to understand what was wrong.

Tom pulled a delicate milk-glass jar out of his pocket; unscrewing the top, he held it under Bear Child's nose.

"It smells like lilies—what is it?"

"Just a scented grease."

The others watched all this, their curiosity incandescent. Even Bear Child's mother, Walking Spirit, who'd always favored Takes-the-Pipe, could hardly restrain herself. So Tom handed the jar to Walking Spirit, who almost stuck her nose in it trying to get a good whiff. Then the jar went around the circle, each of the women sniffing politely. The jar came back to Tom, who poured a few drops of lotion onto Bear Child's palm. He rubbed the grease into one, the other, then he coated the backs of her hands.

"When you'd like more, you must ask me."

She nodded, thrilled yet shy.

"Good afternoon, Bear Child. Good afternoon, Walking Spirit." With excess lotion still on his hands, Tom took leave of the womanly smell and Bear Child's inspiring presence.

At dawn on September sixth Tom and Buck's Heart reached the Missouri River at a spot several miles south of Fort Randall. From there Tom drove the wagon north along a rutted old wagon road, while Buck's Heart pushed his pony through the undergrowth, staying as close to the river as the vicious berry and briar tangles and the steep ravines would let him. Finally Buck's Heart found a small clearing that gave onto a miniature beach. The wagon road ran close to the clearing, and they only had to back through twenty yards of underbrush. The slope up from the water was steep, but the sand was pebbly and the footing seemed secure. After Tom backed the wagon down the bank to test it, he bathed and changed into a white linen suit. They hobbled one of their fast ponies under a pin oak, tied Buck's Heart's spotted gray to the back of the rig, and took the main road north. They were in Fort Randall by two. Which was just as Tom planned.

He left Buck's Heart lying in the back of the wagon, his hands behind his head, feet up on a siderail, apparently without a care in the world. In his white suit Tom strolled the main street to the machine shop which serviced the Missouri steamboats. Through the plate-glass window Tom ogled the vertical drill press and a treadle lathe. The lathe had a giant red and yellow flywheel with dark blue hubs; this flywheel was six feet in diameter, and when it revolved Tom thought, without doubt, it was the most beautiful carrousel he'd ever seen.

In the town library he asked for newspapers of the past two months and read or skimmed every item on the Civil War. The South was doing too well—the Union defeat at Bull Run had burst that thin bubble of optimism and ended the talk of the war being over in six months. The South was getting men under arms more quickly than the Union. In spite of Coughlin's herculean efforts, northern military forces were not effectively organized.

One article stopped him: on August twenty-fifth, Matthew Sherrin had led a battle at Lyon, Missouri. Against a larger force of rebels, Sherrin had split his forces and personally commanded the attack. Meanwhile, his associate—Tom couldn't help putting himself in Lieutenant Jonathan Garner's place—attacked the Confederate right rear. Sherrin's initial charge almost carried, but due to poor communications and Garner's inability to follow up the assault, the Confederates rallied. Sherrin was hit, but not seriously. The battle was inconclusive.

Tom paged through the rest of his stack—as of the day before, the rebels still held strongholds in southern Missouri and Jefferson City, while the Union controlled St. Louis and the Mississippi.

"So Matthew's doing his job," Tom concluded as he pushed back his chair.

Tom was still wondering if he could have helped Matthew turn the tide at Lyon when he sat down in a cafe, ordered coffee and started to sip slowly. For the next hour and a half he listened to every word spoken in the cafe, paying particular attention to the conversations among the young men. Finally he picked out two clerks whose tone was so belligerently pro-Union Tom figured they'd bought substitutes to fight for them.

"Pardon me, gentlemen," he said, leaning their way. They were startled by this impeccably dressed Indian who spoke perfect English. "I couldn't help overhearing your patriotic sentiments."

The two clerks glanced at each other uncertainly. Neither was twenty years old. "I was pleased to hear you speak so fervently of our Union. That isn't done enough these days." He eyed them suggestively while his fingers worked his frock coat lapel, two and two. His hand went to the band of his slouch hat, two and two. Tom scratched the table twice, then twice again. No response.

"Allow me to introduce myself," he said, getting up. "Caspar Browning." Tom paused to let them swallow that. "Ah, I was born a Sioux through a grandmother who had the misfortune to be removed from her prairie home and wedded to a Brule chief." The boy-men accepted Tom's pronouncement a bit dully, not knowing what he was getting at.

"May I sit down?" They were too slow to refuse. "Yes, gentlemen, these days it's harder to find unallayed patriotism than you'd think." He examined them as if to determine what mettle they were composed of. One politely said that even in Fort Randall there seemed to be considerable indifference about the war.

"I would venture to say that both of you are disappointed that you haven't had the opportunity to fight." It was too direct, but Tom figured if he lost them he still had time to try again. However, both quickly admitted they desperately wanted to go to war. Certain personal problems had arisen—

Tom led them into a discussion of the problems of the war, saying that there were few well-informed Northerners left who still believed the fight would be over in six months. One of the young men said that, as far as he figured, the campaign was badly run. Tom agreed, confiding that political considerations were always getting in the way of successful prosecution. He plied them with information he'd just picked out of the newspapers, but by dropping a few highly placed names and using a little strategic double-talk made it seem he was privy to all sorts of extremely sensitive facts: Grant should have been appointed the head of a unified command, but a certain general and the Secretary of the Navy opposed it, or rather, him; Fremont had to be removed in the Department of the West—he was an engineer, not a military strategist, and too old as well. "I expect," Tom said in conclusion, "that you two gentlemen would do just about anything to help the Great Cause."

His auditors agreed enthusiastically. One asked, "Just what are you doing in town?"

"Some business."

"About the war?" the other whispered, trying to be discreet.

Tom actually sneaked a glance to his right. He looked at them to imply that, even if he wanted to, he couldn't talk about it. But he did say, "These days it's not incorrect to say that wars are fought far from the battlefield."

He could almost hear their pulses accelerate. "I'd estimate you both can keep a secret. Otherwise—" this was meant to establish their complicity—"otherwise we couldn't be talking this way." Tom looked around again, then reached into his vest pocket. He casually wrapped the identification papers in his newspaper and slipped the bundle across the table. Each got a glimpse of the official-looking documents Tom had forged on Coughlin's stationery, which confirmed that he was indeed Caspar Browning, on Special Assignment from the 7th Ohio Cavalry under direct orders of the Secretary of War.

"Suppose, just theoretically suppose you were given a chance to help the cause of free men. I don't have to ask you what you'd do, do I?" No, they agreed, he wouldn't have to ask. "This is an absolute secret between you and me. No one else is to know—wife, girlfriend, or mother. Total silence. Swear?" Gravely they agreed, though both were clearly nervous at the prospect of actually doing something. "I don't foresee any physical danger. The assignment's more subtle than that." That relieved them. "We'll meet in the alley behind the post office at 9:15. Come there by indirect routes. Separately. Alone. Understand?"

"Let's synchronize our watches. I have 7:12." They matched his 7:12. "See you then, my friends. At 9:15 for the cause. Not a moment before."

"Or after," said the livelier one.

At 8:15 Buck's Heart was posted on the roof of a low shed behind the hotel, the Henry rifle resting on his knees. At 8:45 Tom forced the door of the machine shop and loosened the floor screws under the lathe and the drill press. At 9:15 he heard them approaching from opposite directions, almost in step. Tom waited until they were standing in the shadow of the post office before he came out from behind the barrels. He asked two questions: "Did you talk to anyone?" "Are you alone?" They answered correctly.

"Now let me explain," Tom said quickly. "Southern agents are swarming all over Fort Randall. Their objective is to disrupt federal shipping on the Missouri. My orders are to move out two pieces of heavy equipment before they can disable or destroy them." His men appreciated the scale of the enemy's intentions.

Tom led them across the street—they passed under Buck's Heart, skirted the wagon in position by the back door. Inside they freed the drill press and carried it out. The drill press was almost too easy. But the lathe weighed nearly three hundred pounds and the beautiful flywheel made it top-heavy. With his helpers under the heavy end and Tom steering, they finally maneuvered it to the back door. But the machine would not go through. Twice they reangled it without getting anywhere, then Tom decided to take the flywheel out first.

They had inched the flywheel halfway out the doorframe when they heard heavy footsteps coming down the alley. They froze, the red and yellow semicircle sticking out in full view. A man with an unsteady gait stopped by the post office, leaned against the hitching rail, unbuttoned his fly and took a noisy piss. It went on for what seemed hours. Tom's men were still doubled over, knees bent, balancing the weight on the floor when the man lurched around, took a few uneven steps, stopped, remembered to button up, did so, then weaved back from where he'd come.

"Let's try it again," Tom ordered when the drunk was gone. They gouged the doorframe, they banged the wall, they sweated and cursed and fought with that off-balance load until the flywheel came free. Then, by kitty-cornering the body of the lathe back and forth, slowly they inched it through, taking the bottom hinge with it. Tom let them rest a minute–they were exhausted and dripping sweat–before he urged, "We've got to hurry." He barely had breath to speak.

Again they heaved together and carried the lathe down the single step and across to the wagon. They shifted their hands to lift it higher–coming up to the tailgate the lathe tottered, but they did get it onto the lip. That unbalanced the load–the drill press shifted toward them, the wagon began to rear. "Hold it there! Hands under it!" Tom whispered fiercely as he jumped onto the wagon bed. The wagon complained as it settled back down. Slowly they stepped the lathe forward until its three hundred pounds rested over the rear axle.

Up went the tailgate, a piece of canvas was roped over the machinery. Tom told the brighter one to trail the wagon, and took the other fellow up on the boot. One full block behind Buck's Heart brought up the rear, moving from shadow to shadow.

Tom drove along the wharf slowly, looking for the right barge. The *Dora* and the *Applepicker* seemed his only possibilities, but the *Applepicker* lay too near the tied-up river steamer. So Tom turned the team around, then leisurely came back along the piers. It seemed years since he'd smelled the tar, the pitch, the moldy stench of rotting wood. Laughter and the squeal of a fiddle mingled with the soft wet smacks of water kissing the pilings. "The right accompaniment," Tom judged, wondering if Charlotte was whirling around a dance floor in a full white dress, if Hyde was trying to catch some sleep in a field tent in Kentucky, if Elizabeth was knitting as she rocked.

No one was aboard the *Dora* when Tom came alongside the second time. She was a medium-sized barge with low sideboards, certainly strong enough to hold his wagon's fourteen hundred or sixteen hundred pounds. The problem was getting the wagon down the greasy, fatigued gangplank, which didn't leave much room on the sides and sloped down sharply to the deck. After comparing the width of the five-board gangplank to the distance between his wagon wheels, Tom jumped up and down on the plank a few times, though that was more for his men's consumption than anything else—it wasn't that he had many options.

Tom unhitched the army horses and led them on board, gauging the sway in the plank under their weight. "O.K., let's go ahead. If anything comes up, just act like you know what you're doing."

With Tom at the front of the wagon, they swung it around, maneuvered it back and forth until it came into line with the boards. When everything was set, he wished for two strong competent men instead of the two he had, crossed his mental fingers, and gave the signal.

The plank bowed viciously as the wagon came on to the edge. His helpers were at the rear on either side, braced to keep the weight centered on the plank while doing their best not to get run over. Up front, Tom strained to keep the tongue in line. Inch by inch they backed it down until, just over halfway, the front wheels began to turn to the left. "Hold it, hold it right there! Can you hold it?" Tom planted his feet in the crack between the boards and, using his body as a lever, pushed with all his strength until the yoke grudgingly swung back to center. "Just a little more," he half cajoled, half commanded, alarmed by their shallow panting.

His fingers were pincushions for splinters, his sides ached from the strain of bracing himself against the weight, but he held the yoke steady. The wagon rumbled down the last couple of feet, the two at the rear just scampering clear. The barge bucked, which smashed waves against the pilings. The horses shuffled. But the bucking calmed, and finally the barge settled. The real work was over.

"Thanks, fellows," Tom said genuinely when the wagon was secured with guide ropes. He patted one of them on the shoulder. "Good work. Real good work."

They were raising the gangplank when they saw a lamp moving toward them. It came on with mesmerizing slowness, spinning dark spokes out from the squat pilings, scattering the shadows of kegs and barrels and crates all over the pier. On it came, the yellow light eerily singling out letters on signs, on storefronts, until it turned up their pier and stopped a few yards from the *Dora.*

"Where's John?" the voice asked.

"Not sure. Up there?" Tom jerked his thumb in the direction of the steamer. In the uncertain light Tom made out only the spiky gray-white hairs on the underside of his questioner's chin. The barge shifted, apparently lifting the man up and down. Nothing in the entire floating city seemed stable.

"What you up to?" the interrogator continued.

"The usual," Tom returned indifferently. He waited a moment, not wanting to rush it. Then he bent down over a pile of thick rope. "Can't stand here gabbing all night. Got to get underway before morning."

"O.K., O.K.," said the other, clearly disappointed. "Don't have to get so damned huffy."

The lamp moved off through the dark dwarf city.

The other two were impressed, but Tom had no time for that. Tapping the gangplank with his boot he said, "Never know when we'll have to off-load to get around a rebel patrol." He thanked them sincerely, said a few words about the dignity of the Union cause, shook hands and said good-bye. They helped push him off. Though they'd worked and sweated together for hours, Tom realized he had forgotten what both of them looked like.

A half mile downstream Tom caught two quick flashes from Buck's Heart's lantern. "All's well so far."

Two miles below Fort Randall the Missouri swung north in a perfect bow, then flowed south again. Tom was just guessing about the channel—he knew enough to keep to the right, watch for markers, and keep a sharp eye out for other boats. Someone else might've found this blind maneuvering daring or foolhardy or both, but Tom didn't give it a thought. After the evening's intrigue, it was relaxing to rest his hand on the hand-smoothed tiller and let the current take him. The moon was not up, but the sky was lanterned with stars; the sky felt like another river.

He exchanged nautical greetings with a barge that passed. Then, coming around another bend, a high-fronted scow suddenly loomed in front of him.

"Hey! You're going to run that bank!"

"It's O.K.," Tom shouted back. "Didn't want to crowd you on the turn."

"*Dora* there? That you, John?"

"Sick." Tom's sense of freedom kept enlarging, for he was almost parallel with the scow now, separated by twenty yards of black water. He moved into the shadow of one of his army horses. The other man, he felt, was staring through the darkness at him.

"Ted?" came the questioning voice

"Yep," he slurred. "That you, mate?"

"Billy here." Tom felt buoyant, the crickets and bullfrogs chimed in chorus, celebrating his escape. "Have a good night, Billy boy."

"You bet. Be in Randall soon."

Tom thought, "He's going to see a woman." By then he was out of range.

Here he was, in the peace and exquisite calm of a summer evening, carrying away tools to make war—the two most important pieces of equipment for his mission. Yet no one had been hurt. Lulled by success and the river breeze, Tom felt almost innocent. Those two faceless young men would have quite the tale to tell their grandchildren.

The dark willows and cottonwoods slipped by, sentinels on silent parade. North, South, red, white—how could such simple labels make such a fateful, fatal difference. The labels fit so badly. Yet, it seemed the more formless or inadequate or misshapen the terms were, the more fanatically people clung to them. Given man's infinite possibilities, something which Tom felt a moment before and which he knew every man, woman and child glimpsed at certain moments of grace or friendship with themselves, it seemed a waste to pay good lives for such a hopelessly inadequate fit. He passed a sternwheeler laboring upstream, showering the night with bursting comets and rainbow sparks which drowned in the darkness below. "Red man, white man—they don't even describe the colors." His sadness prompted him to smile.

Downstream Tom's eyes blurred with fatigue; he got edgy. Without a moon all the coves looked alike. Two sharp flashes broke his mood, then another pair of flashes, and Tom spun the tiller toward the shore, knowing Buck's Heart stood waiting for him behind the light.

The offloading went quickly. They shoved the barge back into the Missouri and sent it on its way south. Tom was tired, but they drove all night. Toward dawn Buck's Heart went ahead to find cover. They rested until it was dark again; Tom slept eleven hours. Traveling only at night, they reached the Cheyenne camp in three days.

They were welcomed like heroes; a feast was held that evening. The villagers showed little interest in Tom's drill press, but everyone wanted to work the treadle and watch the spokes of the red and yellow flywheel spin round and round.

Next morning he was up early to start tooling up the lathe for rifling his gun barrels. The bore was .42 of an inch, with six grooves and six lands; the grooves and lands were to be .10 inch, the groove's depth was .005. The twist of the grooves had to increase from one turn in 120 inches to one turn in 33 inches at the muzzle end. All this was exacting work. Tom took two full days to get the lathe set up for production. Small Deer spent three days collecting the hardwood Tom needed for his jigs and rifle stocks.

In five days he turned twenty-four rifle barrels out of the bar stock on hand. Then Tom tooled down and set up the lathe to cut the magazine; that took another few days' preparation plus four days' work. When his treadle leg ached, Tom pictured that Hartford gun factory with its overhead leather conveyor belts providing continuous power to the rows of lathes and drill presses. He wished a genie would send him two lathes, one for the barrels and one for the magazine. He wished for more, finer and stronger bar stock, trained assistants, hotter fires, but with every teeth-clenched wish he made, he worked more fanatically, determined to change the odds.

In the evenings he visited Bear Child. Often, now, he was first in line. Takes-the-Pipe was always a perfect gentleman. Mountain seemed to have dropped out of the running. But Walking Spirit still opposed Tom. Which was Lightfoot's fault, for he'd stepped up his attacks on "the mad half-white man who stands all day at the devil's wheel." That was bad enough, but Cries-for-Perch objected too. Since Tom had not been initiated into a warrior society, in the official eyes of the tribe he was not a man. He who wanted his deeds to stand beside Laughing Child's, who was about to embark on the greatest raids in Cheyenne history, he was officially considered an overgrown boy.

WARRIOR

WHEN TOM ASKED TAKES-THE-PIPE to sponsor the raid, his old friend accepted with undisguised pleasure. Tom knew it wasn't mere courtesy, but also the opportunity Takes-the-Pipe needed to convince himself of the worthiness of his rival.

Back in his lodge, Tom removed Mohe's eagle feathers from the parfleche Shell had just made for him. He took the last five trading blankets out of the chest, turned his buffalo robe fur-side out and said aloud: "Please indulge me a little longer, Grandfather. I am anxious to get all this metal out of your house, but cannot until the cave is ready. I ask your patience again. I hope it's the very last time."

Holding the blankets against the stem of Mohe's catlinite pipe, he walked through camp, keening as he went. He sang of dead warriors, sang of the war path ahead of him, and the raids from which he would return, if all went well, with many rich prizes. As he marched by familiar lodges, Tom knew that this place and this hour had long ago been prepared for him. Rumbling Wings' prophetic insight into his vision had made room in the future for him. Not a moment of his time had been wasted, for today he was fulfilling those terms laid down so long ago. The villagers remained silent, for everyone appreciated the appropriateness of the moment–Tumbling Hawk had finally caught up with his fate.

He stood at the entrance to the sacred lodge of the shaman and wailed his song:

"I am going in search of the enemy;
When I find him, there will be fighting;
Perhaps he will kill me.
Even so, he must die."

Inside he could hear the clotted breathing of the old man. He sang the song three times before a voice called him in.

Smoking was not easy for Rumbling Wings, but he took Mohe's old pipe, packed in the medicine tobacco, lit the pipe, and drew on it. Tom offered Rumbling Wings the blankets and the shaman accepted. These were not personal matters. In the Cheyenne world there was no one, no way to trick a man out of his birthright.

"I feel I should have been here many years before," Tom said when he'd finished the pipe.

Rumbling Wings looked up at him through countless years. "You are here now. That brings it round again."

Next night Tom sang the wolf songs, leading his father, Takes-the-Pipe, and Buck's Heart round and round the fire. And that final morning he bathed in the holy pool, then purified himself in the sweat bath. Before the sun nudged the horizon line, Tom and his party were riding south.

Around their campfire that evening, the four warriors smoked and prayed and sang the holy songs of war. As Man-Who-Runs-the-Farthest had done so many years before, Tom stayed awake until his followers were asleep. He sang a prayer, then in a hushed voice said, "Hear me, you who hear all voices. I speak like a child, not knowing how to speak to you, yet knowing you will hear my heart. I want to do great things, greater than have yet been attempted. With me are three men I love, who have eased me back to a place I had almost forgotten. I would like to repay them a little.

"I would gladly trade my life for these lives. But that is not the question and I will need much time. Keeping me alive is nothing, Spirit, next to what will happen if I do not succeed. If I die, they—all of them—will die too, and the good they represent will go out of this world. As far as I can reach down and take hold of the things that are in my heart, my intentions are honorable. I will do my best."

He praised the virtues of Big Road and Takes-the-Pipe and Buck's Heart, and asked for their safe return. Then he slept.

A hard day's ride took them within striking distance of Fort Kearney. At dawn Buck's Heart was dispatched to find out where the woodcutters were working. The Buck was back at midday—they were on the Loup Fork with only six guards. Tom was delighted.

That afternoon the four Cheyenne moved into position on a thickly forested ridge above the woodcutters, Tom and Buck's Heart to the left of the detail, Big Road and Takes-the-Pipe on the right. They sat quietly for two hours, listening to the chunk of the splitting axes and the men's voices drifting lazily up the hill like an audible haze. The deer flies were voracious and thick, but they let them bite at will. When the cutters began to load their tools into the supply wagon, Tom sighted the Henry on the lieutenant, breathed in, held that breath, and slowly squeezed the trigger.

The hammer hit the percussion cap, sent the lead spiraling down that engineered tunnel of lands and grooves. Tom knew all the specifications—25 grains of powder, 216 grains of lead for the ball. But never before had he connected his line of sight with that invisible line of force to a man. It was very remote and impersonal, too easy killing a man. The shot caught the young lieutenant high on the cheek and blew away a chunk of his face.

Takes-the-Pipe's shot cracked back at them off the canyon wall. The sergeant staggered from the impact, his knees sagged softly; butt hit the ground first, then he started a slow somersault which he never finished. For an inept moment the other soldiers froze, then they desperately scrambled for cover. Tom felt a convulsing contempt for their awkwardness. It wasn't fair that such specimens had all the advantages on their side. Still the round he fired wasn't aimed at anyone, and Takes-the-Pipe followed by shooting into the air.

The next morning the four Cheyenne hardly needed the field glasses as they lay on the southern ridge and watched the detachment of eighteen soldiers scour the slope directly opposite them. The blue uniforms poked about in bramble and thicket, checked the ravines, slowly weaved up and down the northern ridge. They were young, rode poorly, looked skittish. Just as Tom guessed, as he had hoped, the western outposts had few men to spare.

The Cheyenne held their position when twelve uniformed riders splashed across the Loup to the south bank. The Cheyenne lay still until the soldiers fanned out and started up the southern slope. Big Road, Takes-the-Pipe, and Tom slipped away to the east, leaving Buck's Heart to dally on his pony at the top of the ridge. He was to be the human lure, to draw the soldiers west while keeping them on the southern ridge. The other three would first move east, then Takes-the-

Pipe would make his way back to their original position on the southern ridge while Tom and Big Road would sneak in behind the six sentries the soldiers had posted on the northern ridge. Then the fun would start.

Moments later, Tom heard a shot, some shouting, hooves, then a sprinkling of rifle fire. The shots drifted west. Buck's Heart was running his pony down the ridge, drawing those twelve soldiers after him.

Ten minutes passed before Takes-the-Pipe picked up the Henry rifle and the binoculars. "Good hunting," he said cheerfully and started back toward the position they'd just abandoned.

Father and son took an hour to loop east and cross the stream and work back along the northern ridge. The northern slope was sliced up by steep gullies; the brush was thick; hawthorn and ubiquitous blackberry slowed them. Occasionally they heard a cluster of shots coming from far off.

They'd picked a sentry who worked a path just below the crest of the ridge—they expected him to come up over the peak at a point only yards from where they took cover. Apparently he was tired, for he did not appear. They waited, listening to his high, wheezy breathing approach, then fade off just below their line of sight. Then he came up—the head first, flushed pink, the soggy hair dribbling over his forehead like dark wax. He was about eighteen, puffy, and looked like he anticipated danger from all sides, but was afraid to look too closely lest he be right.

But the sentry didn't come all the way. He glanced ignorantly into the scrub juniper, turned back, and stopped just below the crest, the back of his head peeking over the ridge line.

Tom signaled to his father that he was going, then eased himself ahead on his elbows, pushing with his knees. He made the first bush, a bare snip of piñon. Tom waited coolly. Only the accident of his capture had kept him from becoming a warrior, he knew. Rumbling Wings predicted there'd be honor enough. "So this one is deaf too," Tom thought, calculating the strides that separated him from the pink insensate sentry and waiting for the instant when his body would start him. The sentry settled his weight onto the rifle barrel; Tom came into a half crouch.

From the ridge Takes-the-Pipe viewed in binocular close-up what Big Road witnessed twenty yards away. Eight years had passed since Man-Who-Runs-the-Farthest had taken that white sentry, but Tumbling Hawk executed the same rite—the left hand whipped under the chin, snapped back the neck. The knife blade entered the soldier's artery, then disappeared to the haft. The body seemed to come to attention, then Tom let it slowly slump down, using his right leg for support.

Big Road helped Tom drag the man over the hill, where they stripped off his uniform. The tunic fit Big Road snugly, but he did manage to get one button buttoned. Son and father came up to the crest of the hill, Big Road armed with the sentry's single-shot carbine. Big Road cupped his hands over his mouth, tucked his tongue, and whistled like a goshawk.

There was a pause, then Takes-the-Pipe's shot rang across the canyon. It caught a second sentry in the throat; he slapped a useless hand over the wound as he fell. Tom picked off the next guard. An answering shot cracked back from the southern rim. Round by round they made their way east up the valley, firing in turn. In two minutes seven sentries lay dead or wounded.

Big Road made that shrill whistle again, then father and son raced a half mile to the laurel grove where their ponies were hid. As they galloped to the edge of the sandhills, the wind was strong—hard on the eyes but otherwise helpful; their tracks would be covered in half an hour.

Not long after they set up camp, Buck's Heart came in, grinning and looking as fresh as when the day began. It was pitch-black when they heard the goshawk. Big Road returned the signal, then Takes-the-Pipe walked into camp leading his pony.

"You spaced your shots well," Tom said after they'd handed him the cold supper.

"Like you said, I counted ten before each shot." He started to toll the numbers off on his fingers.

They slept five hours, were up under a starry sky. It was cold in the sand hills. After another snack of dried buffalo meat, Tom ran through the plan for the last time. "The soldiers think there are three of us—at least three. They'll overreact and send out fifty, at the most sixty men. I can guarantee they'll be poorly commanded. But they will have the Pawnee scouts, so we'll have to be careful—especially you, Takes-the-Pipe."

The young chief liked his part in the day's business.

"Takes-the-Pipe, keep ahead of them. Keep moving and, whatever happens, don't let them turn you. The rifle will make them think there are a lot of you." Takes-the-Pipe patted the Henry to indicate there were many of him; his bandolier held forty of Tom's homemade bullets, the pouch over his shoulder another fifty. "Space your shots if you can. You'll be that much more effective if they don't know about the repeater. But, if you get in any trouble, use it! That's what it's for!

"Buck, you have what you need?"

Buck's Heart held up his wire cutters.

"Buck's Heart will get the ponies to their relay stations. You know where they are. Pass the checkpoints—if it's possible. We'll meet at the mesa."

They said good-bye. Buck's Heart led away his three extra ponies. Takes-the-Pipe stalked off, back straight, his elbows bent just that fraction short of locking. Then father and son erased the signs of their camp and started south through the sandhills.

Tom, who felt overdressed in his old frock coat and black trousers, told his father he looked quite handsome in the cavalry uniform. In fact, Big Road had slept in it the night before. The father thought he could suffer the discomfort to learn firsthand about his son's white world.

From the cover of the elders, they watched the column of soldiers leaving Fort Kearney. With the binoculars Tom picked out a full colonel, three majors, one brevet-colonel. One by one he counted the soldiers—when he reached 60, his anxieties skyrocketed. At 72, he thought, "Did too goddamn good a job picking them off. Idiots think we're an army. Takes-the-Pipe has 7 reloads at 15 shots each, 105 rounds. Lousy margin—too slim, too slim." While the mounted double column continued to file out of the Fort, Tom frantically reasoned that as Takes-the-Pipe moved around he'd get time to reload; the terrain would break up the soldiers into small units; killing a few would discourage the others. But none of this calmed him as Kearney disgorged still more soldiers. "83, 84," he tolled, sweat tipping the line where his hair met his forehead. They might have come fresh from the giant storehouse, these gay toy soldiers—the regimental flag waving, sword hilts glinting, blue uniforms immaculate.

Then, finally, "91, 92." Ninety-two soldiers were too many, far too many. They'd outsmarted him by over-overreacting, something he hadn't counted on. He should've had a fall-back position, some way of calling it off. But it was too late now—they'd have to go ahead with it and count on luck. Hyde used to say about luck: "Not much of a strategy, especially when it's all you've got."

In a buffalo wallow, father and son sprinkled each other with dust, then layered the animals' coats with dust, and sat down to wait. Tom kept thinking there was something mindless in the white commander's excess—92 men chasing a single repeating rifle. Seventeen whites had been killed in the Dog soldiers' battle with the Waschita when he was a boy. From Indian Bureau records Tom had counted 235 Indians massacred in retaliation raids—almost 14 Indians per soldier, 14 to 1.

Tom and Big Road waited until the column crossed the river before they galloped toward Fort Kearney and into the parade ground, scattering lounging soldiers, drowsy dogs. Tom left his father outside and rushed into the low log building he remembered so well, shouting, "I've got to see the commanding officer! Where's your C.O.?"

An orderly scurried out of the anteroom and a moment later Tom stood before a young Major Thurston.

"Sorry to burst in on you, Major, but Scout Rhodes and I have just ridden from Bloomington with these orders." He thrust the forged papers into the young man's hands, and gestured toward the window where his father stood.

Major Thurston tried to look composed as he read that rebel troops had crossed into Nebraska from Kansas and were now massing at Alma, forty miles southwest of Grand Island. The orders were addressed to Colonel Smithfield, but in the event of his absence, the Commanding Officer at Fort Kearney was ordered to dispatch three hundred men to the Republican River at a point just west of Bloomington. The order was signed by the Commander of the Western Armies, General Hugo Keller.

Behind his superior's borrowed desk, Thurston couldn't help feeling that fate had dealt him a deadly hand. His first impulse was to stall. But Tom threw on more fuel: "Your men will be the only force between the Confederates and the river. General Keller's afraid they'll roll right on to the Mississippi if he doesn't get reenforcements. There's word that Crittenden's army intends to meet up with Johnston's."

Thurston nodded sullenly.

Tom attended that nod. "Has your telegraph been cut?"

"Yes. Lost it this morning about seven."

Tom said: "Those damn rebs!" He thought: "Good work, Buck's Heart." "Sir," he continued quickly, "I know you're busy, but I've got to move supplies down to General Keller. Will you sign this authorization?"

If he'd read the list, Thurston would've been suspicious. At the very least he would've asked himself, why in the world did Keller need bar stock and compression pins? So everything hung on an elementary piece of psychology. Tom watched the major eye the first few legitimate articles, then saw the eye quickly skim the rest of the page, not heeding the confession that lay in his hands. He didn't even bother to read the second page, just scribbled at the bottom, "Havelock Thurston, C.O."

"Thanks," said Tom, deliberately removing the paper from the big desk. "If it's O.K., I'll load later. I'd rather travel at night, sir. Don't want to take any chances with the general's supplies. Not with the telegraph down and rebels behind every cottonwood."

Thurston glanced up quickly, annoyed that the subject had been referred to again. But Tom was all sympathy, so Thurston calmed himself. "Of course. Take all the men you need to load—whoever's left."

They shook hands. Tom looked at the major as if he had confidence in the other's ability to weather this crisis. It was the least he could do for Thurston, who'd catch untold amounts of hell for what he'd failed to read and failed to see.

As Big Road and Tom stood in the shade of the officers' porch, unable to speak to each other, Tom kept worrying about Takes-the-Pipe and wondering what his father thought of the soldiers mounting those mammoth horses, the lieutenants shouting orders, and the column with its standard raised getting underway. He had smuggled his father into this world, and now he wanted to decipher each minute part for him, explain what it was like the first time he'd heard the dry squeak of saddle leather, the jangle of swords. He wanted to tell Big Road what talking to Thurston had been like—the moment he knew he had him, when all he had to do was keep up his pace and sweep the unsuspecting major along. That might take their minds off Takes-the-Pipe.

As the troops moved out, Tom's eye kept settling on the powder magazine. "Get my stuff out, then blow the whole thing. One good blast would wipe out all their supplies. That might pay them back for some of the bets they fix. Like pledging Indian lands in perpetuity, then whisking them away in a year, like retaliating for an Indian raid at the rate of fourteen to one." He saw forty-foot flames licking the slate roof, the white soldiers throwing child's pails of water at the unquenchable hell fire which ate up their weapons of destruction. With the war for bigger stakes under way, the western outposts would never be fully resupplied. Of course, if he blew the magazine, the Army would come after him with everything they could spare. They'd have to, if only as a point of honor. Tom wasn't ready for that yet.

Two hours later, Fort Kearney was all but deserted; less than fifty men remained in the dusty compound. Not until then did Tom and his father move to the storehouse to supervise the loading. There, for the first time, Big Road saw the white man's wealth arrayed in bins, piled up on top of itself, as his son had seen it years before.

As Tom watched the soldiers load in the steel bar and rod, brass rod and bar, the iron, the boxes and boxes of bullets and cartridge cases, casks of powder, compression pins, all those blanks, even the light-tempered steel for the springs, as he watched this giant handout, he felt like dancing. Tom took five hundred boxes of ammunition, another anvil, and emery, and grades of file, and every other thing he would cram into two large wagons, including five hundred pounds of coal.

"It's all there," he said to the sergeant in charge, checking the last item off his list. "Thank you for being so helpful." The burly redhead with a dished face not unlike Coughlin's saluted. Minutes later they were heading south toward Bloomington with their escort.

There were twelve men—twelve boys in the escort, a horror which Tom would have given anything to avoid. But he couldn't argue that the two fully loaded wagons could go it alone at night, not after he'd peopled the country southeast of Kearney with Confederate troops.

At 2:30 A.M. the convoy stopped for a couple hours' sleep. Two sentries were posted, two boys from Omaha, one quite pleasant. The company bedded down, wiggled their bodies into the loose sand. A few minutes later Tom heard snoring. "Funny how white men snore." White men lived with such extraordinary security that they could make noise in their sleep. "Perhaps," Tom thought in grisly anticipation, "that's why they're so terrified of death."

Tom and Big Road took the sentries silently, with hunting knives. Then they shot the rest with two six-shot revolvers—five men apiece. Very fast, very simple. Only the last two pairs really got the chance to stir, the thick shadows lurching up, then subsiding. There was no anodyne for the simple horror of it.

Tom and Big Road were relieved to be in separate wagons as they turned north and drove away from the dozen corpses. All night they pushed the teams furiously, barely pausing to speak even when they crossed the Platte at a spot twenty miles east of Forty Kearney. They found Buck's Heart waiting at the table-rock ravine, the second checkpoint. He signed that his work had gone well; he'd cut the telegraph in four places; he'd stationed Takes-the-Pipe's relay ponies along the ridge. No, he knew nothing about Takes-the-Pipe, though he was certain he'd heard the Henry's report all through the afternoon.

They drove north through the shifting loess till daylight threatened, when Tom sent Buck's Heart ahead to find a hiding place. They slept soundly the entire day. That evening Tom's band reached the red-rock mesa, their last rendezvous site. They waited an extra day, but Takes-the-Pipe did not appear. At nightfall, reluctantly, they pushed on.

At camp they were welcomed as heroes. The warriors fingered the bullets and steel stolen right out from under the soldiers' noses while they listened rhapsodically to Big Road's descriptions of his son's fierce bravery and inspired leadership. Underneath their transport lay the dark suspicion that Takes-the-Pipe had paid with his life for the iron and steel and cartridge cases.

Prudence told Tom: not so soon after Kearney; wait until all the new equipment is set up in the cave and the flue is venting; work out the plan for the cave's fortification. But a louder voice shouted: you've already lost a great friend and ally, one of the few men who could have helped. You've also lost the brass-frame repeating rifle. And every day you wait you give up more surprise—surprise being one of your few working weapons. The whites know who you are—at this point that certainly doesn't require genius. Tom decided to move right away.

Two evenings later, in the council meeting he called for that purpose, Tom asked for volunteers to come with him on a long and arduous series of raids which would begin in a week, with the Moon of the Changing Leaves, and last till the heavy snows came. If Takes-the-Pipe returned, he would lead one of the bands. If the great young chief did not come back, if he had been killed, the raiding parties would spread revenge for his death from the Missouri to the Platte, from the Misi Sipi to the Rockies. It was time to drive the white invader from the Cheyenne lands; it was time to avenge all the tribe's fallen brothers.

The council lodge erupted: every warrior there—thirty-five of them—asked to go along.

While his warriors prepared for these raids, Tom and Small Deer worked feverishly in the Black Hills cave. That first morning Tom announced, "I want twenty-four finished repeaters before we walk out of here." They raised that idol of two dozen repeaters before them, and by the end of the second day had completed twenty-six plunger springs and mainsprings; by the third afternoon they'd worked out all the dimensions of the carrier blocks. But each carrier block took Tom at least three hours to swage, which was too slow and forced a change in his plans. Since he didn't need all the rifles for his first attacks, he decided to finish the first dozen. After the raids on the Missouri forts, he'd come back to the cave and spend a week completing the second dozen. The break would give his men a last chance to see their families before Tom took them away for a month or more. If the Missouri raids went well, this meant sending them home at the height of their enthusiasm.

Without the Henry for comparison, it was difficult to be absolutely certain of some measurements, but Tom worked from the patent plans and tested every dimension with gauges and calipers. The emery and the new files helped. They had the stocks finished by the sixth day—Small Deer was a genius with wood. All that last night they worked, Small Deer assembling the swaged parts while Tom ground out pin after pin. Just before dawn they came out of the cave into the cool air.

Through their absurdly exhausting week, they'd kept up the argument about the relative merits of the bow and the rifle; neither had converted the other. Which made it that much more extraordinary to Tom that Small Deer had stuck with him—flying in the face of his professional interest on an act of faith for a thing in which he didn't believe. Yet Small Deer had slaved away at his side, gone without sleep, watched the calluses grow and pop on the few remaining soft spots on his hands.

"How alone I'd be without him," Tom thought. "Small Deer..." Emotion and fatigue thickened his voice.

Small Deer's thin handsome face waited for Tom to finish.

"We have twelve rifles now—and everything we need for the next twelve but the carrier blocks."

"We haven't fired them."

But Tom knew they'd work. He'd been over pin and screw, checked and rechecked every millimeter of the twelve finished repeaters. After proving twenty-four sets of sixty-six parts, he knew that each set was perfectly interchangeable.

They fired six rounds from each rifle, savoring the reports like starving men at table. Standing above those buddha-bellied columns of cracked basalt, the two friends sent seventy-two rounds cutting through the lightening mix of night and day sky. Tom would've liked to fire a thousand bullets, but he could not waste the ammunition.

"Twelve rifles, old friend. And twelve more just behind them."

"You said the more guns you had, the more soldiers would come after you."

"The more guns I have, the more it will cost them."

Back at camp they learned that Bear Child was ill. She had been delirious for three days. Tom rushed to her lodge, but was told to wait outside. Lightfoot was in and out all day; never once did he honor Tom with a glance. Shell brought Tom some broth, but he had no appetite. Late that evening Bear Child's fever broke. Tom was admitted after Lightfoot had gone.

She lay on a pile of ragged trade blankets, looking pale and exhausted. Her V-fronted shirt bunched slightly over the slope of her breasts. Tom wanted to lay his tired head there. But Cries-for-Perch, Walking Spirit, and her two sisters were only a few feet away.

"This sudden illness, Bear Child . . . I was so worried . . ."

"I was mourning because I know Takes-the-Pipe is dead. He will never come back." Tears wanted to fall, but she was too exhausted to cry.

"You must believe I did not want that," he whispered.

"I know, Tumbling Hawk. I felt very sad for you too, thinking about what some would say." She paused. He thought her fierce hot eyes looked into his heart. "I fear for you. Please come back."

Tom looked at the others, but they had turned away. He bent over and kissed her forehead. Bear Child tilted up her mouth and he kissed her, tasting a small part of her being. Tom left, feeling that someone had pulled the plug inside his stomach and he had started draining out.

Like Fort Laramie, the town of Fort Randall had outgrown the original walled post and now sprawled down to the waterfront. In the fine drizzle, the low ugly profile of the fort looked like an overturned turtle, those squat sentry posts at the corners like legs thrust uselessly into the air. He left eight shadows leaning against warehouse, crate and piling, and trudged up the dock, the keg on his shoulder. It was really so simple—if anyone asked, he was carrying beer.

By Addison's Chandlery Tom thumped down the keg. Inside were all the ropes and blocks, those beautifully tooled brass fittings and all that canvas. He waited four minutes, staring down into the window that came up just above his waist. This time he didn't have to rehearse the venom—no telling himself that the white pieces of paper that cluttered officers' desks killed red men, that white men killed Indians for stealing a milk cow. The light drizzle draped a thin gray blanket over the world.

Then he heard Big Road's sparrow hawk—once, twice. That meant Plenty Crows and another eight men were in position on the south side of the fort, away from the main gate. Tom immediately speared the plug of the keg with his knife, looked around again—no one was out in the rain—and began to soak the dry siding of the chandlery with the kerosene. Then he worked his way back down the pier to Big Road's position. At the stroke of ten Tom lit a cigar, took a puff and dropped it onto the puddle of kerosene.

It sputtered momentarily, then a trail of flame gullied down the wharf, turned a corner, and flared wildly up the dry siding of Addison's. In two minutes the north end of the pier was ablaze.

Soldiers began to rush by, many half dressed, shouting jumbled directions. Tom waited another minute, then started to move against traffic. Slowly he made his way toward the fort. Behind him the illumination grew brighter in small leaps, as though someone were turning up a giant lamp.

By the south wall, Plenty Crows signaled him that everyone was in place. Tom lit another match and touched the flame to a kerosene-soaked rag at the end of a stick. With that rag Plenty Crows lit the tip of the first arrow, then one by one the warriors filed by until seven arrows were burning. There was no one to notice a few tiny flames in the middle of the conflagration. Then, all at once, the thick gray sky was streaked by lines of fire.

Even before the walls of the fort caught, Tom heard the sharp coughs of the Henrys coming from the wharf. The unarmed soldiers went down in rows, caught between that north wall of fire and Big Road's repeaters. Dead men were silhouetted as they fell, dead men were licked by lurid flame. It was eery retribution—the fort, the waterfront, the whole world consumed in fire, the gray air torn by pain. Tom led his men away when the first boats caught—the water itself appeared to burn.

Within a half hour all eighteen braves had reached the rendezvous site. Not a single man had been wounded.

They rode hard through the rain and, just before dawn, two groups of nine warriors simultaneously struck at Fort Sully and Fort Bennett. At Fort Sully Tom had difficulty starting the fire on the wet roofs, so they shot their fire arrows at the walls. At Fort Bennett, a brisk east wind coaxed the fuse of the stable toward the powder magazine. Big Road mounted and yelled to his men to ride off as fast as they could. They were a half mile away when the explosion jiggled the earth—the flash froze the string of riders against a blood-red dawn. Big Road slowed his pony then—there was no point in racing when no one was left to pursue.

It was late afternoon when Tom and Big Road reached the cave and found Small Deer sitting on the lip of the basalt, looking tired and despondent. Small Deer tried to explain: on his own he'd gone ahead with the next carrier block. He thought he'd done it just as Tumbling Hawk had shown him. And the rifle had worked—for three rounds; then it stopped. Now it would not shoot bullets one after another.

"It's all my fault," Small Deer insisted, his thin face unnaturally long. "I have ruined all your work."

"Not at all," Tom answered. "Without you there wouldn't be any work. Don't worry, Small Deer. We'll fix it."

Tom tried the lever, which worked. But the shell wasn't ejecting. So he took his own rifle apart, then the other one. Piece by piece he compared breech pins, springs and spring catch, and the carrier blocks, where he thought the trouble would be. Instead, he found that the carrier block was perfect and its spring was slightly bent, which made it catch the cartridge too close to center, thus making it impossible to eject the spent shell. They worked with the spring for the next hour until Tom decided it was useless and he'd be better off making some new ones.

"I'm glad we found the trouble now, Small Deer, instead of waiting until the Waschita were shooting at us."

Small Deer was happy it wasn't his fault, and still happier that Tom could fix it. Later, when the rifle passed the firing test and the crisis really was over, Big Road told Small Deer about the raids, those three forts going up in flame. He told them both what Riding High Wolf had whispered: "It was wonderful. I would have been proud to die there."

After reading two newspaper accounts of the raid on Fort Kearney, Hyde was absolutely certain Tom was behind it. The colonel fired off a rambling but stiffly impersonal ten-page letter to Secretary of War Coughlin, in which he explained that the cunningly escalated attacks on the woodcutters were a ruse to draw the soldiers out of the fort. His letter continued:

> The Commanding Officer of the 8th Iowa Cavalry did not understand he was up against only a few, and possibly a single red man until one of his marksmen circled the ridge and picked off one of the Indians from behind. The Indian was armed with a 15-shot Henry breechloading rifle, the weapon currently undergoing tests by your ballistics department.
>
> The lure had accomplished its purpose—to allow, as I have said, the presumed leader of this party to walk boldly into Fort Kearney and drive out with the stolen supplies he requested. Disguised as an agent

under orders to the Union, this man stole from the Kearney stores the munitions itemized in Colonel Smithfield's report of 3 October 1861.

In the last 4 months—as I believe your office has been informed—a treadle lathe and a drill press have been stolen from the machine shop of the Missouri steamers in Fort Randall by a man identified as an Indian who speaks with an impeccable eastern accent. This is obviously the same man who identified himself as a Union agent and subsequently massacred his twelve-man escort.

His intention, I am certain, is to build weapons on the model of the Henry brass-frame repeater. I dread to speculate what even a small number of well-led Cheyenne armed with adequate repeating rifles might do against the youthful volunteer units on the western frontier armed with their single-shot rifles and converted flintlocks.

If this sounds like idle surmise to your office, let me insist that my engineers inform me that the manufacture of such weapons, though not a simple undertaking, is not an impossibility—given the machinery and materiel this renegade has with him now.

The Army's virtually unbroken record of successes against the Indian has been due, in large part, to:

1) our superior discipline and deployment
2) superior coordination and communications
3) superior equipment
4) the Indian's unshakable adherence to his traditional attack tactics, which apparently are a part of his religion—he will not fight at night, in winter, he circles our circles. If one or more of these advantages were overcome, not only the entire civilian population west of Omaha would be threatened, but perhaps the very outcome of the Rebellion as well.

I have no desire to sound alarmist, Mr. Secretary, but I fear the right leader could make the language of the treaties quite literally true. If he could get set up in good defensive position, he could hold a good deal of territory "as long as the grass shall grow and the rivers flow."

The Secretary's big freckled hands gripped the edges of his desk. Hyde could not bring himself to mention the boy's name. Hyde would consider each life taken by Tom a life he'd taken himself as surely as if he'd loaded the gun and squeezed the trigger. "What a wedding present," Coughlin thought, remembering the first time he'd seen them together how glad he'd been that his dear friend had a son, how excited he'd been that they finally had the basis for a just strategy against bigotry and senseless devastation. There were so many hideous ironies—the crushing end to the dreams of Indian progress; the rumor that Charlotte Harris was soon to be engaged; the fact that, after Hyde's brilliant Kentucky campaigns, his promotion to brigadier-general was almost through the pipe. The marriage. How much pleasure would they take in that now? Forever they would insist that Tom's defection was their fault. Both of them would believe that, Coughlin thought. How hard for such people not to take blame on themselves when they tried to the limits of their ability, yet things went desperately wrong. Mrs. Hastings said nothing aged a man like defeat. Hyde recently had three: the transcontinental railroad route, which would be routed up the valley of the Lodgepole, just forty miles south of Laramie, right through the middle of Avery's land; his foundering windmill project; now this, losing his son. They'd all lost a son. Coughlin, too, felt betrayed, lost, confounded. It was as though his son were fighting for the South. Yet, even if his child had turned traitor, Coughlin knew he could not set out after him like an ordinary enemy—as Hyde seemed to be doing. Then, it was Hyde's duty as a soldier—more so, as the very source of the threat. "Children," he muttered, more sad than bitter. "You never know . . ." But then he and Dorothea had never had children.

The raids on the three Missouri forts slashed Coughlin's slim cord of hope that Tom would limit the scale of his outrages. In one night 114 people had been killed—87 soldiers, 18 civilian males, 6 women, 3 children. At Fort Bennett the second largest powder magazine on the upper Missouri had exploded and had taken most of the town along with it. The newspaper accounts were lurid, ghastly.

Three days later Coughlin received the note he'd been expecting. It had no heading, no date, and simply began:

> Whip up public opinion all over the East, Jim. Greeley should be the primary one. Enlist every yellow journalist you can. We'll need every means at our disposal to eliminate this monster. We cannot let him get dug in. Every day counts. Someone—Greeley will do—must paint a picture of the entire Plains about to burst into flame. Play up the grisly senseless deaths. Mobilize public opinion. Attribute every one of the fiendish actions to a heinous southern plot.
>
> I'm one of the best Indian fighters in the country, you know that. If I can have 25 Pawnee scouts and the men I list, plus 1000 foot soldiers, I could run this thing personally from Kentucky without going within 500 miles of the Plains. From where I sit I can pull the strings. I am the

best and truly the only one to fight him because I created him and taught him every trick he knows.

Theoretically, Coughlin had to agree that Hyde was the best man for the job. But the tone of the letter was so unsettling that the Secretary made a discreet inquiry to see if the brigadier-elect was really up to commanding his forces. Hyde's adjutant wrote: "The colonel spends more time alone now, sir. Occasionally he seems a bit more remote. But at all times he is composed and alert and his mind is active with strategies for the contingencies you list."

THE GREAT PLAINS ON FIRE

DURING THE LAST TWO weeks in October Tom's raiding parties set fire to cultivated fields from the Missouri all the way south to the Platte. They spread black char over the tawny prairie, painted the Plains' sky fiery red. Near Yankton they burned five hundred acres of crops, nearly an entire valley; the smoke was visible from the Omaha courthouse, one hundred twenty miles south. Tom split his raiders into bands of three or four or five or six, armed each band with one or two of his repeating rifles and let them slaughter every head of cattle, every sheep, chicken, goat, or horse in reprisal for white man's slaughter of game and buffalo. Whenever they crossed a telegraph line, they cut it down; if they had time, they chopped the wire into pieces and burned the poles. They ravaged ranches and way stations, destroyed ferries. At Fort Kearney again, Tom blew up the powder magazine. The next night Julesburg went up in smoke.

From Julesburg they hit Chug Water, then Hillsdale. The town of Cheyenne they completely razed, killing twenty-four people. Above Denver they struck at a silver mine, killed eight miners and took the payload off to a cave on Bald Mountain. Tom planned to buy steel with the silver when the right time came. When he met resistance from troops or vigilantes, Tom slashed at their flanks with his fast, mobile cavalry. The repeaters shredded them. Trapped in a canyon near Sedgwick, Tom left seven repeaters as a rear guard, then scaled the walls with nine of his men and wiped out all twenty-eight soldiers. His horse was shot out from under him in one skirmish, but he held onto his rifle as he fell and came up firing.

By November, southern Cheyenne, Blackfeet, Crow, Absaroka, and Sioux were riding with Tom's bands. One morning Tom sat on the bank of the Platte and explained, no, he was sorry, but he couldn't stay and smoke the pipe all afternoon, he had to be off to kill more whites. Each red man they met was invited to the spring meeting to be held at the lower fork of the Powder River. The Moon of the Grass Appearing would convene the greatest gathering of red men the world had ever seen. It was then Tom would announce his plan to hold the Plains forever.

Having driven the settlers back into the larger forts and towns, Tom scattered raiding parties all along the Overland Trail. The Sioux helped him patrol the Platte between the Loup River and its tributaries. The southern Cheyenne and Arapaho guarded the south fork to Denver. By the eleventh of November, Denver's supplies were running low; they had received no mail in three weeks; there was terrified talk of the cholera. During those first two weeks of November not a single wagon got more than twelve miles west of Omaha. Nothing moved out of Kearney. In a month five hundred whites had been killed; Tom had lost twelve men, six rifles. In thirty days, Tom had accomplished more than fifty years of Indian wars.

But the campaign had its price. Though the discipline held—there was no grumbling—fatigue was widespread; the men missed their homes, their women, their families. They were not used to such a prolonged campaign, not used to so much killing.

Tom paid too. At the beginning he loved to think of himself as a demonic force, "a red devil with firepower." His speeches to the warriors were passionate, ringing exhortations to take the fight to white man while he was at his weakest; pledges to hold the Plains for the children of the red men, their children's children. He kept himself at fever pitch by ticking off the abuses, the massacres, the humiliations, land grabs, treaties broken. In time the rabidness wore out; the killing, the slaughter obscured anger and hatred. Then he began to dwell on old friends' pain—Charlotte reading headlines about her former lover, coming down to breakfast to face her father, her brother; Elizabeth trying to fathom the reasons for his bloodlust, she who always told him to turn his red cheek. He still killed, but he did so mechanically, without ardor or speeches. The first light snow came on November 29. Tom welcomed it. His men were right—it was almost time to rest.

A piece of paper was lifted from the top of the central stack of papers on the Secretary's desk. The heavily inked stamp read: URGENT—TOP PRIORITY. This paper moved quickly from the large desk of the Secretary of the War Department to the smaller desk of his First Undersecretary, and then on to the First Undersecretary's clerk, who copied its text onto four apparently identical sheets of paper. The URGENT–TOP PRIORITY stamp was reduplicated on the four, so that all five papers commanded the same haste.

Nonetheless, the original paper took up residence on top of another pile of papers in the INCOMING BOX, its URGENT legend doing nothing to unsettle the adjutant clerk's unhurried lunch. After lunch, it started on its way again. At the same time, one copy of that original was making its way toward the office of the President of the United States; a second headed in the direction of the Adjutant General; the third to the Cabinet officer in charge of liaison with the War Department, and the fourth to the military archives. At one point the archives copy was carelessly brushed off a desk, floated innocuously to the floor where it remained for a quarter hour until reclaimed by a clerk who carefully expunged the boot print it was wearing. The copy on its way to the Cabinet officer incorrectly got into a general's office, but he eventually discovered the error and shoved it back into the perpetually flowing stream of paper.

Between any two adjoining desks in any office there is a great gap, a gap as great as the distinction between one man's sense of urgency and another's. But this paper with the established English characters on it, which might've become a window frame or an ax handle or a piece of newsprint–or might've remained a tree–this one had the curious force of arranging for men's deaths.

Killing always has a degree of priority. But in times of civil war, with all the URGENT–TOP PRIORITY papers screaming for lethal top billing, ear and eye are apt to dull. In such times to differentiate true from false urgencies is difficult. Thousands of documents insisted to too many clerks that the message carried was vital, that the history of the nation itself might be changed if its urgent command went unheeded. How to weigh relative urgencies then, with pieces of paper so alike in size, color, texture, and weight? Did the clerk who took out his code book to read this priority stamp, did he really understand what it meant to be dealing with this A-4? Or what might happen if one particularly well-educated renegade, a singularly smart Indian, properly equipped, properly trained, were to hold a remote corner of the world sufficiently difficult to approach, sufficiently productive to support a bare subsistence for himself and a handful of others? Doubtful. Men's inability to make distinctions functions as fully in times of crisis as on ordinary sunny days.

Yet in spite of the various mishandlings and delays these five virtually identical pieces of paper were subject to as they made their way through the bureaucratic maze, one of them—it happened to be the original—had a consistently winning role in a game like rock/scissors/paper—it kept popping up, resurfacing, floating to the top, insisting on its dominance in the hierarchy. Consequently, it was passed, shuffled, handed off, and, though crimped at the edges, forwarded up the paper chain of command. It passed all the right desks as higher and higher—in a manner of speaking—it rose.

When Tom and his men got back to camp, they were feasted for seven days and seven nights, which surpassed the greatest celebrations the old men could remember. But then five hundred white deaths were much to honor. After that week of feasting, the band prepared to scatter.

In council that last night Tom told his warriors they'd fought gloriously. The Cheyenne were now disciplined soldiers, not the unorganized "flock of blackbirds" a white general had once called them. He would spend the winter making as many rifles as possible. In the spring the raiding parties would strike with more men, with fifty or even sixty rifles. Other Indians would join the Cheyenne until the red men of the Plains swept over white man like spring floods. Next year would begin the Great War, which would drive the whites off their lands forever.

Tom distributed sixteen of the two dozen completed repeating rifles among the leading warriors—Plenty Crows, Able-to-Reach-the-Cloud, Hankering Horse, Strong Left Hand. Then he thanked everyone again and wished them a good winter's rest. He told Small Deer how much he'd miss him. He bade wistful farewell to Bear Child, who was to escape the harsh winter by going south to her mother's Arapaho family. Even Lightfoot turned out to say good-bye and congratulate Tom, though he added that he still had no faith in the new ways. Lightfoot seemed altered, much older; it was certain that Rumbling Wings would not live out the winter. Having set things in order, Tom went off to his Black Hills cave with Big Road and Shell, Buck's Heart, and two young braves.

There was no need to organize Hyde's press campaign. "The scourge of the Plains" was as hot a news item as the war. Scores of stories were written about Tom Hyde's bloodthirsty and savage demonic genius. He was "invulnerable and endlessly elusive, everywhere at the same time, clawing at the outlying ranches and settlements with a thousand talons." Sermons were delivered against him; prayer groups were formed. A man in St. Louis was almost lynched for suggesting Tom Hyde was doing what he believed right. Cartoons adorned the editorial page—one with a savage-looking Indian dressed in a frock coat, a ferocious smile on his face as he shot women and children with the rifles in his twelve hands. Another showed a savage-looking Indian with thick lips, a top hat, and a loincloth scalping a woman in her boudoir.

In the South, Tom Hyde was declared a hero. Strategists tried to use his name to keep the Civilized Tribes in the rebel fold. It was rumored in the northern press that he'd been offered a generalship by Jefferson Davis. Two congressmen accused Hyde and Coughlin of creating this monster and called for their resignations. When the furor grew loud enough, President Lincoln intervened. Of Hyde, he said, "I need this man." Of Coughlin: "Ask for his resignation and you ask me to cut off my sword arm." Of both men Lincoln said: "They had about as much to do with this Indian going renegade as I did."

During the month of Tom's devastating raids, every new attack provoked an eight- or ten-page letter from Brigadier Hyde. Yet not once in the two hundred pages that crossed Secretary Coughlin's desk was there a whimper about Hyde's own feeling, not a hint of what Elizabeth felt. Since Hyde decreed himself deaf and dumb to his own pain, Coughlin felt bound by that silence. They referred to Tom only as "him" or that "renegade" or "agent."

By early November Hyde thought he could read his opponent's mind. Hyde knew Tom knew snow wiped out his greatest advantage—mobility. He'd use the winter to hole up somewhere with a few men and rest and fortify his position; and try to make more rifles with the latest batch of supplies he'd stolen. Chances were that Tom assumed that the Army would not—or could not—move troops through the snows. Which brought Brigadier Hyde to his obvious conclusion: they had to do the unexpected. By spring, it might be too late. They had to move that winter.

By mid-November Hyde had drawn a rough rectangle on his map of the western territories—the Platte and its lower fork were the southern boundary, the Missouri River, the eastern, the Cheyenne River, the north, and a line drawn between Fort Laramie and Denver, the west. All Tom's movements fell within that rectangle. Hyde suggested that the War Department send all available scouts to comb the area until they came across his winter camp or heard from other Indians where he was hiding. Once they pinpointed the location, Hyde wanted one hundred to two hundred men taken off each stalled winter battle line until he had a force of one thousand troops. One thousand men would descend on the boy in the dead of winter. That was his plan, and Hyde offered it with considerable slack, knowing he'd be lucky to get as many as seven hundred men.

Coughlin thought enough of Hyde's mid-November submission to telegraph the brigadier: WILL SUBMIT YOUR LATEST TO THE BOSS AT EARLIEST OPPORTUNITY. As he reread the reports of Tom's latest successes, it crossed his mind that only the son of the best fighting general in the United States would recognize the military potential of the Indians. Given their speed and horsemanship, it was brilliant to arm them with repeaters and use them for guerrilla attacks and assault forces to slash through supply lines. The raids on the Missouri forts, the strikes that isolated Denver, cutting off traffic all along the Oregon Trail, and blocking navigation on the main western artery, all this required planning, rigid discipline, perfect execution, and timing. Coughlin couldn't help thinking that Tom and the brigadier were carrying on their own Civil War. He felt like a voyeur sneaking a peak at a deadly private chess match.

On November twenty-seventh Coughlin wrote to his friend:

DEAR BEN,

This morning I saw the President about your latest revised plan. I'm always amused to read those articles about his tendency to vacillate. Every time he calls me in, he tells me what to talk about. Invariably he has an agenda firmly in mind, not decisions so much as a set of priorities. These can be modified if he hears a convincing argument he's overlooked, but mostly it is: "What do you think about this? Indeed. I thought so." Or: "Now I'm told such-and-such, do you agree?"

This morning he looked tired. He talked about the hoopla press gentleman Lee of Virginia is getting, then he said that you, Ben, did "a brilliant job at Belmont to save Oglesby's command" and "It's the kind of action that makes the history books but never the newspapers." (I quote verbatim.)

Finally I did get the opportunity to present your plan for dealing with the Plains threat. When I convinced him the threat was very real indeed, he wanted to know how many troops it would take. I told him you wanted 1000; he asked if we could spare 600. I said yes. He said, "Do it!"

So much for his indecisiveness.

Coughlin went on to suggest some forts and battle lines from which men could be removed and told Hyde they could be detached for four weeks at the most. He did not tell the brigadier that Lincoln had asked him why Hyde volunteered to run the counterattack against the renegade. Coughlin replied that the brigadier knew the boy's mind and believed it was his duty to deal with the problem. Lincoln said, "Not an easy position for either of you, is it?"

Coughlin answered: "It will be less comfortable for all of us if we don't mop this up soon."

The heavy snows came the second week in December, and by then the needs of Tom's band had contracted, their metabolisms slowed. Every few days they had to recut the hole in the white blanket and spin out those threads of trail. They stalked their food on foot, using the bow. Tom didn't want to call attention to the camp. He and his assistants worked a long half day. He knew what had to be done, he knew he had the whole winter to do it. He was calmer now.

Shell was queen of the camp. She cooked for them, drew water, carried firewood, happier than she'd been in years. She had been wrong; her son had not failed, but triumphed gloriously; she accepted her mistake as if she'd been given a gift. In late December she caught a bad cold and had to stay in bed for five days. Big Road was her nurse, cooking the buffalo broth, doing the household chores, making her comfortable. The boundaries between their work were more flexible than Tom remembered.

One evening during that cold he heard Shell whisper to Big Road: "How do I look?"

He said: "Red-nosed, but very beautiful."

Tom began to notice how his parents handled each other's complaints, how they avoided blaming each other, how they softened embarrassments and steered around humiliations. When Big Road broke Shell's bone awl, she volunteered: "Don't worry. I can make another." One day his father was in a testy mood because one of the boys had forgotten to clear the snow away for the ponies and, to make matters worse, had left the picket ropes in the pasture. While Big Road was muttering to himself, Shell slipped out of the lodge, walked the half mile up the hill in the dark, got the ropes out of the tree, and brought them back. Tom loved the way they moved by each other, how they came together to kiss, the way his father's hand seemed molded for her arm or behind. These things are small, but domestic life is built of tiny accords. Tom watched carefully, suddenly eager for the lesson of how two people create happiness for themselves and each other. The tone, the particulars of their life helped him remember his childhood. It also helped him understand more about the life he could lead with Bear Child.

In this quiet time, Tom began to see the failings of the white world with less rancor. At first he was afraid that feeling might signal a weakening of purpose. But that wasn't it. Each world had given him something, had taken something else away. The white world's power came from their dog-eat-dog assumptions, and they glossed their struggles for power and money with Christianity—the perfect god, the love-thy-neighbor ethic for a people so imperfect and so unloving. The Indians worked to perfect accords among themselves and Nature as they knew it, which left them powerless against intruders who did not behave as they did, and powerless against a Nature altered by time and those intruders. Yet Rumbling Wings was right that white man paid for today without figuring in tomorrow's costs. So Tom began to sense that, in the long run, white man would disappear too, if not in that wave the old shaman talked about, then perhaps by some hotter dispensation. Tom's further problem was that the promise of the future didn't help him much in the present.

The daily routine played a silent song in his head, the rhythm of a noiseless ceaseless stream. For the first time since his childhood, the pressure he'd always generated was diffused. He watched the winter dump more white sky on them; he heard the wind trumpet over the hills, calling on its cavalry charge: the trees were its advance guard, rattling saber branches against armored silver trunks; the bushes quailed before its power. He'd pause by the lodge entrance and watch the wind spur on outriders of snow. At the end of the day he'd sit and watch the clear light fade, its frozen edges mingling with the thick dark. Nothing disturbed the peace slowly descending on him. In spring that peace would thaw; in spring, he'd flower.

There was much Tom Hyde didn't know. He didn't know that the young Lakota brave who had wandered into camp just after New Year and took the evening meal with them was a scout from Fort Kearney on assignment from the War Department, and that he and a Pawnee had spied on Tom's camp with their field glasses. He didn't know that on January 17, 1862, forty-five Crow, Pawnee, Blackfoot, and Sioux scouts led by sixteen Indian fighters trekked north from Fort Laramie to seal off the western escape routes out of the Black Hills. Nor would he have guessed, in his ugliest nightmare, that 625 men had disembarked at two landing places on the Missouri River. The three hundred men under General Halleck took the northern route to Buffalo Gap, following the White River overland. Their scouts went ahead on snowshoe, trampling a track for the horses and men.

Tom felt secure in his hideaway—it was deep in the Hills; only Small Deer knew the exact location, and he was spending the winter two hundred miles east on Old Lodge Creek. Tom wanted to be certain his cave remained a secret. Just in case, he had arranged a makeshift rock fortification just above the bisalt ledge. He had camouflaged the entrance to the cave and set up his two tepees around on the south side of the hill. He had eight repeaters and two thousand rounds of ammunition. In two weeks he'd have twelve more rifles. The deeper the snows got, the more insulated he felt.

On January 23, General Booth's 274 men, some of whom had come from posts as far east as Pennsylvania, left the junction of the Missouri and Cheyenne rivers and marched south behind their snowshoeing scouts. They killed every Indian and wiped out every village in a two-mile swath along their advance.

On January 28, 1862, the southern tip of General Halleck's White River command touched the northern tip of General Booth's forces, who'd marched down the Cheyenne. Then they all started west, closing in on the Black Hills. Their advance was slow and heavy and dull, their movement mechanical as each man tramped in the footsteps of the man ahead of him. Not one of the enlisted soldiers knew where he was going.

About twelve miles east of Buffalo Gap, the troops got caught in a heavy storm. They bivouacked where they stood for a day and a half. Eight men froze to death; six lost toes; fingers had to be amputated. Late the second day of the storm they moved on in heavy blowing snow, their lieutenant leading the way by compass, each soldier holding on to the belt of the man in front of him.

The first day of February broke piercingly clear; the temperature was hovering near 15 below zero. By noon the Army scouts had taken their positions on the circumference of a two-mile circle, and for the rest of the day they watched Tom's small party moving through their daily round. That night the Army moved. By dawn 635 men had drawn a mile-round noose around Tom's camp.

On February 2, 1862, Tom Hyde didn't feel like hunting, so he didn't go out with Big Road and Buck's Heart. Instead he sat cross-legged and watched his mother split a piece of sinew with her fingernails, then wet it in her mouth. She rolled the sinew on her knee with her palm, picked up the new bone awl and whittled the tip of the sinew to a fine point. She stopped humming and looked up. "There are very few things in which I can place my faith anymore, Tumbling Hawk. The older I grow the fewer they become." She tried to hum again, but her mouth was set too firmly, and she looked funny.

Tom didn't understand. "You believe in Big Road."

"Yes. That's one of the few things I can understand, like this sinew in my hand." It seemed odd to hear this coming from the philosopher of small detail.

"That's why you and Big Road are so close?"

She shook her head. "No. That's only the beginning." Her son wanted to understand her, but Shell couldn't explain.

Suddenly Tom felt restless. "I'm going up to make some bullets."

"Fine," she said.

Tom took the steep path which curved up and around the hill. Snow was everywhere; the air had that dry hard bite which made him think he could chew on it. There was no wind, so the slim-edged smoke ribbons curled straight out of the lodges into the sky. This morning he'd let the apprentices start late. After all, he still had two months of winter. He was in no hurry; he could even make time for those domestic truths.

He'd been in the cave a half hour when he heard the first shots, a light peppering like the sound of a schoolboy rolling dice. Only this seemed to come from four or five places at once, like four or five walls being hit with light dice. They were all generally from the south—the way his father and Buck's Heart had gone.

He'd barely had that thought when a thundering wave of sound rocked the cave. His torches flickered as though the blast of terrible sound had sucked out the air. Tom stumbled to grab a rifle and rushed to the opening.

Below, as far as he could see, were scores of soldiers, dark blue muffled cylinders staining the pure white snow. He looked south without hope, knowing he could not see the two tepees on the other side of the hill, knowing that she was dead. His father and Buck's Heart—dead too.

The rifle reports picked up, shredding the settled air, leaving it gutted, in tatters. "How many times can they die?" Tom screamed to himself as he pictured the scraps of hide dangling, the lodgepoles snapped like matchsticks. Poised on his toes he stood at the sill of the cave for a long moment, then ran back inside. Cool and deliberate, he collected his ammunition and brought the boxes out, then ran back, picked up all eight rifles and carried them out. He lay down next to his rifles and ammunition, behind that thin screen of rocks.

Scores of men, maybe hundreds, were marching toward him, filling the bumps and hillocks with heads and shoulders, rising to thighs and knees and snowy boots again, moving awkwardly through the drifts, yet all coming in order, like pieces on an assembly line. He emptied the first repeater; seven faceless men fell. But the waves of yellow pantstripe and blue greatcoat still came on.

"How many men?" he wondered, grimly admiring the planning, the execution. "All this for me?" Tom faced a vast mechanical monster, which, Hydra-like, produced a head each time he destroyed one. All that cost, planning, paperwork, the scouting, secrecy, and transport needed to bring them here for this moment. Yet tomorrow they'd be gone. Tom could see the silent force behind the soldiers, invisible to all others—men in coats at large mahogany desks, inkstained clerks with pens poised, that endless stream of paper.

How could he have left the camp undefended? His terrible sorrow was that he'd never look at Big Road or Shell or Buck's Heart again. "Just as well not to have to say good-bye, not to have to listen to the young braves tell me how proud they are to die."

"All questions are about how a man lives." Every one of them, Rumbling Wings said. Tom took that to mean there are only ends, no means, that all means are constantly being converted to ends. Before him a gaping insatiable mouth yawned open, come to chew up his bones. "No man should require all this to bring him down. I'm not that good." His palms were wet, his forehead cold with coward's sweat. The wet hands had trouble holding the rifle steady; he managed to keep firing, yet even as he fired, the swarms of uniforms reached the foot of his hill.

Tom had the feeling that white man's ultimate destruction lay hidden somewhere in those numbers, that the lesson was there for him to find—like his mother's last words about her life—and he cursed the fact they wouldn't give him time now.

As he fired at the bulky greatcoats, it came to him: "When they can't waste, they'll die." Elizabeth's garbage—the first obscene feeling he'd ever had was that moment when he'd lusted after white man's power to waste and rejected the eternal balancing act the Indian practiced. Maybe the right place lay somewhere in between. But white man's arrogance would blind him to that. Pumping round after round into the blue wave spreading over the white ground, Tom grew furious. It wasn't fair for him to die now that he understood. It wasn't fair for one man to face a power without limit. They had no sense of proportion; they turned everything into a horrible joke, made it meaningless.

Dark red blotted the shimmering silver snow; the crust slowly ate up the color. Dark red spread up the hill toward him. Their bullets were bouncing off his rock defense, ricocheting madly. He started a letter to Charlotte:

> It was wonderful to love you, Charlotte. How awful to have been parted by something which seems so ridiculous to me now. You will think it's easy for me to say that, but whatever caused me to take you to the hotel—my desire for you or stupidity or insensitivity, your being spoiled—they had very little to do with our uniqueness together. Having lived away from those reasons you offered yourself, I can see how small and insignificant a rundown hotel room really was—if, indeed, that's what our fight was about.

Five guns were empty—Tom wanted to keep two ahead. But he found it hard to reload and keep firing. There was a deadly delay, his fingers went numb, he could not get the bullets to slide down into the magazine. All his practiced mechanical dexterity was slipping away. "I'll make them bleed, take as many..." Saying it, Tom felt a heavy swell of despair; his arms went muscleless, their undersides recumbent beanbags. "Makes no difference how many I get today if I'm dead tomorrow." His rifle was silent now. The unmolested wave sped up as it swept up the hill. "Only success or failure, no well-played futility for me." Tears flushed his eyes. The amplitude of time he'd had that morning had shrunk to a few minutes.

Suddenly he began firing again, at blue blurs. A lieutenant went down, the man beside him toppled. Because of Tom's failure, his people's way of life was dead, gone forever. It was as simple as that, this time the cause was perfectly traceable. Tom prayed to Mohe, to Big Road, to all his fathers to forgive his arrogance, stupidity, and carelessness.

Now terror fused his spine—death's taste filled his mouth. He cried scalding tears at a world so hateful as to live on without him. At that moment Tom knew he'd cancel the whole world for himself, sell his own and other's souls to devils, white men, whomever, for just a couple minutes more. Not to do better, not to improve his sacred work or even to defeat the horror closing in on him, three hundred yards away, nothing as noble as that. But just to hang on to his senses, to exist for a little while longer, whether as wretch or hero. He understood that he was a coward too; it was just that he'd never faced the truly terrifying questions before.

All those yellow stripes on their pants legs—why couldn't they keep them in line at least? They came slowly now, even those he could feel sneaking up from behind, pouring over the top of the hill. There was even time to think about things he had left to do–instructions to Small Deer he'd omitted, a note he'd failed to write to Elizabeth's cousin for a box of sandalwood soap. In the spring he'd planned to trade pelts for powder. The silver from that Denver mine would buy steel from a white renegade trader. Then there was the great meeting of the Plains tribes. The bugles calling in the kill reminded Tom he meant to teach Small Deer how to blow the bugle calls so that they could confuse the cavalry when they fought them. There was a thick smell in the air now, faintly familiar–blood and those musty woolen greatcoats.

He was firing faster, his thoughts shooting out of his head like bullets. And inside Tom felt incipient wholeness growing like a bubble being blown inside him. Shell had sensed it was there less than an hour before, but she could take him no further. There was an instant when Tom looked into the mad contradictions within himself and realized that he held them all there inside him, like chaos within night and day. Nothing he did, nothing he was, could be alien to him–it was he, Tumbling Hawk/Tom Hyde/Tumbling Hawk.

He wanted to stand up and preach to his executioners, to give them the curse and the imprecation of his now dead people, he wanted the chance to explain what he uniquely understood. He was sorry he would not be present to witness the passing of their empire, but he knew it was inevitable, and he hoped that the spirit of his ancestors would be strong enough to be there. He had no use for excuses now; he called on Mohe to bless his attempt–the soldiers heard it as a war cry.

Tom continued firing–he could see their eyes above their mufflers. He felt very much at home behind that rock sill, for the distance between his worlds had shrunk to nothing.

They found him with his eyes open: What did it mean to stare at not just your own death but the death of all those around you, now and forever? As a man, as a warrior, you took it along with the whole raft of inevitables the world pushed at you. Feeling your own strength and your own potential to be stronger, you understood how ineffective yours was against all other strengths–their strength. The why of that eluded you.

One of those standing over him looked into those open eyes. "Vicious devil, ain't he?" the soldier said as he raised the butt of his rifle and rammed it into Tumbling Hawk's cold face.

* * *

Elizabeth walked out of her house into the light snow, wondering if it was over. Ben had been too fair-minded to keep any of his plans from her, so she knew his strategies step by hideous step. She knew when the Indians and scouts left Fort Laramie, knew when the troops steamed up the Missouri, when they disembarked and started the overland trek. Yesterday when her newspapers told her nothing, she knew that the War Department was holding the story until all the troops were back on their battle lines. The news would come today, she thought, and, if not, then tomorrow. As she approached the Laramie General Store and Post Office, she'd already accepted his death—that was as certain as the sun going down.

The street was painfully quiet, disturbed only by her steady step and a dog's distant bark. There were three empty sleighs in front of the post office, their horses dusted white. As Elizabeth stepped onto the plank sidewalk, she saw Mrs. Topfield, the grocer's wife, nod a warning to someone inside.

Elizabeth's entrance hushed the large room—the men seated around the stove gave up lying to scrape their boots and sneak glances her way; the women at the counter fell silent. Elizabeth removed her gloves, shook the snow off her cape and bonnet. The smug round features of Mrs. Bostick, Mrs. Topfield's frazzled triumphant eyes reminded Elizabeth of those first slow walks down Main Street with Tom; and before that when rumors of impropriety dogged her steps. She'd born those impositions without a whimper; she would do the same now. But she felt indignant that they were always poking their noses into other people's business and always getting it wrong. Those faces at the counter or tilting back in the chairs, they loved the fact that Tom had gone renegade. They loved being able to point a finger and say: "See, see, the chickens have come home to roost." She found it odd they felt proud when their worst articles of belief were confirmed. "Oh well," she thought with great fatigue, "we won't be here much longer."

Elizabeth took the fat bundle the postmistress held out to her. There were two letters from Ben, an envelope bulging with what she suspected were newspaper clippings. Probably, they'd already heard the news of Tom's death. "Good day," she said to all, outwardly unflappable, and strolled out.

With the boy dead and Ben in Kentucky, she had no reason to stay in Laramie. Soon she'd go East. When the war was over—if it ever was going to be over—Ben would get a command in Pennsylvania or New York, or even New England. People in the East would know less about

Tom, and have less at stake. Not that she and Ben would ever really escape the issue. The hope was that time would diminish its hold on them.

She walked back along Main Street through a snow so fine she wasn't certain if it was really snowing or just blowing off the store roofs. The gray light diffused through the sky gave no hint of its source. She greeted Mr. Mudgins, one of the few Laramie merchants who still was a friend. Avery, an underfed apparition at his new plate-glass window, wafted her an oily smile.

Elizabeth carried the fat bundle of mail up the steps of the white frame house and, inside, along the same path on which Ben had pursued her for thirteen years, down the hall and through the sitting room. She placed the pile on the table reserved for her knitting and sat down in her rocker. Starting at the top, Elizabeth made her way down through the newspaper accounts of Tom's death.

The *Tribune*'s coverage was the most self-righteous, bloodcurdling, and the most complete. The *Tribune* spent three days on the "manhunt," with long feature pieces on the planning and setting of the trap, and profiles of General Halleck and General Booth; eyewitness accounts of the end. She read it all, read that Tom had murdered twenty-two men on that last day. Her tears brought no relief. She kept crying, wishing she could stop, but not stopping. Behind all the self-congratulation on the secrecy and dispatch and coordination, on "the brilliant deploying of the few available troops," Elizabeth could read her husband's thoughts, just as she read them in between the icy martial terms with which he detailed his plans to her; she could feel his pain even as he lectured himself about the demands of duty.

How close this dead child had brought them, Elizabeth thought, as her rocker pumped up and down. Without Tom she never would have overcome the inertia of all those years. Tom was the one who'd made this marriage. He'd pressed so hard and unremittingly that, unaware, he'd worked on her until one of her deepest, most heartfelt convictions seemed arbitrary and willful, altogether selfish. He made her feel that she and Ben were close enough to chance that part too. So a movement, so hard to initiate oneself, was started by Tom's push; so her curiosity to understand someone else's desire—Ben Hyde's—became a need.

On November 11, 1860, Ben asked Elizabeth to marry him for the seventeenth time. She said, "I'm not going to say no, Ben. I'm going to consider your proposal." He looked as surprised as she did at these unrehearsed words. Then Hyde realized the answer was yes. She could feel him wanting to get up, cross that space between them, and take her in his arms. And this time, for the first time, she did not turn her mind away from the question. She wanted him to, she wanted him to....

They decided to put off the legal ceremony until the end of the summer so that Tom could be there.

For some, Elizabeth believed, lovemaking was a matter of passion; some had a wellspring inside which gushed up and carried them away somewhere. For her, at her age and with her inexperience, lovemaking was a matter of the right will and the right moment—a complex of delicately balanced yearnings and long-denied impulses, fears, and embarrassments, many of which were far too obscure for Elizabeth to begin to comprehend. Ben had brought her a concerned passion. And so another motion had started. She felt, not like a young girl, but like a winter field unthawing. And the feelings were there, percolating up to assure Elizabeth and her husband that the step they had taken was a fitting one. It was, in fact, deeply moving to them both.

She rocked, drawing the settling motion of her adult life closer to her. Her mind kept turning over Tom's death, a finger probing the blistering, suppurating wound. There was no question he had to die—anyone who took all those lives had to die. That was the oldest biblical injunction. But underneath religion and reason and her husband's slightly unhinged, impersonal letters, Elizabeth intuited—no, drove herself to find the grain of reasonable complaint under Tom's madness.

It wasn't hard for her to understand the boy's rage and frustration, not when one considered what everyone could see lay ahead for the Indians. And hadn't Mr. Bushnell insisted it was wrong to take a Cheyenne boy out of his world and turn him into, into—whatever Tom had become. Even in those early days when their progress seemed so remarkable, hadn't she sensed the odd and terrible strain Tom labored under, as though there was some unpredicted physical stress that would later develop into a structural failing? Now she could give more meaning to those pained troubled eyes that searched hers for comfort; Elizabeth remembered just how little she'd metered out to him, because to give too much would have been to lie. All that bombarding him with glass and maps and drawings and machines and words, they were all just magic tricks to confound an innocent child. Or the day Tom came back instead of riding away to the Cheyenne—there was no happiness or peace in the boy's countenance then, only a grim commitment to a dream that someone else said existed. All his cheery letters from Arundel, and the summer he came back to Laramie and let that remark slip about Mr. Bovie being the kind of man he could not honor: then she knew. His hurts were so deep, so untranslatable. He was—had been—such a remarkable boy.

It was different for Ben. As long as he lived he'd never make any attempt to understand. And yet both of them had been at fault. How willingly she'd let herself be hoodwinked by Hyde's arguments about what had to be done—how willingly she'd hoodwinked herself. Elizabeth remembered that running discussion with her husband about pushing the boy too hard, about the beauty of the Cheyenne beliefs—how insufficient Hyde's answers looked at this moment, with the child lying out there with scores of bullet holes through his body. If she'd known more about the questions then, if she'd argued better, if Ben had been more honest or better informed or less blinded to the way Tom saw the world, if she hadn't let her mind stop and accept ignorance as a badge of her station, perhaps, just perhaps, it wouldn't have ended with this empty unquenchable pain. Perhaps they could've given the boy some truth to help him believe a little more in their world.

Elizabeth rocked hard, tilting the room. For the first time she let her mind roam freely in her hatred for what had cost so much. She realized that, all along, she and her husband had taken most, that the boy had done nothing but give till, in the end, he'd lost all. Everyone used him—they did, Greeley did, the government certainly did. They'd offered him up to all bidders, thinking they could control the bidding. The bidding had gotten out of hand. And Elizabeth was the only one left to make the final tally—the boy was dead; the man she loved unable to speak the name of the boy who'd made their marriage; Coughlin and Mrs. Hastings crushed; the truth to be kept from Dorothea for all time; the townspeople—and thousands like them all over the country—content with those smug gloats fixed on their faces. Elizabeth knew that they'd failed Tom—that their teaching was too arrogant, too full of itself; it left out too many things, like the signal thump of the rabbit he'd told her about. "This world does not work the way we told him. There are no beings higher or lower than anything else. Nothing marches in a perfectly straight line, for nothing can be said to have gotten anywhere—there is no progress—until a thing is ended." Looking at this ending, Elizabeth was certain they hadn't come very far.